Praise for N

"McKenna provides heartbreakingly tender romantic development that will move readers to tears. Her military background lends authenticity to this outstanding tale, and readers will fall in love with the upstanding hero and his fierce determination to save the woman he loves."

—*Publishers Weekly* on *Never Surrender*

"Full of intensity and action-packed romance. There is great chemistry between the characters and tremendous realism, making *Breaking Point* a great read."

—*RT Book Reviews*

"An action-packed, compelling story, and the sizzling chemistry between Ethan and Sarah makes this one good read."

—*RT Book Reviews* on *Degree of Risk*

"Lindsay will pull you into *Breaking Point* and captivate you with her smooth writing, fast paced action, and the palpable attraction between Gabe and Bay."

—*Harlequin Junkie*

"Lindsay McKenna will have you flying with the daring and deadly women pilots who risk their lives… Buckle in for the ride of your life."

—*Writers Unlimited* on *Heart of Stone*

A US Navy veteran, *New York Times* bestselling author **Lindsay McKenna** was a meteorologist while serving her country. She pioneered the military romance in 1993 with *Captive of Fate* (Silhouette Special Edition). Her heart and focus is on honoring and showing our military men and women. Creator of the Wyoming Series and Shadow Warriors series for HQN Books, she writes emotionally and romantically intense suspense stories. Visit her online at lindsaymckenna.com.

Look for more books by Lindsay McKenna in Harlequin Romantic Suspense—the ultimate destination for heart-racing romance and high-stakes suspense! There are four new Harlequin Romantic Suspense titles available every month. Check one out today! Also look for Lindsay's titles in HQN Books.

New York Times Bestselling Author

LINDSAY McKENNA

His Woman in Command

and

Operation: Forbidden

HARLEQUIN® ROMANTIC SUSPENSE CLASSICS

ISBN-13: 978-0-373-60668-9

His Woman in Command and Operation: Forbidden

Copyright © 2014 by Harlequin Books S.A.

Recycling programs for this product may not exist in your area.

The publisher acknowledges the copyright holder of the individual works as follows:

His Woman in Command
Copyright © 2010 by Lindsay McKenna

Operation: Forbidden
Copyright © 2011 by Lindsay McKenna

Printed in U.S.A.

HARLEQUIN®
www.Harlequin.com

CONTENTS

HIS WOMAN
IN COMMAND

To ROMVETS, a group of women who have served or are currently serving in the military. This list comprises women who are aspiring writers and published authors. It's an honor to be among you. www.RomVets.com

Chapter 1

"Twenty bucks says you can't get that good-lookin' woman to come over to our table and have a beer with us," Staff Sargeant Neal Robles challenged.

Captain Gavin Jackson, leader of a ten-man Special Forces team, squinted in the semidarkness of the officers' club—a tent on the most dangerous border in the world: between Afghanistan and Pakistan. It was the last day of their two weeks of rest between month-long assignments in the field. Tomorrow, they'd be back out in the badlands border area hunting Taliban. Gavin sat with his nine men. The pitcher of frothy cold beer in front of them went quickly.

The woman in question had just entered the spacious tent, catching the attention of every man in the room. She was about five foot eight, with short, curly black hair framing an oval face and high cheekbones. She was olive-skinned with light gold eyes. Then there was her killer mouth that Gavin wanted to capture and kiss. The frumpy green one-piece flight uniform that told him she was a pilot couldn't hide her assets. Curvy in all the right places. Gavin felt his body harden with desire.

He didn't know why. His relationship with another woman army pilot had crashed and burned a year ago. Gavin had sworn off women for now and women army pilots forever. Squirming in his seat, the wooden chair creaking, he shrugged as Neal Robles grinned like a wolf over the dare.

"Why her?" Gavin grunted, lifting the cold mug of beer to his lips.

Robles's dark brown eyes gleamed as he whispered, "She's hot, Cap'n."

"She's the *only* female in here," Gavin drawled. Indeed, the huge dark green canvas tent was packed with men— A teams coming in for a well-deserved rest, logistics, pilots or mechanics to support their missions. Women pilots were few, but they did exist. Automatically, Gavin rubbed his chest in memory of Laurie Braverman, the U.S. Army CH-47 Chinook driver that he'd fallen in love with. They'd broken up because of their mutual inability to compromise. A war of egos had eventually destroyed their relationship.

"She might be the only one," Robles asserted, "but you gotta admit, Cap'n, she's something." Robles looked at the other enlisted men around the table, all of whom bobbed in unison to agree with his observation.

Tugging on his recently trimmed beard, Gavin gave them an amused look. His team knew about his hard luck with Laurie, especially since he'd been a growly old bear for a month after their spectacular parting.

"You know," he said, "it's damned hard enough to survive the border villages. Now, you want to collectively throw me at *another* driver?" *Driver* was a common slang expression for any pilot whether they flew fixed-wing aircraft or helicopters.

Laughter rippled through his team. Gavin was fiercely protective of his men. They'd been together over here nearly a year, and they were tighter than a set of fleas on a mangy Afghan dog. He wanted to bring all of them back off this tour alive so they could go home to their families. He had visited the base barber this morning, got a wonderful hot shower, a trim, clean clothes and joined his men at the canteen tent. Although they were in the U.S. Army, their clothes were decidedly Afghani. With their beards, wearing their wool *pakols,* or caps, they melted into the mountainous area less a target as a result of their wardrobe. They all wore the traditional turban. The loose, comfortable-fitting top with long sleeves had pajamalike trousers of the same color, and the traditional wool vests were worn over it.

"Naw, she doesn't look like she's a man-eater like the last one you tangled with," Robles said. The table broke out in collective laughter once again. More beer was poured. A bartender came over and delivered another pitcher of cold beer, the froth foaming up and over of the top.

Gavin couldn't disagree and his gaze wandered to the woman leaning up against the makeshift bar and ordering a cup of coffee, not beer. She was probably on duty, Gavin assumed. He watched her hands. They were long, narrow and beautiful-looking. No wedding ring. But then, what did that mean? Nothing, because military combatants were forbidden to wear jewelry of any kind. So, she could be married. Frowning, Gavin felt his assistant CO, Dave Hansen, give his right shoulder a nudge.

"Go on, Gavin," he said in his slow Texas drawl, "she looks pretty docile. Invite her over. We'd all like the company of a good-lookin' woman to remind us of what's waiting for us at home. We're harmless. Just tell her we're voyeurs."

Gavin scowled at his team. "Since when are you willing to throw me to the lions? Don't I treat you right out there?"

Guffaws broke out and Gavin couldn't help grinning. They all desperately needed a little fun. The border country was violent and lethal. They'd spent thirty days in the mountains hunting out pockets of Taliban in caves. Not that the local villages along the border ever cooperated. Most of them were terrorized by the Taliban. And the tribal people had been forgotten by the government in Kabul decades ago. Out there, Gavin knew, no fiercely independent Afghan could be trusted once your back was turned on them. They'd just as soon put a bullet between your shoulder blades as look at you because of what the Taliban had done to them. Gavin's team had had several firefights with the Taliban on their last mission. If not for the Apache helo drivers coming in with heavy fire support, they wouldn't be here enjoying this beer with one another.

Gavin sat up and sighed. He knew his men needed a reprieve from their deadly work. They all had PTSD symptoms. Why not waltz up to this gal and ask her to join them? "Okay," he growled at them, "I'll go throw myself on her mercy for the likes of all of you and see what she says."

The men clapped and cheered as Gavin stood up. He smoothed down his vest and adjusted the thick leather belt around his waist that carried a dagger and a pistol. Out in the field, he'd have body armor on, but not now. He adjusted the dark brown wool *pakol* on his head. To anyone seeing these men riding up on their tough mountain-bred ponies, they looked like a group of Afghan men. Of course, here in the canteen tent, they were out of place, but everyone on base knew Special Forces A teams dressed like Afghans.

Giving his group a wink, Gavin said, "Okay, men, keep it down while I work some magic." They all nodded solemnly, lifted their glasses of beer and beamed excitedly like little children waiting for Christmas to arrive. Gavin shook his head and walked across the creaking plywood floor toward the bar. He noticed that although men were hanging around the bar, all of them gave the woman pilot some room to breathe. Not that they weren't looking at her. But none made a move on her. Why? They were support and logistics men and worked in the camp, so they might know something about this woman pilot he didn't.

Coming to the bar, Gavin stood about two feet away from her. The scalding look she gave him with those lion-gold eyes surprised him. He was clean, for once. He didn't smell of sweat and fear. His black hair and beard were neatly trimmed and combed. Maybe she didn't like A teams or Afghans, Gavin decided. The way her full mouth thinned, her hands tense around the white ceramic mug of coffee, told him everything. She really didn't want this intrusion into her space.

"I'm Captain Gavin Jackson," he said, pushing aside his fear of rejection. He looked at the upper arm of her green flight suit. "We've never seen a patch with a black cat on it. I was wondering what squadron you're with." That was a safe icebreaker, Gavin thought.

Nike Alexander, at twenty-six, did not want any male attention. Just a year ago, she'd lost Antonio, an officer in the Peruvian Army who had died in a vicious fire-fight with cocaine dealers. She glared icily at the man, who was decidedly handsome despite his rugged appearance. "I'm with the Black Jaguar Squadron 60," she snapped.

"I've been out here on the front nearly a year. I've never seen this patch. Is this a new squadron?" Gavin opted for something simpler than trying to get this good-looking woman to come over to their table for a beer. He was frantically searching for ways to defuse her tension.

Shrugging, Nike lifted the coffee to her lips, took a sip and then said, "We're basically Apache pilots in an all-women flight program. We got here three weeks ago."

"Oh." Gavin didn't know what to think about that. "All women?"

Nike's mouth twitched. "We're black ops." His thick, straight brows rose with surprise. While it was true there were women pilots in combat, no women-only squadrons existed. "We're top secret to the rest of the world. Here at camp, they know what we do," she added to ward off questions she saw in his large blue eyes.

Under other circumstances, Nike would be interested in this warrior. Clearly, he was an A-team leader. She knew these brave and hardy Special Forces teams were on the front lines, finding Taliban and stopping their incursion into Afghanistan's space. His hands were large, square and roughened by work and the forces of the weather.

"Ah, black ops," Gavin murmured. He saw the wariness in her gold eyes. "You're new?"

"I arrived a week ago."

"Welcome aboard," he said, holding out his hand toward her. This time, he was sincere. Anyone who flew the border risked their lives every time they lifted off from this secret base.

Looking at his proffered hand and then up at him, Nike couldn't help herself and slid her hand into his. He grinned like a little boy given a Christmas gift. Despite the neatly trimmed beard that gave his square face a dangerous look, he seemed happy to meet her. Well, they were both in the army and that meant something. Her flesh tingled as his fingers wrapped gently around hers. She admired his deeply sunburned face, laugh lines at the corners of his eyes. A wild, unexpected surge of excitement coursed through Nike. What was *that* all about? Why was her heart pounding? She broke the contact and pulled her hand away.

Oh, he was eye candy, there was no doubt. The boyish, crooked grin made him even more devastatingly handsome, Nike decided.

"What's your name?" Gavin asked. He forced his hands off the bar, unexpectedly touching her olive-tone skin. The brief contact sent crazy tingles up and down his arm. The close proximity to this woman intoxicated him in quite another way. Gavin fully realized he was more than a little tipsy from the beer he and his team had been guzzling. But he was still alert, still fixated on this new person of interest.

"I'm Captain Nike Alexander," she informed him

in a clipped and wary tone. She'd just arrived with her squadron from the USA and wanted to focus only on the mission before them. As an all-women squadron they had a lot to prove—again. They'd done it in Peru, now it would be here. She didn't want to tangle with some sex-hungry A-team leader who hadn't seen a woman in God knew how long. Still, a secret part of her wondered what Gavin would look like without that beard. Not that he wasn't handsome with it; maybe she was just more interested than she cared to admit.

"Nike," he murmured, rolling the name around on his tongue. "That's different." He squinted and gave her a measuring look. "Are you...American?" Her husky voice had a trace of an accent. When she frowned, he knew he'd asked the wrong question.

"I was born in Athens, Greece, Captain. I was invited from my country to train and work for the U.S. Army." She turned and showed the American flag on the left shoulder of her uniform.

"Greek." That made sense, although he'd said it as if he were stunned by the information. Seeing the frustration in her large, clear gold eyes, Gavin asked, "Wasn't Nike a goddess in Greek myths?"

"She still is," Nike said in a flat tone. "I was named after her."

"I see." Gavin stood there, his brows dipping. "So, you're part of a black ops, you're a female pilot and you're from Greece." Brightening, he shared a look with her, his smile crooked. "That makes you a pretty rare specimen out here in our backcountry."

"You're making me feel like a bug under a microscope, Captain. Why don't you mosey back to your team. I'm not interested in anything but my mission here."

Her tone was low and dismissive.

Gavin kept his smile friendly and tried to appear neutral and not the leering, sexually hungry male he really was. It was now or never. "Speaking of that, Captain Alexander, we were wondering if you might not come and join us? My boys and I are going back for thirty more days in the bush tomorrow morning. We'd enjoy your company."

Easing into a standing position, Nike glanced over at the table. Nine other bearded men in Afghan dress looked hopefully in her direction. English-speaking women who were not Muslim were a rarity in this country. Of course they'd want her company. "Captain, I'm not the USO. And I'm not for sale at any price. If you want female entertainment I suggest you find it somewhere else."

Ouch. Gavin scowled. "Just a beer, Captain. Or we'll buy you another cup of coffee. That's all. Nothing else." He held up both his hands. "Honest."

"I appreciate the offer," Nike said. She pulled out a few coins from her pocket and put them on the bar next to the drained cup of coffee. "But I must respectfully decline, Captain." She turned and marched out of the tent.

"That went well," Gavin said, his grin wide and silly-looking as she exited. He walked over to his men, who looked defeated.

"You crashed and burned," Robles groaned.

Jackson poured himself another glass of beer. "She's got other fish to fry." He said it as lightly as he could.

The men nodded and nursed their beers.

At twenty-eight, Gavin understood that a little fun

and laughter was good medicine for his men. Silently, he thanked Nike Alexander for her decision. What would it have been like to have her come over and sit with them? It would have lifted their collective spirits. They were starving for some feminine attention. Oh, she probably realized this, but didn't get that his invitation was truly harmless. Gavin had seen a lot of sensitivity in her face and read it in her eyes. However, she was protective, if not a little defensive about sharing that side. He couldn't blame her.

Gavin told them what he'd found out. His men were like slavering dogs getting a morsel tossed to them. In Afghanistan, Muslim women could not talk directly to any man. Consequently, it was a world of males with males and the women were hidden away in their homes. Gavin missed being stateside. Even though he'd crashed and burned with Laurie Braverman on his first tour here, he still hungered for conversation with an intelligent woman.

As he glanced toward the flap of the tent where Nike Alexander had marched through, Gavin lamented her departure. Clearly, she thought he was hitting on her. Well, wasn't he? Digging into the pocket of his trousers, he produced a twenty-dollar bill and threw it across the table to his medic. "Here, Robles. Satisfied?"

Chuckling, Neal took the twenty and hoisted it upward. "You tried. Hey, Cap'n, this will give us another round of beer!"

The men clapped and hooted, and Gavin grinned crookedly. His team needed this kind of blowout before they got dropped in the badlands again. As he took one more look to where Nike had left, he wished he'd had a little more time with her. Would they ever meet again? Hope sprang in his chest. Nike was a fascinating woman, pilot or not. Gavin shrugged off any romantic thoughts and took a deep swig of beer. Chances of *ever* seeing Nike Alexander again were next to nothing.

"Nike," Major Dallas Klein-Murdoch said, "sit down and relax. Welcome to BJS 60."

Nike settled in front of her commanding officer's desk. Every incoming pilot to the squadron did a one-on-one with the CO. This morning, it was her turn. Dallas Klein's reputation with the original Black Jaguar Squadron, for which she had flown in Peru, was legendary. Nike was only too thrilled to be here under this woman's command. They'd had a stint together in Texas chasing Mexican drug-runners before this latest assignment. There, Dallas had fallen in love with ATF agent Mike Murdoch. The Pentagon had then sent Dallas and her new husband to Afghanistan to oversee the latest Black Jaguar Squadron. Murdoch was now a captain in the U.S. Army and worked as a strategy and operations officer for the all-women Apache combat pilots that comprised BJS 60. And while the pilots were all female, some males in the ranks took care of the Apache helicopters. Nike was glad that Dallas was assigned here with her new husband. Taking off her baseball cap, Nike sat down and grinned. "Like old times, isn't it?"

Dallas laughed. "Better believe it." She reached for a file folder and handed it to Nike. "Here are your orders. We have twenty women Apache pilots here and ten helicopters assigned to us. The last two helos are being flown in today to this base. My executive officer, XO, is going to be Captain Emma Trayhern-Cantrell."

Raising her brows, Nike said, "From *the* Trayhern family?"

"The very same. Shortly after you left Peru, Emma was assigned to BJS in Peru and flew Apaches down there for six months before I was able to convince the Pentagon to have her assigned here. She's a chip off the old Trayhern block—a real woman warrior."

"Whose child is she?" Nike wondered.

"Clay and Alyssa Cantrell-Trayhern's oldest child. Emma has three younger sisters, two of whom are in the U.S. Naval Academy right now. They're due to graduate next year. They're twins. Clay and Alyssa were Navy pilots and flew P3 antisubmarine aircraft for twenty years. Emma, whom you'll meet sometime today, is a long, lean red-haired greyhound with blazing gray eyes. I'm glad to have her on board. She's a natural XO."

Chuckling, Nike opened the folder. "Emma sounds perfect for this black ops."

"Oh, she is. Her grandfather is the original black-ops figure behind the scenes," Dallas drawled, smiling. "Let's get down to business. I'm seeing my pilots individually to give them their orders."

"Fire away," Nike murmured, studying the papers.

"First of all, BJS 60 remains an all-women U.S. Army force," Dallas began, leaning back in her chair. "The women I chose for this new squadron have more than one flight skill. For example, you are licensed to fly fixed-wing, single-engine planes as you did on the U.S.-Mexico border with me. And you're also certified to fly the CH-47, which is the workhorse helicopter used here in Afghanistan." Dallas looked over at the lean, wiry pilot. "Every woman in BJS 60 has multiskills in aviation. There may be times when I want you to fly the CH-47 and not the Apache."

"Being multitalented has never been a problem for me," Nike said, grinning.

Dallas leaned back in her chair. "We are under General Chapman and we work indirectly with the national Afghanistan Army. BJS 60 is going to be a 'sparrow-hawk' team that will be called upon in emergencies when the regular Apache pilots from the other two squadrons are not available. In other words, we're going to pick up the slack to ensure that Special Forces A teams get immediate help and support out in the field. Our jobs will vary depending upon what General Chapman's operations officer decides for us. One day you could be flying a CH-47, another, you'll be back in the seat of an Apache helicopter. Mike, my husband, is working as a liaison between Chapman's people and us. We're going to try and get as much air time as possible in the Apache, but we also know our pilots will be flying other helicopters, too."

Nike nodded. Instantly, she pictured Captain Gavin Jackson, who was a man's man, supremely confident. Someone she was drawn to, but Nike wasn't willing to admit that to herself now or ever. "I ran into one of the A teams over at the canteen a little while ago."

"Yes, they're our front-line defense here on the border," Dallas told her. "These men go out for thirty days at a time. They are hunting Taliban and stopping terrorist insurgence from getting into Afghanistan. This is one of the most dangerous places in the world for our troops—the mountains and the border around the Khyber Pass, which connects Pakistan and Afghanistan."

"And we thought Peru was dangerous," Nike joked, turning the page in the file for her assignment.

"Yeah," Dallas said grimly. "This is worse. Let's talk about your assignment tomorrow morning. Part of a new project that's being initiated by the top generals now assigned to Afghanistan is winning the hearts and minds of the border villages in this country. Tomorrow BJS 60 pilots will be assigned to certain A teams to fly them into Taliban-controlled villages. The dudes in Washington, D.C., have finally figured out that if we don't make these boundary villages pro-American, we've lost the battle to stop terrorists from coming into this country from Pakistan."

"Why are these villages pro-Taliban?" Nike wondered, perplexed.

"They aren't. First of all, Afghanistan is composed of fiercely independent tribal systems. Even the Russians, who threw ten times the troops into this country, couldn't defeat the Mujahideen. Afghans don't count on anyone to help them. They have survived thousands of years with their tribal clans. In this century, the Afghan government, which has tried to force these different tribes or clans to acknowledge them, has failed to solidify them. The central government has always ignored the mountain villages along the border, anyway. They never poured any money, medical help, education or food from the government into these villages. Basically, the Kabul government didn't think ignoring these border villages was a problem until Osama bin Laden surfaced. Now, it's our biggest problem thanks to the government's blind eye."

Tightening her lips, Dallas added, "Kabul has Afghans who defy their own central government. They remain faithful only to their tribe and their chieftain or sheik. The Taliban uses force against the villagers, attacks their women and creates hostility among the tribal people. That is why these border villages don't stop Taliban and terrorists from coming and going through their valleys. They hate them as much as we do, but they lack the resources to stop the Taliban from being the bullies on the block. And Kabul officials never sent out troops to protect these border villages from the raiding Taliban, so the villagers are understandably distrustful of the central government. And your demeanor toward these villagers will be as follows. If you, as a person, do something good for an Afghan, they will call you *brother* or *sister* until they die. They are completely loyal to those who treat them humanely and with respect. That is what I want you to cultivate as you interface with the villagers. This is the only way we are going to win their hearts and minds."

"Nice to see these outlying villages hate the Taliban as much as we do. I'll be happy to 'make nice' with these village folks," Nike said.

"This new program the general has just initiated is beginning to bear fruit. Starting tomorrow, you're going to fly an A team to Zor Barawul, a village that is located five miles away from the Pakistan border. This A team will stay thirty days to try and win the trust and respect of these villagers. This operation, which is along all of the border, is to get villagers to realize that Americans are here to help them. We're not coming in like the Taliban with guns blazing and using brute force upon them. Furthermore, the medic in each of these A teams will be bringing in all kinds of medicine for villagers. We want to gain their trust with positive and consistent care. The only medical help these people have had in the last sixty years has been from Christian church missions and Sufi medical doctors who try their best to go from village to village helping the people."

"Sufis? I thought they were Muslim."

"Yes, they are. Sufis are the mystical branch of the Muslim religion. They are about peace, not war. Love and compassion instead of hatred and prejudice. We need more of that here and the Sufis are leading the way."

Nike raised her brows. "Then Sufis are the antithesis of the Muslim terrorists, aren't they?"

Dallas nodded. "Yes, and the Taliban is willing to kill the Sufi doctors who give their life to serving the village people, if they can. The terrorists are one end of the Muslim religion, Nike. They don't represent the middle or the other end, which is the Sufi sect. Now, General Chapman wants to expand upon that humanitarian mission and bring in A teams to support what they're doing."

"Isn't that dangerous—to put an A team down in a Taliban-controlled village?"

"Yes, it is," Dallas said. "But the new general, who is taking over the country insofar as military help for the Afghans, sees that this is the only way to change the border."

Nike was disappointed that she wouldn't be flying the Apache right off the bat. She kept that to herself. "I wouldn't want to be an A team, then," Nike muttered.

"Fortunately, all you have to do is fly the CH-47 transport helicopter and drop them and their supplies off to the village and fly back here. I'm assigning you to six A teams that will be dropped along the border.

When they need anything, you'll be at their beck and call via radio. If they request more medicine, you'll get the supplies from our base here and fly it in to them. If they need food, blankets or clothing, same thing. If they need ammo or weapon resupply, you'll be on call to support that, too."

"Sounds pretty routine," Nike said, hoping to have an Apache strapped to her butt so she could give the troops air support.

Shrugging, Dallas said, "Don't be so sure. The possibility of a Taliban soldier disguised as a villager sending a rocket up to knock your helo out of the sky is very real."

"Except for a tail gunner, I won't have any other weapons at my disposal to ensure that doesn't happen," Nike griped, unhappy. Each CH-47 had an enlisted tail gunner who doubled as the load master for the helicopter.

"We'll be flying Apache support for you," Dallas promised. "We're not going to leave you out there without proper air protection." She saw the unhappy look in Nike's eyes and understood her resignation. Nike was a combat warrior, one of the finest. But not all her BJS 60 pilots were accredited to fly the CH-47 as she was. "Look, don't go glum about this assignment. See what unfolds. Your work, as mundane as it might seem, is high-risk and important."

"I think I'll strap on a second .45. You can call me two-gun Alexander."

Dallas grinned at the Greek woman's response. Picking up another file, she said, "The border area is the Wild West and Dodge City, Nike. For real. It doesn't get any more dangerous than here. Here's your first assignment—the A team you're flying out at 0530. Once you drop them off, you fly back here and we'll give you the next village flight assignment."

Opening the order, Nike gasped. "Oh my God."

"What?"

Nike looked up, a pained expression crossing her face. "I just had a run-in with this dude, Captain Gavin Jackson, over at the canteen."

Smiling slightly, Dallas said, "I hope it went well."

"Not exactly."

Chapter 2

Their air commander was Captain Nike Alexander.
Gavin couldn't believe his eyes that morning as his
team trooped across the tarmac to the waiting CH-47
that would take them to the Taliban-controlled village
of Zor Barawul.

He didn't know whether to give her an evil grin of
triumph or simply keep a poker face. As he approached
the opened rear of the CH-47's ramp, she was coming
out of the right-hand seat, helmet dangling in her hand.
When their eyes met, she instantly scowled.

Ouch. Gavin threw his pack behind the seat and
pushed the rest of his gear beneath the nylon webbing.
Looking up, he noticed her pursed lips and her narrowed
golden eyes—on him.

"Don't worry," he told her teasingly, "I'm not infec-
tious."

Nike couldn't help but grin. Despite Jackson's ragged Afghan clothing and that beard, he was undeniably handsome. A part of her wanted him. The merriment dancing in his dark blue eyes made her heart race just a little. "Don't worry, I'm vaccinated against guys like you." He merely smiled at her obvious warning. Damn, why did he have to be so good-looking?

Nike threaded between the other nine men who were settling in on either side of the cargo hold. She strolled down the ramp toward her load master, Andy Peters. The sergeant stood at the bottom waiting for everyone to get settled before he started loading the many boxes. Her boots thunked hollowly against the corrugated aluminum surface. On one side rested a fifty-caliber machine gun that Peters would put into a hole at the center of the ramp. Once airborne, Andy would drop the ramp, the ugly muzzle of the machine gun pointed down at the earth below them. Peters's job was to take out any Taliban who fired up at them or tried to launch a rocket or grenade at the bird. She nodded to short, stocky Andy, who was all of twenty years old.

Nike could feel Jackson's gaze burning two holes between her shoulder blades. He was watching her. Intently. Like a wolf on the prowl. Hunting *her*. Well, it would get him nowhere.

The brisk, early April morning was chilly. New snow had fallen overnight, leaving about six inches on the tarmac. There was barely light on the eastern horizon, the silhouette of the sharp mountain peaks highlighted. She had a dark green muffler wrapped around her neck and dangling down the front of her bulky dark green winter flight suit. As her fingers slowly froze, a mist came out of her mouth when she spoke to Andy.

"All here and accounted for?"

"Yes, ma'am. Ten-man A team." He consulted his papers on a clipboard, and then he looked over at an approaching truck. "We'll be loading all the supplies and medicine in just a moment. We're on schedule."

After consulting her watch, Nike nodded. There was a timetable to keep and she was a punctual person by nature. "Very good, Sergeant. I'll do my walk around the helo while you're getting all those boxes on board."

"Of course, ma'am."

Scanning the area, Nike appreciated the towering mountains to the east of the small base. The village of Nar was two miles away. As the dawn grew brighter, she could see the mountains were still cloaked in heavy snow. Closer to the bottom, they appeared a dark blue color. Rubbing warmth into her arms, Nike wished she'd put on her flight jacket to keep her upper body protected against the gusting breeze coming off the mountains. She'd left the jacket on the seat in the cockpit of the helo. The sky was a deep cobalt blue above the back-lit peaks. It would be a good hour before the sun, still hidden behind the peaks, would crest them. Nike noticed the last of the stars above her, twinkling and appearing close enough to reach out and touch. Most of these nap-of-the-earth flights were flown just above one hundred feet above the land. All flights departed early in the day when the dark-green-colored helicopter could be hidden in the mountain shadows from an ever-present enemy lurking below.

The canopied olive-green military truck backed up toward the chopper with Peters's hand signals to guide it. Two men hopped out of the cab once the truck halted.

Nike went to the starboard side of her helo to begin her check of all flight surfaces.

"Want some company, Captain Alexander?"

Startled, Nike turned on the heel of her boot. Gavin Jackson stood less than a foot away, a shy smile on his face. She hadn't heard him approach. *Stealth.* That was what hunter-killer A teams were all about: you must not be seen or heard in order to kill your target. Gulping convulsively, Nike pressed a hand to her neck. "You scared the hell out of me, Captain!"

"Oh, sorry," he said, shrugging. And then he brightened. "Call me Gavin when we're alone like this."

Scowling, Nike continued her slow walk along the two-engine helo. "I'll think about it," she said. Nike scanned the rivets in the plates for signs of wear or loosening. Craning her neck, she checked for hydraulic leaks from either of the two massive engines on each end of the bird.

Undeterred, Gavin fell into step with her. "Don't you think it's kismet that we've met twice in less than twenty-four hours?"

Giving him a long, dark look, Nike growled, "More like damnable karma if you asked me."

"Ouch."

"Oh, get over yourself, Captain Jackson." Nike faced him, her hands on her hips. He was about six foot two inches tall and it killed her to have to look *up* at him. His blue eyes were warm and inviting. Without thinking, her gaze fell to his smiling mouth. He had a very, very male mouth. And for a moment, Nike realized he would be a damned good kisser. But a lover? Just because he was a man didn't mean he automatically had the kind of maturity that Nike demanded. And why on earth was she even *thinking* along those lines with this rude dude?

Snorting, she jerked her gaze up. "Listen, hotshot, cool your jets. You're obviously starved for a warm female body, but remove me from your gun sights. I'm not interested."

Dark brows rising, Gavin backed off and held up his hands. "Whoa, Nike—"

"It's Captain Alexander to you." Nike flinched inwardly when she saw his cheeks beneath his beard go ruddy with embarrassment. He had enough humility to blush. Jackson wasn't really the ego-busting officer Nike had first thought. Hands still resting on her hips, she added with less acidity, "We have a job to do, Captain. I'll do mine and you do yours. All I have to do is fly your team into a village, drop you off and then I'm out of your life."

"That's not very optimistic," Gavin observed. Her face was a mask of wariness. And yet, he sensed a crack in that facade. Oh, it wasn't anything he could point to or see, but Gavin knew his little-boy expression had gotten to her. There wasn't a woman alive who wouldn't melt under that look. Of course, it wasn't really a ploy. Gavin was a little boy at heart when he could get away with it.

"War is *never* optimistic, Captain."

Shaking his head, Gavin said, "Now where did you pick up that attitude?"

"In Peru. Chasing druggies for three years. Give no quarter, take no quarter. That's my maxim, Captain."

"I like it," Gavin said, properly impressed. The corners of his mouth moved upward. "You're a brazen woman, Captain Alexander, and you make my heart beat faster."

Nike ignored the comment, though it secretly pleased her. She finished her inspection of her helo. Maybe he'd get the message and leave her alone. She felt Jackson approach and walk silently at her side. When she halted to touch the metal skin to inspect something more closely, he would wait without a word.

What kind of game was this? Nike thought for sure if she gave him "the look" that he'd disappear inside the helo. Nope. Not Gavin Jackson. He still had that thoughtful and curious expression on his face. His blue eyes gleamed with humor. In his business, there wasn't much to be merry about, yet he looked amiable, approachable and drop-dead handsome.

"You know," Gavin said conversationally as she halted at the Plexiglas nose, "there isn't a man on this godforsaken base out in the middle of nowhere that isn't happy about BJS flying into town." He rubbed his hands. "An *all-women* squadron. That's really something."

"We're black ops," she warned him. Jackson seemed absolutely joyous over the prospect of ten Apaches with twenty pilots and a mostly all-women crew coming to this base. No wonder. "Not sex on legs."

"Ouch. Double ouch."

"Oh, give me a break, Captain. That's all you see us women as—bedding material." She moved around the nose to the port side of the helicopter.

"That's not fair."

A burst of sharp laughter erupted from Nike. "It's the truth, isn't it? Who said anything in life was fair?"

Nodding, Gavin moved with her, his hands behind

his back and face thoughtful. "I see you as sharing more than just my bed."

"Oh sure," Nike said, eyeing him. She ran her cold fingers across the metal. Rivets would come loose under the constant shuddering and vibration of the blades turning. Never did she want any of these light aluminum panels to be ripped off midflight. It could cause a crash.

"No, seriously," Gavin pleaded. Leaning down, he caught her golden gaze. "I'm dying for some feminine companionship."

"Intelligent conversation with a woman? I like that."

The jeering in her tone made Gavin chuckle. "That's all I want, Captain Alexander—just a little conversation."

Nike shot him an I-don't-believe-you-for-a-second look and continued her walk around. As she leaned under the carriage, she checked the tires. The tread was thick and obviously new. That was good because when she landed this bird on rocky terrain, she didn't need a blowout. Tires had to be in top-notch condition.

"We have *nothing* in common except for this assignment, Captain Jackson."

"Are you so sure?"

Straightening to her full height, Nike grinned. "*Very* sure." He stood there with a quizzical expression on his features. And she had to admit, he had a nice face. She liked looking at him, with his wide brow and high cheekbones. He had a prominent nose and a solid chin hidden beneath the dark beard. His lips reminded her of those on a sculpted bust of Julius Caesar. They were his best attribute aside from his large, inquiring blue eyes. She found it tough to think of him as someone who could easily pull a trigger and kill someone if needed. Jackson just didn't seem like the killer type.

"Why don't you give me a chance to prove otherwise?" Gavin pleaded as they neared the rear ramp. He knew he could win her over. The men had just finished loading fifty boxes of supplies for the village. The truck fired up, the blue diesel smoke purling upward in thick, churning clouds. He halted. So did she. Nike seemed to be considering his challenge. *Good.*

Why did he want to engage her on any level? Hadn't he had enough with Laurie and her inability to compromise? Never mind he'd fallen head over heels in love with her. He'd been able to take her stubbornness in stride. Her ego was considerable and dominating like his. And that was what had broken them up. Two headstrong egos unable to bend. Laurie had brought out the worst in him. And he was as much at fault in the breakup as she was. Gavin felt men and women were equals—not one better than the other. Laurie, however, had felt that all women were inherently better than any man and that grated on Gavin, too.

"This attention is flattering but I'm busy," Nike told him with finality.

"Are you married?"

"That's none of your business, Captain." Nike glared at him. "Let's get this straight—I'm your pilot. I fly you in, drop your team off and leave. I come back with any supplies you radio in to ops. Nothing more or less. Got it?"

Sighing, Gavin said, "Yes, I got it. I wish it was otherwise, though." True, Nike had a helluva ego but didn't seem as stubborn as Laurie. "You're an interesting person. How many women have been flying against South

American drug cartels?" He gave her a warm smile. "See? We really do have something to discuss. I'm kind of an interesting dude myself."

"Oh, I'm sure you think that," Nike said, laughing. She shook her head and moved up the ramp.

Gavin stood watching her pull on the helmet and get situated in the right-hand seat in the cockpit. Nodding to the load master, Gavin mounted the ramp.

His men were grinning expectantly at him as he made his way to his nylon seat right behind Nike. He held up his hands in a show of surrender and they all laughed. Gavin didn't mind making himself the target of fun or prodding. His team had had a two-week rest, and now they were going out again. This time, he hoped, to something less dangerous, but he wasn't sure of that.

The ramp groaned and rumbled upward until finally the hatch was shut with a loud clang. Darkness, except for the light coming in through the cockpit, made the inside of the helicopter gray. Gavin watched his men strap in, their weapons in hand, their faces belying their real thoughts. He prayed that as they approached Zor Barawul nearby Taliban soldiers wouldn't be firing RPGs at them as they came in for a landing. He knew from the premission briefing that the townspeople hated the Taliban. But were they pro-American? There was no way to know except to walk in, offer humanitarian aid and see what happened next. They had no script written for this newest idea by General Chapman.

After pulling on his helmet, Gavin plugged in the radio connection and heard Nike's honeyed voice as she talked with the base air controller for permission to lift off. She had already engaged one engine on the helo and then the other one. Gavin had found out at the briefing with his people that her usual copilot had food poisoning and there was no one to replace her. Nike was flying alone, which wasn't a good thing, but Gavin had seen it happen.

If they weren't wearing helmets, the noise created by the helicopter would be horrendous and would destroy their hearing in a short time. The bird shuddered and shook around him. The deck beneath his booted feet constantly shivered. If his men had any worry about a woman flying this huge, hulking transport helo a hundred feet off the earth, they didn't show it. Flying nap-of-the-earth took a helluva lot of skill. Gavin wondered how many hours she had of flight time. When Nike had finished her conversation with the tower, Gavin piped up, "Captain, how many hours do you have flying this bird?"

All his men heard the question, of course, because they, too, had helmets on and were plugged in to the inter-cabin radio system. Gavin saw the load master at the far end turn and give him a questioning look. He also heard the explosion of laughter from Nike.

"Oh, let's see, Captain, I got my helo-driver's license at Disneyland in Orlando, Florida," she drawled. "Does that count?"

His men were guffawing in reaction, but no one could hear it over the noise of the vibrating helo around them. Jackson chuckled. "I feel better, Captain Alexander. So long as Mickey Mouse signed off on your pilot's license I feel safe and sound."

Jackson thought some of his men were going to fall out of their nylon seats they were laughing so hard. He joined them. And then he heard Nike joining their collective roar of laughter. She had a wonderful, husky tone and it made his body ache with need. What kind of magic did this Greek woman have over him?

"Actually," Nike said, chuckling, "it was Minnie Mouse who signed it. You have a problem with that?"

"No, not at all. Now, if Goofy had signed it, I'd be worried."

Even the load master was giggling in fits, his gloved hands closed over the fifty-caliber. Unaccountably, Gavin felt his spirits rise. If nothing else, Nike Alexander gave as good as she got. Even more to her credit, she could take a joke and come back swinging. Looking into the faces of his men, Gavin felt a warmth toward the woman pilot. Did Nike realize how much she'd just lifted everyone's spirits? Probably not. But he would tell her—alone—and thank her for being a good sport on a deadly mission.

"Okay, boys," Nike said, catching her breath, "let's get this show on the road. Sergeant, once we're airborne, lower the ramp and keep that .50 cal ready to shoot. We're not in Disneyland and where we're going, the bad guys are waiting. Hunker down, you're about to go on the wildest roller-coaster ride you've ever taken. I'm ready to rock...."

For the next fifty minutes, Nike's full concentration was winding between, around and down into one valley after another in the steep, rugged mountain range. When they roared past Do Bandi, another village, she knew they would soon be climbing steeply. Zor Barawul sat in a rich, fertile valley ringed by the snowy mountains. On the eastern side of those mountains lay the Pakistan border where Taliban hid. The valley was a well-known Taliban route. They boldly passed through it because the Afghan villagers could not fire on or challenge them. If they did, the Taliban would come in and kill men, women and children.

The sunlight shone in bright slats across the mountaintops as she brought the Chinook up steeply, pushing with throttles to the firewall to make it up and over the snowy slope that blurred beneath them. How badly Nike wanted a copilot to do all this other work, but that wasn't her luck today. Captain Emma Trayhern, the XO who was supposed to fly with her, had caught a nasty case of food poisoning and was laid low for the next twenty-four hours. Her CO, Dallas Klein, had faith in her to handle this mission all by herself. Helluva compliment, but Nike would have preferred a copilot, thank you very much. The sunlight made her squint even though she wore a pair of aviator's sunglasses. The bird rocked from one side to another as she aimed the nose downward at top speed and skimmed headlong down a steep, rocky slope and into another valley.

Nike could see herds of sheep and goats being tended by young boys here and there on the bright green valley floor. They would look up, wave as the CH-47 streaked by them. The herds of animals would flee in all directions as the noisy Chinook passed low overhead. Nike felt sorry for the young herders who would probably spend half a day gathering up their scattered herds. What she didn't want to see was yellow or red winking lights from below. That would mean the Taliban was firing a rocket up at them. *Not good.*

The mountains were coated with thick snow even in April. The lower slopes showed hopeful signs of greenery sprouting after enduring the fierce, cold Afghan winter. The helicopter vibrated heavily around Nike as she flew the bulky transport through the valley. Shoving the throttles once more to the firewall, she urged the helo up and over another mountain range and down into the next valley. And, as she glanced out her cockpit window, it was comforting to see an Apache helicopter with her women friends from BJS 60 flying several thousand feet above her, working their avionics to find the enemy below before they shot her Chinook out of the air. She might not have a copilot, but she had the baddest son-of-a-bitch of a combat helicopter shadowing her flight today. That made Nike smile and feel confident.

The village of Zor Barawul contained two hundred people and sat at the north end of a long, narrow valley that was sandwiched between the mountains. On the other side lay the border of Pakistan. As in all villages Nike had seen, the wealthy families had houses made of stone with wooden floors. Wood was usually scarce. Those less well-off had homes made of earth and mud with hard-packed dirt floors. Some who could afford it would have a few rugs over the earthen floor. Roofs were made from tin or other lightweight metals. The poorer families had thatched material on top.

As they passed over all kinds of homes, Nike felt the sweat beneath her armpits. Fear was always near since at any moment, they could be fired on. As she located the landing area, she ordered her load master to bring up the ramp. Moments later, she heard the grind and rumble of the ramp shutting. The ramp had to be up in order for her to land.

Nike brought the Chinook downward and gently landed it outside the village. The earth was bare and muddy. Nike let out a sigh of relief. They were down and had made it without incident. She powered down, shut off the engines and called to her friends in the Apache flying in large circles outside the village. This was Taliban-controlled territory and the Apache was using its television and infrared cameras to spot any possible enemy who might want to shoot at the Chinook after it had landed.

The whine of the engines ceased. The women in the Apache reported no activity and continued to circle about a mile from where she'd landed. Nike thanked them and signed off on the radio. The Apache would wait and escort her back to base as soon as everything was unloaded. Unstrapping the tight harness, she pulled the helmet off her head and stood. Andy had removed the fifty-caliber machine gun and set it to one side. He opened the ramp and it groaned down. Once the ramp lip rested on the muddy ground, Andy signaled the A team to dismount.

As she glanced to her left, Nike caught sight of Gavin. This time, he was grim-faced and not smiling. *Right.* He understood this was a very dangerous place. No one knew for sure how the villagers would respond to their landing. Bullets or butter? For a moment, Nike felt a twinge in her heart. Jackson looked so damned responsible and alert. This wasn't his first dance with the Afghan people. She saw the grimness reflected in the flat line of his mouth as he gathered his gear and slung it across his shoulder.

His other team members were already moving down the ramp. Several took the cargo netting off the many boxes and prepared to move them outside the helo. What were the people of this village thinking of their arrival? Were they scared? Thinking that the U.S. Army was going to attack them the way the Taliban did? When the Russians had invaded Afghanistan a decade before, that's exactly what they had done. People here justifiably had a long memory and would probably not trust the Americans, either.

"Hey, do these people know you're coming?" Nike called to Jackson.

"Yeah, we sent an emissary in here a week ago."

"So, they know you're on a mission of peace?"

He took the safety off his weapon and then slung it across his other shoulder. "That's right. It doesn't guarantee anything."

Worriedly, Nike looked out the end of the Chinook. She saw several bearded older men in turbans or fur hats walking toward them. "Well, they don't look real happy to see us."

Gavin glanced out the rear of the helo. "Oh. Those are the elders. They run the village. Don't worry, they always look that way. Survival is serious business out here."

"They're carrying rifles."

"They sleep with them."

Smiling a little over the comment, Nike walked down the ramp and stood next to him. "Do you ever not have a joke, Captain?"

Gavin grinned over at her. Nike's hair lay against her brow, emphasizing her gold eyes. He heard the worry in her voice and reached out to squeeze her upper arm. "You care...."

Nike didn't pull away from where his hand rested on her arm. There was monitored strength to his touch and her flesh leaped wildly in response. Seconds later, his hand dropped away. "Oh, don't let it go to your swelled head, honcho."

"Hey, I like that nickname."

"It wasn't a compliment."

Gavin chuckled. "I'll take it as such."

"Ever the optimist."

"I don't like the other choice, do you? Thanks for the wild ride, Captain." He gave her a salute and smiled. "How about a date when we get back off this mission?"

"That's not a good idea." Nike saw the regret in his deep blue eyes.

"Okay, I'll stop chasing you for now." Looking out the rear of the helo, Gavin said, "I'll be seeing you around, lioness."

She felt and heard the huskiness of his voice as he spoke the word. *Lioness.* Well, that was a nice compliment. Unexpected. Sweet. And her heart thumped in reaction. She hated to admit it but she really did care. But before she could open her mouth, he turned and walked nonchalantly down the ramp and into the dangerous world of the Taliban-controlled village.

Suddenly, Nike was afraid for Gavin and his team. The ten elders approached in their woolen cloaks, pants and fur hats to ward off the morning coldness. They looked unwelcoming and grim.

Well, it wasn't as if she could help him and she had to get back to base. A part of her didn't want to leave Gavin. Nike looked up and saw the Apache continuing its slow circuit at about three thousand feet. *Time to move.* Grabbing her helmet, she gave Andy a gesture that told him to lift up the ramp. He nodded. As soon as they were airborne, he'd lower the ramp once more and keep watch with his hands on that machine gun.

Settling into her seat, Nike pulled on her helmet,

plugged it back in and made contact with the Apache once more.

"Time to boogie outta here, Red Fox One. Over."

"Roger, Checkerboard One. All quiet on the western front here."

Nike chuckled and twisted around. The ramp ground upward and locked against the bird, causing the whole helo to shudder. Andy gave her a thumbs-up and put on his helmet. All was well. Turning around, Nike began to flip switches and twist buttons. As soon as she was ready to turn on the engines, one at a time, she'd get harnessed up for the harrowing one-hundred-foot-high flight back to base. It wasn't something Nike looked forward to.

And then, her world came to an abrupt halt. A glaring red light began to blink back at her on the console—the forward engine light. Scowling, she flipped it off and on. *Red. Damn.* That meant either a problem with the engine or a screw-up with the light itself. Nike could do nothing at this point.

"Red Fox One, I have a red light for the forward engine. I can't go anywhere. Can you contact base to get a helo out here with a couple of mechanics? Until then, I'm grounded. I'll radio Operations and get further instructions from them. Over."

"Bad news, Checkerboard One. Stay safe down there. Out."

Well, it didn't take long for Nike to get her answers. Major Dallas Klein, who was in ops, answered her.

"Stay where you are. We can't get a mechanic team out until tomorrow morning. Stick with Captain Jackson and his team. Your load master will remain with the helicopter. In the meantime, go with the A team.

We'll be in touch by radio when we know the time of arrival to your location. Over."

Great. Nike scowled and responded. "Roger. Over and out."

Now what? She gestured for Andy to come forward because he had not been privy to what was going on. Shaking her head, Nike felt a sense of dread combined with unexplainable elation. She was stuck here with Jackson, who clearly would be delighted with her company. *Double damn.*

Chapter 3

Jackson walked toward village elders. The knot of men stood watching them. But before he could talk with them, Nike appeared at his shoulder, her face set and disappointed.

"What's wrong?" he asked, anchoring to a halt.

"My helo has engine failure and I've got orders to stay the night here with you and your team. My load master will remain with the bird. A mechanic team will be flown out to fix it tomorrow morning."

She didn't seem too happy about the news but joy threaded through Gavin. "Engine failure." He tried to sound disappointed for her. "Sorry about that, Captain Alexander."

Nike tried to avoid his powerful stare and glanced over at the knot of elders. They were a sour-looking bunch. Every one of them wore a deep, dark scowl of suspicion. She returned her attention to Jackson. "Let's look at the positives. This engine failure could have happened en route. We're damned lucky to have landed before the problem."

"And here I thought you were a doom-and-gloom pessimist." Jackson grinned and desperately wanted this moment alone with her, but the elders had to be properly greeted.

Nike shook her head and muttered, "Jackson, you're a piece of work."

He smiled quickly and then resumed his serious demeanor toward the elders. "Thank you."

"It wasn't a compliment."

"As always, I'll take anything you say as a positive."

"Get real," she gritted between her teeth so that only he could hear her. On either side of them, the team had fanned out, hands on their weapons but trying not to appear threatening to the elders.

"Do me a favor?" Gavin said.

"Depends upon what it is."

"These elders have strict laws regarding their women. I'll be speaking to them in Pashto. They may have a problem with you not wearing a *hijab,* or scarf, on your head. That scarf is a sign of honoring their Muslim beliefs. So, if it comes to pass that someone hands you a scarf, wear it."

Nike nodded. "No problem."

"Thanks, I needed that."

"Judging from their looks, you're going to need more than a scarf on my head to turn this situation into a positive, honcho."

Gavin said nothing. Nike took a step back, partly hidden by his tall, lean frame. The elders looked aged, their weathered faces deeply lined. Their skin was tobacco-brown, resembling leather, because of their tough outdoor life. Nike knew the elements at the top of the world in this mountain chain were unforgiving and brutal. Villages along the border had no electricity, no sewers and sometimes little water. These rugged Afghan people eked out a living raising goats and sheep. At this altitude, poppy crops wouldn't grow because the season was too short. Winter came early and stayed late. Nike had found out through the weather officer at BJS ops that snow started in September and lasted sometimes into June. That was why they couldn't grow crops and relied heavily on their animals for a food source.

The elders had good reason to be serious-looking, their hands hidden in the sleeves of their woolen robes, chins held high and their dark eyes assessing the A team. These proud and fiercely independent Afghan people had few resources. Beneath their threadbare woolen clothing, Nike saw the thinness of all the elders. There wasn't a fat one in the group. Their leanness was probably due to the hardships of living in such a rocky, inhospitable place. She felt compassion and respect toward them, not animosity.

Gavin had been given an in-depth briefing on Zor Barawul before arriving at the village. Photos had been taken and the elders were identified in them. He recognized the chief elder, Abbas, who separated himself from the group. He was in his sixties and every inch like his name, which meant "angry lion" in Pashto. They approached each other like two competing football-team captains staring one another down. Tension sizzled in the cold morning air between the two groups of men. Walking forward, Gavin extended his hand to Abbas, who wore a dark brown turban and cloak. The man's face was as narrow and thinned as a starving lion's, horizontal lines deeply carved across his broad brow. Gashes slashed down on either side of his pursed lips. Ordinarily, the Afghan custom of greeting was to shake hands and then kiss each other's cheeks as a sign of friendship.

That wasn't going to happen here. Gavin fervently hoped that Abbas would at least shake his extended hand. The elder glared at him and then down at his hand. No, that wasn't going to happen, either. Gavin pressed his right hand over his heart, bowed referentially and murmured, *"Salaam-a-laikam."* This meant "peace be with you," and was a greeting given no matter if the person were Muslim or of some other faith. It was a sign of respect and of the two people meeting on common ground.

Scowling, Abbas touched his chest where his heart lay and murmured, *"Wa alaikum assalam wa rahmatu Allah,"* in return. That meant "And to you be peace together with God's mercy."

Gavin could see that Abbas was surprised by his sincere and knowledgeable greeting. His scowl eased and his voice became less gruff. "We told your emissary last week, Captain Jackson, that we did *not* want you to come to our village. The Kabul government has always ignored us. There is no reason you should be here at their invitation. If the Taliban finds out we are dealing with the Americans, they will come back here and kill more of my people. We are a tribe and as such, do not recognize the government as having any power or control over our lives," Abbas said in Pashto, his arms remaining tightly wrapped against his chest.

Halting, Gavin allowed his hand to drop back to his side. *"Sahibji,"* he began in Pashto, "we do not come as representatives of the Kabul government. I realize you do not acknowledge them. The American people have donated all of this—" he turned and swept his hand toward the stacked boxes "—as respect for your tribe. Americans believe in peace and when they found out that your children needed help, they sent these boxes of medicine to you." Gavin kept his voice sincere. "There is also food and blankets for your people, if you will accept their heartfelt generosity."

Gavin knew that Afghan people, when given a sincere gift, would never forget the heart-centered gesture and would be friends for life with the givers. They were a remarkable warrior class who judged others on their loyalty and honor. They held an ancient set of codes based upon Islamic belief and here, in these mountains, the villagers practiced these morals and values to this day. That was one of the reasons the Russians had never been able to break the spirit of these proud people. The more they tried to destroy the Afghan tribal culture, the more stubborn the people became. Gavin felt General Chapman's operation to win the hearts and minds of these people, one village at a time along the border, was much wiser and more humane. Gavin knew the Afghans would respond to honest gifts given from the heart, for they, above all, were a heart-centered people.

Abbas's thick black-and-gray brows lifted slightly as he looked longingly toward the boxes. Then, his mouth curled as he swung his gaze back to the captain. "And for this you want what?"

Shrugging, Gavin said, "The opportunity to earn your friendship over time. Judge us on a daily basis and allow us to earn your respect." He knew that the Afghan people were a proud people and that they were slow to give their trust. It was earned by deeds alone—not by any words, but actions.

"I have families who are sick and ailing," Abbas said abruptly. "Even if there is medicine, there is no doctor. So what good is all of this?"

Gavin turned to his medic, Staff Sergeant Neal Robles. "This is Sergeant Robles. He is my paramedic and one level below a medical doctor. We have brought him to help your people. We are here on a strictly humanitarian mission. We are not here to cause stress or fighting."

Grunting, Abbas lifted his chin a little higher. He stroked his salt-and-pepper beard. Looking over at the paramedic, he demanded, "And this man can do what?"

"He can give vaccinations to all your children. Many Afghan children die unnecessarily of diseases and our vaccinations can stop that. He can examine a male and treat him accordingly. We have brought antibiotics, as well."

At that, Abbas's brows lifted in surprise. Hope flared in his narrowed eyes.

Gavin saw his response. Abbas knew antibiotics were as valuable a commodity as opium made from the poppy fields of southern Afghanistan. The elder understood, thankfully, that antibiotics could save a life. But in this remote village, there was no way to get them nor was there the help of a doctor to dispense the lifesaving drug. Gavin was sure that Abbas had seen any number of children, men and women die of ailments that could have been stopped and turned around by antibiotics. "Sergeant Robles will train a man and a woman whom you suggest to use the antibiotics that we will supply to you. Your village will always have them on hand from now on." Gavin could see the surprise and then the gratefulness in the man's narrowed dark eyes.

Abbas heard the elders of the village whispering excitedly over the officer's last statement. Turning, he saw them eagerly nod over receiving such a gift. His tribe had suffered severely for years beneath the Kabul government, the Russians and now, the Taliban. Drilling a look into the captain, Abbas growled, "My people have died without the help of our own government. They do not care whether we exist. If not for a Sufi brother and sister who are medical doctors who visit our village twice a year, many more would have died." He jammed a long, thin index finger down at the hard brown earth where he stood.

"The United States of America is trying to change that," Gavin told him in a persuasive tone. "We are here on a mission of mercy." He walked toward the boxes, printed in English and Pashto. "Come and see. This is not the Kabul government nor my government. This is from the American people who do not like to see anyone's children die. Look at the gifts from my people to your villagers. There is clothing, blankets, food and medicine. All we ask is to be able to distribute it and have our medic help those who ask for medical attention."

Abbas walked commandingly over to the bounty, his lean shoulders squared, head held at a proud angle. He reached out with long brown hands and placed them on the tops of several of the cardboard boxes. Walking around the fifty cartons, he stopped, read the Pashto lettering on one and then moved on. The rest of the elders came to his side at his gesture. Gavin watched the group of men carefully read each label and check out the gifts.

Gavin turned and to Nike spoke quietly, "Listen, I need a favor. There are women here who need medical attention. Abbas isn't about to let Robles touch any Muslim female since it's against their religion. Can I volunteer you to help him?"

"But I don't have any medical training," Nike whispered.

"Doesn't matter. Robles will teach you the basics."

She saw the pleading in his eyes. "I don't want to hurt anyone with my lack of experience."

"Don't worry, that won't happen."

Abbas strode over and gave Gavin a brusque nod of acceptance. "Allah is good. The gifts are indeed welcome, Captain Jackson. *Shukria,* thank you."

"You're welcome, *malik sahib,*" Gavin murmured, touching his heart and bowing his head respectfully to the elder.

Mouth quirking, Abbas looked directly at Nike and jabbed a finger toward her. "And this is the woman who will help Dr. Robles?"

Gavin didn't want to correct the elder. To do so would be a sign of disrespect. Besides, it would humiliate Abbas in front of the others and he had no wish to destroy what little trust he had just forged between them. "Yes, sir. Captain Nike Alexander will assist Dr. Robles, if you wish. With your permission, she will care for the women and girls of your village."

"I wish it to be so," Abbas said in a gruff tone. "My wife, Jameela, will bring her a *hijab* to wear over her head. She must respect Islam." He folded his arms across his narrow chest. "You are welcome to remain

here and help my people, Captain Jackson. We are a
peaceful tribe of sheep- and goat-herders. I will have
my second-in-command, Brasheer, help you." He eyed
Nike. "This woman is not allowed among your men.
She will remain at our home. My wife will give her a
room and she will remain in the company of women
and children only."

"Of course," Gavin murmured, and he explained that
Nike would be a transiting visitor because the helo was
down. "You are most gracious," he told Abbas, giving
him a slight bow of acknowledgment. "We would like
to stay as long as you need medical help."

"I approve. Captain, you shall honor me by being
my guest at every meal. We will prepare a room in our
house for you. Your men will be housed at the other
homes, fed, and given a place to sleep."

"Thank you, *malik sahib*. You are more than generous. We hope our stay improves the health of your
people." Gavin could see the hope burning in the old
man's eyes. As an elder, he carried the weighty responsibility for everyone in his village. It wasn't something
Gavin himself would want to carry. Abbas must realize what these gifts would do to help his people. And
he knew he was weighing Taliban displeasure over it,
too. The Taliban would punish the village for taking
the offered supplies and the old man took a surprising
risk. With such humanitarian aide, this village might
become less fearful of the Taliban and provide information to stop the terrorists from crossing their valley
in the future. For now, no one in the villages gave away
that information.

Gavin finished off the details of where the boxes
would be taken and stored. All his men could speak

Pashto. Robles was as fluent as Gavin and that would work in their favor. The other elders took over the management of the boxes while his A team became the muscle to carry the cartons toward the village.

Gavin watched as the elders left, parading the groups of carriers and boxes back into their village like conquering heroes. "Do you know any Pashto?" he asked Nike.

"I have problems with English sometimes and I'm Greek, remember?"

"So, I guess that's a no." Grinning, Gavin felt the tension melting off his tense shoulders. Just looking into Nike's gold eyes made him hungry for her again. Black curls framed her face and Gavin had to stop himself from reaching out and threading his fingers through that dark, shining mass. "Pashto isn't that difficult. Most villagers don't speak English. I'll get one of my other men to help interpret from a distance. You can always go outside the home and talk to him out in the street and he can translate. He won't be allowed in where there is a female."

"That sounds like a workable strategy." She narrowed her eyes on Gavin. "So how did it go with Abbas? He looked like he'd just won the lottery when he read some of the labels on that shipment."

Gavin laughed a little while keeping alert. Taliban came through this valley all the time, and he knew that with an American A team here, word would get out to their enemy. "The elders' main concern is the health of their people. We've done this type of mission in southern Afghanistan for the last year and it was a great success. The key is in establishing trust with the Afghans."

Nike nodded and noticed how Jackson remained

alert. She was glad the .45 pistol was strapped to her left leg. And wearing a bulletproof vest gave her a strong sense of protection. She hated wearing the chafing vest, but this was Dodge City and bullets could fly at any time. "I thought I saw tears in his eyes. He kept stroking the tops of the boxes that contained the antibiotics. It reminds me of a Greek proverb—*Upon touching sand may it turn to gold.* Only this time, his gold is the life-saving drugs for his people."

Grimly, Gavin agreed and said, "I'm sure he's seen many of his people die terrible, suffering deaths that could have been avoided if they'd only had antibiotics available to them."

"Pnigese s'ena koutali nero," she agreed softly in Greek.

Cocking his head, Gavin said, "What did you just say?"

"You drown in a teaspoon of water. Another one of my Greek sayings I was raised with. It's the equivalent to your saying that for want of a nail the horse's shoe is lost, and for want of a shoe the horse is lost, and for want of a horse, the battle is lost." She held up her finger. "Antibiotics are a small thing, but in his world, they're huge," Nike said. "Why was Abbas pointing at me earlier?"

"His wife, Jameela, will bring you a *hijab* to wear. Just be grateful to her for the gesture. Muslim women always wear the *hijab* any time they're outside their home. In Arabic it means *covering* or *concealing.*" His mouth pulled into a devilish grin. "The best part is Abbas inviting us to stay at his home. The men and women are always separated. You'll be on the women's side of the house and have your own room. You'll also eat separately, too."

"That's a little strict."

"I agree, but we have to be aware of their religious laws. Afghans see that as a sign of respect. And respect can, we hope, earn us friendship with them."

Nike said, "Okay, boss, I can do it. Not exactly military issue, but in black ops you have to be flexible."

"Good. Come on, I see a woman coming toward us. She's got a red *hijab* in hand, so that must be Jameela."

When Gavin placed his hand beneath her elbow, Nike was surprised. She felt a sense of protection emanating from him. It was like a warm blanket surrounding her and she couldn't protest the nice gesture. The entire village, it seemed, had come out to view the boxes. Indeed, word had traveled fast. Women, men and children stood as the elders marched past them with the A team carrying some of the boxes. There was crackling excitement and expectation in the air.

"Women are pretty well hidden here from the outer world. When they're inside their homes they don't have to wear a burka or *hijab.* And there's real power among the women. They treat one another like sisters. Even though you may think the women have it bad, they really run the place. They have a lot of power in the household and in the village decisions in general. The women learned a long time ago to stick together as a unit. United they stand and divided they fall. Woman power is strong among the Afghan women and I think you'll enjoy being a part of it," Gavin told her conversationally as they walked toward Jameela. The elder's wife wore a black burka. The black wool robe swathed her from her head to her shoes. A crosshatch opening revealed her cinnamon-colored eyes.

"Don't expect me to wear one of those things," Nike warned him with a growl. "All the women are dressed like her. I'm not going to wear a burka. I'll stay in my uniform."

"They won't ask you to don a burka, so don't worry. Little girls don't start wearing them until around age seven. Until then, they've still got their freedom from the burka."

Nike grumbled, "I have a really hard time thinking any woman would be happy wearing a burka."

"Try to be gracious and don't stir up trouble with Jameela—she's the chieftain's wife. There's an unspoken hierarchy here in these villages. She's boss of the women and children. Jameela wields a lot of power even though she's hidden under that burka. Don't ever underestimate her position and authority. In reality, the women have equal power to any of these men. It may not appear to be like that, but from what I've seen, it is."

"*All* women are powerful," Nike reminded him. She felt his hand slip away as they walked to meet the tall, thin woman swathed in the black wool robe.

"No argument from me." And then Gavin turned slightly, gave her a wink and added teasingly, "Especially you…"

Nike had no time to retort. She felt heat rising in her face. Gavin chuckled with delight. Focusing on Jameela, Nike searched the woman's spice-brown eyes between the fabric crosshatch. It was Jameela's only opening into the outside world. Nike felt at odds with the woman, who stood about five foot six inches tall.

Only her hands, reddened and work-worn, told Nike of her hard, unrelenting life.

Gavin bowed in respect to Jameela and offered the Islamic greeting to her as they halted about six feet from one another. Jameela whispered softly the return greeting to Gavin and to Nike, who bowed slightly, pressed her hand to heart and said, *"Salaam."* She didn't know what else they said to one another, but at one point, Jameela leaned forward and gave Nike the *hijab*. She made some gestures indicating she should wrap it around her head.

Nike gave her a friendly smile and put it on. Once the knotted scarf was in place, Jameela's eyes crinkled as if she were smiling. Perhaps she was grateful to Nike for honoring their customs. Not being able to see another person's body language or their facial expressions was highly disconcerting. Nike realized in those minutes how much she truly assessed a person through nonverbal means. Jameela remained a mystery to her.

"I speak...English...little..." Jameela said haltingly to Gavin and Nike, opening her hands as if to apologize.

Nike was delighted and grinned. She saw Gavin smile and nod.

"Where did you learn English?" Gavin asked her politely. He knew that Jameela shouldn't be talking to him. Under the circumstances, he felt it was all right but not something to be done more than once outside her home.

"When I was little, my parents lived in Kabul. I was taught English at a Christian missionary school." Shrugging her small shoulders beneath the burka, Jameela laughed shyly. "Coming out here, I could not practice it. So, I am very poor at speaking your language, but I will try."

"Thank you, *memsahib*," Gavin told her quickly in Pashto. "My friend, Captain Nike Alexander—" he gestured toward her "—is here to help the women and children. Perhaps you could interpret for her? She does not know Pashto."

Jameela nodded in deference toward Nike. "Of course, Captain, I would be happy to. Please, apologize to her that I speak broken English?"

Gavin nodded. "Of course, *memsahib,* but you speak English very well. I know Captain Alexander will be grateful for your English and translation help. Thank you."

Jameela bowed her head slightly, her long hands clasped in front of her. Nike could have sworn the Afghan woman blushed, but it was hard to tell with the burka like a wall between them.

"You are the first Americans to come here," Jameela told Gavin in a softened tone. "There are Sufi twin brother and sister medical doctors, Reza and Sahar Khan, who visit us once every six months. The Sufis are heart-centered and they help us greatly. The Khan twins travel from the northern border of Afghanistan and follow it all the way to the south helping the villages along the way. Then, they turn around in their Jeep and come back north to do it all over again. We bless them. The Sufis are a branch of Islam who are dedicated to compassionate love toward all, no matter what their beliefs."

"Yes, I'm aware of the Sufis' nature," Gavin told her in Pashto. "I'm also aware that the Taliban hate them. The Sufis practice peace at all costs and the Taliban has been known to kill them."

Jameela nodded sadly. "That is so, Captain Jackson.

But Doctors Reza and Sahar Khan are welcomed by all our villages along the border, regardless. We greet them and bring them into our villages on two white horses. We place flower wreaths around their necks and sing their praises. That is our custom of honoring their courage to care for us regardless of the personal danger they place themselves in. They have saved many of our people over the years."

"I've heard the Khans mentioned by other villagers," Gavin said. "I hope one day to meet them. They're heroic people and give the Sufis a good name around the world for their courage and generosity."

Jameela hesitated and then said, "My husband is afraid Americans coming here will invite another Taliban attack upon us. Surely you know this?"

Nodding, Gavin said gently, "I understand that. We hope to win his trust over time, *memsahib.* And my team will be in your valley here to protect you from the Taliban. Our mission is to show that the American people are generous and care, especially for those who are sick."

Jameela looked toward the sky. "Allah be praised, Captain. You have no idea the prayers I have said daily to Him, asking for more help. If you stay in our valley then the Taliban won't attack us. Our Sufi brother and sister constantly travel. We understand they can only visit us twice a year." She gestured gracefully toward the village. "Captain Alexander, you will come with me, and I will put you to work. Captain Jackson, you may join your men."

"Of course," Gavin said, and he winked over at Nike. "I'll catch up with you later. And I'll have Sergeant

Robles alerted to your requests. Just relax. It will all work out."

Nike wasn't so sure, but said nothing. She didn't want this humanitarian mission scuttled because of her lack of medical knowledge. As she walked with Jameela, she said, "Are your duties the same as your husband's in running this village?" Nike knew little of the Afghan culture and didn't want to make a gaffe. Better to ask than to assume.

Jameela nodded. "My duty first is to my husband and our family. After that, I am looked upon to provide leadership to the women of the village in all matters that concern us."

"I see," Nike said. She suddenly had a humorous thought that couldn't be shared with Jameela. Wearing a bright red scarf, a dark green flight suit and a pistol strapped to her waist, she must look quite a sight! The women of the BJS would laugh until it hurt if they could see her in her new fashion garb. Still, Nike wanted to fit in, and she would allow the course of the day to unfold and teach her. Often, prejudices and misunderstandings from one country or culture to another caused tension and she would not want to create such problems.

As Nike followed Jameela down the muddy, rutted street, she was struck by the young children playing barefoot on such a cold April morning. The children's clothes were threadbare with many patches sewn in the fabric. They shouted and danced. Their gazes, however, were inquisitive and they stared openly at Nike. What an odd combination she wore—a man's trousers with the prescribed headdress of a Muslim woman. Fired with curiosity, the group followed them down the middle of the wide street where mud and stone homes sat close to one another.

As Nike smiled at the children, she regretted not knowing Pashto. Their eyes were button-bright and shining. Little girls and boys played with one another just as they would in the States or in her homeland of Greece. But then, as she glanced farther up the street, her heart saddened. A little girl of about six years old stood on crutches near a large stone home. The child had only one leg. Nike remembered that damnable land mines covered this country. Most of them had been sown by Russians, but of late, it had been the Taliban, too. Had this child stepped on one? Nike's heart contracted. There was no doctor here to help her. No painkillers. No antibiotics. How had she survived?

"Jameela? That little girl over there? Who is she?"

"My youngest daughter, Atefa. Why do you ask?"

Gulping, Nike hoped she hadn't made a fatal mistake by asking. "I…uh…she's missing one leg. Did she step on a land mine?"

"Yes, as a four-year-old." Jameela's voice lowered with anguish as she pointed outside the village and to the east. "Afghan national soldiers laid land mines everywhere outside our village two years ago. They wanted to stop the Taliban from coming through our valley." Choked anger was evident in her quiet tone.

"How did Atefa *ever* survive such a terrible injury?" Nike asked softly.

"Allah's will," Jameela murmured. "Everyone said she would die, but I did not believe it. Dr. Reza Khan and his sister, Sahar, found her near the road where it happened. They saved her life and brought her to the village in their Jeep. Then, we had Farzana, our wise woman, tend her with the antibiotics the doctor left. Also, Dr. Sahar knows much about herbs and she directed Farzana how to use them."

"That's an amazing story," Nike said, her voice thick with unshed tears. People like the Sufi medical doctors inspired her. She'd never heard of Sufis or that they were Muslim. Nike decided she was very ignorant of Muslims in general. What if the Sufi doctors hadn't been on the road driving by when Atefa had been injured? Nike watched as the child hobbled toward them on carved wooden crutches. "She's so pretty, Jameela. What does her name mean?" Nike wondered.

"It means *compassion* in our language. Little did I know when my husband and I chose that name for her that she would, indeed, bring exactly that to our family and village. My husband wants her to go to a school in Pakistan when she's old enough. He feels Allah has directed this because she was saved by Sufis."

Atefa had dark brown, almond-shaped eyes; her black hair was long and drawn into a ponytail at the back of her head. She wore a black woolen dress that hung to her ankle; her foot was bare. To Nike, she looked like a poor street urchin. But then, as she scanned the street, she realized all the children shared in the same impoverished appearance as Atefa. The children were clean, their clothes were washed, their skin was scrubbed clean, their hair combed, but this was a very poor village.

"Maybe," Nike told Jameela, briefly touching her arm for a moment, "there is something that might be done to help Atefa before she goes to her school."

Chapter 4

"How are things going?" Gavin asked as Nike finished ensuring her helo was protected for the night. She'd just sent Andy into the village to grab a bite to eat at Abbas's house before staying with the bird during the coming darkness.

She turned, surprised by Gavin's nearness. The man walked as quietly as a cat, never heard until he wanted to be. His cheeks were ruddy in the closing twilight. "Doing okay." She held up her gloved hands. "Today, I became 'Dr. Nike' to the women and children in the village." She laughed. The look in his narrowed eyes sent her heart skipping beats. She stood with her back against the Chinook, for the metal plates still exuded the warmth of the sun from the April day.

"Yeah, Robles said you were doing fine. He's proud that you can give vaccinations. You're a fast study."

Nike grinned. "I had to be! I wasn't given a choice."

The jagged mountain peaks became shadowed as the sun slid below the western horizon.

"From all accounts, old Abbas seems to be satisfied with our efforts."

"Him." Nike rolled her eyes. "That old man is married to a woman thirty years his junior!"

"That's not uncommon out here," Gavin said. "Wives die in childbirth and there's no medical help to change the outcome. The man will always marry again." He grimaced. "And let's face it, there are many widows around and they need a man in order to survive out here."

"Jameela said Abbas has had two other wives before her. Both died in childbirth." Shaking her head, Nike muttered, "Things were bad in Peru, too. BJS did a lot of flying into the jungle villages to deliver health care when we weren't chasing druggies. This place is a lot worse."

Gavin enjoyed being close to Nike. About six inches separated them and he wished he could close the gap. The best he could do was keep them talking. "These people deserve our help. You look kind of pretty in that red *hijab*. Do you like wearing it?"

"No, but I respect their traditions. At least Abbas didn't demand I climb into one of those burkas."

"Indoors, the women wear more casual clothes and no *hijab*," Gavin told her. "It's just when they go out in the community that they put on the burka or *hijab*."

"That robe looks like a prison to me," Nike muttered. "I asked Jameela today what she thought of the burka and she liked it. I couldn't believe it."

"In their culture, most women accept that their body and face are to be looked upon only by their husbands.

The way the men figure it, if the woman is hidden, she's not a temptation to others."

"Why don't their husbands show some responsibility for what's between their legs? Then a woman would be safe to wear whatever she wants."

"Yeah, I can't disagree with your logic, but that's not the way their world turns, and sometimes we have to fit in, not try to change it."

Nike felt the coldness coming off the mountains in the evening breeze. "I feel absolutely suffocated by their culture's attitudes toward women. You don't find an Afghan woman flying a combat helicopter."

"No doubt." Gavin saw her put her hands beneath the armpits of her jacket to keep them warm. He took a step forward and allowed his heavily clothed body to contact hers. Her eyes widened for a moment. "I'll keep you warm," he soothed.

"Right now, I'm so damned cold I'm not going to protest."

Chuckling, Gavin continued to look around. "Things seem to be quiet. I've been working with Abbas most of the day. You know, he won't admit that the Taliban comes through their village, but we have satellite photos as proof."

"Is he pro-Taliban? Or just afraid of them like everyone else?" Nike absorbed the heat from his woolen Afghan clothes. For a moment, she wondered what it would be like to slide her hands beneath the folds and place her hands against his well-sprung chest. It was a forbidden thought, but tantalizing, nonetheless.

"I'm pretty sure he's afraid of them. There aren't many village chieftains or sheiks who get in bed with the devil and the Taliban is all of that," Gavin said, his mouth quirking. "He told me that the Taliban came in here and ordered their girls' school shut down. He's a man of education, and he didn't like being ordered to do that. Abbas continues to teach the girls and women of his village behind closed doors in defiance of their orders. He's a man of strong principles and morals. He believes women deserve education just as much as any man. And Abbas is enlightened compared to other village leaders."

"He was a teacher?" Nike found that inspiring for a man who lived in such a rugged, isolated area.

"Abbas was born here in this village. His father sent him to Kabul for higher schooling. He graduated with a degree in biology. When Abbas returned home, he helped the village breeding programs so that their sheep produced better wool. That helps to raise their economy because better wool demands a higher price at market. And he increased goat-milk output. He's done a lot in the region and he's respected by everyone because of this."

"Wow, I'd never have guessed. No wonder he's the head elder."

"Looks *are* deceiving." Gavin watched the high clouds across the valley turn a dark pink as the sun set more deeply below the western mountains. "He's carrying a lot of loads on his shoulders, Nike. Abbas takes his responsibilities as leader seriously. He's got a lot of problems and few ways to resolve them. When I asked him about medical and health help from the Afghan government, he got angry. Over the years, he's made many trips to the capital to urge them to bring out a health team every three months to these border villages, but he could never get them to agree to it. And

Afghan people are superindependent. They really have a tough time looking at a centralized government to rule over them."

"That's awful that the politicians in Kabul wouldn't help these people. Can you imagine *that* happening in the USA or Greece? There would be a helluva uprising."

"Abbas doesn't accept his government's lack of care," Gavin said. "When you realize Afghanistan is cobbled together out of about four hundred different clans or tribes, you can see why they wouldn't place trust in a Kabul government. Our job is to try and persuade Abbas that his own government does want to work with him."

"How are you going to convince him Kabul's listening and willing to pitch in some medical help out here in the border area?"

"I told Abbas that the report I write up regarding our visit will be given to the health minister of the government. This minister is trying hard to change old, outdated policies. I pointed out to Abbas other border villages south of him already have intervention, supplies and funds on a routine schedule from Kabul."

"Does he believe you?"

"No, but over time he will."

"And you and your team will stay here four weeks?"

"Yes. From the satellite photos, we know that the Taliban uses the north end of this valley twice a month. We've set up to be here when they try to cross it a week from now."

"And then what?" Nike grew afraid for Gavin and his team.

He shrugged. "Do what we're good at—stopping

them cold in their tracks and denying them access across this valley."

"What will Abbas do?"

"I don't know. He knows if we stop the Taliban from crossing, they could take revenge on this village. This is what Abbas is worried about."

"He's right about that." Nike leaned against Gavin a little more. The dusk air had a real bite to it. His arms came around and bracketed her. For a moment, she questioned her silent body language. Why had she done this? Something primal drove her like a magnet to this military man. Fighting herself, Nike finally surrendered to the moment. She had been too long without a man in her life, and she was starved for male contact. Yet, what message did this send to Gavin? Was he reading her correctly or assuming? Unsure, Nike remained tense in his embrace.

"Comfy?" he teased quietly. Surprised by Nike's unexpected move, Gavin hungrily savored her nearness. He had wrapped his arms around her but resisted pressing her tightly against himself. Right now, just the fact she'd allowed this kind of intimate contact was enough of a gift. Even though they sparred like fighters in a ring, he'd seen something in her gold eyes that he could never quite accurately read. Maybe this was the result of that smoldering look he'd seen banked in her expression. Only time and patience would tell.

"Yes, thank you."

Gavin wasn't about to do anything stupid. She had given herself to him in a way that he'd never entertained. Maybe it was the pink beauty of the clouds across the valley that had inspired her in this wonderful moment.

"What are you going to do here?" Nike asked.

"We know from satellite reconnaissance that the Taliban uses the north end of this valley at the new moon, when it's darkest. We'll be intercepting them if they try it next week."

"There's only ten of you. There could be a hundred or more fighters crossing that border and coming down into this valley."

"Are you worried?" Gavin ventured.

"Any sane person would be."

Laughing quietly, Gavin closed his eyes for a moment and simply absorbed the curves of Nike's womanly body against him. What an unexpected reward. It was precious in his world of ongoing war and violence. A sweet reminder of peace, of love and nurturance. Something he hadn't experienced for a long time. "You're right," he admitted. "But we look at it this way—our base camp where you're assigned isn't that far away. We have BJS here with Apache helos to help us out if we're attacked. We know you gals will hightail it in our direction and drop the goods on the Taliban so we'll survive to fight them another day."

"I have never met such an optimist," Nike said.

"I don't like the other possibility. Do you?" Gavin asked. He watched the clouds reflect pinkish light across the valley. In the background, he could hear the bleating of sheep and goats from their pens within the village. At dusk, boys tending the herds brought them into the village to protect them against wild animals and roving Taliban. Both two- and four-legged predators were always hungry for village meat.

Feeling uneasy and caring too much for Gavin even

though she didn't want to, Nike said, "No, I don't like the alternative. This is a dangerous mission."

"Yeah, it is. We're out in the wilderness and the bad guys are right over that mountain to the east of us." He lifted his gloved hand to point at the darkened peaks. Bringing his hand down, he wrapped his arms around her once more. "Don't worry, we know our job, Nike. We've already survived a year here."

"And you're on your second tour."

Hearing the flatness in her tone, Gavin nodded. "We're slowly making a difference. I'd give my right arm to find bin Laden. All of us would. It would change the tempo of this war against the terrorists."

Nike understood army hunter-killer teams were all about finding terrorists and Taliban. "So, how are you feeling about this more peaceful assignment of working in this village as an ambassador of goodwill?"

"I like it."

"But it takes you off the front lines."

"Not really." Gavin looked to the north of the village. Kerosene lamps were lit and the mud and stone homes that had windows glowed golden. He liked dusk, even though from a wartime perspective, it was a killing time, when the enemy sneaked up and took lives. "With General Chapman coming here to Afghanistan, the priority has shifted to focus on these boundary villages. If we can get these people to trust us, they will let us know when Taliban are coming through. The villagers could be our eyes and ears. If we can stop the Taliban's advancement into this country, that's a good thing for everyone. In the end, it will save a lot of lives."

"I like your general's philosophy."

"So do I. If I could, I'd have world peace. As it is, there's world war."

Nike shook her head. "I grew up in a peaceful Greece."

"And yet, Greece has had its fair share of revolutions, too."

"Granted." Nike observed the pinkish sky, now fading. Darkness began to encroach across the narrow valley. "I wish for the day when there are no more wars anywhere. No more killing. I've seen enough of it. All people want to do is live in peace and get on with their lives."

"It's the same here," Gavin acknowledged. "Abbas was saying that all he wanted for his people was to be left alone to eke out their survival in this valley. He's grown old before his time because of the Russians and now the Taliban intrusion."

"Afghanistan needs decades of peaceful downtime," Nike agreed. But there had been none for them.

A wonderful sense of happiness bubbled up within her but it warred with sadness at her loss of Antonio. Suddenly bothered by her proximity to Gavin, she frowned. "I don't know what's going on between us," she admitted quietly.

Gavin gazed down at Nike. Even in the semidarkness he could see the worry register in her face. "Why try to decipher it? Why not just let it be natural and flow?"

Her stomach was filled with those butterflies. The only other man to make her feel this way had been Antonio. "It's not that simple," she told him.

"When I first saw you, I thought you were the most beautiful woman I'd ever seen. Most of all, I liked your gold eyes," Gavin confided softly. "You have the look of a lioness."

Her heart beat a little harder. Gavin was sincere. Or at least, he sounded sincere. That meant she had to take his compliment seriously. Antonio had been so much like him: a gentle warrior, a man of philosophy, of much greater depth and breadth than most men. "Thank you. My grandmother had the same color eyes. They run in the women of our family."

"You're feeling tense. Why?"

Nike pulled out of his arms and faced him. Oh, she didn't want to do that, but if she remained in the protection of Gavin's arms, she would lose all reason. Did this man realize the mesmerizing power he had over her? She searched his hooded blue eyes. The shadows of the night made his face dark and fierce-looking. "Look, I've got a lot of past history, Gavin, and I don't want you to think the wrong things about us."

Hearing the desperation in her tone, he nodded. "What happened to make you feel this way?"

It was the right question. Again, Nike squirmed inwardly. She'd talked to no one about the loss of her beloved Antonio nearly two years ago. Only Dallas, who had been executive officer of BJS in Peru, knew the full story. She had been her confidante, her healer up to a point. A heaviness settled into Nike's chest and once more she felt old grief discharging from her wound. Opening her gloved hands, Nike said, "I fell in love with a Peruvian army officer whose job it was to locate and capture drug-runners." The next words were so hard to say, but Nike felt driven to give Gavin the truth. "Antonio was an incredible person. He had graduated from Lima's university in archaeology, but the men in his family all had served in the army. So he went in and I met him when he was a captain. He loved his country and he saw what the drug-running was doing to it. Without fail, he would volunteer for the most dangerous missions to eradicate the dealers."

"He sounds like a fine man," Gavin said. "Courageous."

"Yes, well, that courage got him killed," Nike bit out. Looking down at the dark, muddy ground, she added, "I told him that he was going to get killed if he kept it up. But he wouldn't listen. And then…it happened. Two years ago."

Gavin measured the look in her wounded eyes and heard the hurt in her husky voice. Reaching out, he placed his hand gently upon her drooping shoulders and whispered, "I'm sorry. He must have been one hell of a man to get your attention."

Tiny ripples of heat radiated from where his hand had momentarily rested on her shoulder. Looking up, Nike searched Gavin's narrowed, intense blue eyes and shook her head. "Listen, I learned the hard way—in our business if you fall in love with a military person, you're going to lose him."

"That's not always true."

"Yes, it is."

Gavin heard the stubbornness in her tone. Looking into Nike's eyes for some hint that it wasn't the truth she really believed, he felt a sinking sensation in his gut. Something hopeful and newly born shattered in his chest. After all, he had been burned but good by Laurie Braverman a year ago. Gavin had sworn off military women for another reason. He hadn't lost someone he loved to death. He had lost her because they simply could not compromise with one another.

"Maybe you just need time," Gavin counseled gently, removing his hand. He ached to kiss Nike. The set of her full lips, the way the corners of her mouth were drawn in, told him the pain she still carried over the death of the Peruvian captain.

"No," Nike said grimly, "time isn't going to change my mind." She stared up at him, her voice firm. "You need to know the truth. I shouldn't have led you on. I'm sorry."

"I'm not sorry at all, Nike. Look, we all need someone at some time."

His mouth was so beautifully sculpted. Good thing he couldn't read her mind. He had the lips of Apollo, the sun god. And wasn't Gavin a bit of sunshine in her life? Nike didn't want to admit that at all. But he was. All day, she'd longed to have a few quiet, uninterrupted moments with him. She was hungry to find out who he was, his depth and what mattered to him. Far more curious than she should be, Nike said, "I can't need any man who is in the military, Gavin. Never again."

Looking toward the village that was barely outlined by the dying light, the windows gleaming with a golden glow, Nike sighed. "You deserve to know the truth."

"And I'm glad you trusted me with it." Gavin smiled down at her upturned face. Her lips parted and almost pleaded to be touched by his mouth. "It's a good first step, don't you think?"

Seeing that gleam in his eyes, Nike knew Gavin wanted to kiss her. Yet, he hadn't made a move. The tension swirled between them and her heart screamed for his kiss. Her past resurfaced, frightening her. If she surrendered to her desire for Gavin, she would be right back where she was before—heartbroken. "There are no other steps," she warned him.

"I don't believe that," Gavin said, his voice a low growl. Reaching out, he took that step forward, his arms coming around her shoulders. Surprise flared in her golden eyes, her need of him very readable and yet, as he closed the distance, Gavin could see her fear. As he gently brought Nike against him he wondered if she would resist. If she did, he'd instantly release her, of course. Gavin didn't want that to happen and he sensed she wanted him, too. He leaned down, searching, finding her parted lips.

The world exploded within Nike as her arms swept across his shoulders, his mouth capturing hers. It was a powerful kiss, yet gentle and welcoming. His lips were tentative and asking her to participate fully in the joy of connection. The moisture of his ragged breath flowed across her face. The whiskers of his beard were soft. Gavin's mouth guided her and slid wetly across her opening lips. He cajoled, passing his tongue delicately across her lower lip. Instantly, Nike inhaled sharply as the throbbing sensation dove deeply down between her thighs.

He smelled of sweat, of wool and the sharp, clean mountain air. She reveled in his weather-hardened flesh against her cheek. His arms were cherishing and Nike surrendered as he swept her hard against his body. Their breaths mingled as they explored one another like hungry, greedy beggars. Well, wasn't she? It had been two long years since she'd kissed a man. And how different Gavin's kiss was! Nike tried not to compare him to Antonio. Gavin's mouth wreaked fire from within her as his lips molded hotly with hers. One hand moved sinuously down the back of her jacket, following the curve of her back. His other hand held her close. Her nipples hardened instantly as he deepened their kiss.

Nike was starved! Her entire body trembled just as he reluctantly withdrew his mouth from her wet lips. Nike saw the glint of a hungry predator in his eyes as surely as it was mirrored in hers. Knees like Jell-O, Nike felt weak. Inwardly, her body glowed brightly and she yearned to know his touch upon her aching breasts, and how he would feel entering her.

All of these crazy sensations exploded through her now that they stood, watching each other in wonder. The night air was cold and their breath was like white clouds between them. Nike noted the satisfaction glittering in Gavin's narrowed eyes. He held her gently and didn't try to kiss her again.

"Now," Gavin rasped, "let's start all over. I'm me and you are you. I'm not the man from your past. I'm the one standing with you here in the present. Judging from the kiss, I think we have something to build upon. I'm a patient man, Nike. I wasn't looking for a woman, but you walked into my life." His hand against the small of her back tightened. "And I'm not about to let you walk out of my life."

Chapter 5

Nike hadn't slept well and was finishing up breakfast with Jameela and her three daughters. Chapatis, a thin pita bread, had been filled with vegetables and seasoned with curry. She had trouble focusing on food when she kept remembering Gavin's kiss. It was completely un-expected—but welcome. Groaning inwardly, Nike re-membered all her nightmares of Antonio's death. He'd been shot to death in the jungles of Peru. She'd sworn *never* to fall in love with a military man again. Not *ever*.

So why had she kissed Gavin? Why did she still want him? Nike had seen the predatory look in his eyes. She could have easily brushed him off. Why hadn't she? *First things first: stop thinking about it.* Nike watched as the older daughters of the family cleared away the dishes and went to clean them in the kitchen.

Jameela was helping six-year-old Atefa wrap her leg,

which had never had any surgical intervention. The little girl's leg was missing below the knee. Jameela had her daughter lie on the rug as she carefully wrapped the red, angry-looking stump with soft cotton fabric. Once it was tied in place, Atefa sat up and took her handmade crutches.

"Have you sought help for your daughter's missing leg?" Nike asked the mother.

"When it happened, we were shocked. My husband tried to get help from our government. He pleaded and begged a regional official to bring a doctor out here to help her," Jameela responded.

Nike frowned. "I'm so sorry. Who planted those mines?"

With a grimace, Jameela whispered, "The Afghan army did, to stop the Taliban."

Surprised, Nike blurted, "Why?"

"They hid them along the edges of our fields where we plow. They didn't want Talibans coming in here."

The whole conflict and mind-set of the Taliban didn't make sense. As soldiers, they could only do their part and hope families would be saved. Nike had to get to work pronto. Getting up, she shrugged on her coat and put the red scarf in place around her head. It was 0700 and dawn crawled up on the horizon. A mechanic team would arrive this morning to try and assess what was wrong with her CH-47. Every minute on the ground kept the helo a target of the Taliban. She had to get out and relieve her load master so he could come to Abbas's house and get breakfast.

"I'll come back later," Nike promised the woman. "Right now, I have to check my helicopter and relieve my sergeant."

Jameela stood and nodded. "Of course."

In the freezing cold of the spring morning, Nike hurried down the muddy, rutted street. The men were already busy. A donkey hauled a wooden cart filled with wood brought from the slopes of the nearby mountains. She saw no one from Gavin's team, which was just as well. Right now, Nike couldn't bear to see him. She was too confused about what happened between them, that part of her wanted it to happen again...

Andy was delighted to see her and climbed out of the CH-47. He rubbed his gloved hands to warm them up. Even though Nike had provided heavy bedding for him, she knew it was no fun to sleep in a helo in freezing weather. After motioning for him to hightail it to the awakening village for breakfast, Nike took over watch of the helicopter. He handed her the binoculars.

Around her, the valley awakened. The brownish-red haze above the village came from the many wood fires prodded to life to feed a family in each of the mud-brick and stone dwellings. Above, the sky was a pale blue and she could see the tips of the mountains illuminated as the sun peeked above them. When the first rays slanted over the narrow valley, Nike could feel the warmth caressing her.

Dogs barked off and on. It seemed as if everyone had a dog or two. She never saw any cats and wondered why. Her breath was white as she exhaled. This was a very cold place even in the spring. But then, they were at eight thousand feet, so what did she expect? Moving around the helicopter, which sat out on a flat, muddy area, Nike looked for movement below. There didn't seem to be any, but she didn't trust the naked eye. The binoculars around her neck were a better way to search for the enemy.

Standing behind the helo for protection against sniping, she scanned the slopes below her. Nike noted small herds of sheep and goats being prodded out of the village center and down to the green grass below. It was a tranquil scene. The sun's emergence had already upped the temperature by several degrees. Several dogs herded the animals farther down into the flat of the valley floor. It all looked so peaceful.

By the time Andy had gotten back to resume his duties, Nike was more than eager to go back to Jameela's home and grab another hot cup of the delicious and spicy chai tea. The woman had shared her secret recipe with Nike. Chai was individual to every family and Jameela's was legendary among the villagers. With some gentle persuasion, Nike got Jameela to divulge her recipe. Chai consisted of strongly boiled tea with goat milk, a pinch of brown sugar, cardamom and nutmeg. Her mouth watered just thinking about it.

She gave Andy a welcoming smile. He grinned as he walked up to her.

"Nothing?" he asked.

"No." Nike handed him the binoculars. "Keep watch. Captain Jackson was saying that the Taliban come through the northern end of this valley at the new moon, which is next week."

"Under cover of darkness," Andy said, placing the binoculars around his neck.

"Most likely, but you never know."

"I wouldn't know a Taliban from a villager. They all dress alike."

Grimly Nike said, "The villagers know they cannot

approach this helo. So, if someone does, you draw your pistol and assume it's the enemy."

"Yes, ma'am. I just hope no one approaches," Andy said unhappily.

"I'll ask one of Captain Jackson's men to relieve you once an hour," Nike responded with understanding.

"Thanks." Andy looked up at the helo. "I'll sure be glad to get out of here and back to base. I didn't sleep hardly at all last night."

"Neither did I." Nike smiled a little. Looking at her watch she said, "The team's supposed to arrive at 0800. That's not long from now."

"Can't be too soon. I'm spoiled," Andy said with a grin. "What I'd give for some bacon and eggs now. Not that the hot grain cereal wasn't good. It was."

Chuckling, Nike lifted her hand and walked back toward the village. Her heart thumped hard when suddenly she saw Gavin walking down the street, his rifle over his shoulder, looking as though he was hunting for someone. When he noticed her, his mouth lifted in a smile. He was the last person Nike wanted to see, but she couldn't turn around and avoid him.

"Good morning," Gavin called, catching the wariness in Nike's narrowed gold eyes. Those lips he'd caressed yesterday were pursed with tension. Over their kiss? He wasn't sure. Maybe she was upset over something else?

They met near the last mud-brick home. Both were aware that they might become targets and stepped into the alleyway between two homes for more protection. "I had sweet dreams," he told her.

"I didn't."

The flatness of her voice startled him. "Sorry to hear

that. Everything okay?" He hooked a thumb toward her helo. Maybe Nike was discouraged over the fact her bird was down.

Nothing was okay, but she couldn't stand here discussing her personal stuff. Instead, she said, "You've seen Atefa? Abbas and Jameela's little girl who lost a leg to a land mine?"

"Yes."

"What are the chances of flying her and her mother out to Kabul to get some medical help with a prosthesis?"

Shrugging, Gavin said, "I could make some calls and find out."

"I'd appreciate that. That kid lost her leg to a land mine. She needs some type of medical help. Why can't the U.S. supply her with a prosthetic limb?"

Assuming Nike's worries were over the little girl, Gavin relaxed. Several black curls peeked out the sides of the red scarf she wore around her head. Nike looked even more vibrant and breathtaking to him. "There's no reason we can't. I've already radioed Kabul to tell them to get a medical doctor out here in the next two weeks."

"What about dental? A *lot* of people here have tooth problems," Nike said. She was relieved to be talking business with Gavin.

"Good idea. I hadn't gone that far with my plans for this village. Usually, it takes us a good three to four days to assess their health needs. Then I create a report and suggest a plan of action. After that, other medical or health teams are flown in to supplement the initial work we're doing right now."

"I see." Nike wasn't familiar with the tactics, but it sounded like a logical approach. "I think if you can help Atefa that it will go a long way to lessen Abbas's distrust toward us."

"Yeah, the old codger is definitely questioning everything we're doing," Gavin agreed quietly. "I'll give a call this morning to the medical people in Kabul. Several American programs help children who have lost limbs to land mines."

Warming to his concern, Nike tried not to look at his mouth. Memory of the kiss came back hot and sweet. Frowning, she said abruptly, "Look, what happened yesterday is in the past, Gavin. I don't have time for any type of a relationship right now."

Gavin heard the desperation in her husky tone and trod carefully. "It was a shock for me, too," he admitted. "I came out of a relationship with a woman helicopter pilot about a year ago. I swore off military women." He gave her an uneven grin. "Until you came along."

Nike held up her hands. "Listen, I'm stopping this before it starts. I do *not* have room in my life." His blue eyes became assessing and furrows gathered on his brow. He took the Afghan cap off, pushed fingers through his short, dark hair and settled the cap back down on his head.

"It's not that easy, Nike. You know that."

"It is that easy." Feeling frantic, she couldn't face the stubborn glint in his eyes. "One kiss doesn't give you access to me or my life."

"That's true," he murmured. Gavin knew if he could just bring her back into his arms, capture her mouth, he'd persuade her differently. That time would come. But now, she was too scared, too prone to push him away. He had to let her go…a little bit. "I'm a patient person. Let's just take this a day at a time?"

"No." Giving him a hard look, Nike said, "It's *over*, Gavin. I'm sorry but I am not going to lose someone I love to a bullet. My heart just can't handle it. Do you understand?"

"Yes, I do," he answered honestly, feeling bereft. In his heart he knew that whatever they had would be long-term. Looking into Nike's eyes, however, he saw the fear and grief entwined. There was nothing he could do. Time to give up. "Wrong time and place."

"Exactly." Taking a step back, Nike said, "You're a nice guy, Gavin. Maybe if we'd met a few years earlier... Oh, who knows? Just be safe, okay?"

As he watched Nike walk away, Gavin scowled. It felt as if someone had grabbed his heart and torn it out of his chest. Rubbing that sensitive area, he wondered how this beautiful Greek woman had captured him so easily. Gavin decided it was her personality. Nike had compassion for others, which his ex had lacked. Laurie had been out for herself and to hell with the rest of the world. By contrast, Gavin had seen Nike's care for others, whether it was concern for her load master, the people of this village or even his team.

"Well, hell," he muttered. Stepping out from between the homes, Gavin thought of the long day ahead. He was especially edgy because, according to headquarters, tonight was when the Taliban would start coming through the valley, and his mission would be to stop them dead in their tracks. Had the Taliban heard of their landing here, and were they coming in early instead? Ten men against a hundred of the enemy was not good odds. Gavin would not make the village a target. No, his team would take the fight with the Taliban elsewhere. He was glad of one thing: Nike would be out of here and safe. Her helo would be fixed and she'd be gone. That was important to Gavin.

Nike wanted to whoop for joy. She was sitting in the right-hand seat, her CH-47 idling along, both engines working once more. The mechanic team had arrived via Chinook and by noon, the damage to the front turbine was fixed. Andy, who was sitting in the copilot's seat, grinned like an idiot, but she understood why.

With her helmet on, she spoke into the microphone set close to her lips. "Okay, we're good to go. Did you contact Captain Jackson and let him know we were taking off?"

"Yes, ma'am, I did. He said for you to have a safe trip back to base."

Relieved, Nike gave him a thumbs-up. To her right, the first Chinook was taking off. Above them, an Apache circled to ensure no enemy was close to the U.S. Army helicopters. It felt good to have that firepower and she could hardly wait to get back to civilization. Andy left the seat and walked to the rear. Once she took the helo skyward, the ramp would be lowered and he'd be sitting out on the hip with the machine gun, watching for possible Taliban attacks from below.

Even though the helo shook and shuddered around her, Nike loved the sensations. Strapping in and tightening her harness, she radioed to the other helos. Within a minute, the rotors were at takeoff speed. Just feeling the Chinook unstick from the surface made Nike feel good. She saw a number of women and children at the village's edge watching in wonder. It was impossible to lift a hand and wave goodbye to them. One of her hands was on the cyclic, the other on the collective. Together, these kept the helicopter in stable, forward movement.

Most of all, Nike was relieved to leave Gavin behind. She felt guilty, but pushed all that aside. As the helo moved out over the green, narrow valley below, she followed the other Chinook at a safe distance. Within a minute, they'd begin their nap-of-the-earth flying, one hundred feet over the terrain in order to avoid being brought down by their enemy. Pursing her lips, Nike focused on the business at hand. For at least an hour, she wouldn't have to think about Gavin. Or about his kiss that had rocked her world.

"Any word from that A team in Zor Barawul?" Nike asked the communications tech in the ops building. It was nearly midnight and Nike couldn't sleep. She was worried about Gavin and his team interdicting the Taliban in the valley.

The woman shook her head. "Nothing—yet."

"Okay, thanks," Nike muttered. She shoved her hands into the pockets of her trousers and walked out of the small building. Above, the stars twinkled brightly, looking so close Nike could almost reach out and touch them. There wasn't much light around the camp, which helped keep it hidden from the enemy. She had a small flashlight and used it to get to her tent.

Just being back on the roster and assigned an Apache helicopter made Nike feel better. At least she was off the workhorse helicopter list. Despite this, worry tinged her happiness. Five minutes didn't go by without her thinking of Gavin or remembering the heated kiss they'd shared.

"Dammit," she breathed softly. Why, oh why couldn't

she just let that kiss go? Stop remembering the strength of his arms around her? The pressure of his mouth caressing her lips as if she were some priceless object to be cherished?

Upon reaching her tent, she pulled the flap aside and then closed it. The warmth from the electric heater made all the difference in the world. Each of the twenty women Apache pilots got a small tent with a heater and a ply-board floor. The cot wasn't much, but it was a helluva lot better than what she'd had at the village.

Because she was on duty for the next twenty-four hours, Nike remained in her clothes. She took off her armor and boots and laid them at the foot of her cot. She had to sleep, but how? She worried about Gavin and his team. Had they discovered the Taliban coming across the valley yet? Lying down, she brought her arm across her eyes. And then, in minutes, she fell asleep— a small blessing.

Chapter 6

"This week, you're assigned to the CH-47," Emma Trayhern-Cantrell, the XO, told Nike as they sat together at an ops table. "You're going to be bringing in supplies to several boundary villages. And we're short on copilots, so you're flying without one."

"Thanks," she told her XO. Nike nodded and tried to hide her disappointment. For a week, she'd flown the aggressive Apache and done her fair share of firing off rockets and rounds to protect A teams up in the mountains hunting Taliban. Because she loved the adrenaline rush, it was tough to be relegated to a lumbering workhorse instead.

Her XO handed her the list of villages along with the supplies to go to them and the times of delivery. Emma Trayhern was all business. She had the red hair of a Valkyrie with large gray eyes and a soft mouth. She had her uncle Morgan Trayhern's eyes. However, Nike already knew that this Trayhern child was no pushover even if her face spoke of openness and compassion. Emma was an Apache pilot and as tough as they came.

"I know you're bummed. CHs don't rock." Emma tried to smile. "There's always dirty work along with the rockin' Apache. You're just lucky enough to have skills in the CH-47."

"Yeah," Nike said grumpily, folding up the orders. "I wish they'd give us another Apache or two."

Shaking her head, Emma said, "They're stretched to the max over in Iraq. We get the leftovers. It sucks, but it is what it is."

"I'm not so philosophical," Nike said, rising. It was near dawn, a red ribbon on the eastern horizon outside the ops hut. Already, the air base was in full swing and with plenty of action.

"You hear anything about your guy? Captain Jackson?"

Giving Emma a frown, Nike said, "He's *not* my guy. How did that rumor get started?"

Grinning, Emma folded up the huge map and left it on the ops table. "Blame your load master, Andy."

"Blabbermouth," Nike muttered.

"We were expecting the Taliban to go down through that valley near Zor Barawul, but they didn't. I told Dallas that I thought someone from the village probably sneaked off to tell them the A team was in town, so they took another trail into the country."

"I wouldn't doubt it," Nike said. She put the paper into the thigh pocket of her dark green flight suit. "When I was there overnight, there was a lot of wariness toward Americans."

"Well," Emma said, "you'll be delivering the last load of the day to them. If you get a chance, stay on the ground for an hour and find out what's going on. I like to get eyes and ears out there on those villages. Dallas wants to keep a check on them and whether they get slammed by the Taliban."

"Good idea." Nike wasn't too sure she wanted to spend an hour on the ground to visit with Gavin. She saw the curiosity in Emma's eyes. "I'll do my best."

"Do it at each stop, Nike. We want you to talk to the leader of each team and get their latest assessment."

It wasn't a bad idea, Nike thought as she put on her black BJS baseball cap. "Okay, will do," she promised. "This is going to be more like a milk run."

Emma walked her to the door. "I hope you're right. But be careful. Those four villages are not on our side. Yet."

"Getting food, medical personnel and medicine in to them on a regular basis will help," Nike said, opening the door. The crisp air was barely above freezing. Nike would be glad when June came. Everyone said it got warmer at the beginning of that month. In the mountains at eight thousand feet, a local gardener told her that there was less than a ninety-day growing period. This made gardening tough, which was why most people had goats, chickens, sheep and few vegetables. Certainly, fruit was scarce, too.

Clapping her on the shoulder, Emma reminded her, "Be careful out there. Dallas does *not* want to lose any of her pilots."

Grinning, Nike gave her a mock salute and said, "Oh, not to worry, XO. We're a tough bunch of women." She decided to swing by the base exchange and picked up four boxes of dates and four pounds of candy for the kids. Dates were a delicacy usually eaten only at the time of Ramadan. Poor villages couldn't afford such a wonderful fruit and Nike wanted to give it to the wife of the chief of each village. The meaning of her exchange would go far with the women of the village to cement a positive connection. And the children would love the sweets. That made her smile because the Afghan children were beautiful, so full of life and laughter.

Gavin was surprised as hell to see Nike walking toward him from the helicopter. She'd covered her short, shining dark curls with a black baseball cap. He grinned, feeling his heart open up.

"Hey," he called, "this is a pleasant surprise."

Her lips tingled in anticipation. Nike could see the happiness burning in his blue eyes as he approached her. While part of her wanted to rush into Gavin's arms, she halted a good six feet from him, hands on her hips. "Just dropping off supplies, a doctor and dentist, and getting the lay of the land and giving Jameela a box of dates as a goodwill gesture."

Gavin sensed her unease but kept his smile. "Dates. That's a great idea." He added, "I missed you."

Though wildly flattered, Nike couldn't get on a personal footing with him. Lucky for them, there was all kinds of activity around the unloading of the helo. A number of men carried the cardboard boxes into the village. The doctor and dentist were led into a group of awaiting men and boys. "My boss wants me to spend an hour with you getting a sense of how things are going at the village. She's compiling an ongoing dialogue with the generals above her on where each village stands."

Raising his brows, Gavin said, "You ladies are on top of things." He gestured for her to follow him. "Come on, we'll go to the team house, have some chai and chat."

Nike did not want to be alone with Gavin. He was too damned masculine. She wished for the thousandth time her traitorous body would stop clamoring for another kiss from him. Her mind was in charge and no way could she get involved again. Ever. "Okay, but this is business, Captain."

"No problem," Gavin said smoothly.

Walking at his shoulder, a good twelve inches between them, Nike said, "You never got that attack you were expecting. I'm glad."

Gavin dodged the muddy ruts made by the continuous donkey-cart traffic through the village. "Yeah, we're relieved. But suspicious." The sun had warmed the village and children played in the late afternoon. Dogs ran around barking and chasing one another. Women in burkas were here and there, but mostly, they moved the window curtains aside to stare at them walking by.

Nike saw a number of barefoot children with mud up to their knees. She smiled a little. They were tough little kids in her opinion and yet, so huggable. She started handing out the bag of candy she carried in her hand. In no time, every child in the village surrounded them. Nike made sure each child, no matter how little, got a handful of jellybeans. When it was gone, they disappeared with their treasures. She turned to Gavin. "I'm glad for you it's been quiet around here. Why do you think that happened?"

Gavin nodded as they sauntered toward the stone home on the left. "We think the Taliban got tipped off by someone here in the village and they decided to take other paths into the country."

"But that doesn't guarantee anything for long," Nike said.

"True, but we're making progress. Abbas is softening his stance toward us. He's still worried the Taliban will see him consorting with us. And I think someone in the village was scared to death of the same thing, intercepted the Taliban and told them to take another track. That way, it would look like this village was still helping the Taliban. It's a real balancing act out here for Abbas." Gavin halted and gestured to a large mudbrick home. "Here we are. Come on in. I'm ready for some hot chai."

Inside, the hard-packed earth had been swept. Everything was clean and neat. The men's equipment stood up against the walls in neat rows. There was a stove in the corner with plenty of wood, the tin chimney rising up and out of the roof. The windows were clean and sunlight made the room almost bright, if not cheerful.

"Have a seat," Gavin said, taking off his hat and putting his rifle nearby. He shrugged out of the dark brown tunic and then removed his body armor. "Feels good to get out of this thing," he muttered. "I live in it almost twenty-four hours a day."

"Armor is the pits," Nike agreed. She saw several small rugs and pillows near the stove. Taking a seat on one, she watched as Gavin went through the motions of putting water in a copper kettle and then sitting it on top of the stove. Her heart pined for his arms around her, his mouth cherishing her lips. For now, she fought her desire, crossed her legs and folded her hands in her lap.

"If your CO wants to know about this village," Gavin

said, pulling a tin of loose tea off a shelf, "tell her that we've got about a twenty-percent pro-American base here now. The men are starting to open up to us."

"Is that all?" Nike pulled out a notebook and a pen from her left pocket.

Gavin filled the tea strainer and gave her a one-raised-eyebrow look. "Is that all? It's only been a week. I think that's pretty amazing."

Jotting it down, Nike said, "I've brought a medical doctor and a dentist and hygienist with me. That ought to encourage a little more loyalty."

He poured hot water into two tin mugs and then dipped in the strainer filled with loose tea. "If we could gain loyalty like that, all we'd have to do is hand out money and buy them off."

"I understand."

"Honey?"

"Yes, please." She watched as he poured goat's milk into the mixture and pulled another tin from the shelf. He ladled out a teaspoonful of golden honey into each cup. Another tin contained a spice mixture and he put a pinch into the steaming chai. There was something solid and steady about Gavin. He had a confidence born from experience in the field. Everything he did had a sureness to it. Nike realized that he was the kind of leader anyone could trust completely. That was just another reason to like him way too much.

Gavin brought over the steaming mug. "Chai for two," he teased. He set his cup on the ground and brought up a small gold rug and pillow, sitting opposite her. "And I know Jameela's chai rocks, but she isn't about to give her secret recipe to anyone." He chuckled.

"She gave it to me. I loved staying at her home. At the

base I keep trying different chai mixtures to duplicate it, but so far, no luck." Nike sipped the delicious chai. "Hey, this isn't bad, Jackson." She tried to relax, but being so close to him made her squirm endlessly. Not to mention Gavin seemed even more handsome with his long-sleeved cotton shirt and brown Afghan trousers. His beard, as always, was meticulously shaped and trimmed. Even his hair was longer in order to emulate the Afghan men's hairstyle. His skin was so suntanned he could easily have passed for an Afghani.

"So, did you miss me?" he inquired with a wicked grin.

Nike refused to meet his eyes. Her hands tightened imperceptibly around the tin mug. "I didn't have time."

"Pity," Gavin teased. He saw how uncomfortable Nike had become. Yet, her cheeks reddened and there had to be a reason for it. "Well," he said conversationally, "I sure missed you."

"I wish you wouldn't."

"Why?"

"You know why, Gavin. I just can't fall for another military man."

"Oh, that's right—you think I'll die in combat."

"There's a damn good chance of that."

"Well," he pointed out, "look at you. You have an Apache strapped to your butt and you're always a fair target for the Taliban, too."

"That's different."

"How? A bullet is a bullet."

"You're infuriating. Were you on the debate team at your college?"

"Actually, a university. And yes, I was on the debate

team for four years. I like arguing." He flashed a smile
even when revealing this nugget of truth.

"Of course you do." Nike couldn't help but smile
back, all while trying to steady her racing heart. "Which
university?"

"Princeton. Where did you get your degree?"

"The University of Athens."

He gave her a warm look. "Congratulations."

There was an uncomfortable pause and Nike could
feel him warming up for some heady declaration. Why
couldn't this be a business meeting? Well, she knew
why but just couldn't face it.

Sipping his chai, he sighed. "I've dreamed about you
every night. About our kiss."

"That's your problem." Nike had to look away, until
she realized she was being a coward.

"I don't believe you mean that." Gavin searched her
narrowing gaze. "You're scared, Nike. That doesn't
mean there isn't something between us. I grant this is
a lousy place to become aware of it. I'm interested in
you for all the right reasons. And I know why you're
gun-shy. But can't you give us a chance?"

His words were spoken so softly that Nike felt her
heart bursting with need of him. This was a side to him
she'd not been aware of until now. "I'll bet you are a
damned good used-car salesperson, too."

Laughing heartily, Gavin finished off his chai, got to
his feet and made a second cup for himself. "Thank you
for the compliment. Frankly, I'd rather sell you on me."

"I got that." She sipped her chai and wanted to run
away. The room became smaller and smaller and Nike
felt trapped. Or maybe she was trapping herself.

"My team is coming back in a week to base camp,"

he told her conversationally, sitting down once more. "We get two days off. I'd like to take you to Jalalabad, to a nice little restaurant I know about, and have dinner with you. How about it?"

"I don't think so, Gavin."

"Are you sure? I see some hesitation in your eyes."

Setting the cup down next to her knee, Nike said, "I just can't."

Nodding, Gavin said nothing. His instincts were powerful and he knew she liked him. Just how much, he didn't know. He'd tried to play fair and that hadn't worked. Honesty wasn't necessarily the best policy with Nike, who was jumpy and wary. While he understood her reasons, Gavin wasn't about to back down. He watched as she drew out her notebook and pen once more.

"Ready for my village assessment?" he asked her. Instantly, he saw Nike's face relax. So long as he remained on a professional, hands-off basis with her, she wasn't distrusting.

"More than ready." Nike looked at the watch on her wrist. "I have to lift off in thirty minutes."

"No problem." Gavin launched into the many details, names, events and places that he knew her CO would want. It was still an unadulterated pleasure to be with her. She was a feast for his eyes, balm for his heart and Gavin felt as if her presence pumped him full of life and hope again.

Nike just about ran out the door of the house when they were done. She did not want Gavin to trap and kiss her. If he ever kissed her again, she'd melt away in his arms, completely defenseless against his heated onslaught. Moving out into the late-afternoon sunshine, she saw that the shipment of boxes had been removed from the CH-47. Next, she visited Jameela at her home and gave her the box of dates. The woman nearly cried, threw her arms around Nike and hugged her.

"You are my sister," Jameela whispered, wiping her eyes as she held the precious box of dates.

Feeling the warmth of true friendship, Nike reached out and squeezed her hand. "All women are sisters," she told her with a grin.

Jameela nodded and understood exactly what Nike was saying. In this man's world, ruled by men and where women were considered secondhand in every way, they needed to band together and support one another. "The next time you visit, you must have time to have chai with me," Jameela said.

"Ah, I love your chai," Nike said with a laugh. "And yes, if I get this mission again, I'll ask my CO for a half hour more and we'll sit and talk over chai."

Bowing her head, Jameela's eyes burned with warmth. "I would like that, my sister. Allah keep you safe."

"Thank you," Nike murmured, meaning it sincerely. "I can use all prayers." She left the house and hurried down the muddy street. She wanted to do nothing more than get out of here and away from that man who drove her to distraction.

Nike ordered Andy into the helo to raise the ramp, and she settled into her right-hand seat. Just the act of putting on her helmet and running through the flight list before takeoff soothed her taut nerves. From time to time, Nike would give a quick glance out the window, looking for Gavin to show up. He had a way of quietly walking up to her so that she never heard him coming. Not today.

Within minutes, they were airborne. Some small part of her was disappointed that Gavin hadn't come to see her lift off. Moving the heavy two-engine helo into the blue sky, Nike now had to focus on more important things—like surviving this flight back to base.

As she flew nap-of-the-earth throughout the region, she never took the same route twice. Consequently, the route through the mountains was always different and filled with unexpected new difficulties. Nike was glad for the challenge. It kept her mind—and her heart—off Gavin. Still, even as she flew, she wondered what would happen when he and his team came back to base for a two-day rest.

Chapter 7

Nike was halfway back to base when she got orders to turn around and head back to Zor Barawul. Stymied by the clipped radio message, she had no choice but to do so.

As she landed near dusk, the sun tipping the western mountains, she saw Gavin standing with Jameela and her daughter, Atefa. The whirling blades of her helicopter kicked up heavy clouds of dust.

By the time she got out of her harness and placed her helmet on the seat, Gavin was at the rear of the ramp.

"What's going on?" she asked.

"The medical doctor just approved Atefa to be flown to Kabul to be fitted for a prosthesis." He grinned. "I called your base and asked that you return. Sorry to do this. I know it's damn dangerous flying in and out of here."

"Don't worry about it," Nike said, looking out the ramp door at Jameela, who stood with a protective arm around her young daughter. "Is Abbas in favor of this?"

"He is. That's the best news." He searched her face. "I've already talked to the CO of the base. We need to fly them in now and preparations are under way to give them a tent and food for the night. Tomorrow morning, the three of us will be flown to Kabul."

"You're coming along?" Her heart beat once to underscore that news.

"Yes. I'm leaving Sergeant Bailey in charge while I'm gone."

"But..."

"The threat of attack here is always high," Gavin said, reading her concern. "I've gotten permission from my superior to do this because they feel this particular village is essential in the fight against the Taliban."

"And Jameela and Abbas trust you." Nike nodded. "It makes sense." She managed a slight smile. "Have you warned them about the rough ride and nap-of-the-earth flying we'll be doing?"

"I have. What I want to do is get Jameela and her daughter strapped in behind you and I'll ride shotgun in the copilot seat if that's all right with you?"

Her smile turned devilish. "Sounds good to me. If I get shot you can take over flying."

Gavin recognized her black humor and chuckled. "Right. I have a pair of gold-plated tin wings from a United flight attendant that makes me pilot material. Will that do?"

"You're a piece of work, Jackson."

"But you like me anyway, right?"

Seeing the glimmer of warmth in his eyes, Nike

waved a hand at him and walked down the ramp. "There's no way I'm answering that one." She gestured for the pair to come forward. After giving Andy orders, she walked back into the bird. Gavin had passed her on the ramp, walking down to meet the twosome. Nike noticed most of the village had turned out to watch. She had to remind herself that these people, cut off from the outside world, hadn't seen helicopters since the Russians tried to ransack their country decades earlier. The CH-47 was a curiosity among them, especially the younger children.

Jameela walked slowly and kept a hand on her curious daughter as they boarded the helicopter. Nike finished off her radio message to her base and then turned around. Lifting her hand, she waved hello to Jameela, who was draped in her black burka. Nike could only see her wider-than-usual eyes. The woman must not ever have flown in any type of aircraft. Feeling for her, Nike went back, knowing that a smile might make the woman feel more at ease.

As Jameela grabbed her hand, Nike said, "It's okay, Jameela. Everything will be all right." She leaned over and gave Atefa a hug. The little girl was dressed in her finest, most colorful robe, her black hair brushed to perfection. Atefa's eyes shone with excitement.

Jameela gave the ramp door a desperate look and still gripped Nike's hand.

"She's scared to death," Nike said to Gavin, who had come up behind her.

"I know. Show her to the nylon seat behind your seat. I'm sure being near another woman will help calm her fears."

Nike didn't disagree. She took Jameela to the nylon

webbed seat and asked her to sit. The woman did, with great reluctance. Nike had to guide her carefully to the seat so she wouldn't trip and fall over her burka.

After getting the harness in place around Jameela, Nike attended to Atefa in the next seat. Andy took the girl's crutches and tied them down next to their two stacked suitcases strapped down on the deck of the helo. Atefa's eyes were huge as she scanned the cargo hold of the helicopter. Nike kept smiling and murmuring words of encouragement as she ensured they were strapped in.

Next came the helmets. They had none that would fit Atefa, so Andy brought over a pair of earphones and clapped them over her head so she would have protection from the horrendous sounds within the airborne helo. Jameela pulled on hers and was hooked up to the communications system. This way Gavin could continue to answer her questions and soothe her throughout the flight.

In minutes, the ramp groaned and squealed as it came up and closed. The cargo hold was thrown into semidarkness. Patting Jameela's shoulder, Nike went to her seat, pulled on her helmet and got ready to take the bird up.

Andy sat down next to the twosome and Gavin explained to Jameela that he was there to support her through the flight. Jameela seemed less intimidated when Andy strapped himself in next to her. Nike's large, broad seat back on one side and the young man on the other seemed to calm her fears, Gavin thought.

After climbing into the copilot's seat, Gavin picked up the extra helmet and put it on, opening communication between the four of them. As she rapidly went through the preflight checklist, Nike's gloved hands flew across the instrument panel. She was focused on this flight, not on the man next to her. He must have understood the gravity of this dangerous flight and wasn't about to distract her. For that, she was grateful.

The flight back wasn't any different from any other, but Gavin had his hands full with Jameela, who screamed into the helmet's mouthpiece whenever they dived and wove through the mountain passes at a hundred feet. Nike couldn't afford to pull her focus off her flying. The CH-47 shook and shuddered like a dog shaking off fleas as she guided it up and down and then twisted around the mountains to plunge down into the next valley.

By the time they arrived at the base, Jameela was frantic. Atefa, however, was laughing and throwing her arms up and down. For the child, it was like a fun roller-coaster ride.

By custom, no man could touch the woman, so it was Nike who unharnessed Jameela and Atefa, taking off the helmet and earphones and walking them down the ramp into the dusk. Andy brought along the suitcases. A medic met them at the bottom of the ramp in a golf cart, ready to whisk them to a tent for the night.

By the time Nike had them settled, it was pitch-dark. Gavin met her outside the tent.

"They all set?"

"Yes. Finally." Nike quirked her mouth. "What a day."

Gavin nodded and fell into step with her as they headed to the chow hall on the other side of the base. "Couldn't have done it without you. Thanks. I know Jameela feels better because she knows you and trusts you." No lights marked the camp after night fell. To have it lit up was to invite attacks by the Taliban. Each of them had a small flashlight to show the way between the rows of green canvas tents.

The cool night air revived Nike. She was always tense after such a flight. It felt good to talk about little things, and, even though she didn't want to admit it, she was glad to have Gavin's company. After chow, she'd go to ops and fill out her mission debrief report.

Inside the large, plywood-floored tent, the odor of food permeated the air. Nike found herself hungry, so they went through the line and ended up at a wooden picnic table in the corner. She eagerly sipped her hot coffee. Gavin sat opposite her.

"You a little hungry?" she teased Gavin, who sat opposite her, digging into roast beef slathered with dark brown gravy.

"Listen, when you eat as many MREs as we do, real food is a gift," he said, popping a piece of beef into his mouth.

Nike could only imagine. There were mashed potatoes with that thick, brown gravy, corn with butter and a huge biscuit. She ate as if she'd never seen food. Normally, she didn't have such a large appetite, but tonight, she did. "This hits the spot," she told him.

"Mmm," Gavin mumbled, barely breathing between bites.

Nike grinned. "If you don't slow up, you're going to choke on that food you're shoveling down your gullet."

Chastised, Gavin had the good grace to flush. He slowed down a little. "You have no idea how good real, hot food tastes."

"I probably don't. I'm spoiled. I might fly every day

or night, but I can come here and get good chow. I hate MREs."

"Everyone does," he said between bites. He took his third biscuit and pulled it open. After putting in several slabs of butter, he took a big bite.

Nike saw the absolute pleasure the food gave him. She knew these A teams were out in the wilds for a month at a time, sometimes more. This unexpected trip was a real present to Gavin. She tried to ignore how handsome he was, even with the full beard.

"Do you mind wearing your disguise?" she wondered, pushing her empty plate to one side. She held the white ceramic mug of coffee between her hands.

"No."

"It's got to be different from the spit and polish of shaving every day."

"Oh, that." Gavin touched his neatly trimmed beard. "I bet you wonder what I look like without it?"

"No…"

"Sure you do." He grinned.

"I was just wondering how you liked going under cover."

Shrugging, Gavin finished off his third and final biscuit. "Doesn't bother me. Usually, when we're out for a month, we're riding horses and doing our thing."

"So you've all learned how to ride."

"That or fall off." He laughed. Scraping up the last of the gravy, he sighed. "That was damn good food. I wish I could take this back to the guys."

"You and your team go without a lot of things," Nike said, feeling bad for them.

"Luck of the draw," Gavin said. He wiped his mouth with his paper napkin, pushed the plate aside and then picked up his cup of coffee. "I'd rather be on the ground than threading the needle with that hulking helo of yours. That must take some starch out of you."

"Sure it does. Seat-of-the-pants kind of flying. I don't mind doing nap-of-the-earth. I do mind getting shot at."

Chuckling, Gavin felt the warmth of the food in his belly. How lucky he was that Nike had shared such a meal with him. He felt happiness threading through him like sun shining into a dark valley. "Makes two of us. I felt for Jameela. The poor woman is probably going to refuse to step into the CH-47 tomorrow morning."

"We'll have to persuade her that the flight to Kabul will be smooth and quiet, unlike the snaking flight from her village."

"I don't know if she'll believe me," Gavin said.

"She'll get on board because her daughter is going to be fitted for a new leg."

"I appreciate all you did. If you hadn't been there, this would have been a lot tougher. Muslim customs don't allow any man to touch a woman."

Shaking her head, Nike muttered, "I'm glad I was there, but I can't see how their women live in such a state. I know I couldn't."

"Different realities, different belief system," Gavin said. "We don't have to like it for ourselves, but we have to understand and respect them for it."

"Glad I'm a woman from a democracy, thank you very much."

Gavin smiled. "Dessert? I saw some great-looking cherry pie over there. Want some?"

"Sure."

He got up. "Ice cream on it?"

In that moment, Nike saw he was like a little boy in

a candy store. The light dancing in his readable blue eyes made her heart melt. "Why not?"

"Be right back."

She watched him thread his way through the noisy, busy place. This was the dinner hour and the place was packed with crews. There were a few A teams, as well, all dressed in their Afghan clothing. Still, as she allowed her gaze to wander around the area, Nike thought Gavin Jackson stood head and shoulders above any other man present. Maybe she was prejudiced. Maybe she liked him more than she should.

Feeling uneasy for a moment, Nike didn't question why she decided to have a meal with him. If she was really sincere about not ever wanting to love a military man again, she'd have left him at the chow hall and disappeared. But she hadn't. *Damn.* Rubbing her face, Nike felt torn. The problem was, Gavin was too easy to like.

His eyes were shining with triumph when he came back with two large plates. His had two pieces of cherry pie and scoops of vanilla ice cream. Setting hers down in front of her, he gloated, "I couldn't help myself. I love cherry pie and ice cream. My parents have a farm in Nebraska and I grew up picking sour cherries from our trees so Mom could make these mouthwatering pies."

"You're something else," Nike murmured. She watched him sit down and launch into the dessert without apology. Indeed, he was a little ten-year-old boy and not the man sitting there. His expression was wreathed with such pleasure that Nike couldn't help but laugh.

"So, you're a Nebraska farm boy?"

"Yep. My folks have a five-hundred-acre farm. They raise organic wheat, corn and soybeans for the growing green market. Of course, they were doing this decades earlier."

"And you helped with all the farming?"

"Me and my two younger brothers," Gavin said, shoveling in another bite of cherry pie. "They're still at the farm and will take it over when Dad decides to retire."

Cocking her head, she asked, "So, what made you come into the military, then?"

Shrugging, he wiped his mouth. "The excitement. I get bored real easy and watching corn grow wasn't exactly my kind of fodder."

"So, this is your career?"

"I plan to put twenty in, retire and then do a lot of things I couldn't do before."

"Like what?"

He gave her a wistful look. "I like to travel. I want to see the countries of the world, large and small. I enjoy meeting people of different beliefs and religions. I always learn from them and it makes me a better person in the end."

"I'd never have thought that of you."

"No?" Gavin asked, lifting his head and giving her a thoughtful look. "What did you think?"

Uncomfortable, Nike said, "I don't know. I just never thought that much about it." *Liar.*

"I see. Well, how about you? You're Greek by birth. How did you get into the U.S. Army to fly Apaches?"

The pride in his tone washed across Nike. Plenty of men distrusted her because she was a woman in the pilot's seat of an Apache. "My father was in the Greek military for twenty years and then went into flying for a commercial airline. I grew up wanting to fly. He made sure I had flight lessons on single-engine airplanes from the time I was fourteen years old. Later, I wanted to fly helicopters, so I got my license when I was seventeen. My mother didn't want me to go into the military, fearing I'd die."

Gavin nodded. "Not a prudent choice from her perspective."

"No, but I was a tumbleweed of sorts. I didn't want to do things girls were supposed to do. All I wanted to do was get in the sky. I loved the challenge of flying a helo versus a fixed-wing aircraft. When I was up in the sky, everything in my life went right."

"On the ground, things got muddied up?"

"You got it."

"Was there a program for flying the Apache?"

"There was, and I took advantage of it. After I graduated from school in the U.S., I was assigned to the Black Jaguar Squadron down in Peru. I spent several years chasing the druggies and loved every moment of it. From there, I got assigned to chasing druggies along the U.S.–Mexican border. Dallas, who was already there, got me assigned to her unit. When she told me the Pentagon was going to approve a second all-women BJS squadron, I wanted to be a part of it."

"And here you are. That's pretty impressive."

"Thank you. Women can do anything they want if they dream high enough."

"Obviously, you're one hell of a dreamer."

She chuckled and relaxed completely. Talking to Gavin was like talking to her best friend. "I don't think everyone dreams of being in combat, though. I like the challenge of it. I don't like thinking about getting killed. No one does."

"So, what other dreams do you have?"

She took a sip of her coffee. "I'd like to go back to Apache school in the U.S. and teach. I think I'd be a good instructor."

"So, you dream of twenty years in the military, too?"

"I guess I do, but I'm focused only on the present. My mother is always urging me to get married, have kids and come back to live in Greece. I told her I was too young for all of that. I've seen people get married too early, get bogged down with children, and then they're forty-five before they ever have a life of their own. I love kids, and I want them, but not right now. I want to use my twenties and thirties to explore what moves me in life. After that, I'll settle down."

"Sounds like a plan," Gavin said before his expression became serious. "You said the man you loved was killed in combat down in Peru?"

"Yes." Nike hesitated.

"I know what it's like to lose someone you care for. In my first deployment here in Afghanistan, I lost two of my men from my team."

"I'm sorry." And she was. Nike saw his straight, dark brows dip in grief. "I'm just now coming to terms with the loss of Antonio."

"I'm sure we'll both remember those we loved forever."

She liked his sensitivity. "Love can't be destroyed."

"I found that with their loss, I became overprotective and superconservative when I was out in the field. I didn't want to lose any more of my men."

"That's understandable."

"Well, it got to the point where my own men got frustrated with me. I was scared. So, I pulled back, and I lost my will to go out and be the risk-taker I was before. At the end of my first tour, my men finally had to sit me down and let me have it. They told me that risk is a part of our nature, that avoidance wasn't going to help them live or die. Eventually, I realized they were right," Gavin murmured. "I was afraid to connect with life again. My fear paralyzed me in a lot of ways I couldn't see then. I do now, but my men had to gang up on me and force me to see how I was reacting."

She saw the caring in Gavin's blue eyes as he held her gaze. "I can see why you became so gun-shy, so to speak. I hope you don't blame yourself for what happened."

"I try not to." Gavin sat up and moved his shoulders as if to get rid of accumulated tension. "It didn't want to take another chance and that kept me from my job, from living. My men saw it and came to my rescue."

"They are good friends to you, then."

"And I want to be a friend to you, Nike."

His words, softly spoken, made her heart hammer suddenly. Gazing into his eyes, Nike could feel him wanting to reach out and touch her hand. "A friend?" she asked stupidly.

"You're afraid to get back into life because you lost the man you loved. I know you want to protect yourself." Gavin smiled warmly, the expression making her ache inside. "But life isn't like that. You can't help who you do or don't fall in love with. It's chemistry and a million other things all rolled into one."

"Where is this going?" She tried not to look at him but it was impossible

"I'd like to be your friend, but you won't let me."

"You want a lot more, Gavin. I can't give that to you."

Sighing, he nodded. "I know. The problem is, I like you. I'd like to get to know you better on your time and terms. I'm not the kind of guy who hops from bed to bed. You're different from any woman I've ever met. You're courageous, you have steel nerves and you're intelligent. All those things draw me to you. I didn't plan this, it just happened."

His honesty made her feel guilty, especially since there was so much she liked about him. It had been a long time since someone had touched her on such a deep level. "Gavin, you're a nice guy, but I just can't."

Getting up, she left the chow hall as quickly as she could. Her heart was hurting and the grief still roiled within her. The cold night air gave her the slap in the face she needed. She felt bad that she had stomped all over Gavin for being honest. Nike didn't like herself very much as she made her way to her tent. Weaving through the tent city, she noticed the stars twinkling above. They were cold, distant and beautiful. If only she could feel that distant and cold toward Gavin.

Every time the guy looked at her, she found herself shaky, needy and sexually hungry. Was Gavin right? Was this all about her own fear of loss? Of course it was. Nike halted in front of her tent and shut off the flashlight. In the distance, she heard an Apache revving up to take off on a night mission. The wind was cold and she shivered. As she recalled Gavin's story about losing his men, she realized he was trying gently to tell her something about herself.

With a muffled curse, Nike turned, pulled open the flap on her tent and went inside. She sat on the cot and took off her flight boots. Tears burned in her eyes and she wiped them away almost instinctively. She was

drawn to Gavin Jackson whether she wanted it or not!
A sense of guilt and a need to run flooded her.

The worst part was Gavin had no unlikeable qualities. This fact compelled her to throw her boots across
the floor. They made thunks as they struck the plywood.
Leaning over, elbows on her thighs, Nike pressed her
hands to her face. She wanted to keep crying. Of all
things! It had been two years since she'd cried and that
was at Antonio's funeral.

"Damn you, Jackson."

Chapter 8

The July heat was arid and scalding. Nike had grown up in the dry heat of her homeland, Greece, so she felt right at home. Red-haired Emma Trayhern-Cantrell and she trotted across the tarmac to their waiting Apache helicopter. The crew quickly opened up the canopies. Word had just come in that an A team near the village of Bar Sur Kamar was under heavy attack.

Time was of the essence. Nike was the AC, air commander. She leaped up on the step and quickly situated herself in the forward cockpit. Her heart pounded in time with the snaps her harness made as she fastened it. Emma climbed into the rear seat, behind Nike. A blonde mechanic by the name of Judy cinched them in and gave them a thumbs-up before removing the ladder and hauling it beyond the range of the helo's blades.

"Ready," Emma told Nike from the rear seat.

"Good to go," Nike said, pressing the microphone to her lips. The sun beat down upon them. "Let's shut the canopies first. It's hotter than hell."

Once the canopies were locked down, Nike was able to turn on the air-conditioning. The coolness flowed past her helmeted face as they went through the pre-flight checklist in record time. The Apache quivered to life, its rotors swinging in slow arcs. Nike powered up and the blades began to churn. As she looked through the dark shield over her eyes, Nike snapped off a salute to the women on the ground. The chocks were removed from the wheels and they were ready to take off.

For the last two months, Nike had been able to fly the Apache exclusively. She loved being off the roster for assignments with the slow CH-47. As she placed her gloved hands around the cyclic and collective, she lifted the massive, deadly assault helo off the tarmac and into the air.

"I'm punching in the coordinates," Emma told her.

"Roger."

"I'm tuning us in to the A-team commo link so we can monitor them going in."

Lips compressed, Nike felt the helo moving powerfully through the desultory late-afternoon air. "Roger." The land grew distant as she brought the Apache up to seven thousand feet. With this bird, she didn't have to fly nap-of-the-earth. The Apache had every conceivable device on board to locate possible firing by the Taliban. This bird ruled the air in Afghanistan.

Her gaze flicked over the large panel in front of her. Nike watched airspeed and altitude and constantly craned her neck to spot problems. She heard scratchiness through the helmet earphones. Emma switched to the A-team frequency, which would enhance communication. In the past month, attacks on the army hunter-killer teams had escalated. They always did in the summer when travel was easier for both sides.

Her mind turned back to Gavin. She hadn't seen him in two months and was relieved he'd gone back into the field. After she'd dropped Jameela and Atefa into Kabul, her days of ferrying were over. Atefa now had a new leg and was doing fine.

The vibration moved through her hands and up into her arms. But despite her return to more comfortable surroundings, Nike couldn't stop thinking about Gavin. She felt the weight of the armored helicopter around her. Too bad she couldn't choose who to love. Not that she loved Gavin, but she kept seeing—feeling—that one, unexpected kiss in her mind. She'd replayed their conversations too many times to count. How sad was that? Nike could convince herself that she didn't care, but right now she admitted how worried she was for him and his team. It wasn't unusual to fly three missions a day in support of those out in the field. Each time the temptation came to nose around for Gavin and his men, she hesitated. Nike couldn't stop her dreams— the ones where she explored his body, her lips moulded against his, those strong hands ranging over her heated flesh. How many times had Nike awakened from sleep, breathing raggedly, aching for him? Too many.

They topped a mountain range, some snow left on the very tops, the blue-purple rock below. As they came over the valley, communications blared into her helmet.

"Red Dog One to Alpha One, over."

Nike gasped. *It was Gavin!* The moment she'd dreaded had come. Gavin's team was under attack!

"Alpha One, this is Red Dog One, over," Emma's calm voice responded.

"We're getting another attack! I've got two men down. One will die if I don't get medevac pronto! Do you have us in range? Over."

The desperation in his voice shook Nike as nothing else ever had. Hands tightening on the flight controls, she saw the puffs of mortars fired at a hill on the other side of the valley. She knew that the A teams set up lonely outposts in valleys to intercept the paths Taliban took into Afghanistan. Gavin must have been ordered to Alpha One. This valley was a hotbed of enemy attacks.

Pushing the Apache, Nike said, "I've got them in sight. Prepare the rockets."

"Roger," Emma said.

"Alpha One," Emma called, "we're on our way. Give me the coordinates of your position. Over."

Nike heard the back-and-forth between Emma and Gavin. The Apache screamed down out of the sky and Nike watched the firings at the top of the hill where Gavin and his team were pinned down. Her heart raced. Sweat trickled down the sides of her face as she brought the helicopter in line to fire the rockets.

"Ready and on target," Emma called.

Tension reigned in the cabin. "Fire at will," Nike said.

Instantly, the Apache shuddered as the first rocket left. Then a second, third and fourth. Nike watched with visceral pleasure as the rockets struck their targets. Rocks, dirt, flame and other debris exploded upward one, two, three and four times. The hill suddenly had tons of dirt gouged out of one side of it.

"On target!" Gavin yelled, triumph in his hoarse voice.

Emma continued to speak to the A-team leader. It was Nike's job to circle the entire hill. They had infrared aboard that would show body heat where the Taliban was hidden below in the tangle of thick brush. Emma also worked the infrared and continued to give her flight changes so that she could fire the Gatling gun beneath the belly of the helo at other pockets.

In moments, the Apache came on station and Nike held it at an angle, hovering about five hundred feet above a particularly thick grove of trees. Emma released a fusillade of fire, the Apache bucking beneath her hands as the Gatling gun spewed forth the bullets. Nike watched the bullets chew up the landscape like a shredder. Tree limbs exploded, bushes were torn up and she saw about twenty of the enemy scattering in all directions to get out of the line of fire.

It was then that Nike realized just how overwhelmed Gavin and his team had been. She estimated about a hundred of the enemy on all sides of the hill. Her headphones sang with communications between the team, Emma and ops. The sunlight lanced strongly into the cockpit and Nike didn't like it. This time of day was hard on the eyes, making it tougher to see. Fortunately, Nike had a television screen in front of her and she didn't have to crane her neck and squint. The television feed showed a number of other hiding places for the enemy.

Over the next five minutes, they systematically took the Taliban charge apart. The .45 pistol she carried on top of her flak jacket made it tough to draw in a deep breath of air. As Nike danced the Apache around the hill, they spotted another force of about fifty men coming down from the slope of a mountain behind the hill.

Whistling, she said, "They *want* to take that hill."

"No joke!" Emma said. "We're running low on ammo. Want to call in another Apache for support?"

"Roger that," Nike said grimly, and she switched the commo to another position to call ops with the request.

"Red Dog One, this is Alpha One," Nike said. She kept looking around as she brought the Apache to a thousand feet above the hill and continued to circle. This was the first time Gavin had heard her voice.

"Nike?"

She grinned. "Roger that, Red Dog One."

"I need immediate helo evacuation." Gavin's voice registered his surprise. "I've got one man with a severed artery. I've got a tourniquet on it but Burkie'll bleed out before the medevac can get here. Can you land, give up one of your seats and take him on board? Over."

The request was out of the ordinary and completely against regulations. Emma's gasp showed her shock, but what could they do? It would take forty minutes for medevac to arrive on station. By that time, his team member would be dead. Nike knew all the men, and her throat tightened. It was Emma's call. She was the XO. She had the position and power to override any rule.

"Emma?"

"I know," she said, her voice desperate. "Dammit!"

"We've got the Taliban on the run. The hill's clear and we've scattered the fifty coming down to join them. I think we'll be okay to land. We can do this before our backup arrives."

"Are you volunteering to stay behind?"

Nike hadn't thought that far. "I guess I am. Can you clear this request and give permission?" she begged.

"We shouldn't do this," Emma said grimly. "It's against our orders. Dallas will hang us."

"I know, but there's a man dying down there. There's enough room to land and take off, Emma. I can set this girl down, hop out and we can get the guy on board. It'll be easy for you to fly him back at top speed. I don't think the Taliban will regroup. We've killed most of them."

Nike held her breath. If Emma approved the illegal pickup and leaving a pilot behind, it was her ass on the line. Emma was one hell of a pilot and a damn good leader. If anyone could persuade Dallas this was the right decision, it would be Emma.

"Okay, okay, let's get down there. I'm going to rig some static for a call to ops requesting permission. They won't give it to us, but we'll pretend we heard otherwise."

Nike wanted to cry for joy. "We'll stick together on this."

Chuckling, Emma said, "We're BJS and crazy wild women, anyway. This might not be in the flight rules for the boys flying Apaches, but for us, it's no rules at times. Peru taught us that."

Nike understood. How many times down in Peru were the flight book and rules thrown out the window? Too many times to count. If nothing else, BJS was a fly-by-the-seat-of-your-pants squadron. It shouldn't be any different here, either.

"Red Dog One, this is Alpha One. Clear off an area north of your position on the hilltop. We're coming in to land. Once down, I have to shut off the engines. Bring your man once the blades have stop turning. Over."

"Thank you, Alpha One. We'll get on it pronto. Out."

Nike heard the incredible relief in Gavin's voice. Knowing how tight he was with his men, that they were family to him, Nike felt moisture in her eyes. She blinked away tears as she noted the men scrambling to the north end of the hill to pick up anything that the blades might kick into the air. If there was anything lying around, the power of the blades could throw it up in the air and turn it into weapons against them.

Emma rigged the shorting-out communications call with ops and made it sound like static. She laughed darkly. "Okay, we're indicted now. Ready to land?"

"Yes."

Banking the Apache, Nike swooped down and brought the helo to a hover fifty feet above the clearing.

"You can take a hop back on the medevac that's already under way."

"Roger that. No way do I want to stay on that hilltop tonight." Nike brought the Apache down until its tri-wheels hunkered on the earth. Dust clouds kicked up in every direction until the blades had stopped. She pushed open the canopy, climbed out and leaped to the ground.

Two men were carrying a third between them. The injured man's left leg had a tourniquet, midthigh. Blood stained his entire pant leg down to his boot. Gavin trotted up, his face grim, rifle in hand. There were splotches of blood all over his uniform. He'd probably dragged his friend out of the line of fire.

Emma had thrown open her cockpit canopy and stood on the seat to give the men directions.

Nike met Gavin's eyes and ached for the fear and

grimness in them. He handed her the rifle and then lithely leaped up on the Apache. Together, the three men got the unconscious soldier into the cockpit. Nike watched as Gavin quickly harnessed him up. Within two minutes, Emma was ready to take off. Gavin locked the canopy back into place and gave her a thumbs-up.

Nike handed Gavin his weapon as he leaped off the Apache. Together, they all moved away.

"Are you all right?" Gavin demanded as they stood back and hunkered down.

"I'm fine."

"Thanks for doing this," he said.

"No problem." She was kneeling down in a foxhole dug deeply enough to keep them hidden. The dust from the Apache kicked up and the shriek of the engines was like music to her ears. Coughing, Nike shut her eyes and covered her mouth as the thick dust rolled by.

Within three minutes, the Apache was hotfooting it across the valley toward base. The thunking sound of the blades beat in echoing retreats across the valley. Nike told Gavin that a medevac was on the way, and Gavin nodded. "That's good to hear. You're going to be on it."

"Yes, I will be."

He wiped the sweat off his brow. His hands trembled as he put another clip of ammo into his weapon. "You just saved our bacon. At least a hundred of those bastards were down there."

"I'm glad we made the difference." Nike sat down in the hole, dust all over her flight suit. She saw the rest of the men in other foxholes across the top of the hill. Huge craters had formed from mortars fired earlier by the Taliban. The sun slanted powerfully across the hill, making it difficult to see on the western side.

"I've got two other men wounded, but they're walking and firing." He locked and loaded his weapon, craned his neck out of the hole and gazed down the side of the chewed-up hill. Sitting back down, he conferred with his assistant and told him to keep watch, this was merely a lull in the fighting.

Nike sat next to him, her heart lifting with joy to see him alive. "How long have you been up here?"

"Too long. It's been twenty-eight days so far, Nike." He managed a grin. "Why? Do I smell bad?"

Nike chuckled. "This isn't exactly the Ritz."

"I'd give almost anything for a hot shower." He met and held her gaze. "But right now, I'm the happiest man on earth. You're here. With me. Amazing."

Laughing softly, Nike said, "Okay, I missed you a little, too."

"Really?"

She liked the amusement in his crinkled eyes. "A *little*," she stressed. Right now, Gavin looked more like an eagle on the hunt than the laid-back soldier she'd met at base camp two months ago. She reminded herself that he'd been under attack, his adrenaline was up and he was in survival mode.

Gavin wanted to grab Nike and crush her against him. He could smell the shampoo she'd used this morning in her hair. Any fragrance compared to the hell he'd seen on this hill over the last three weeks was welcome.

"Are you wounded?" she said, pointing to his leg. Besides being dirty and torn, he had some fresh blood on his right thigh.

"What? Oh, that. I'm fine. It was just some shrapnel from a mortar."

"You should be medevaced out, too."

"No way."

Frowning, Nike began to really study the rest of the team. They were all wounded to some degree and oblivious to it. All their attention was riveted on the base of the hill where the next attack might come from. The courage these men displayed amazed her.

"How long has this attack been going on?"

"Four days off and on. Today they attacked en masse," Gavin said. He pulled out a canteen and guzzled water. Droplets leaked out the corners of his mouth and down his beard. After finishing, he looked over at her. "They want this hill back. From here, we can see everything going on in this valley. Since we got here over three weeks ago, we've called in ten strikes on them as they tried to cross the valley at night to get into Afghanistan."

"No wonder they're pissed," she said, giving him a grin. His blue eyes lightened for a moment and Nike could feel his desire. She could almost feel it surrounding her. And then, he glanced away and the moment was broken. She wanted those seconds back.

"Yeah, just a little." He stretched his head up above the hole to study the slope for a moment. "I'm glad you're going to be out of here by dark."

"Why?"

"They'll attack then. Damn good thing we have night scopes to pick up their body-heat signatures or we'd have been dead up here a long time ago."

He said it so matter-of-factly, and yet, for Nike, the words were a shock to her system. Gavin Jackson dead.

For the first time, it really struck her that it could happen. Before, Nike had felt he was such a confident leader, that nothing could bring him down. Now, sitting here in a foxhole with him, she felt very different. And she was scared to death.

Chapter 9

There was nothing to do but wait. Nike remained in the foxhole while Gavin made his rounds, running and ducking into the next foxhole to speak with his men. Their only communication was by yelling. He and his second-in-command had radios, but that was it.

Nike kept cautiously peeking over the top of the foxhole, watching below and wondering if they'd destroyed enough of the enemy to keep them at bay for another hour. She wasn't sure. Wiping her mouth, which tasted of dust, she took one of the canteens in the foxhole and drank some water.

Luckily for her, she had her radio and could remain in contact with ops and any flights coming their way. Still, she felt dread. Was this how Gavin and his men felt all the time? The waiting? The wondering when the next attack would come? She couldn't conceive of living in this type of nonstop stress. Her admiration for the A team rose accordingly.

The top of the hill was about the size of a football field, although rounded. The hill was steep and not easy to climb. There had been a wooden lookout at one time, but it had been splintered into oblivion by repeated enemy mortar rounds. The scrub bush that coated the sides of the hill was massive and thick. Nike had seen it from the air and knew men could quietly sneak up almost to the edge of the top of the hill. Her adrenaline pounded through her. What would happen at night?

She could hear Gavin's voice drifting her way from time to time. The foxholes were deep and the nine remaining men stayed in a circle at the top so intruders could be spotted coming from any direction. The afternoon sun was nearly gone and was dipping behind the peaks. As much as she tried to stifle it, Nike was scared for all of them, not just herself.

When Gavin leaped back into the hole, she noticed he'd put his Afghan hat back on. He wore body armor beneath the dusty white shirt, soaked with sweat beneath his armpits. It gave him a little protection from flying bullets.

"Like my digs?" he asked casually, putting his weapon next to him and taking another swig from one of the canteens.

"This is a special hell," Nike said, frowning. Searching his sweaty, dirty face, she added, "I don't know how you take this kind of stress."

"It's not fun," Gavin admitted, twisting the cap back on his water.

"Has this hill been a U.S. outlook for some time?"

"Yes. And with great regularity the Taliban drops

mortars on it hoping to kill us." He gestured toward where the wooden tower had once stood. "We build the look-out tower and they come back and bomb it to oblivion."

She shook her head. "I never realized the kind of danger you were in."

"No one does until they're up to their butts in it," Gavin said, grinning. He took his weapon and made sure there was a round in the chamber. With the rag in his pocket, he tried to clean most of the dust off the weapon.

"Will they attack?" Nike asked.

"I don't know. Depends upon how much damage you were able to do to them."

"Do they attack every day?"

"No, but since two days ago, they've made a concerted effort to take back this hill." Gavin made circular gestures above his head. "This hill is the key to the whole valley, Nike. It sits at one end and with our binoculars and infrared scope, we can see anyone trying to cross it at night."

"How are you being resupplied?"

"We aren't," he said, frowning. "We're low on ammo and water. Usually, we get a flight in here twice a week. We're in dire need of resupply right now."

"And you can't get it because…?"

"The Taliban keep firing at the helicopter transport that's supposed to supply us. Oh, there's always an Apache with it and they lay down fire, but this time, it hasn't worked. If the transport can't land to resupply us, well…"

"Have you made a call to your commander about this?" She felt her throat tighten with concern.

Gavin wiped his brow with the back of his arm. "Yes." He looked at his watch. "I figure in about twenty minutes we should see a medevac, a transport and an Apache come flying in."

"Then what?"

"Well, we're going to swap out A teams. A fresh team will come in with supplies and we'll be airlifted out of here."

Relief spread through Nike. "That's good news."

Grunting, he said, "Not for the team coming in. It's one of the hot spots on the border and no one wants this assignment."

Nike gulped. "Is anyone else in your team injured besides yourself?"

"Oh, we all are more or less," Gavin said.

Nike couldn't believe how calm he was about it all. She noticed again the dark red blood that had stained half the trouser across his right thigh. "Are you okay? It looks like your wound is bleeding more."

"I caught a flesh wound," he said. "It's nothing. I'll be okay."

She sat there digesting all the information. "I never realized how…dangerous…"

Chuckling, Gavin reached out and patted her shoulder. "Hey, it's okay. You Airedales fly above the fray. It's ground-pounding soldiers like us who stare eyeball to eyeball with the bad guys."

His touch felt so good. Suddenly, Nike realized just how much she liked Gavin. Despite the terror, the trauma and the possibility of another attack, he was joking and seemingly at ease about his lot in life. This was real courage.

"You're right, Gavin. I sit up there and I'm not connected to the ground below."

"Well, saves you a lot of PTSD symptoms," he told her wryly. He sat with the rifle between his drawn-up legs, arms around it.

"That's not even funny," she muttered.

"You know what I do when things are quiet like this?"

She heard a wistful note in his voice. "No. What?"

"I think about you. About us."

A bit of ruddiness crept across his cheeks. It was hard to believe that Gavin would blush but he did. "Us?" Her pulse started as he gave her a warm look.

"Yeah." Looking around at the foxhole and then up at the blue sky, Gavin said, "It helps me hold on. When things are bad, I remember that kiss."

So did she, but she wasn't about to admit it. "Oh."

Gavin gave her an assessing look and added, "I swore that if we got off this hill alive, I was going to hunt you down."

A thrill moved through her, though Nike tried to stay neutral. "This isn't fair, Gavin."

"What isn't?"

"You know my past. I lost the man I loved to an enemy bullet. I can't go through that again."

Hearing the desperation in her voice, Gavin reached out and gripped her hand. "Hey, life is dangerous. Not just to military people, but to everyone."

"Especially to the military." Nike jerked her hand out of his. She felt stifled and trapped. Her heart yearned for Gavin, but her past experience had done too much damage. Nike pleaded, "I'm afraid to love anyone in the military ever again, Gavin." There, the truth was out.

Gavin absorbed her strained words. Every once in a while, he'd look up and over the crater to peruse the hill below, but everything seemed quiet. "I appreciate your honesty, Nike. A lot of people allow fear to run their lives in different ways. There's the woman who won't leave a marriage because she fears losing the security. There's the man who fears leaving his job for another one." Shaking his head, he held her narrowed golden gaze. "Fear is everywhere all the time, Nike."

"What do you fear?"

He smiled. "Being alone. See? I have my fear, too."

"Why fear being alone?" She searched his pensive face.

"My mother nearly died when I was a little kid. As a ten-year-old I lived through days and nights when she didn't come home from the hospital. My father tried to help me, but I felt this terror that I'd never see her again. She'd had appendicitis with complications, but as a young kid, I didn't realize what had happened. My father, bless him, tried to keep the three of us cared for, but he had a job. We ended up with a babysitter and not a very good one at that."

"It would be hard for a young child to have a parent suddenly gone from their lives like that."

"It was. I look back on that time a lot. My mom nearly died, but my father never let on how bad it was. I was in school, and that helped. I used to come home and look for her, thinking she was playing a game of hide-and-seek with me."

Nike's heart ached for his pain. "That must have been very hard on everyone."

Picking up a clod of dirt, Gavin crushed it in his fist and let the soil sift between his fingers. "That was one of the most defining moments of my life. I felt abandoned and afraid."

"But she survived?"

Nodding, Gavin said, "Yes, she came back ten days later. We couldn't visit her in the hospital because of the type of infection she had. And she was in a coma, so we couldn't talk to her on the phone. My dad kept telling us she was all right, but none of us believed that."

"Wow," Nike whispered, "that was awful for her and you kids."

He leaned back against the dirt wall. "Yeah, it was. And when she did come home, she was very weak. Nothing like the mother I had known before. I don't know who cried more—us or her when she was brought in the door on a gurney by the ambulance crew."

Nike sat digesting it all. "And she did recover?"

"Fully. It took about six months though. She looked like a skeleton and we all thought she was going to die. My father lost his job because he had to stay home and take care of us. We didn't have the money for a full-time babysitter or a nurse. I remember waking up with nightmares." He sighed. "It was always the same nightmare—Mom was dead. I'd go into her room and she'd be on the bed, dead."

"How awful." Reaching out, she let her hand fall over his. She could feel the grit of dust beneath her fingertips. "I'm so sorry, Gavin."

He enclosed her fingers and gave them a gentle squeeze. "Hey, every family has their trauma and heartache."

"That's true," Nike admitted. Her hand tingled over Gavin's touch. She couldn't deny any longer she was powerfully drawn to him. "So how did this affect your life?"

Gavin chuckled and made another quick check down the slope on their side of the hill. Sitting down, he said, "My fear is abandonment. My whole life has revolved around the possibility of loss. When I joined Special Forces after graduating, I made damn sure I would never abandon my men or leave them without help."

"Unlike the ten-year-old who was abandoned by his mom?"

"Yep." Gavin sighed. "And I got into some pretty stupid relationships with women because of it, too."

"You wouldn't abandon them?"

"No, but they abandoned me in many different ways. I always seem to pick strong women who have no problem having affairs with other men."

"Ouch," Nike murmured. "That has to hurt."

"Yeah."

"Did that ever stop you from having a relationship?"

Giving her a warm look, Gavin said, "Oh, it would for a while, but then I'd jump back into the fray and choose the same kind of woman all over again."

"I don't see how you could keep going back and trying again," she said.

"What's the other choice? Becoming a monk in a cave in the Himalayas?"

Nike laughed along with him, feeling the connection to him deepen. "Well, at least you have the guts and courage to jump back in and try. I don't."

"Maybe you just needed time," Gavin said.

"Two years."

He shrugged. "Well, everyone is different, Nike. Was Antonio the first man you've fallen in love with?"

She nodded. "Coming from a strict Greek upbring-ing, I was taught that love comes along only once. My parents have been married since their twenties. They're very much in love with one another to this day. I wanted that for myself. I wanted that happiness."

"But it isn't working out that way for you."

Nike nodded. "I used to think happiness would just happen."

"I don't think happiness is a guarantee in our life," Gavin said ruefully.

"No," Nike said grimly, looking up at the darkening sky. "That's how I see it now."

"So your world view got shattered when he died."

"Just like yours did when you were ten."

"Life does things to all of us," Gavin said. "I guess what I got out of my mother and father was that hope springs eternal. He never gave up on her. He would hold us, promise us that she was coming home. For whatever reason, the ten-year-old me wanted to see her before I would believe him."

"You can't be hard on yourself. You were only ten, scared, and suddenly you had your mom ripped out of your life."

"I learned then that nothing in life is safe."

"You're right about that." Nike sighed. She sat digest-ing his words. *Nothing is safe.* Sitting here in a foxhole on a hill in Afghanistan proved that. "I feel safe when I'm flying an Apache."

"That's only because you haven't ever been shot down."

"Mmm," she agreed. Rubbing her brow, Nike gave him a frustrated look. "I'm too much of an idealist. I think everything is safe and fine until it blows up in my face."

"Right," Gavin murmured. "But we all get those left hooks that life gives us. The point is to get back up, dust off your britches and move back into the fray."

"And you've done it time and again."

Gavin nodded. "Yes, I have."

"Don't you get tired? Exhausted?"

"Sure I do." He gave her an uneven grin. "But then, hope infuses me, and I start all over again. I open back up and do the best I can."

Rubbing her armor-clad chest, Nike confided, "You're a far braver person that I have ever been, Gavin."

He looked at his watch. "I have an idea."

"What?"

"We happen to like each other. In about ten minutes, those helos will be flying into the valley. How about when we get back to base, we start all over?"

Nike felt fear along with a burst of elation. "What are you talking about?"

"My team will get two weeks' R & R. I'd like to get to know you when things aren't as frantic or dramatic as they are right now. Can we get together and just talk?" He opened his hands and grinned wolfishly. "I promise, I won't hit on you. Maybe what you need is a gentle transfer from the fear of losing someone into making friends once more."

"I don't know, Gavin."

"Look at us," he said persuasively. "We're sitting here in a foxhole together just talking. I like hearing about your life and how you see things. I know you're enjoying yourself."

"Yes, I am."

"This proves that we can be friends."

"That's not what you really want," she challenged, feeling that old panic again.

"No, but I can be satisfied with friendship, Nike. In all my other relationships, I never had what we have. I like it. My parents used to tell me that the strongest base for a relationship was being friends first. I'm just now, with you, beginning to understand that statement."

"You were never friends with the women in your life?"

"Not really. And that's where I may have made a huge mistake."

Uneasy, Nike said, "Antonio and I were the best of friends." She saw him digest that statement.

"Maybe," he said, a bit of wistfulness in his tone, "you're the best thing ever to happen to me."

Quirking her mouth, Nike said, "I wouldn't be so sure of that."

Gavin heard the sounds of rotors and craned his neck to the west. "Oh, I am. Hey, here comes our rescue party. Two Apaches. That's even better."

About that time, Gavin's radio blared to life. Nike heard her CO's voice. Dallas was flying one of the Apaches, which meant she and Emma were probably in a helluva lot of hot water. And Dallas was on the flight schedule today. She'd soon find out.

Gavin gave directions to the medevac and transport, a CH-47, about where to land on the hilltop. Before they did, the Apaches made a sweep of the entire area to ensure the transport could land without being fired upon. For the next ten minutes, the two Apaches used their infrared cameras to look for warm bodies in the area. There were none.

Gavin stood up as the CH-47 came in for a landing. Holding out his hand, he said, "Come on, Nike. We get to go home—together."

She gripped his hand and stood up. Standing there, rifle on his shoulder, he looked incredibly strong and courageous. If nothing else, Nike felt like a true coward in comparison. Right now, she had her CO to worry about. If Emma couldn't sell the reason for letting off the pilot to take an injured soldier on board, her career could be in real jeopardy. Watching the CH-47 hover and slowly come down, Nike wasn't sure what to expect.

Chapter 10

Once Gavin had helped her onto the ramp of the CH-47, he backed away, which surprised her. The other A team trundled off and quickly left the area of the rotor blades. Some of Gavin's A team came on board and the rest went on the medevac. Nike turned, confused.

"I'll see you back at base tomorrow," he called, stepping away.

The ramp started to grind and groan as it came up. Nike realized that Gavin was probably going to fill in the next team and she sat down. She dutifully put on the helmet, but couldn't shake the disappointment that he wasn't coming back with her. She understood why, but it didn't help her fear. The Taliban could attack again. At night.

The CH-47 lifted off, the shuddering familiar and comforting. Closing her eyes, she leaned back and tried to relax. The pilot would be doing the roller-coaster nap-of-the-earth flying, and she hung on. Her mind turned to consider the inevitable: Dallas Klein, her CO, was probably pissed off as hell at what she and Emma had done. They'd broken every cardinal rule in the Apache flight book. Who knew what kind of punishment Dallas would dole out?

The moment Nike stepped into the BJS 60 headquarters, the staff looked up, their expressions grim. A sergeant, Carolyn Cannon, said, "Major Klein wants to see you right away, Captain Alexander."

I'll bet she does. Nike nodded. Normally, Emma Trayhern-Cantrell, the XO of the squadron, would have been at her desk, but there was no sign of her. Girding herself, Nike marched up to the closed door, knocked once and heard "Enter." Compressing her lips, Nike gripped the doorknob, twisted it and entered.

To her surprise, Emma stood at rigid attention in front of Major Klein's desk. Cutting her gaze to her CO, Nike knew she was in a lot of trouble. The older woman's eyes blazed with rage.

Coming to the front of the desk, Nike said, "Reporting as ordered, ma'am." Sweat began to gather on her brow and her heart pounded with adrenaline. Nike had never seen Dallas this angry.

"Captain, what the *hell* were you thinking when you left the cockpit of your Apache? You know damn well neither pilot is to *ever* leave that helicopter for *any* reason unless it's on fire."

Nike looked straight ahead to the wall behind her CO. "Ma'am, Berkie…er…Sergeant Berkland Hall, the communications sergeant, was bleeding to death. Captain Jackson said he'd die before a medevac got there to rescue him. Berkie...er...Sergeant Hall's wife had their first child three months ago. I—I didn't want to see him die. I wanted to see him live to get home to see his new baby. Ma'am..." Right now, that all sounded like a decision based on too many emotions, but Nike stuck to her guns.

"Captain Trayhern-Cantrell says she ordered you out of the cockpit. Is that true?" Dallas growled.

Gut clenching, Nike realized Emma was being true to her word to take the fall on this breaking of rules. Nike didn't want to leave Emma at the center of the problem. "Er... Ma'am, it was a mutual decision."

"Mutual?" Dallas yelled. She glared at Emma. "Dammit, you're XO of this squadron! You have no business making any 'mutual' decisions!"

Emma shot a fearful glance at Nike and then said, "Yes, ma'am."

Dallas got up and prowled the small office, glaring at both women. "I have my XO, who is supposed to be the poster child for following rules, breaking them. And then I have one of my best pilots agreeing with her to break those rules, too." Hands behind her dark green flight suit, Dallas stalked around her desk.

"There are men dying out there every day, ladies. We are not medevac. If you want to be medevac you should have damned well volunteered to do that kind of service work. Our job—" and she punched an index finger in their direction "—is to protect and defend. The Apache is *not* a medevac!"

Swinging her attention to Emma, she added, "Dammit, Trayhern-Cantrell, what if you'd got shot coming back? What if you'd needed Nike on the instruments if the Taliban started firing at you? What if, God forbid, we'd needed the two of you on another call on the way back?"

"You're right, ma'am," Emma whispered contritely.

"I don't want to be right!" Dallas exploded. "I want you to know what is right, Captain! You're a damn poor example for our squadron. It makes all of us look bad."

Emma's lips thinned and she said nothing, her eyes straight ahead.

Nike cringed inwardly. In all her years knowing Dallas as the XO of the Black Jaguar Squadron down in Peru, she'd never seen her fly off the handle as she was doing. That was how serious this was, Nike realized. At the time, it had seemed like the right decision to make. She didn't know yet if Berkie had survived or not. She'd come straight here to HQ from the helo.

"Of all the harebrained decisions the two of you have ever made, this goes over the top." Dallas glared at them. "What am I to do? If I don't punish you for your decision, then one of my other pilots will get it into her head that it's okay to climb out of the cockpit on a mission to give up her seat to another injured soldier."

Wincing, Nike felt the blast of her CO's anger. Oh, it was justified. The only question now was what Dallas Klein was going to do to punish them for their blatant transgression. She could feel two spots burning into her cheeks as her CO watched her.

"All right," Dallas flared, her voice suddenly deadly quiet, "neither of you leave me any choice. Captain Trayhern-Cantrell, you're stripped of your status as XO. You've just proven you aren't up to the task of reinforcing the rules that we must all live under here in combat."

Nike winced. She knew that punishment would go

on Emma's personnel jacket and it could stop her from making major someday. There was nothing Nike could do about it, and she felt terrible.

"Yes, ma'am," Emma croaked, shock in her tone.

"Remember, Trayhern-Cantrell, you did this to yourself. You made the decision! You shouldn't have allowed that A team captain to influence you as he did. You've clearly shown that you don't have the backbone to enforce the rules."

"Yes, ma'am," Emma whispered.

Heart breaking, Nike heard the pain in Emma's tone. She knew that Emma came from a military dynasty, a very famous one. There were so many medals and awards for valor in the Trayhern family, and now Emma was giving it a black eye. Emma must feel awful about this. Guiltily, Nike knew it had been her idea to pick up Berkie.

"Ma'am," Nike spoke up strongly, "Emma is innocent in all of this! I—"

"That's not true, ma'am," Emma piped up quickly, giving her friend a panicked look.

"Quiet!"

Nike grimly shut up, as did Emma. Her attempt to save her friend was not going to work. When Dallas had been a young pilot, she had to have made some stupid decisions, too. She'd probably been in a similar situation herself.

Breathing hard, Dallas said, "Do you realize what you've done? We're a covert black ops. We've come here with an incredibly spotless record of positive work as an all-female squadron. And you two decide to screw it up with this stupid, completely avoidable mistake."

Nike'd known the chewing-out was going to be bad,

but not this bad. She felt guilty that her desire to save Berkie would give all the women of this squadron a bad name, but still couldn't be sorry for her action. Her decision broke the rules, but wasn't wrong by moral standards. With that resolve, Nike was prepared for the worst. What made it tough was how Emma selflessly threw herself under the bus. She didn't have to, but she did. Nike felt awful about that.

"What the hell am I going to do with the two of you?" Dallas spat. "It isn't like I have women pilots standing in line to fly Apaches! But I can't trust the two of you in the cockpit, either." Glaring at them, Dallas shook her head.

"I'm sorry, ma'am." Emma's voice was quiet and apologetic.

Nike absorbed the brittle tension that hung in the small office. She was sure the office pogues outside could hear everything. It was completely unlike Dallas to scream at anyone like this.

"Captain Trayhern-Cantrell, you're demoted. It will be reflected in your jacket and haunt you for the rest of your military life. You have not done your proud military family any favors with your poor decision-making. From now on, you will be just one of the pilots in the squadron. One slip-up—and I mean *one*—and I'll send your ass back to the States and you can be reassigned into a mixed-gender helicopter squadron flying transports. You got that?"

"Yes, ma'am."

Nike tensed inwardly as Dallas swung her glare to her.

"And you, Captain Alexander. I have a terrible feeling this was all your idea and that Captain Trayhern-

Cantrell was the patsy for your desire to help that man. War is not pretty. I thought you would have got that in Peru, but obviously, you didn't. You let your compassion for that man affect your judgment. I can no longer trust you in the cockpit of an Apache, can I?"

"No, ma'am, I guess you can't," Nike whispered.

"There's no *guess* about it, Captain Alexander." Dallas fumed. "Dammit, you leave me no choice. From now on the only time you'll have your ass strapped into an Apache is to keep up your flight skills. I'm assigning you permanently to the transport squadron here on base until you can be trusted to fly an Apache properly. I need every woman I have to man the Apaches and you've now left me a pilot short. I'm calling back to the Pentagon to see if I can find another female pilot to replace you."

Nike closed her eyes, taking her CO's words like punches. She had never anticipated this. Her Apache days were over. "Yes, ma'am," she croaked.

"I can't trust you, Captain Alexander. That's what this really comes down to, isn't it?"

It was useless to try and fight for herself. "Yes, ma'am," Nike said.

"Has it ever occurred to you that I could court-martial you, drum you out of the U.S. Army and send you back to Greece?"

Horrified, Nike opened her mouth and then snapped it shut. The fury in Dallas's eyes burned through her.

"I could do that, Captain. But dammit, that would be another blow to BJS 60 and frankly, I don't want that on our record. I wanted to make a positive record of our performance as an all-women squadron here in

Afghanistan. So you're safe on that score and damn lucky," she gritted out.

Closing her eyes, Nike swallowed hard. She opened them and stared straight ahead at the light green wall behind her CO. "Thank you, ma'am."

Dallas sat down. She scribbled out a set of orders. "Captain Alexander, you're officially transferred to the transport squadron based here. All you are going to do is fly CH-47s. Maybe that will remind you of your bad choices and how you've hurt our squadron. Fly with those realities in mind." She thrust the papers at Nike. "Now, both of you, get out of here. Dismissed."

"I'm sorry," Nike told Emma once they were back in their tent area. The night was dark and they had their flashlights. "I didn't think...."

Emma put her arm around Nike's slumped shoulders. "I'm sorry, too. I don't care if I lose the XO position. I know the rules are there for a reason. We made a choice and got caught, was all."

"There were times in Peru when we would take a sick child or adult out of a village and fly them to Cusco," Nike grumbled. "And Dallas damn well knew we did it. We'd leave one of the pilots behind, radio in to the cave and let them know what we were doing and nothing was ever said by Dallas or the CO."

"Yes, but it's different here," Emma said. "Down there, we had no other military ops around us. Here, the eyes of the whole base watch our every move because we're an all-female squadron."

"Humph," Nike growled. They stepped carefully through the ruts made by a storm the night before. "Dallas knows we did that stuff down there."

"Yes, but she's CO now. And the men are watching us," Emma said. "Dallas didn't have a choice in this and I knew it."

Giving her friend a sharp glance, Nike said, "You knew she'd bust you out of XO position?"

Giving her a slight smile, Emma nodded. "Sure. That's what I would have done if I was CO. I was just hoping she wouldn't have been so hard on you, that she'd put a reprimand in your personnel file and let it go at that."

"Dallas knows I was the one who thought it up, that's why."

Halting at a row of tents, they turned. It was chow time and most of the women were gone. Nike was glad. Word would spread like wildfire. By morning, the whole camp would be aware of their new orders.

"I'm not hungry," Emma said, halting in front of her tent, next to Nike's. "Are you?"

Nike laughed sourly. "The only thing I want is a stiff damn drink of pisco to burn out the tension in my gut."

Emma grinned. Pisco was the drink of Peru. It could kick like a mule once it was gulped down. "Yeah, that sounds pretty good right now. I'll bet Dallas has a stash of it hidden somewhere."

Nike's spirits rose over her indomitable friend. "I don't think she's going to share it with us, do you?"

Giggling, Emma said in a whisper, "Not a chance."

"I'm going over to the med tent," Nike told her. "I don't even know if Berkie made it or not."

"He was in terrible shape," Emma admitted quietly. She put her hand on Nike's shoulder. "I'm going to lie down and try to sleep. I feel like I was in a dogfight and lost."

Nike nodded. "Yeah, it hurts, doesn't it? Well, we did this to ourselves. Dallas did what she had to do."

"Gosh, Nike, you can only fly CH-47s now. That's terrible! I never thought Dallas would go that far."

"I know," Nike whispered glumly. "What bothers me is that if she replaces me, I'll never get back into the squadron. I could finish out my tour here in Afghanistan flying transports. That sucks."

Emma nodded. "Putting an aggressive combat pilot to fly a bus is a horrible punishment."

"It could have been worse," Nike reminded her solemnly.

"Well, all we can do is be good pilots from here on out and do the best we can. Over time, this thing will settle out and be forgotten."

"I hope so," Nike said. What would she tell her parents? They would be shocked. "I still am not sorry we did it, Emma."

"I'm not, either," Emma told her. "If Dallas knew that, she *would* court-martial us."

Depressed, Nike agreed. "Well, it's our secret for the rest of our lives. We can't tell our families, either. You know how word gets around...."

"Mmm," Emma agreed. "My dad is going to hit the roof and God, my mom is going to be scraped off the ceiling, too. And my uncle Morgan is going to...well, who knows what he'll do...."

Nike knew that Clay and Aly were very proud of their daughter. The Trayhern family created warriors for the military and Emma was no slouch. She was one of the finest Apache pilots ever to go through the school. And her uncle, Morgan Trayhern, was a genuine military hero who was highly respected within that world. "I'm really sorry about that."

Emma shrugged. "They'll understand. I'm not sure Uncle Morgan will, but I know my parents will forgive me and just tell me to keep my head down and do good work."

"What do you think your uncle will do?" Morgan Trayhern was in a position of power running a black-ops company that helped the U.S. government in many different ways.

"Ugh, I don't know."

"He has influence," Nike said hopefully. "Do you think there's anything he can do to help you take the black mark out of your jacket?"

Emma placed her hands on her hips and looked up at the stars overhead. "Probably not. He'll probably agree with Major Klein's decision. He's not a rule-breaker, Nike."

Nike snorted. "I'll bet he broke plenty of rules when he was in the military. He just didn't get caught like we did, is all."

"Listen, head on over to the clinic. Find out about Berkie. I sure hope he made it."

"I'll let you know." Nike opened her arms and impulsively hugged Emma. "Thanks for everything. If Berkie made it, it's because of you."

Releasing her, Emma grinned. "Let me know, okay? Come back, and if I'm sleeping, wake me up?"

Nike watched as a medic behind the desk rifled through a bunch of papers. He then consulted the computer, scanning for the name Berkland Hall.

"Yes, ma'am, he's alive," the young blond medic finally said as he tapped the computer screen. "He's resting in stable condition at the hospital at Bagram Air Force Base. Says here they're going to be transporting him back to the States tomorrow morning."

"Thank you," Nike said, relief in her tone. She left the busy medic tent and headed back out into the darkness. Tears burned her eyes. Berkie would live to see his newly born daughter. His wife would have a husband. A sob ripped from her and Nike pressed her hand against her mouth, afraid that someone nearby might hear her. She couldn't cry here.

There was a spot on the north side of the base where Nike went to sit and clear her head. This night, after this horrible day, she went to her rock, turned off her flashlight and simply allowed the darkness to swallow her up. She loved looking at the myriad stars since they reminded her of her home in Greece. Right now, she felt alone and depressed. And she worried about Gavin, hoping the Taliban weren't attacking the hill tonight. Because she was between squadrons, there was no way for her to know. Until she took her orders to the new CO of the transport squadron, she couldn't ask anyone about anything.

Touching the BJS 60 patch on her right shoulder, Nike knew she'd have to take it off tomorrow before going to the CO of the transport squadron at 0800. For all intents and purposes, she had been drummed out of BJS 60 in shame. She wrapped her arms around her drawn-up legs. She had no one to thank for this but herself. Inside, she was a mass of contradictory emotions. Berkie was alive because they'd broken the rules. A little baby and a wife would have a father and husband to complete their lives. It had been a hell of a decision, and Nike didn't mind paying for it personally. She hated that Emma had stepped in and taken part of the blame, but that was Emma. Nike had often seen her wearing the mantle of the Trayhern dynasty and sometimes, it weighed heavily on her. *What a mess.* Nike had ended up getting Emma's fine career smeared permanently.

It all seemed overwhelming in that moment. She balanced out her grief over the decisions that Major Klein had made against Berkie being alive. What was a life worth? Everything, in Nike's mind. Lifting her chin, she saw a meteor flash across the night sky. How was Gavin? Was he safe? When would he fly back here to be with his team?

Nike realized that she truly missed Gavin. The wonderful, searching talk they'd had last night was burned into her heart's memory. She was such a coward when it came to trusting love.

Love?

Snorting, Nike released her arms from around her knees and stood up. *Am I falling in love with Gavin? No, that couldn't be.* Hadn't she been punished enough in one day's time? Did she need this awareness like a curse upon her, too?

Shaking her head, Nike couldn't assimilate all of the day's unexpected turns and twists. Yet, as she turned and shuffled back toward the tent city hidden in the darkness, Nike still missed Gavin. If he was here, she could confide in him. He would understand. Right now, Nike ached to have his arms around her. Right now, she needed to be held....

Chapter 11

Gavin sat in the medical-facility tent on a gurney. The doctor had cut away most of his blood-soaked pant leg, inspected the bullet wound that had created a three-inch gash across his thigh. The place was a beehive of activity this morning. It was raining and he was soaked after coming off a helo that had brought him back to the base.

"Well?" Gavin asked Dr. Hartman, a young black-haired man with blue eyes.

"Flesh wound. You're lucky, Captain Jackson," Dr. Hartman said, looking up.

"Shoot me full of antibiotics, sew me up and authorize me back to my team," he told the doctor.

Hartman grinned a little. A female army nurse came over with a tray that held the antibiotic, a syringe, needle and thread plus some scrubbing material to ensure that the wound was free of debris. "I know how you Ateamers like to stick together, Captain," Hartman said, picking up a syringe that would locally anesthetize the wound area first.

"It's just a flesh wound," Gavin said. He sat on the gurney, his good leg hanging over the side. While the army would give him three weeks at the base to let the wound heal properly, Gavin didn't want it. His team would be ordered out without him and that bothered him greatly. He felt protective of his men; they were his friends. Gavin didn't want them subjected to someone else's leadership.

"Mmm," the doctor said, swabbing down the area with iodine. He stuck the syringe around the edge of the open wound.

Frowning, Gavin said, "Look, Doc, I don't want a three-week R & R back here because of this." He jabbed his finger down at the wound.

The doctor waited for the anesthetic to take hold and smiled at Gavin. "I know you don't want to get separated from your team, Captain, but this is bad enough to do it. If I release you back to your team and you go out on a mission and rip the stitches out, the wound will become reinfected."

"Not if you give me a steady supply of antibiotics to take," Gavin said. He could tell this doctor had just come over to the front. And he was probably a by-the-book kind, to boot.

Shaking his head, the doctor took the debridement sponge and squirted iodine into the wound cavity. "Sorry, Captain Jackson, I won't authorize that. Your wound is too deep. You're lucky it didn't go into your muscles. Take the three weeks of medical R & R and go to Kabul and chill out."

That was the last thing Gavin wanted. He felt no pain or discomfort from the debridement as the doctor meticulously scrubbed out every bit of the open wound. "Look, Doc," he pleaded, "I don't want my men going out there without me. They're safer under my leadership."

"Can't do it. Sorry." The nurse handed him the needle and thread and he began to close the wound one stitch at a time.

"How about you give my entire team a three-week R & R? Then we can go into Kabul together. They need a break."

Hartman's mouth curved slightly. "You're a pretty creative type, Captain Jackson."

"Look, my men need updated vaccinations. Couldn't you authorize my team off-line for that extra week because of that?" Gavin was giving the doctor the excuse he needed to authorize such a ploy. However, it was the veteran doctors who had spent a year in either Iraq or Afghanistan that understood what he was really asking for. Gavin had hope that if Hartman was a vet of the war, he'd do it.

"You know, Dr. Hartman," the nurse medic spoke up, "we are way behind on vaccination checkups for all the teams. I can accommodate their needs and rotate them through here." She smiled over at Jackson. "We've got forty-nine A teams in here. Maybe if you authorize Captain Jackson's team to stand down, I'll put them at the end of this roster. It would take a week to get around to vaccinating them. And as you know," she added, giving the young doctor a serious look, "we can't send these teams out there in summer without updated vaccinations."

Hartman nodded and considered the medic's request. "So, we're behind on vaccinations?"

Gavin couldn't believe his good luck. The woman was an officer like himself, a registered nurse, and had to be in her forties. He guessed she'd seen more than one tour at the front and was wise to the ways of getting things done for the troops when necessary. He gave her a nod of thanks, and she grinned back.

"Yes, sir, we are. Now, I could arrange this with your approval. The army isn't going to take notice of such things. One A team out of forty-nine that stands down for a week isn't a burp on the Pentagon's radar."

Hartman finished the knot, seeming pleased with his work. He put the needle and thread on the tray. Snapping off his latex gloves and tossing them on top, he told the nurse, "Do the footwork and I'll sign it."

Gavin watched the doctor quickly walk away to the next patient. "Thanks for catching on," he said to the nurse.

The woman set the tray on the gurney and began to place the dressing over the stitched wound. "Don't worry about it, Captain Jackson. He's green."

"Yeah," Gavin said grumpily, "I knew that."

She quickly bandaged his wound. "There. You're all set." She pulled off her gloves and dropped them on the tray. "I'm due for a break, so I'll go back to our office and get the orders created for you and your men."

Giving her a warm look, Gavin said, "You're a real angel." He read her name tag, G. Edwards. "Thank you, Lieutenant Edwards."

"My name is Gwen. And don't worry about it."

"Truthfully," Gavin told her in a quiet tone, "none of us really need any updated vaccinations."

Chuckling, Gwen took the tray and gave him a merry look. "Oh, I knew that, Captain Jackson, but Dr. Hartman doesn't. He arrived here two weeks ago and doesn't have a clue yet. I'll make sure your team is sent to Kabul for an extra week, and, of course, by the time I get around to your vaccination records, your wound should be plenty healed up. That way, we can release you and you can go back into action as a team."

"I owe you," Gavin said. "Thank you."

She winked. "Not to worry, Captain. You and your A teams are incredible and I'll do what I can within my duties to assist you when and where you need help. Enjoy Kabul for me."

Gavin felt like yelling triumphantly. Of course, he couldn't. As he watched Gwen move away and thread through the fifty or so gurneys and medical teams, he grinned. He slid off the gurney, realizing he must look funny with one pant leg gone and the other still on. He'd go back to his tent, tell his men what had transpired and change into a new set of trousers. After that, he'd go to the medical-unit headquarters to get his team's temporary orders for Kabul.

Walking out of the huge tent, Gavin saw the turbid gray clouds roiling overhead. In the summer, sudden thunderstorms could pop up and they were the only rain the desertlike area would receive. Some thunder rumbled far away and he walked carefully through the mud and puddles toward the row of tents where the A teams were housed.

As he did, he received some strange looks, but that was okay with him. His mind turned to Nike. How was she? Where was she? He'd been on the hill for two days acquainting the new A team with everything they needed to know. Gavin could have opted out of that role because of his wound, but he didn't. The medic on the other A team had kept him supplied with antibiotics, ensuring his wound would not become even more infected. Of course, Doc Hartman didn't know that and Gavin wasn't about to tell him, either. And certainly, no A team would push him off the hill, either. So many times, men who were cut, scratched or even suffering from flesh wounds like himself would not seek immediate medical treatment. They just didn't have the time or place to be picked up by a helicopter to get that sort of help.

Sloshing through the muddy ruts and divots made by men's boots, Gavin reached tent city. In no time, he told his team what was up, and there was a shout of triumph about going to Kabul for three weeks instead of the usual two. It was a well-earned rest for them, Gavin knew. Inside his tent, he got out of the destroyed pants and put on a new pair. As always, he'd remain in Afghan garb even in Kabul. Kabul wasn't safe for any American. And blending in with beards and Afghan clothes was a little insurance. Still, Kabul was considered barely stable and they would all carry weapons for protection. The Taliban was making a major push to take back the region.

Gavin headed off toward the BJS 60 squadron area. He knew where their HQ was and wanted to find Nike. He wondered if she was out on a flight or here at the base. Wherever she was, he had to know how she was. It didn't take him long to find the tent that housed the all-women Apache team.

Each tent had a door. He opened the ops door and

stepped inside. Removing his Afghan cap, he walked over to the red-haired woman at the desk.

"Excuse me, I'm looking for Captain Alexander."

The woman's huge gray eyes regarded him with a disconcerted look. He glanced down at the name tag on her green flight suit: E. Trayhern-Cantrell.

"Oh...and who are you?"

"I'm Captain Gavin Jackson. Nike and I know one another." He hooked a thumb over his shoulder. "I just arrived off a mission and I wanted to catch up with her. Can you tell me where she is?"

Grimacing, Emma looked around. Lucky for them everyone was over at the chow hall for breakfast. "Er, Captain," she began, her voice lowered, "there's been a problem."

Alarm swept through Gavin. "Is Nike all right?" He had visions of her being blown out of the air by a Taliban missile or her Apache burning and crashing.

Holding up her hand, Emma said, "No, no, nothing like that. Nike told me about you. So, I'm going to give you the straight scoop." She leaned forward and said, "Nike has been transferred out of here."

His brows shot up. "Why?"

"Captain, when we flew that mission to your hill-top and Nike gave up her seat so that Berkie could get the medical help he needed, we broke every rule in the book. We weren't supposed to do that, but we did."

"I don't understand. You saved his life by doing that," Gavin said, instantly flustered.

Emma stood and came around the desk. She didn't want anyone to hear this. "Captain, Nike and I took the fall for that decision. I lost my position as XO and she got transferred to the CH-47 squadron here at the camp."

Disbelief swept through him. "You mean...her CO got rid of her? She can't fly the Apache anymore?" Gavin was horrified.

"Captain, Nike came close to being court-martialed for what she did. Fortunately for both of us, the CO doesn't want to give the squadron a black eye by letting that happen. So, she sent Nike off to a transport squadron. She can fly an Apache once every seven days to keep up her skills, but that's all."

Gavin shook his head, reeling from the information. "But she did nothing wrong. She saved a man's life, for God's sake!"

Emma held up her hand. "I agree with you, Captain, but there's nothing we can do about it. Nike could have been sent home to the U.S. or back to Greece. Her CO could have done a lot of things and didn't. This was the least slap on the hand that Nike could receive."

Stunned, Gavin stared at the tall, lean pilot. "I—I don't know what to say. I'm sorry this happened to the two of you. But my man's alive and on his way stateside now because of what you did. Doesn't your CO see that?"

"Our CO, Major Klein, is pretty savvy, Captain. She had no choice in this. If she'd let it go and the word got out on it, that would be bad for the squadron. She had to act."

"Dammit," Gavin whispered, shaking his head. He looked up at Emma. "I'm really sorry about this, Captain. I didn't think saving my man's life would screw up both your careers."

"Don't worry about it," Emma soothed, touching his

slumped shoulder. "Neither of us is sorry we did it. And we didn't apologize for our actions in front of our CO, either. We are taking our lumps for this, but that's just part of being in the military."

Gavin knew it meant a hell of a lot more than that. Each woman's personnel jacket would have the reprimand in it. For the rest of their careers every time they tried to go to the next officer pay grade, that reprimand would be there. Rubbing his brow, he muttered, "This isn't right. Are you sure I can't do something to take those reprimands out of your jackets?"

Emma looked at him warmly. "Oh, how I wish you could, but you can't. One person cannot undo this type of reprimand. You're bucking one of the oldest rules in the Apache book—neither pilot ever leaves the helicopter unless for safety reasons."

Gavin sighed. "I didn't mean to screw your career for you, Captain. Or Nike's. I know how much she loves flying the Apache and she's damn good at it."

"No disagreement there," Emma said. "What I'm hoping is that because it's summer and things heat up with the Taliban during this season our CO won't be able to do without her piloting skills. Right now, the CO can't find a replacement for her, which means one Apache is on the ground."

The ramifications were brutal and Gavin rubbed his beard. "So, she's officially with the transport squadron flying CH-47s? Permanently?"

"Yes, until further notice."

Gavin ached for Nike and wanted so badly to tell her he was sorry.

"You might go over to the transport HQ and find

her there. She's still in our tent city but I don't know if she's home or out on a mission."

Grunting, Gavin put on his Afghan cap. "I'll do that, Captain. Thank you." He lifted his hand in farewell.

Of all things! Gavin tramped angrily through the mud and glared up at the clearing sky. In two days, Nike's whole career had been upended—by him. By his request. Even worse, he wondered if she'd be pissed off as hell at him and never want to see him again. Threading in and out between the tents, he finally found the BJS 60 group. In front of one tent was a young woman with blond hair.

"Excuse me, I'm looking for Nike Alexander's tent. Can you point it out?"

"Sure, right next to mine," she said, pointing to it.

"Thanks."

"She's not there."

Gavin looked at the name tag on the woman's flight suit: S. Gibson. "I'm Captain Gavin Jackson."

"Oh, yes, the A-team leader." She thrust out her slim hand. "I'm Sarah Gibson."

Gavin knew that his Afghan clothes might get him mistaken for a local instead of U.S. Army. No locals were allowed on the base for fear that the Taliban might get on the base in disguise. His skin was deeply suntanned and he could pass for an Afghan-born citizen. He didn't know how Sarah could tell his nationality except by how he spoke the English language.

"Sarah, do you know where Nike is?" His heart beat a little harder.

"No, I'm sorry, I don't," she said, shaking her head. "Since she got rotated out to the transport squadron, we rarely see one another. When I'm flying, she's here. When she's flying, I'm off duty."

Nodding, Gavin said, "Then I'll go to the transport HQ."

"If you don't learn anything, I can pass Nike a message for you. She always spoke of you in glowing terms."

Not now she isn't, Gavin thought grimly. "Could you tell her I'm back on base and doing fine? My team and I will be sent to Kabul for three weeks' R & R. Probably tomorrow morning. I'd really like to see her before I go." *And tell her just how damn sorry I am that I got her into this mess.* Even if Sarah gave her his message Nike might be so angry at him that she wouldn't care.

"Of course, Captain Jackson, I will." Sarah smiled brightly. "If you'll excuse me, I'm going on duty. Enjoy the R & R. I'm jealous."

Gavin tried to quell his fear as he walked into the HQ of the transport squadron. It was a busy place with mostly male pilots coming and going, although he saw several female helicopter pilots. But Nike wasn't one of them. Standing near the door, Gavin searched the area to find out who might have the daily squadron flight roster. One man in back with red hair and freckles was at a huge chalkboard containing the name of every pilot and the flights for the day.

Aiming himself in that direction, Gavin quickly perused the names, twenty of them, on the huge green board. The very last name was *N. Alexander.* He smiled momentarily as he approached the enlisted man, a U.S. Army tech sergeant.

"I'm Captain Gavin Jackson," he began as an introduction.

"Yes, sir. What can I do for you?" the red-haired youth asked.

Reading the last name on his flight suit, Gavin said, "Sergeant Johnson, I need some info. You recently had Captain Nike Alexander rotated into your squadron. I'm trying to track her down. Can you help me?"

Johnson nodded. "Yes, sir." He turned and pointed to her name. "Right now, she's flying ammo and food to Alpha Hill in this valley." He read the chalked assignment on the board. "She left an hour ago. Should return, if all goes well, in about an hour from now."

Gavin realized Nike was resupplying the hill and the A team he'd just left that morning. How badly he'd wished he'd seen Nike.

"She'll be coming back in here once the mission is complete, sir."

Gavin nodded. "Thanks, Sergeant. After she's done with this flight, does she have the rest of the day off?"

Laughing, Johnson said, "Oh, no, sir. In fact—" he held up a sheaf of papers "—I was just going to the next chalkboard. Each one is a mission for each transport pilot. On good days, they might fly once or twice. On bad days, we're landing, loading up again and flying three to four times, depending upon the distance." He peered down at a paper. "She's slated to take an A team out to a place called Zor Barawul."

"Any other flights after that?"

Looking through the rest of the missions for the day, Johnson said, "No, sir, I don't see any. If all goes well, Captain Alexander should be done and out of here by chow time."

"Good. Thanks, Sergeant." Gavin turned on his heel and left the busy squadron headquarters.

Moving out into the muck and puddles left by earlier thunderstorms, Gavin sighed. He headed back to his own tent city to be with his team, but the whole time he thought about seeing Nike again. What would her reaction be? Anger or pleasure? Gavin couldn't guess and that drove him crazy. He liked to control his destiny and he couldn't control Nike's reaction to him.

The sky was showing blue among the white and gray shreds of cloud as the thunderstorms moved off to the east. Sun started to come out in slats here and there. The temperature rose and it looked like a good day ahead. Mind whirling, Gavin knew that flying transports was even more dangerous than flying an Apache. They were trundling workhorses, slow and unable to move quickly if targeted by the Taliban below. His heart ached with fear for her life. He'd just found her and now, dammit, through his own actions, he might have lost her.

All he could do was be at her tent when she returned. Gavin couldn't quell the anxiety fluttering in his chest. He remembered starkly that one beautiful kiss they'd shared. He remembered Nike's fear of ever falling in love with a military man again. There were so many mountains to climb to reach her. In his gut, Gavin sensed Nike was worth every effort. But would she receive him warmly or with scorn? All he could do was stand at her tent and wait for his fate.

Chapter 12

"Hey, Jameela," Nike called to the woman as she approached the helicopter with her daughter. Nike had just arrived to pick up the current A team deployed to Zor Barawul. The mother was in her black burka, the crisscross oval showing only her eyes. Atefa was still on her crutches but Nike had learned that the medical facility at Bagram Air Base near Kabul was ready to fit her with a prosthetic leg.

Behind her, the load master, Sergeant Daryl Hanford, worked to unload all the medical and food supplies for the village. He got help from the new A team just arriving at the village.

"Hello," Jameela said, reaching out to grip Nike's extended, gloved hand.

Nike knew not to hug Jameela. That would have been against Muslim rules. Instead, she kissed each side of Jameela's hidden face, which was a standard greeting.

Jameela laughed and they pressed cheeks. Nike had been studying Pashto, and she knelt down and smiled into Atefa's bright and happy face. The little girl had a new set of crutches from America, far better than her old ones. "Hello, Atefa."

Shyly, Atefa smiled.

"Ready to go to Kabul?"

The little girl prattled on in Pashto. Nike had no idea what she was saying. Easing to her feet, she turned and looked at the progress at the CH-47. It had been unloaded, and Daryl waved to her to indicate everything was ready for takeoff. Since she didn't stay on the ground too long, Nike gestured for Jameela to bring her daughter forward.

They walked slowly, Jameela on one side of her daughter and Nike on the other. The storms of last night had made the once-flat spot a mire instead of a dust bowl. Half the village had gathered to watch them. Nike had been informed that Jameela would remain at Bagram, the air base outside the capital, for three weeks. Luckily for her, Nike would get to stay the night at the base.

Nike helped strap Jameela and her daughter into the nylon seat. By now, they understood it would be a roller-coaster ride until they could get away from the mountains and onto the brown desert plains. As Nike belted in and worked with her copilot, Lieutenant Barry Farnsworth from Portland, Oregon, she quickly went through the preflight checklist. Her heart lifted. She might have been kicked out of BJS 60, but at least she'd get a night at Bagram Air Base. That, she was looking forward to with relish.

* * *

At the O Club on Bagram Air Base outside of Kabul, Gavin nursed a cold beer and tried to get past his disappointment. Nike hadn't shown up at her tent. He'd gone looking for her but then one of his men had found him and told him they had fifteen minutes to get their gear together to catch a flight to Bagram for their R & R.

He looked around at the wooden tables filled with officers from all the military services. The long, U-shaped bar was made of plywood with plenty of bar stools. The room was crowded, with music, chatter and laughter. He should be happy, he thought, taking a swig of the ice-cold beer. The bubbles on his tongue from the beer always made him smile. There weren't many perks in this war, but getting a cold beer was one of them. It washed the mud of the war and their thirty-day missions out of his throat.

Gavin rested his back against the bar. For whatever reason, his gaze drifted to the main door of the O Club. It was nearly dark except for the lights around the entrance. For a moment, he thought he dreamed Nike Alexander entering in her olive-green flight uniform. It couldn't be! Heart pounding, Gavin slid off his stool, shock rolling through him. How did she get here? He didn't think. His instincts took the lead and he moved toward Nike.

Knots of men and women crowded around the many tables. It was tough to get around all of them. When Gavin managed to meet Nike, he saw her eyes go wide with shock.

"Gavin?" Nike blinked twice. Her pulse raced; she couldn't believe her eyes. Gone was his beard and his

Afghan clothes. He was a suave urban American male in a pair of blue jeans and a short-sleeved white shirt. Even more, Gavin Jackson was drop-dead handsome. His jaw was square, his mouth sensual. The merriment in his blue eyes captured her. When his mouth curved, she felt heat shimmer from her breasts all the way down to her toes.

"You look different" was all she could say in her surprise over seeing him again.

"And you look beautiful," he said. Reaching out, he cupped her elbow. "Come on, I see an empty table in the corner. Let's grab it. I'll buy you a beer."

Head spinning, Nike followed and she soon found herself sitting at a small round table. It was fairly dark in this corner, with just enough light to see Gavin. Damn, but she couldn't stop looking at him. She'd never really seen his body because of his bulky Afghan clothes. Now he moved with the litheness of a cougar on the prowl. His arms were heavily muscled, his chest broad and powerful. Maybe it was his legs, those hard thighs, that made her throat go dry. She couldn't believe how dynamic and confident he appeared now. As Gavin turned, smiled at her with two beers in hand, Nike felt that she was in some kind of crazy, wonderful dream.

"Here you go," Gavin murmured. He set the beer in front of her, took a chair at her right elbow and sat down. Nike was wide-eyed and her curly black hair was wild, showing that she'd just recently flown. "Can you talk or are you still stunned?" He grinned.

Wrapping her hand around the chilled bottle of beer, Nike took a long swig. She closed her eyes and simply allowed the bubbles and the taste of the hops to wash down her dry throat. Once she set it down and found her voice, she gave him a silly grin. "I just can't believe you're here."

Gavin had the good grace to flush and gave her a bashful smile. "I never expected you to waltz through that door, either."

Nike took several more sips as his words registered. A waitress came over and she ordered a hamburger and French fries. So did Gavin. Nike rested her elbows on the table and stared at him. "How's your leg wound? I didn't know you were off Alpha Hill."

Feeling giddy, Gavin relayed the chain of events, during which he ordered another round. "Nike, I talked to Emma Trayhern-Cantrell and she told me what happened. I'm so sorry." How badly Gavin wanted to reach out and squeeze her arm, but he didn't dare. This was a military O Club and fraternization was not allowed. You could get drunk and fall on your face, but no kissing, holding hands or anything serious with the opposite sex. The exception was when the jukebox prompted couples to dance and the floor became crowded.

"Don't worry about it, Gavin. Emma and I knew we were breaking every rule in the book for Berkie."

His eyes were sad. "Then it's true? Your CO booted you out of BJS 60?"

"For the time being," Nike said, relishing the taste of her second beer.

"I didn't realize what this might do to your and Emma's careers," he muttered with sincere apology.

"I've lived long enough to know I'm not always going to do things right. Berkie was special to me. Well, all your guys were. When you said he was bleeding to death, all I could think about was his wife and baby daughter. I couldn't stand by and let him die."

"Well," Gavin said, his voice hoarse with emotion, "Berkie is on his way stateside. I don't know if you heard his update, but he's going to make it. Right now, he's on a C-5 Galaxy flight headed for Walter Reed hospital in Maryland. I know that Vickie, his wife, is flying in from Louisiana to meet him at the hospital after he gets through the entry process."

"Wonderful!" Nike said. "Is she bringing his daughter? I know he's only seen video of her on the computer."

"Yep," Gavin answered after taking a swig of his beer, "Francesca is going to be in her mother's arms when she's allowed to see Berkie. It's going to be one hell of a reunion."

Nike sighed with deep contentment. "Thanks for sharing all that with me, Gavin. It makes what we did worth it ten times over."

"Don't tell that to Major Klein. Next time, she'll crucify you."

"Oh, she's not like that usually," Nike said, smiling. "Dallas had to do it, Gavin. If she allowed us to get away with it, other pilots in other situations might think about abandoning their seat for another injured soldier. No, she was right and we were wrong. I'm willing to take the fall and so was Emma."

"You two are tough women warriors," Gavin said. His hand ached to hold hers.

"How long are you here for?" she asked. Gavin's face was deeply shadowed by the sparse light and it made him even more handsome—and so dangerous to her pounding heart. "And what happened to your beard?"

"I managed to wrangle three weeks here at Bagram for my team." He touched his chin. "I shaved it off today after we arrived. I'll have to let it grow back out. In three weeks, my mug will be covered again."

"You must have run screaming to the base barber." Nike chuckled. "Your hair is military-short, too." Indeed, his black hair shone with blue highlights beneath the light. There was a predatory quality to Gavin's face, especially with those large blue eyes. But it was his mouth that made her melt like hot butter. He couldn't know how much his looks influenced her wildly beating heart and no way would she ever admit it to him. Just sitting here at the table, their elbows almost touching, was like a fantasy.

Gavin grinned. "My team hit the barbershop post-haste," he agreed congenially. Touching his short hair, he said, "We just wanted to get cleaned up and feel like American men for a while."

"Over in the barracks where I'm staying, there's actually a tub, not just a shower in the room. I can hardly wait to get over there and take a long, luxurious hot bath. At our base it's outdoor stalls with piddling water coming out of the showerhead. This is real luxury."

"Bagram is beloved by all military branches," Gavin told her. "I know you're four months into your one-year tour here, but I'm sure you'll look for every chance to get a night or two at this base."

"That's one of the perks of being a transport pilot," Nike agreed. "In fact, tomorrow morning at 0700 I'm flying a supply of ordnance back to our camp."

Frowning, Gavin knew the CH-47 would be filled with ammunition of all types. "That's a dangerous run." If the Taliban got lucky and shot bullets—or worse, a missile—at the lumbering helicopter, it could be blown out of the sky. He'd seen it happen on four different occasions and nothing was ever found of the crews. Nothing. Heart contracting, he kept his mouth shut. The possibility of her dying in a situation like that nearly undid him. And yet, every day, every hour, they were in combat and bad things happened to good people.

Nike nodded and finished off her second beer. The waitress brought two oval plates filled with hamburgers and French fries. After putting dollops of ketchup and mustard on her hamburger, Nike ate it with complete enthusiasm. For the next few minutes, there was silence because they were eating like there was no other pleasure in the world.

"Aren't we a couple of starved wolves?" she chortled. Between French fries she added, "Down in Peru, in our cave where BJS squadron lived, we had a pretty good chow hall. Our CO made sure that we got fresh fruits, veggies and eggs from Cusco. I always liked taking our transport helicopter into Cusco. My copilot and I would spend the night in that high-altitude city, do the tango, drink pisco and have a wonderful Peruvian meal. Then, we'd stagger back to our hotel and fall into bed. The next morning, we looked like hell, took hot showers and got into our civilian clothes to be driven back out to the airport." Chuckling fondly, Nike said, "We lived hard and died hard in Peru. We didn't lose that many women or Apaches, but our job was just as dangerous as it is here in Afghanistan."

"You traded jungle for desert. And instead of druggies, you got the Taliban."

"Bad guys exist all over this globe, unfortunately," Nike said. She finished off the French fries and gave him a silly grin. "I feel good. There's nothing like American food."

"But you're Greek."

"I know, but over the years of being in the States and then with the original BJS, I really got into American junk food." She patted her waist. "Good thing I come from a family of thin people. Otherwise, I'd be over the weight limit to fly the Apache." Nike chuckled.

"Do you really think you won't be allowed back into your Apache squadron?" he asked, getting serious. A shadow appeared in her eyes and she pursed her lips. It rankled his conscience that he had been the cause of her career demotion. Gavin knew the military very well. With that kind of reprimand in her personnel jacket, Nike could easily be overlooked for the next rank. Well, he had to live with the consequences of his actions whether he liked it or not.

"I don't think that Dallas will find another female pilot coming out of the Fort Rucker Apache training school," Nike said. "Not that many women wind up in the flight program and there's a lot of resistance to their being in the combat helicopter."

"Surely your squadron's exploits have shown them otherwise?"

"Over time the boys at the Pentagon stopped refuting our abilities." Nike grinned. "It's like pulling teeth, but we'll get more women into the Apache program. Like Maya, our CO down in Peru, said, we have to hold the energy and keep our intent clear. We know women can do the job as well as any man. Flying the Apache isn't about brawn. It's about brains and coordination."

A slow song came on the jukebox and Nike suddenly felt self-conscious.

"Come on. Dance with me. I like the idea of holding an Apache pilot with brains." Getting up, Gavin extended his hand so that Nike couldn't protest. He saw her eyes flare with several emotions, among them a desire to dance with him. He could feel it.

"Come on," he urged, gripping her hand. "You can do this. You're one of the bravest women I know, so don't say no."

Nike felt herself coming out of her chair. The dance floor was crowded as she followed Gavin out to the middle. When he turned and placed his hand on the small of her back and drew her closer, she came without resistance.

"See?" he whispered in a conspiratorial tone. "This isn't so bad, is it?" He led her expertly around on the floor.

Laughing a little, Nike said, "Did I have a horrified look on my face?"

Gavin drowned in her golden eyes. "Hey, you said you danced with the Latin boys down in Cusco, so why not here, too? How can I compete?"

"You don't have anything to worry about on that score," she said. He kept about six inches between them. Even though he could have used his hand to press her up against his body, he didn't. He gave her space that made her panic subside. Besides, Nike told herself, why not dance with Gavin? He was damn good at it.

"Oh? So I stack up pretty well?"

"Absolutely." He gave her a mirthful smile and she enjoyed the happiness in his blue eyes. Why not let go? She had in Cusco. She'd blown off the tension and danger and death that always surrounded them. Dancing with Gavin was a wonderful antidote to her flying in this country, too.

"I can tango, too," Gavin informed her, his grin

increasing. "My mother loved ballroom dancing. I grew up knowing all of the different styles and steps. Competing as an amateur was her hobby."

"Well," Nike said, impressed, "you're good."

"You have no idea," he told her in a roughened tone, his lips near her ear.

Her flesh tingled wildly in the wake of his warm breath as it caressed the side of her face. For a moment, his hand squeezed hers a little more firmly. An ache rose in her body. She was so hungry for him that it wasn't even funny. Two years celibate had left her more than hungry, but she'd want Gavin in any condition. Something still made her hesitate. This wasn't love, right? This could just be a physical release. That's all she needed. At least, that's what she told herself.

"So," Gavin said quietly, "what's going on behind those beautiful eyes of yours? I see you want me."

"You are such a brazen dude."

He whirled her around and then brought her back into his arms. "I want this night with you, Nike. There don't have to be any strings, if that's what you want. One night together, that's it."

She looked deeply into his eyes and considered his request. "Just sex. And friendship."

Nike knew Gavin would be a good lover. She could tell by the way he monitored the strength of his hand around hers as they danced. She was wildly aware of his palm against the small of her back, and the way he sometimes caressed her with his thumb, as if stroking her. It reminded her she was a young woman with real needs. Maybe her grieving really was over and she hadn't realized it. Antonio would always be in her heart and her memory. Nike never wanted that to go away. When she loved, she loved deeply.

Finally, she couldn't stand it anymore. "Okay, let's get out of here. Your place or mine?"

"Mine," Gavin said confidently. He pulled her off the dance floor and smiled. "In the BOQ for the men, we each have a nice room to ourselves. I'll bet you have a roomie."

"Yes, I do. Does yours have a tub?"

"No, but we'll make do." Gavin smiled wickedly and led her out the door of the club.

Chapter 13

Just as they reached the male BOQ—Bachelor Officer's Quarters—an enemy mortar landed somewhere near the revetment area where all the helicopters were parked. Nike jumped and whirled around. Gavin automatically shielded her with his body.

Her eyes widened as mortars began to "walk" in their direction. Fire erupted when a helicopter was directly hit and flames roared into the air. Smoke belched into the dark sky, highlighted by the leaping flames. And then, when the aviation fuel on board the helicopter exploded, a huge reverberation of thunder was followed by a painful, earsplitting boom.

Pressing her hands to her ears, Nike saw Gavin's tense, shadowed face as another explosion rocked a hangar nearby. "They're going to need us!" Nike yelled.

Nodding, Gavin gripped her upper arm. "Where's your flak jacket? You can't go anywhere without it."

He was right. All the festering desire that had bubbled up through Nike had vaporized in a split second. "I'm making a run for our barracks."

"Be careful! Meet me back here when this is over."

Nodding, Nike turned and hotfooted it down the line toward the women's BOQ that sat on the opposite side of the airport. People were running, grabbing their helmets, shrugging on their body armor and wrestling with their weapons. As Nike ran, the wind tearing at her, she saw that the Taliban's attack had been very successful. Three helicopters were on fire and utterly destroyed.

She ran around the end of the base and realized she had no weapon. Somewhere beyond the nine-foot-high fence, strung with razor-blade concertina wire over the top, were several Taliban mortar crews. Nike knew she could be a target with the flames leaping a hundred feet in the night sky behind her.

Changing course, she ran toward the burning wreckage and the fire crews now dousing the area with water. Better to take more time and go around the other end of the airstrip where it was safe in comparison.

Another round of mortars popped off. Nike could hear the hollow ring fired somewhere out in the night. To her shock, the mortars went toward the control tower, right where she was. With a strangled sound, Nike dove for the ground when she stopped hearing the whistle of a mortar screaming overhead. She hit the ground with a thud, the air knocked out of her. Rolling into a ball, her hands over her neck and head, she didn't have long to wait. The air-control tower was a two-story-tall brick building. The mortar landed on the side and about thirty feet from where Nike had burrowed into the ground. The next thing she knew, she felt a whoosh of hot air. In seconds, she was flying through the air, arms and legs akimbo.

When she struck earth once again, Nike yelled out in pain. She hit her shoulder and heard something pop. Barely conscious, she held her left arm tightly to her body, pain arcing up through her shoulder. Had she broken a collarbone? Worse, had she dislocated her shoulder? Groaning, Nike sat up, shaking her head. She spat out the mud and tried to reorient. People were running around like rats out of a drowning ship. Nothing seemed organized.

Holding her elbow tightly against her, Nike knew she had to get medical help. *Dammit, anyway!* Somehow she managed to get to her feet and fought to regain her balance.

The medical building was in high gear when Nike arrived. She saw men with torn pants or blown-off shirts. Some were burned, others dazed and bloody. Hesitating at the door, Nike knew she wasn't as seriously injured. Someone pushed her through the opened door.

"Get in there," a man ordered her in a gruff, no-nonsense tone.

Turning, Nike noted the white-haired doctor in a blood-spattered lab coat.

"Over there," he ordered her, pointing to an area where there were cubicles, each with a gurney.

Not hesitating, Nike headed to the dark-haired army medic with a stethoscope around her neck. Red-hot pain shot from her shoulder into her neck and the next thing Nike knew, she collapsed to her knees while still holding her left arm against her.

Gavin couldn't find Nike anywhere. Panic ate at him. In the grayness of dawn, he saw the black, smoking wreckage of three transport helicopters. He wondered if Nike's CH-47 was among the carnage. As he stood near the air-control tower that had missed several mortar rounds, he noticed how the ground around it was hollowed out in craters.

Where was Nike? He'd been over to the women's BOQ but hadn't found her. Nor was she waiting for him at his BOQ. Worriedly, he searched the red line of the dawn on the flat plain. Firefighting crews were putting out the final flames and smoldering fires around the helicopters. A number of other smaller buildings around the airstrip had been hit, as well. Rubbing his jaw, Gavin tried to search through the hundreds of crews working to reclaim what the Taliban just destroyed.

His heart ached with fear. Had Nike been hurt? Gavin turned on the heel of his boot and headed toward the medical area. Long ago he'd traded in his civilian clothes for a set of green fatigues, his combat boots, body armor and helmet. Normally, Bagram was never hit, but sometimes the Taliban took it upon themselves to get close enough to remind the Americans that no place in Afghanistan was safe from their strikes.

The air smelled of metal, smoke and burning wood. Panic started to curl up from his heart and he felt as though he was choking on fear. What if Nike was wounded? Dead? Blinking, Gavin refused to go there, though he knew that she'd tried to make it across the base to her barracks without any protective gear on. That made her vulnerable.

"Damn," he muttered, halting at the opened doors to the medical building. It looked like measured chaos inside. If the Taliban had struck to take out people, they'd succeeded. The wounded and bleeding sat everywhere on the floor, with medics and doctors working among them with quiet efficiency in triage mode. Peering inside the brightly lit area, Gavin scanned it for Nike. He did not spot her.

His gut told him to keep going, keep looking. He pushed through the entrance, winding his way through the medical teams and the nurses' station. He found an officer, an army nurse, and asked, "Have you admitted a Captain Nike Alexander?"

She looked up. "I don't have a clue, Captain. We haven't exactly had time to sit down and type all these people into our computer yet."

Nodding, Gavin said, "Mind if I look for her?"

"Go for it. Good luck."

After the nurse hurriedly left, Gavin turned and scanned the area. There were several curtained cubicles on the opposite side of the room. The people on the gurneys were all men. He searched every face in the entrance area and no Nike. Okay, if she wasn't here, maybe on the second floor, which was the surgical floor. Gavin picked his way to the stairs at the back of the room and quickly ascended them.

The surgical floor was also mayhem. Gurneys were filled with soldiers and airmen who had been wounded in the mortar attack. Blood dripped from one gurney, creating a large pool on the white tile floor. Medics hurried from one gurney to another checking stats, talking to the waiting patients lined up to go into the next available surgical theater.

None of them were Nike. Gavin couldn't still his anxiety. He knew in his heart he was falling in love with her. And now, she could be dead. *God, no, please don't let that happen,* he prayed as he made his way to the nurses' station.

"Excuse me," he called to a nurse who was updating records. "I'm looking for a woman, Captain Nike Alexander. She may have been wounded in this attack. Can you tell me if she's here?"

The nurse gave him a harried look and stopped writing. She went to a large book on the desk and perused the list. "Sorry, Captain, no one here by that name," she said.

The only place left was the morgue. Gavin stared at her. "Are you sure?"

"Yes," she said firmly, "I'm sorry, she's not here."

Oh God. He stood and numbly watched the nurse return to her work. How could this be? One moment, Nike was walking with him to his BOQ. They were going to spend the night together. She'd been able to scale her fear of loss enough to be with him just once. But Gavin knew Nike wasn't like that. No matter what she said, he understood on a deeper level that she was reaching out to him. To love him. It was going to be a helluva lot more than sex. She cared about him, and he loved her.

He stood at the desk, his mind tumbling in shock and disbelief. He didn't want to go to the morgue. He didn't want to ask about her there. Tears burned in his eyes and Gavin blinked them back. His throat went tight with a forming lump. In that awful moment, Gavin realized that even though his bad relationship with Laurie had stung him, he was ready to try again. And Nike, in her own way, seemed to be working to trust once more, too. Why the hell did this attack have to come now? Gavin knew the answer: war was unpredictable. Death was a breath away. Nothing was stable and nothing could be counted on.

It has to be done. Mouth tasting of bitterness, Gavin worked his way out of the medical building. Last year, two of his men had been killed in a firefight and he'd had to identify them at the morgue here. He'd hated it then. He hated it now.

Dawn was pushing the night away, the red ribbon on the horizon turning pink and revealing a light blue sky in the wake of the cape of retreating night. The whole base felt tense and edgy. Grief ate away at Gavin. He remembered Nike's wish never to fall in love with a military man again for fear he would be ripped away from her. That her heart could not take a second shock like that. Well, now he was in her shoes. Making his way between large vehicles, the smell of diesel in the air, Gavin saw the morgue ahead. It was a single-story building painted the color of the desert. The doors were open. He saw several gurneys lined up with body bags on them. Was Nike in one of them?

Unable to look, he passed them and hurried inside to the desk. A young man of about eighteen looked up.

"Yes, sir?"

Swallowing hard, his voice barely a rasp, Gavin asked, "Do you have a female officer in here? Captain Nike Alexander?" He stood, not breathing, waiting, praying hard that he wouldn't hear the word *yes.*

The man scowled and looked through a sheaf of papers. "No, sir. No one by the name of Alexander, male or female."

Relief tunneled through Gavin. He felt faint for a moment. He'd been handed a reprieve. Releasing his held breath, he nodded. "Thanks," he muttered, and left.

* * *

Nike was just coming out of the BOQ when she spotted Gavin. He looked hard and upset, his eyes thundercloud-black. Worry was evident on his features. She gave him a wan smile and lifted her right hand.

"Gavin. Are you okay? I've been looking all over this base for you."

He saw her left arm in a sling. Halting, he said, "Are you all right? What happened?"

Grimacing, Nike told him the details. "As soon as they took X-rays, the doctor said I'd dislocated a ligament here on my shoulder out of what they call the AC joint. He got the ligament back in, thank God, but I've got orders to stand down for a lousy six weeks." She frowned at her left shoulder. "I can't lift my arm above my chest. That means no flying. I'm stuck behind a desk, dammit."

Closing his eyes for a moment, Gavin felt like a man who had just been given the greatest gift in the world. He opened them and clung to her golden gaze. "I— thought you were dead," he managed in a strangled whisper.

Nike stared at him. And then, it hit her hard and she managed a croak of despair. "I'm so sorry, Gavin." She reached out and gripped his arm. "There was no way to get hold of you."

"I know, I know," he said. Gripping her hand in his, eyes burning with withheld emotion, he rasped, "Nike, I understand your fear now. About losing someone you love to a bullet."

Shock bolted through her. Staring at Gavin, she realized he understood now as never before how she felt about Antonio being ripped out of her life. His hand was firm and warm. She'd been tense and nervous since the attack, but somehow, Gavin's protective presence just seemed to make her feel safe in an unsafe place. "It isn't pretty, is it?" she said in a low tone.

"No. It's not." He searched her eyes that held the shadows and memories of the past. "I looked everywhere for you. I—I eventually forced myself over to the morgue."

"Oh," Nike groaned. "I'm so sorry...."

And then, Nike knew that he really did love her. Gavin might verbally spar with her but the look in his eyes told her the truth. Gulping, Nike shoved all that knowledge down deep inside her until she could deal with what it meant to her.

"It's not your fault. Things get crazy when a base is under attack."

She squeezed his hand. An ache built in her heart as she saw the devastation, the terror, in his gaze. "It's a hell of a way to understand my fear of a relationship with you. I'm sorry you had to find out this way."

"Nike, I don't want to live without you. I'm willing to risk everything to have some kind of a relationship with you on your terms."

His words melted through her pounding heart and touched her. Blinking through unexpected tears, Nike pulled her hand from his. Panic ate at her. This was serious. *He* was serious. There was no way she wanted to hurt him, but she had to. "I'm stuck in this war zone for another eight months, Gavin. What kind of a relationship could we have?"

"Catch as catch can?" he asked hopefully, the corners of his mouth pulling upward a tiny bit.

Hearing the hope, the pleading in his voice and seeing the stark need reflected in his blue eyes, Nike felt the last of her stubbornness dissolve. "I feel scared, so scared, Gavin." That was the truth. Nike felt terrorized by the realization he did love her. It wasn't just a game. It was real. Could she go there again?

"I understand your being scared." Reaching out, Gavin cupped her cheek. "Darling, we're just going to have to learn to be scared together. The last time this happened to you, you were alone. You had no one. Well, now you have me. I grant I'll be gone thirty days at a time in the field, but when we get back to base, we'll be together. I promise you that."

His eyes burned with such intensity that it seared the fright out of her. "All right," Nike quavered, "I believe you, Gavin."

Gavin stroked her cheek, knowing full well that fraternization was strictly prohibited. He could be in a lot of trouble. Worse, he could get Nike into more trouble than he already had. Quickly, he dropped his hand. Her cheeks burned a bright red. "We're going to make the most of this, Nike. We can't let fear tear us apart again. We'll live one day at a time. It's all anyone has."

Nodding, she slumped against the wooden building behind her. "You're right." She sighed. The feeling was there and she wanted so badly to say the words *I love you, too.* But she couldn't. Nike was still imprisoned by her loss as much as she felt this new love.

"I wish I was wrong," Gavin confided, coming close to her but keeping his hands to himself. "At least I get a reprieve from worrying about you. You're stuck back on base, which is a helluva lot safer than flying a helo."

"Don't remind me. I feel stifled in an office." And

then more softly, "I won't stop thinking about you no matter what I'm doing."

Warmth spread across Gavin's chest. "Well," he said with a tender smile meant only for Nike, "it looks like we've made the best of a bad situation here. We might not have had the night we wanted, but we're alive and on the right page."

Despite the ache in her shoulder, Nike wanted to throw her one good arm around him, but that was impossible. "Six weeks…" Inwardly, she was relieved. Gavin was backing off. Maybe she needed that time at the desk to truly rethink her position with him and try to put the past to rest. To allow what she had with Gavin to blossom.

"What's the prognosis on your shoulder?"

"I'm on a mild painkiller for now," Nike whispered, her voice sounding off-key. "The doctor said it would take six weeks because I strained the ligament. They don't heal fast. He gave me a bunch of papers with exercises on them. At three weeks I'm to fly back here for another examination."

"At seven weeks I'll be back to base," Gavin said. "Maybe we could, you know, pick up where we left off before all hell broke loose?"

She grinned. Relief flooded her. Nike was sure she could figure this all out by then. "One way or another. I might not have the range of motion, but that's not going to stop me."

Gavin laughed softly. "Okay, sounds good. Where are you off to?"

"The doctor gave me orders to take the first transport back to our base. My helo was destroyed last night. My copilot will be coming back on the same flight. Once I get home, I need to go see my CO. I'm sure he'll put me on a desk and forget about me for six weeks."

"Wild horses don't do well in corrals," he teased her gently.

"Do you still get your three full weeks here?"

"Yes. They've asked all available personnel to help in the cleanup and I was going over to ops to get orders."

"Wouldn't it have been nice if the doc had told me to stay here at Bagram?"

Gavin rolled his eyes. "That would have been a miracle."

"Well," Nike told him, picking up her helmet bag in her right hand, "I think we've seen plenty of miracles for one day, don't you?"

Gavin took her helmet bag and walked at her side as she headed for the airstrip. "You're right. A miracle did happen—between us."

"I'm still worried," Nike admitted. "I don't think I'll ever get over the fear of losing you, Gavin."

It hurt not to be able to reach out and touch her, hold her hand or place his arm around her just to give her a sense of protection. "You're not going to lose me. I promise. This is my second tour and I've got a year of experience under my belt. That will keep me alive."

How badly Nike wanted to believe that. The demons would resurface. Yet, the glimmer of love burning in his eyes fed her. Gave her hope. Could she really reach out and love him? Or would her fear drive him away?

Chapter 14

"When does Gavin get back to our base?" Emma asked as she sat with Nike in the chow hall. At noon it was packed, the noise high and the smell of cooked food permeating the area.

"Tonight if all goes well."

"Tonight?" Emma shook her head. "I suppose tomorrow he and his team will be flown out somewhere for thirty days?"

Slathering butter on a hot roll, Nike nodded. Her left arm hadn't seemed to make any progress over the last two weeks. She could lift it waist-high and then excruciating pain hit. Eating was an interesting proposition with only one and a half hands available to her. "Yes."

Emma ate her meat loaf after cutting it up into many dainty pieces. The perfectionist in her always expressed itself in many different ways. "That's not fair."

Snorting, Nike said, "When is war ever fair?"

"Or life, for that matter?" Emma rejoined, grinning.

"You got that right." Nike enjoyed the warm butter on the fragrant homemade roll. The late-August noontime was hot. A front was coming in and it was supposed to storm. Nike wasn't looking forward to that.

"Things seem to be falling apart over at BJS," Emma confided.

"Oh?" Nike raised her brows. "What's the scuttlebutt?"

Emma shrugged. "The bad news is that Becky Hammerschlag is the XO and she's terrible at it."

"You were a good one," Nike said.

"Everybody knows that. They keep coming to me, not Becky, with issues to resolve with Dallas."

"I'll bet Dallas isn't happy about that. Or Becky."

"No, not at all. I can't just ignore Becky and go around her to Dallas."

"Jumping chain-of-command is trouble for sure," Nike said. She spooned up some of her macaroni and cheese. "What else is going on?"

"Well—" Emma brightened "—some good news. In a way…"

"I can always use that. Tell me."

"It's good news for BJS but not for you. And it's good news for me, personally."

"Uh-oh," Nike murmured, "Dallas found another female pilot to replace me?" That meant that her secret hope to be pulled back into the BJS 60 squadron was squashed.

Emma nodded. "I'm sorry, Nike. I was holding out hope against hope that the pressures and demands on our services here would force Dallas to ask you to come back."

"Me, too," she said. "Oh, well."

"I'm sorry. We really miss you. You were our best pilot."

"Tell that to Dallas," she said, giving Emma a playful smile. Lifting her right hand, which had the last of the hot roll in it, Nike added, "Look, we knew we were breaking a cardinal rule when we picked up Berkie, but I'd do it all over again."

"I don't regret it, either. I'm just sorry that Dallas chose to focus on you instead of me."

"I'm the one who gave up the seat." She chuckled. "You stayed with the helicopter. Of course she's going to zero in on me."

"I don't think I'd take this as well as you are," Emma said glumly.

"Hey, you have a family military dynasty on your shoulders to carry," Nike chided with a grin. "Me? All I have is some disappointed parents and my big Greek extended family. But they understand and agree that I did the right thing. You? Well, if you'd gotten out of that seat, the media would have blitzed you over a transfer to a transport squadron." Shaking her head, Nike added, "No news about me being transferred as punishment because I'm not famous or in the media's eye like the Trayhern family is."

Emma sighed. "You're right. I've been catching all kinds of flak on the Internet blogs and even on CNN because of my demotion from XO."

"See?" Nike said, poking a finger in her direction. "I know the media is in love with the Trayherns. And what you did was heroic in my eyes. Maybe the media is chewing this up, but we saved a life, Emma. I'll answer for that decision with my God, not with anyone else. Especially not the media."

"Nike, you're one in a million. I'm proud to know you. I'm proud of what we did, punishment be damned. And I couldn't care less about the media sniping at me, but I know it impacts my whole family. That's what I don't like—them going after my mom, dad and sisters."

"Listen, they're Trayherns. They'll roll with it. A military family has the toughest of skins."

"Well, it hasn't done my career any good," Emma said.

"No, but I'm sure you'll distinguish yourself over here, and, in time, all will be forgiven. Me?" Nike grinned. "There's not much chance of me distinguishing myself as a transport pilot of men and ammo. So, as I see it, my days are numbered."

"Nike! You aren't going to leave the military, are you?"

"I don't know. I'm up for reenlistment after this tour. Depending upon how it goes, I may get out. I didn't sign up to be a trash-hauler. I'm an Apache pilot and a damned good one. If the U.S. military can't use my services, then why stay in? I can find better work back in Greece where my talent can be used in the civilian sector."

"Let me talk to Dallas. You can't do this! We can't lose you, Nike! You're too good at what you do."

Nike held up her hand. "It's okay, Emma. I got myself into this pickle. I'll decide how I get myself out of it. Life doesn't end if I can't fly an Apache. I could land a nice, cushy job as a commercial helo pilot."

"Damn," Emma whispered, hanging her head. "You shouldn't even be thinking in those terms."

"We did it to ourselves," Nike reminded her, using the last of her roll to run through the gravy on her plate. "So tell me, you said there was good news for your family?"

"Oh, that…" She grimaced.

"Eat your food, Emma. You're so emotional. You can't let this impact you this way. I'm fine. I'm doing a good job over at the transport squadron."

"But you're not happy."

"I didn't say I was. Life isn't always fun, but we do our best."

"You were happy at BJS 60."

"Yes, I was. What I miss most of all is the camaraderie of the women."

Emma watched Nike eating her food. She seemed at peace despite everything. "The other good news is that my cousin, Rachel Trayhern, has just graduated from Apache flight school in Fort Rucker, Alabama. She's being assigned to BJS 60."

"Wow, you'll have a cousin here with you?" Nike was impressed. "Which family is she out of?"

"My uncle Noah's family. Rachel is one of four children. She's the oldest. My mother, Alyssa, was saying that even though her brother, Noah, was a Coast Guard officer for thirty years, all four of his children are in the military and flying. The flight gene is definitely from the Trayhern side of the family."

"Wow, that's great! Are you close with your cousins? I know in my family, we're tighter than fleas on a dog."

Emma laughed. "Yes, the whole family tries to get together. One year we'll go to Florida where Uncle Noah and Aunt Kit live and the next, we'll go to San Francisco, where my parents live. And then, they'll all try to make it to Philipsburg, Montana, where my uncle Morgan and aunt Laura live. It's a huge dim sum plate and it takes a lot of work to get everyone in one spot at one time."

"Mmm," Nike said, finishing off her applesauce. "I would think so if all the offspring are in the military."

"Rachel is a rock 'n' roll Apache pilot," Emma said, her voice reflecting pride in her cousin. "She's very competitive and aggressive."

"Just like an Apache pilot should be." Nike chuckled. She put her empty plate aside on the aluminum tray and picked up her white mug of coffee. "So, when is Rachel arriving?"

"A week from now."

"I didn't think the military would allow two family members in the same squadron."

"They don't allow brothers or sisters to serve together," Emma said. "They say nothing about cousins." With glee, she rubbed her hands together and gave Nike a huge grin.

"I'll bet your family is thrilled about this development. They must see you as the watchdog who can take care of Rachel while she learns the ropes."

Brightening, Emma began to eat once more. "They are thrilled. I'm excited to have her. We're good friends."

"When Rachel gets here, we must meet."

"Oh, that's a promise," Emma said enthusiastically.

"We can help her get situated with combat and Afghanistan. She could use our experience."

"For sure," Emma agreed. And then, her smile disappeared. "Have you been in touch with Gavin? Do you know when he's coming in from Kabul?"

"No way to get in touch with him. I checked at ops and his team is on a transport that will arrive here at 1700."

"Just in time for dinner."

"Maybe we can have one together," Nike said.

"You deserve a little happiness," Emma told her.

"Thanks," Nike whispered, meaning it. They sat for a while in silence. The coolness in the huge tent area was wonderful compared to the heat and local storms. This place, in some ways, reminded her of home in Greece. The country blistered with dry summer heat and then chilled with icy temperatures in winter, but there was little snow unless one lived in the mountainous areas. Still, Nike looked forward to the moment when she could meet Gavin and his team. Her heart beat a little harder to underscore just how much she'd missed him in the last two weeks.

In the quiet moments at her desk, Nike would allow her heart to feel the love that had taken root within her. She knew he'd hurt her career but she'd forgiven him for that long ago. In the heat of battle, one didn't always think about such things. And in Nike's world view, a human life was a hell of a lot more important than a regulation. Since Bagram, she hadn't been able to stop thinking about Gavin. It seemed as if every few minutes, she'd replay some conversation they had. Or she'd recall that terrorized look in his eyes that told her the raw truth: he loved her. At first, Nike had felt it was a game with Gavin. Now, she knew it was not.

Gavin could hardly keep his face impassive. He watched Nike in her dark green flight suit, waiting as he and his men disembarked from the CH-47 helicopter. It was dusk; the skies were gray and churning. Soon, it would storm. She looked beautiful, her curly black hair about her face, a smile on her lips and those gold eyes shining with what he thought might be love—for him.

As he hefted off his duffel bag, he ordered his team to their already assigned tents. He told them he'd see them later. Turning, he walked with the huge bag across his left shoulder. Once more, he was in Afghan clothing.

"Hey," Gavin greeted her as he walked up to her. "Do you know how much I've missed you and our talks?" He kept his voice low so that others could not hear. It about killed him not to show affection. Her mouth was soft and parted, ripe for kissing.

"I'd like to hug you but I can't," she said with a grin, pointing to her arm.

"How's your left shoulder?" Gavin asked.

She held her hand out and could only move it waist-high. "I can't sleep on that side and I can't lift it beyond here. If I try to lean out and stretch it, I'm in pain. The doctor says the first three weeks are the worst."

Shaking his head, Gavin said, "That's no good. How's the desk job?"

"Boring as hell. How was Bagram?"

"Lonely without you." Gavin drilled a look into her widening eyes. "Is there anywhere we can go to be alone for a while?"

She grinned. "Yeah, my tent. Don't worry, the gals on either side of it won't say a peep about me having a male visitor." That was against regulations, too, but the female pilots protected one another. They would never go to the XO or CO about it. Sometimes, rules were meant to be broken.

"Good," Gavin said. "Lead the way." He hoisted his duffel up on his left shoulder once more.

In no time, they were at her tent. Nightfall was complete and they had flashlights to light their way through the tent city. Wind began to twirl around them as Nike opened up the tent flap to allow Gavin inside. She followed, turned and tied the flaps together. A small fan in the corner sitting on the ply-board floor gave some coolness against the high temperatures.

Gavin set his duffel near the entrance, turned and walked over to Nike. Although she did not wear her left arm in a sling any longer, he was aware of how painful it was to her. Gently, he laid his hand on her right shoulder. "Come here. I've been dreaming of kissing you for two weeks...."

How wonderful it felt to come into his arms. Nike situated herself against him, her breasts beneath her flight suit pressing against his cotton Afghan clothes. His beard was growing once more and she felt the prickly hair against her cheek as their lips met. With a moan, Nike opened her lips and hungrily clung to his mouth. Their breathing changed, became ragged. He held her gently against him, his left arm around her right shoulder. His tongue moved slowly along her lower lip and a shudder of need rippled through Nike.

She wrapped her right arm around Gavin's broad shoulders. He smelled of the heat, and his arm felt strong and capable around her body. Her breasts ached to be touched and teased by him. Nike knew they couldn't dare make love here, even if her injured shoulder would allow it. Frustrated, she broke their hungry, wet kiss.

They stared at one another in the semidarkness. The only light came from a table lamp and it cast a weak beam around the interior of the warm tent. Gavin's eyes burned with need of her. After two years, Nike felt starved for a man's touch. Not just any man. Gavin.

"This is hell on earth," she muttered, reaching out and stroking his returning beard.

Her fingers trailed across his cheek and Gavin groaned inwardly. What would it be like to have Nike touching his body? Nightly dreams had kept him tossing, turning and waking up over that very thing. He caught her hand and pressed it between his.

"Definitely," he agreed thickly. Gavin understood implicitly that Nike was in enough trouble. If he were found in here with her it would be another nail in the coffin of her career.

Nike moved away and went to sit on a canvas chair opposite the bed. "Sit down," she invited, gesturing to the cot.

Gavin did so—because if he didn't, he was going to kiss her again and again. His lower body ached with want of her. Nothing could be done about that right now. Sitting down, he opened his legs, rested his elbows on his thighs and clasped his hands. "I don't know what's worse—not seeing you at all or this."

Smiling, Nike sat back in the chair and cradled her left arm against her body. "I know. It's like going into a candy store and seeing all the goodies behind the glass. You can't reach them. They aren't yours."

Chuckling, Gavin said, "Exactly." He absorbed her quiet beauty. "How are you really?"

"I'm missing you. Our talks," Nike admitted quietly. They both spoke in low tones so no one could hear them outside the tent. It was the first time she'd ever admitted that to Gavin. She saw his eyes flare with surprise and then fill with warmth…and love. "My shoulder is progressing slowly. A lot more slowly than I want. The doctor keeps telling me at the four-week mark I'll have full range of motion back. If that happens, I'm going to be all over my CO to put me back on the ops missions and start flying again."

Gavin saw the frustration gleaming in her eyes. "There's no chance Dallas will take you back into BJS 60?"

Nike shook her head and shared Emma's information from lunch with him. "Hey, it's okay," she told him. "Berkie's alive. I'm okay with that, Gavin."

"I'm not," he growled, unhappy. "You should have been put up for a medal for your bravery, not removed from your squadron."

"I don't want to waste time talking about it, Gavin. I want our time to be about us." Her bold statement scared her but Nike tried to ignore the fear. This was real love. Not a game. And time wasn't on their side right now.

"You're right," he said.

"Where are they sending you?"

"They're dropping us off at the village of Kechelay. It's about two miles from the Pakistan border. We've got an outpost up in the mountains above that narrow valley where the village sits."

Nike tried to restrain her concern. "That's a hot spot right now, Gavin. We have pilots flying into that area and they're getting shot at. In fact, we had one CH-47 that had to remain on the ground at the village. They were off-loading food supplies for the village when the Taliban mortared it."

"What happened to the crew?"

"They were saved. No injuries. The Apache helo with

them blew the Taliban mortar position up, but it was too late. We're out of pocket for a CH-47."

"I know Kechelay is a real dangerous area," he agreed, his voice grim. "We'll be taken to the outpost to relieve another A team that's spent its thirty days up there."

Fear gutted Nike. There was nothing safe about Gavin's job—ever. She remembered Alpha Hill, the memories fresh of Berkie, who had almost died there. His whole team would be put on the line once more. "What are you going to do up there? Be sitting ducks again like you were at Alpha Hill?"

Grinning, Gavin said, "Yes and no. We've got orders to rummage around at night and try to interdict the Taliban flowing through the valley. Kechelay is Afghan and the villagers are deathly afraid of Taliban retaliation on them and their people. Our job is to stop them from getting into that village. They've accepted U.S. food, clothing and medicine. We've got night scopes and goggles, so we'll be the hunter-killer team more than a bull's-eye for the Taliban." He saw the worry shadowing her eyes. The dim light caressed her beautiful face, emphasizing her cheeks and lips—lips that he wanted to capture and hear her moan with need of him. With a sigh, Gavin understood that wouldn't happen until he and his team returned to this base four weeks from now.

"It sounds pretty dangerous."

"It is," he said, not trying to sugarcoat it. "Flying a transport through these mountains and valleys is a crap shoot, too," he told her. "I'll worry about you."

"There's nothing to worry about," she said. "I'll probably be flying a desk until you return. The only thing I have to be concerned about is the Taliban attacking our base, and the odds of that are low."

"True," Gavin said. He smiled a little. "At least I won't have to stress about you."

Nike realized that would be a good thing. She wanted his focus on his duty because it would keep him alive— to come back to her. "I'll be safe here." Her voice lowered. "But I'll be worrying about you, Gavin." Again, the words *I love you* almost ripped out of her mouth. Nike felt she needed more time. And yet, the torture of not telling him that she was changing, that she was making a turn toward him and away from her past, ate her up inside.

Gavin rose to prepare for tomorrow morning's assignment. "Hey," he called, gently touching her cheek, "I have every reason to survive out there." Leaning down, he sought and found her lips. They were soft and yet firm. When her tongue met his, he groaned. This was a special hell. They could kiss but not make love.

Easing away from her mouth, Gavin whispered, "I love you, Nike. I think I did from the moment I laid eyes on you. I know we have a long way to go, and it takes our courage to get there." Straightening, he threaded his fingers through her soft, curly hair. She felt like warm silk. When she lifted her chin to meet and hold his gaze, Gavin said in an unsteady voice, "I'll come back in a month. We love one another. We've got something to build on. It's just going to take time."

As he opened the tent flap and then put his duffel on his shoulder, Nike stood up, her throat clogged with tears. And then Gavin disappeared into the night. Nike suddenly realized that she hadn't told him she loved him. *Why not?*

Closing the flaps and tying them, Nike had no answer except that she was still afraid. The fear of losing Gavin was ten times worse than before, simply because Nike realized she had fallen in love with this courageous soldier. She felt a helplessness similar to that she had felt in Peru. There was no way she could protect Gavin. The border area was rife with violent fights daily. For the second time, she had to wait and hope that the man she loved would return alive. It seemed unconscionable that she'd twice lose a man to war. But as they'd both said, war wasn't fair.

Chapter 15

Nike's pulse raced after she landed the CH-47 at Kechelay. Her copilot, Jeff Perkins, was a green lieutenant and this was his first flight after arriving in Afghanistan. She hooked her thumb across her shoulder.

"Jeff, help our load master with off-loading the cargo. Get it out of here ASAP. I don't want to stay on the ground any longer than we have to."

Jeff bobbed his blond head. "Yes, ma'am, pronto." He released his harness and squeezed between the seats.

Nike sat tensely in her seat, her helmet still on. She unharnessed, feeling uneasy. This was her first flight after being taken off medical waiver. After convincing her CO that her shoulder was healed enough at four weeks, Nike was back on line.

The village of Kechelay had a population of about one hundred. Several starving mangy dogs ran through the recently fallen mid-September snow. It was about three inches deep and the sky above threatened another round of snow showers. The cold air leaked into the helo as the ramp was lowered. Dividing her attention between the three villagers gathering about two hundred feet from the helicopter and her hardworking crew, Nike remained alert.

Somewhere across the valley were Gavin and his hunter-killer team. It was ironic that two days before he was due to be rotated back to the base, she was sent out to the very village where he and his men had been based. Missing him terribly, Nike wished for the hundredth time she'd told Gavin she loved him. Worse, every waking thought was of him. Their kisses in her tent... She wasn't sure what ached more: her heart or her body that wanted to love him and hold him—forever. Miserable, she looked out across the first snow upon the landscape, the tall mountains on the other side coated in white once more. Somewhere over there, Gavin and his men were probably hunkered down and sleeping in the daytime. His work was a nighttime affair and she didn't envy him. It was cold at eight thousand feet and she wondered how successful Gavin's team had been. Judging from the dark looks of those villagers, the fight with the Taliban was fierce in this area. Where were the rest of the villagers? Usually, when a supply copter came in, every able-bodied man was there to help offload the boxes. Why only these three who had hatred in their faces here? Worse, the demand for Apaches at other firefights had left her without any protection on this mission.

Oh, how Nike wanted to see Gavin! Her arm was still sore and she realized she might have been released back to duty too early. Her pleading to the base doctor had convinced him to authorize her to go back and fly. Nike had passed all the tests he'd given, but she'd paid dearly for it later with aching pain. At least now, she could use her arm, and more than anything she wanted to throw it around Gavin's shoulders and kiss him breathless.

"Look out!"

The scream of warning came from Lieutenant Perkins. As Nike jerked around, she heard shots fired at close range. To her horror, the load master, Goldman, slammed to the ground, his head blown open. Jerking the .45 out of the holster, Nike leaped out of the seat and saw Lieutenant Perkins pulling out his .45 and backing up the helo's ramp.

Too late! Several Afghans, Taliban she realized too late, rushed the ramp, firing wildly. Bullets screamed into the CH-47, ricocheting around or exploding out of the thin metal skin.

Nike was lifting her .45 to aim at the leader, a man in a red turban with a black beard and equally black, angry-looking eyes, when she was struck. A bullet ricocheted off the inside of the helicopter and struck the side of her helmet, knocking her unconscious.

Pain throbbed through Nike's head. She groaned as she slowly regained consciousness. The first thing she realized was that her hands were tied together in front of her. Secondly, that it was cold and dark. Sitting up, she blinked through the pain. The left side of her face felt frozen. Reaching up with cold, trembling fingers, she felt dried blood all along her left cheekbone and jaw.

She looked around, gauging she'd been put into a small barn. The bleating of several sheep and goats confirmed this. And then, the memory of the attack on her men and her helicopter rushed back to Nike. She sat up, back against the wall of the rickety barn, remembering everything. Were both Jeff and Terry, the load master, dead? Nike knew the Taliban had initiated the attack. Those three men were not villagers, that was why she hadn't seen the able-bodied men from Kechelay there to help off-load the boxes. Why hadn't she picked up on that clue?

The door opened. Slats of light shot in and momentarily blinded her. Hearing the sheep bleat in terror, Nike squinted her eyes. Two of the Taliban appeared, armed and glaring down at her. "Get up!" one of them growled in stilted English.

Nike tried to get to her feet, but dizziness swept over her and she fell back onto the cold, hard ground. Hearing expletives in Pashto, Nike felt one of the men grab her by the right arm and yank her upward. She bit back a cry and wobbled unsteadily to her feet. But before she could regain her balance, her legs crumbled. There was nothing she could do about it. In the next second, blackness fell like a veil before her and she remembered nothing more.

Gavin was awakened by the GPS radio buzzing at his side, tearing him from badly needed sleep. He fumbled for the device in his pocket. He and his team were hiding in a cave near the valley floor. As he opened his eyes, he noticed it was snowing outside—again. More cold and poor visibility. To add to their troubles, the late-afternoon light was weak.

Gavin punched in a code and lifted the phone to his ear.

"Bluebird One. Over."

"Bluebird, this is Sand Hill Crane."

"Roger, Sand Hill Crane." Gavin rubbed his eyes. Why the hell was ops ringing him when they had at least two more hours of sleep before moving again? "What's going on?" he demanded, his voice thick with sleep.

"Bluebird, we have a situation at Kechelay. The CH-47 transport is overdue. We had a satellite over the area and the bird has been destroyed. We have a three-person crew missing. Over."

The fatigue vanished instantly. "We didn't hear anything, but we're across the valley and sleeping. Over."

"Roger that. You have orders to get over to Kechelay and try to locate our missing crew members. There are two men and one woman. Over."

"Names?" Gavin's heart raced. But then, he told himself it couldn't be Nike because she was still on medical leave.

"Captain Nike Alexander, Lieutenant Jeff Perkins and Sergeant Terry Goldman. Over."

Disbelief exploded through Gavin. "Are you sure?" His voice was urgent. Desperate. How in the hell had Nike managed to get off medical leave? The adrenaline rushed through his veins.

"Positive, Bluebird. We need you in there ASAP. Once you are in position, contact us. We have two Apaches and a CH-47 standing by if you need them. Over."

Son of a bitch! Gavin almost said it out loud. His other men were stirring now at the sound of his voice. Most of them were sitting up, yawning and throwing off the blankets. "Roger that, Sand Hill Crane. Out."

Gavin sat for a moment, GPS in hand, his mind tum-

bling with possibilities. The Taliban hated women in
the military. Nike was in more trouble than the men.
She would be tortured. Set up as an example in the village to stop women from even thinking about their in-
dependence. He pushed the GPS back into the pocket of
his long brown wool coat and turned to his men. They
had to move now. Every minute could mean the lives
of Nike and her crew.

"Tell us everything!"

Nike tried to prepare herself for the coming blow.
She sat in a chair, her arms bound behind her, her legs
trussed. The side of her head exploded with bright light.
Then the pain. Blood flowed out of her nose and into
the corners of her mouth. It felt as if the man's hand had
ripped off her head.

"Enough, Rasheed!"

Ears ringing, Nike spat out the blood flowing into her
mouth and looked up. The left side of her face ached like
fire. Rasheed, the one with the black beard, had been
using his thick, opened hand to slap her into revealing military information. Two other Taliban remained
nearby. Already, she could feel her left eye closing due
to swelling. Thinking that her jaw had been broken,
Nike breathed raggedly through her split lower lip. Fear
ate through her pain. They'd dragged her out of the barn
half-conscious. Her knees had taken the worst of it as
one man on each side had grabbed her uniform by a
shoulder and hauled her between them. Nike remembered, vaguely, many children and women behind burkas staring at them. Fear was etched on the children's
faces—fear for her. Nike knew that when the Taliban
entered a village receiving U.S. aid, they killed inno-

cent people. Right now, Nike was sure villagers hid behind closed and locked doors. She didn't blame them. They had suffered brutality at the hands of the Taliban too many times.

For a moment, there was a hot argument between Black Beard and Brown Beard. Nike wished she knew more Pashto. Blinking, her eyesight blurred, she wondered if she'd sustained a concussion. Had the bullet to her helmet done more damage? Nike couldn't stand as the dizziness was severe.

It was warm in the room. At least she had that. Nike looked out the window and saw that darkness had fallen. White snowflakes, thick and big, twirled against the window. Fear engulfed her. She knew these men would kill her. Tears jammed into her eyes and she shut them, gulping heavily. She would never get to tell Gavin that she loved him. *Oh, God, please, let me live to tell him that. Just that...* In that moment, Nike felt the fear of the past dissolve. And with it, a bright burst of light through her heart—for Gavin. He'd loved her unerringly. He'd never wavered. He'd always been there for her, even though she'd been running away from him. The hot tears burned her cheeks and ran into her lips. The stinging pain intensified as they connected with her split lower lip. Unable to stop the tears, Nike surrendered to them—and to her love for Gavin. She would never see him again. That alone savaged her more than any beating at the hands of the Taliban. She would never be able to tell him she loved him. *Oh, God, forgive me....*

Just as Rasheed reached forward to grab her by her hair once more, the door burst open.

Several men in white gear emerged, their rifles raised and firing. Rasheed had no time to reach for his weapon. He screamed and fell backward against the wall, blood gushing out of his throat. The other two men screamed as they were killed.

Gasping, Nike saw one of the invaders slam the door shut. The weapons all had silencers. The other three men surrounded her. The leader, heavily hidden in his white gear, pulled the hood away from his bearded face.

"Gavin!" she cried.

"Don't move," he ordered her hoarsely, handing his weapon to another team member. Unsheathing his knife, he quickly cut the ropes that bound her.

With a groan, Nike leaned forward. If not for Gavin catching her, she'd have nose-dived into the hard-packed dirt floor.

"Cap'n!" the man at the door whispered. "We gotta get outta here! I saw a light go on four doors down. There could be more Taliban staying here that we don't know about."

Gavin gripped her shoulders. "Nike, where're Goldman and Perkins?"

"Dead, I think," she rasped. Lifting her hand, she tried to wipe the blood flowing across her lips. "They died at the helo. We got attacked by Taliban while they were off-loading cargo."

Gavin grimly looked across his shoulder. "Chances are they burned the bodies when they blew up the helo."

There was terse agreement among the men. Nike tried not to cry.

"Okay, we're getting you out of here. Can you stand?"

"N-no." Nike touched her scalp where her helmet had been. She felt a deep wound in her scalp with blood still oozing. "I took a bullet to my helmet. I got knocked unconscious. I can't stand or I'll fall over."

"Okay, hang on," he urged her. In one smooth motion, he lifted Nike up and across his shoulders. He had her in a fireman's carry with the help of one of his men.

"Comfy?" he grunted to her. Nike hung like a big fur collar around his shoulders, her face near his. One of his team helped him put on his night goggles.

"I'm fine. Let's just get out of here."

Gavin nodded. They doused the lights and quickly stepped through the opened door.

Outside, Nike felt the soothing cold against her heated, throbbing face. Gavin moved quickly, as if she wasn't even around his shoulders. The team was silent. They swiftly moved outside the village, the light snow creating soundproofing as they went. In the dark, with night goggles on, they made their way toward the blackened remains of the helicopter.

Nike hung around Gavin's shoulders as his men quickly searched the smoldering wreckage of the CH-47. In no time, they found the half-burned bodies of the two men. Nike wanted to scream with grief. Her eyes burned as more tears began to fall. She heard Gavin curse softly.

"What now?" she asked thickly.

"We're meeting a CH-47 five clicks from here," he told her gruffly. "We'll put them in body bags and take them with us. How are you doing?"

"I'll live."

"Hang on...."

Gavin stood protectively by Nike as the doctor at the base examined her swollen face and blackened eyes. His team was brought in and a standby A team took over their mission. It took everything he had not to show his rage over her torture by the Taliban soldiers.

"Well," Dr. Greenwood said in a teasing tone to Nike, "this is going to get you two weeks' R & R at Bagram, Captain Alexander." He took gauze and continued to wipe away the dried blood from her jaw. "The X-rays came back. You got slapped around but good, though nothing is broken. That's the good news."

Nike grunted. She closed her eyes because each swipe of the gauze hurt like hell.

Gavin didn't care what the doctor thought so he reached out and held her hand. She sat on a gurney with her legs dangling over the side. Dr. Greenwood looked up but said nothing about their intimacy.

"What I'd recommend is pain pills for the next four days," the doctor said. "By then, the worst of the bruising and swelling will be over."

"Fine," Nike muttered impatiently. "All I want is a long, hot shower."

Chuckling, Dr. Greenwood nodded. "Just a few more minutes, Captain Alexander."

Gavin felt Nike squeeze his fingers in return. How badly he simply wanted to haul her into his arms, hold her and protect her. It wouldn't be long now.

"Your next stop before your shower is ops," the doctor told her, finishing up. "You have to give a preliminary report on your capture to your CO. You're not that injured that you can't do it."

"I understand," Nike said, touching her aching jaw. It wasn't broken, but several of her back teeth were loose. The doctor assured her they'd tighten up in a few days on their own.

"I'll escort you over there," Gavin told her as the doctor wrote a prescription.

"My office will issue you orders to Bagram for two weeks, Captain. Just drop by tomorrow anytime after 0900 to pick them up," the doctor said.

Gavin helped her off the gurney. She was still unsteady and clung to his arm.

"A wheelchair is in order," the doctor said, frowning. "The X-ray didn't show a problem, but you've got all the earmarks of a concussion, Captain. The dizziness should abate a lot by tomorrow morning. Get someone in your unit to check on you every couple of hours. If the dizziness doesn't lessen, come back and see me."

A medic brought over a wheelchair, and Nike gratefully sat down in it. Gavin leaned over and flipped over the foot panels so she could rest her boots. "If I'm still unable to walk straight tomorrow morning, you'll see me, Doc."

"Good night, Captain. Try to get some sleep," Dr. Greenwood said.

Gavin wheeled her out of the ward and into the lobby. He stopped and walked around and knelt down beside her. "Are you sure you feel like giving ops a report?" Searching her puffy, bruised face, he wanted to rage over what had been done to her.

"Positive. I want this behind me, Gavin. Tomorrow morning when I wake up, all I want to know I have to do is board a CH-47 and fly to Bagram."

Gavin gently touched some of her curly black hair near her temple. "I'll take you over to ops and hang out until you're done. Then—" and his voice lowered "—you're coming back to my tent and sleeping with me. I'm not leaving you alone tonight. Do you hear me?"

Nike gave him a blank look. "But I can't even kiss you…"

The wobble in her voice tore at him and tears gathered in her swollen eyes. "Babe, you don't have to do anything except let me hold you all night."

That sounded incredibly good to Nike. She sniffed, tried to wipe the tears off her swollen cheeks. She touched her lips and whispered in an off-key voice, "I want to kiss you…."

"I'm a patient man. Right now, you need a safe place to unwind and let down. You went through a helluva lot."

Nodding, she managed, "I could have died."

Holding her fear-laden gaze, Gavin nodded. "But you didn't. You're here and you're alive."

"I'm a mess."

"Anyone would be after the beating you took," Gavin told her quietly. He slid his hand into hers. "Nike, you're in shock. Heavy shock. I know the symptoms when I see them. I'll be there for you. I promise."

Chapter 16

"This all seems like a nightmare," Nike told Gavin as they stood on the tarmac of Bagram Air Base. The September sky above was a combination of low-hanging gray, scudding clouds and bright blue sky peppered with slats of sunshine. However, it was sixty-three degrees Fahrenheit, and she was wrapped in her summer gear as they went toward ops.

Gavin walked close but kept his hands to himself. "It's over, Nike," he told her. "And you got some good out of it. Major Klein personally told you she was adding you back to the Apache roster. Your days of banishment are over." He saw her swollen face and lips lighten momentarily.

"Yeah, but I have to see a shrink here on base every friggin' day for fourteen days." Dallas had told her she had PTSD, post-traumatic stress disorder, due to her torture at the hands of the Taliban. She didn't deny it, but didn't want two weeks of rest at Bagram with Gavin at her side ruined like that.

"Small price to pay," he assured her. There was a lot of activity on the tarmac because it was early morning, and most flights went out then. Opening the door, they stepped inside the concrete building.

The air-conditioning was welcoming. The place was crowded with pilots, copilots and load masters at the L-shaped ops desk. Everyone was getting their flight plans and orders and making sure the materials that would be flown were really here and ready to be loaded. All Nike had to do was weave through the area to the personnel department where she and Gavin would hand over copies of their R & R orders.

Later, at Nike's BOQ barracks, Gavin stood with her in the lobby. Men were not allowed anywhere but this area in the two-story building. They sat down on a couch in the corner away from the main flow of traffic. "Do you have a plan?" she asked him.

Grinning, Gavin said, "Yeah, I do. I have a good Afghan friend who, oddly enough, is a Christian and Muslim. They're a rarity here, but they do exist. Captain Khalid Shaheen lives in Kabul. He was trained in America on Apaches and is the only Afghan to be flying one for us."

"I didn't know that," Nike said, impressed. "I thought I knew all the Apache pilots. I know there's a squadron based at Bagram."

"He's a part of that unit," Gavin told her. "I made friends with him during my first tour. We were in the south of the country at that time. More than once, Khalid saved our bacon out there against the Taliban. I went to thank him when my tour of duty was done. We became instant friends. He's one helluva guy."

"So, how does this have anything to do with us?"

"Khalid was American-educated. His father is a very prominent and successful importer of Persian rugs. His mother is Irish. He and his family live in Kandahar." Gavin hooked his thumb over his shoulder. "His family has a summer home here in Kabul, as well, but the family stays in the south. Khalid uses the home here in Kabul as his own when they aren't here."

"Mmm," Nike said, "I'm beginning to get the picture. By any chance is your friend going to let us stay with him?"

With a grin, Gavin nodded. "Yes. Now, Khalid is not a promiscuous type. I've told him that we're serious about one another and he's offered two bedrooms to us."

"That's nice of him." Nike smiled wickedly.

"Very nice," Gavin said. "He's flying in the south right now, but he's left the key to his home with his housekeeper, who will cook and clean for us. She'll leave after the evening meal."

"That sounds like a slice of heaven," Nike murmured. "This is more than I ever expected," she said warmly.

"Khalid is a good guy. He stands with one foot in American culture and another in his country, living an interesting religious life in a Muslim world."

"He's got to be special."

"One of a kind," Gavin said. "Why don't you do what you have to do here and then we'll take a taxi into Kabul to his home."

Where had the first week gone? Nike finished taking a deliciously warm bath. Once more, she thanked the mysterious Khalid for his very modern home. Bathtubs were a rarity in Afghanistan. Those who could afford such plumbing had showers only. Most of the populace washed using a bucket or a bowl. Her stomach growled. It was 0800, the September sun barely peeking over the plain of Kabul, the sky a bright blue.

Patting herself dry with the thick yellow terry-cloth towel, Nike went to the mirror. It was partly steamed up, but she could see her face. Seven days had made an incredible change. The swelling was gone. The black under her eyes looked more like shadows and her split lip had finally healed. All her teeth were solid now and her jaw no longer hurt. Touching her cheek, she could still feel some tenderness, but she looked like her old self, more or less. Her hair was curled from the humidity and she ruffled through her black curls with her fingers to push it back into shape.

Sitting down on a stool, she pulled on white cotton socks, shimmied into a pair of jeans and donned a bright kelly-green tee. Khalid's home was cool and comfortable. Silently, she thanked the Apache pilot and wished that she could meet him in person to offer her appreciation for this gift he'd given her and Gavin.

Nike brushed her teeth and put on some makeup to hide the shadows beneath her eyes. After hanging up the yellow towel on a hook behind the door, Nike padded out into her spacious bedroom. If she didn't know she was in Afghanistan, the bedroom would have fooled her. Khalid, it turned out, had fallen in love with American quilts. They adorned every bed in the spacious three-thousand-square-foot home. And some smaller art fabric collages hung on the walls. Of course, his father's Persian rugs were everywhere across the bright red tile floors, too. Gavin had told her that Khalid would haunt the little towns in the U.S. to try and find another beautiful handmade quilt.

Opposite her queen-size bed hung a large quilt sporting rainbow colors and a wedding-ring design. Her room was painted pale orange and the quilt complemented the tone. She'd found out from Gavin that Khalid was not married. He would make some woman very, very happy someday. Not only did he come from a rich family, but he was Harvard-educated and had gone into the military. He worked now to get other Afghan pilots into the Apache program back at Fort Rucker. Khalid fiercely believed his countrymen should be educated so that they could handle any threats. He did not believe the U.S. and other countries should have to continue to shed their blood on the soil of his country. Afghans were independent and tried to pull themselves up by their own bootstraps. That was one of the many reasons Nike respected them.

Running a bristle brush through her hair, she gave herself one more look in the mirror. Today was the day. She and Gavin would make love. They slept together at night and he did exactly what he'd promised: he held her safe in his arms throughout the night. Never once had he made any overtures. He understood as few could that, being beat up as she had, she was in no shape for such things. She was grateful for his sensitivity, which only made her love him more. It had solidified her decision to love him fully, without her past as an anchor.

She found Gavin out in the large, airy kitchen. He was at the counter and had brought down two plates. She sat down on a leather stool at the counter. "Where's Rasa?" The thirty-year-old housekeeper had been with the Shaheen family since her birth. Rasa had never married and had been a faithful servant to Khalid at this house.

Gavin turned. "I gave her the day off." He saw Nike's eyes widen and then her luscious mouth curved faintly.

"I see. Great minds think alike."

"Do they?" He left the plates and sauntered over to the breakfast counter. Leaning on the colorful hand-painted tiles, he held her sparkling golden gaze with his own.

Nike reached out and slid her fingers across his lower arm. Gavin looked incredibly masculine in his bright red T-shirt and jeans. "Oh, yes." His brows rose and a mischievous smile shadowed that wonderful mouth of his. "I don't know about you, but I'd like to schedule a brunch instead of a breakfast. Are you game?"

He picked up her hand and pressed a soft kiss into her palm. "More than game." And then he became serious. "Are you sure? Are you ready?"

"Definitely." She touched her healed lower lip. "Now, I can kiss you." Nike grinned playfully and squeezed his hand. "Let's go."

"Is this a dream?" he asked her.

"If it is, I want to take full part in it," Nike told him. As he approached her, she opened her arms to him. To her surprise, Gavin slid his arms beneath her thighs and back, lifting her off the chair and into his arms.

"Where are you taking me?" She laughed with delight.

"To *my* room," he said, grinning. Nike had placed her arm around his shoulders. Drowning in the desire burning in her eyes, Gavin took her down the hall, pushed open the door and brought her into his room.

Nike's eyes widened. Large, beautiful candles burned on the dark mahogany dresser and the nightstands on either side of the huge king-size bed. "Why, you—"

"I figured it was time," he told her gruffly as he deposited her gently on the bed.

Nike gazed up at him as he stood there, hands on his narrow hips and looking impossibly sexy. "We must have wonderful telepathy. How did you know?"

Touching his chest where his heart lay, he said teasingly, "I felt it here. Just like you did."

"Well, get over here...." Nike whispered, a catch in her voice. She pulled him down beside her on the gorgeous quilt that covered the bed. Its fall colors reminded her of autumn in New England. The bright yellow sunflowers around the border made her feel even more joyous.

Stretching out beside her, Gavin slid his arm beneath her neck as she rolled over onto her back. Heart pounding, he moved to her side. "Do you know how long I've wanted to kiss you?" he said. He leaned down, barely touching her smiling lips. Just feeling the lushness and curve of her beneath him was enough and he closed his eyes. He brushed his mouth lightly against hers.

Nike sighed as his tongue gently moved across her lower lip. She felt as if she were being caressed by a butterfly. Gavin understood this first time was going to be tender and gentle. As the kiss deepened slightly, Nike surrendered completely. She never wanted to go back. It was too good, this feeling of intimacy and deep passion. His warm breath became as ragged as hers. Wrapping her arms around his shoulders, she moaned as his lean, hard body connected fully with hers. The moment was magical as Nike drowned in his mouth and then felt his hand sliding softly against her cheek.

In the back of her whirling mind, Nike realized that as hard as Gavin could be, he had the incredible sensitivity and gentleness to woo her with light touches here and there, a stroke across her cheek, a teasing sip of his mouth against hers. With him, she felt safe. He was healing to her brutalized spirit.

Gavin slid his hand beneath her tee, his fingers lingering slowly along her rib cage. He caressed her flesh and moved under her shirt to the fullness of her breast. He inhaled her gasp of pleasure as he found the hard nipple. Easing the tee up and off her, Gavin allowed it to drop to the floor. For a moment, he had to look into her face, into those eyes. He got lost in their golden depths and how they shone with a hungry need of him. His desire now turning feverish, he leaned down and placed his lips upon the nub. As he suckled her, she moaned and her hips ground into his.

Nike's world exploded into a powerful heat that leaped to life between her legs. Each suckling movement drove her deeper and deeper into starving need of Gavin. Gasping, she pulled off his T-shirt and watched the powerful muscles in his chest and arms. His chest was covered with dark hair, which only added to his sexiness. Giving him a wicked smile, she whispered, "It's my turn." She forced him onto his back and quickly unsnapped his jeans. In a few moments, she'd pulled them and his boxers off him, along with his shoes. As he lay naked, she appreciated Gavin as never before, and she ran her hand admiringly across his hard thigh. She whispered, "You are beautiful, like a Greek god."

Laughing, Gavin sat up and quickly removed her

jeans, shoes and socks. "And you're a goddess," he rasped, pinning her on her back, his hands splaying out across her arms. "And you're mine," he growled, pressing his hips into hers. Nike's eyes shuttered closed as he allowed her to see just how much he wanted her.

"I can't wait," she whispered unsteadily. And she gripped his arms and forced him onto his back. Without waiting, she mounted him.

"I like this," Gavin said, bringing his hands around her hips. He lifted her and gently brought her down upon his hardened length. Her fingers dug convulsively into his shoulders as he arched and slid within her hot, wet body. Groaning, he held himself in check since he didn't want to hurt her. She'd been hurt enough lately, and he wasn't about to be a part of that.

"Easy," he said, holding her hips above his. "Take your time...."

Her world disintegrating, all Nike could feel was a huge pressure entering her. It didn't hurt, but at the same time, she was hungry to inhale Gavin into her. The years without sex made her feel as if she couldn't accommodate Gavin. When he leaned upward, his lips capturing a nipple, she automatically surged forward, engulfing and absorbing him fully into herself. The electrical jolts, the pleasure from her nipples down to the juncture between her thighs, had eased the transit. Now, his hands were firmly and slowly moving her back and forth. A moan rose in her throat and all Nike could do was breathe, a complete slave to this man who played her body like a fine instrument.

The world shuttered closed on Nike as Gavin's hands, his lips and the hard movement of his hips grinding into hers conspired against her. She wanted to please him as much as he was pleasing her, but that wasn't happening. All she could do was feel the heat, the liquid, the building explosion occurring within herself. Her body contracted violently. She cried out, rigid, her fingers digging deeply into his chest. And then, her world became a volcano erupting and all she could do was cry out in relief, the pleasure so intense that it just kept rippling again and again like a tsunami rolling wildly and unchecked within her. All that time as she spun out into the brilliant white light, the sensation of no body surrounding her anymore, Gavin kept up the rhythm to give her maximum pleasure.

How long it lasted, Nike had no idea. She felt herself crumpling against him, felt his arms like bands around her, holding her tightly, forever. The smell of sweat, the sensation of it trickling down her temple, her body still convulsing with joy over the incredible release and him groaning beneath her, was all she could fathom. She had no thinking mind left. The only sensations were relief, pleasure, love and wanting Gavin over and over again. Peripherally, Nike knew he had climaxed and she pressed her face against the juncture of his jaw and shoulder, utterly spent. A loose smile of contentment pulled at her lips. Her hand moved weakly across his dark-haired chest and followed the curve of his neck until she cupped his recently shaven face. She lay against him, breathing hard with him. Just the way he trailed his fingers down her back to her hips told her how much he truly loved her.

"Wow…" Nike whispered. It took all her strength to lift her head enough to look into his face. She thrilled to the thundercloud look in his blue eyes. They burned with passion—for her. "Wow…"

He chuckled, his hand coming across her hips and caressing her. "Wow is right." Just absorbing Nike's gleaming gold eyes told Gavin everything he wanted to know. They lay together, connected, and he never wanted to let her go. Flattening his hand against the small of her back, he slowly raised his hips. He saw the pleasure come to her eyes and to her parting lips. "Give me a few minutes and I'll be ready to wow you all over again."

Grinning, Nike leaned down and moved her lips softly against his smiling mouth. She could feel Gavin monitoring the amount of strength he applied to her. She was fragile in many ways and he sensed that and loved her at that level. Her lower body burned with memory and she loved how he remained inside her. Nothing had ever seemed so right to her. "I'm already ready." Nike laughed breathily.

"It's been two years," Gavin told her, reaching up and framing her smiling face. "You stored up a lot of loving in that time."

Moving her hips teasingly, she could already feel him filling her once more. That was amazing in itself. "I did." She reveled in his hands framing her face. "Maybe we should skip brunch and go to a late lunch."

That moment of her husky laughter, the heat of her body, the look in her eyes conspired within Gavin. "Maybe supper."

"I'm hungry for *you*," she whispered, becoming more serious. "I've wanted you since I first laid eyes on you. I fought it for a long time, but that's the truth." Nike's brows dipped as his hands came to rest on her hips. "I love you. I should have told you that back at base before all that stuff happened. You have no idea how many times I regretted not telling you when I was tied up in that barn in that village. That hurt me the most—not having had the courage to tell you how I really felt."

Whispering her name, Gavin trailed his fingers across her cheek. He saw the tears in her eyes and his heart contracted with pain. "Listen, you did the best you could, darling. Learning to let yourself love again is tough. I understood that." And then he gave her a boyish smile, hoping to lighten the guilt she carried. "I loved you from the moment I saw you. And I knew I'd eventually get you. All I needed to do was show you that you didn't need to be afraid to love me."

Nodding, Nike lay down across him, her head coming to rest next to his jaw. "I'm glad you didn't give up, Gavin. I wanted you, I really did. But I was so scared." She felt him move his hands down across her drying back. It was a touch of the butterfly once more, as if absorbing and taking her pain away from her.

"We're all scared, Nike," he told her, his voice rough with emotion. "And we each had to take the time to surmount those fears. In the end, we're pretty courageous people. We love one another. And yes, we have this tour to get through, but we'll do it. It will be good because we'll get to know one another over that time. Together." He eased her chin up with his hand so that their eyes met. "Together. You hear me?"

Nodding, Nike leaned over and caressed his lips. "Together." She saw a satisfied look come to Gavin's face.

"Marry me."

Shocked and laughing, Nike pushed herself up into a sitting position upon him once more. "You have this all figured out, don't you?"

Gavin eyed her innocently. "Hey, I have a lot of time to think while I'm out there in the boonies for thirty days at a time." Gavin reached up and caressed her curly hair. "I figure that your parents will probably want us to marry over in Greece."

"Got that right," Nike said, laughing. "My parents would have a kitten if you wanted us to marry in the States."

Gavin smoothed his hands down the length of her back and across her hips. "You can e-mail them anytime you want. Luckily for us, Khalid has satellite here at the house."

"Maybe later," she whispered, lying back down upon him and nestling her brow next to his jaw. "Right now, all I want to do is be with you, Gavin. I want to make this next week last forever."

He pressed a kiss to her brow. "Listen, forever is going to last a lot longer than this week. I'm looking forward to a long, long life with you."

Closing her eyes, Nike whispered, "That's all I want, too, Gavin. I love you so much."

* * * * *

OPERATION: FORBIDDEN

To Marchiene Reinstra, Interfaith Minister

Thank you for all your help

Blessings

Chapter 1

Emma was in deep trouble. She'd just signed up for a second tour at Camp Bravo on the front lines of the Afghanistan war. And now this. Her commanding officer, Major Dallas Klein, had just requested her presence. Right now. That couldn't be good. She swallowed hard, and her heart began a slow pound of dread.

"Go on in, Captain Cantrell," the assistant said, gesturing to the C.O.'s office.

Emma nodded, took a deep breath and opened the door. She stepped inside and quietly closed it behind her. "Reporting as ordered, ma'am," Emma said, coming to attention.

Dallas Klein looked up from behind her desk.

"At ease. Have a seat, Captain," Dallas said, pointing to the chair near her desk.

"Yes, ma'am," Emma murmured. Sitting at attention,

she clasped her hands and waited. Her boss frowned as she lifted about ten files and put them into her lap. The woman sifted through them, and Emma instinctively knew they had something to do with her. She almost blurted out, *What kind of trouble am I in now?* but didn't. Compressing her lips, Emma held on to her last shred of patience.

"Here it is," Dallas said, opening one file and pushing the others aside. "Captain, you're the only woman in our squadron that speaks Pashto. You took a one-year saturation course before you came over here. Correct?"

"Yes, ma'am." Emma nodded.

"Good. And you continue to use the language?"

"Of course. I get a lot of practice with the Afghans who are allowed to work here on our base."

Dipping her head, Dallas looked down at the thick sheaves of paper in the file. "Very well, Captain. I've just had a highly unusual request dropped on me. And ordinarily, I would tell high command to go stuff it, but this time, I couldn't." Dallas scowled over at Emma. "You really gave your career a black eye last August by rescuing that Special Forces sergeant off a hill under attack. I know Nike Alexander had the idea, but you were the XO at the time, and you implemented her request."

Emma wanted to roll her eyes. God, didn't Klein forget anything? She remained silent; the major wanted her to respond, but what could she say? Yes, she'd screwed up, but she'd also saved a life. Emma knew when to keep her mouth shut, and she held the major's flat stare. Emma had never confessed to what the major just said. If she had, she would probably have been court-martialed. The better choice was to remain alert but mute.

"Well," Dallas growled, jerking open another paper

from the file, "I have a way for you to save your career, Captain Cantrell."

Brows raised, Emma was interested. "Oh?"

"Actually," Dallas said, "the Pentagon chose you because you speak Pashto, the common language here in Afghanistan. And frankly, I'd like to see you distinguish yourself in some way so you can eventually go up for major and make the promotion." Dallas thumped the file with her index fingers. "I believe this is a very good way for you to salvage your army career, Captain Cantrell. I hope you think so, too."

Perking up, Emma leaned forward. "I'm interested."

"I thought you might be." Dallas opened up the file to another section. "This is a very special mission. What I don't like is that you'll be out of my squadron for six months. You'll be part of a team working on a unique Afghan project known as Operation Book Worm."

Emma almost laughed and struggled to keep a straight face. "Operation Book Worm? Ma'am?" Dallas appeared completely serious, not a hint of a smile or joking demeanor. And God knew, members of the Black Jaguar Squadron played tricks on each other all the time. Black humor was alive and well in this combat squadron. It kept them all sane. Laughter instead of tears.

"This is not a joke, Captain Cantrell, so wipe that smirk off your face."

"Yes, ma'am." What the hell was Operation Book Worm?

"Okay, here's the guts of the mission. You're being assigned to Captain Khalid Shaheen. He's the only Afghan currently allowed to fly the Apache combat helicopter. He's been flying with another Apache squadron in the Helmand province of southern Afghanistan until this operation went active."

Emma's brow bunched. "An Afghan flying one of our Apaches?" She'd never heard of such a thing. And she was being assigned to this dude?

Dallas held up her hand. "Just sit and listen. I don't want you interrupting me, Captain."

"Yes, ma'am."

"Captain Shaheen is a thirty-year-old Afghan. He's responsible for creating Operation Book Worm."

Emma nodded and said nothing. How was this mission going to help *her* career?

"Captain Shaheen comes from one of the richest families in Afghanistan. He is a Princeton graduate and has a master's degree in electrical engineering. He graduated with honors. The army persuaded him to spend six years with them and he proved ideal flying Apache helicopters. The Pentagon is relying on Captain Shaheen to persuade other Afghan military men to come to the United States to be trained at Fort Rucker, Alabama. Once they've earned their wings in Apaches, they will come back to Afghanistan to start fighting and defending their own country."

"Afghanistan does not have an air force."

"No, but Shaheen is the bedrock for starting one."

Emma considered the pilot with new respect. "That's a tall order."

"New ideas start with one person," Dallas said.

"And what is my activity with him?"

"There's more. His sister, Kinah Shaheen, was also educated at Princeton. She's twenty-eight years old and holds a Ph.D. in education. She has made it her mission in this country to provide education to young girls. As you know, under Taliban rule, girls weren't allowed any type of education. Kinah is armed not only with a hell of an education, but her family's money and a fierce determination to get girls back into school."

"Wow," Emma said, "that's an even taller order. I've been here long enough to see how women are suppressed when it comes to education. In the past, the Taliban killed teachers and tribal elders or chieftains of villages who allowed girls to be schooled."

"I know," Dallas said, grimness in her tone. "Kinah and her brother, Khalid, came up with the idea for Operation Book Worm. Khalid is considered a used-car salesman of sorts." She grinned a little.

"You've met him?" Emma was now completely taken by the Afghan brother and sister and their plans.

"Once," Dallas said dryly. "And I can see why Khalid has been able to talk corporations in the United States into donating millions of dollars for this idea. Kinah is no small-time operator, either. Their father is a Persian rug salesman, so talking people out of money is in their DNA."

"But their idea sounds more than saleable," Emma said, excited.

"It has been." Dallas leaned back in her chair. "Between them, they've got ten million dollars to throw at this operation."

"Wow…"

"Yeah, double wow," Dallas agreed. "You'll come into this by virtue of the fact that Khalid is going to use, with the U.S. Army's permission, a CH-47 transport from Camp Bravo. He's qualified in four types of helicopters, by the way. And that's no small feat, either."

Eyes widening, Emma considered that skill. "He must be…"

"He's a genius," Dallas said. "Brilliant, mad and passionate, not to mention a damned fine combat helicopter pilot."

Emma took a deep breath. "He sounds like a Renaissance man. Many skills and talents."

"Oh, Khalid is all of that," Dallas said.

"Why does he need me?"

"He wants to land in each targeted village not only to deliver books, supplies and food, but to show you as an example of what a woman can do. Khalid wants the girls of the village to see a woman who flies that helicopter. He feels that show-and-tell is a quick way to get the girls to dream big and often."

"That's a great strategy," Emma said, understanding the Afghan's brilliant concept. "So, I'm his copilot?"

"You're both aircraft commanders—ACs. You're the same rank. You have three years less time in the Apache than he does, but he wants you in the driver's seat off and on."

"In other words, he has a live-and-let-live policy about swapping out AC status?"

"Yep. You'll find Khalid one of the most fascinating men you've ever met. He'll keep you on your toes. He wanted a woman Apache pilot who spoke Pashto because he wants that woman to be able to speak to the little girls. He wants you to become a saleswoman to encourage their education. And don't be surprised if he has you do impromptu speeches on why little girls should want an education. Khalid wants to fire their imaginations. He wants to shock them from the realm of dreams to that of possibilities."

"I'll be happy to take on this mission, ma'am," Emma said.

"For the next six months, from spring through fall, you'll work with him. He plans on having fifty schools set up along the border villages by the time snow flies."

"But," Emma said, holding up her hand, "haven't you left out one thing? You know all the border villages are wide open to attack from the Taliban? Those villagers live in fear of them. And how does Khalid protect all these villages? Once the Taliban hears of schools for girls, you know they'll attack and kill the teachers."

Dallas nodded grimly. "He's very well aware of the situation, and the U.S. Army is coordinating with him to protect these villages. They'll be moving more Special Forces A-teams *into* the villages. And air force drones will be utilized as flyovers on a nightly basis by our CIA guys stationed here when the Taliban is active. This could be a queen-maker for you, Captain Cantrell."

Emma considered the assignment carefully. If she could successfully work with Captain Shaheen and his sister, her personnel jacket would contain glowing commendations from them. Enough to bury the censure over her decision last year. And then her family, who had a nearly unbroken ribbon of service to America, would no longer have this blight on its reputation. As she sat there contemplating all of this, Emma then wondered: could she get along with this Afghan? He was filthy rich. Princeton-educated. Would he look down on her? Not appreciate what she brought to the table with her own intelligence and creativity? Suddenly, Emma felt unsure.

Dallas signed the orders and handed them across the desk to her. "Here you go, Captain Cantrell. Do us proud." She hesitated for a moment and added, "Be warned: He's a marked man. The Taliban has a huge reward out for his death. This is going to be no picnic for you. Captain Shaheen is landing in—" and she looked at her watch "—fifteen minutes. Be on the tarmac to meet him. Dismissed."

The sun was bright and Emma put on her dark aviator glasses. The breeze was inconstant across the concrete revetment area. The odor of flight fuel was strong. She watched as several ordnance teams drove out in specialized trucks, pulling their loads of weaponry on trailers. An excitement hummed through the area. Emma inhaled it and absorbed the vibrating tension. She loved that feeling, which was probably why she was an Apache combat helicopter pilot.

Some anxiety lingered about the new assignment. If Shaheen was a marked man, on the enemy's top-ten-wanted list, it was more than likely the Taliban would make good on their threat to murder him.

Then there was her own distrust of rich men who thought they could act reprehensibly without recourse. Like Brody Parker. Brody had been a rich American in Lima, Peru, and she'd met him when flying in for the original Black Jaguar Squadron. A year after falling helplessly in love with him, Emma found out he was married, with children. Stung to her soul by the lies that men could tell, she'd made a point of avoiding the opposite sex since coming to Camp Bravo. It was a clean start. She didn't need another rich, lying bastard to deal with.

Shaheen landed the Apache on a three-point landing about a hundred feet away from where Emma stood.

It was a perfect landing—gentle and not bouncy. Her eyes narrowed as she saw the ground crewman place the ladder against the bird and climb up after the rotors stopped turning. He hefted the canopy upward on the front cockpit after it was unlocked by the pilot. Emma was confused; she saw no pilot in the back seat. No one flew the Apache with just one pilot unless it was an emergency.

When Khalid Shaheen climbed out of the cockpit, he handed the crewman his helmet, and Emma smiled to herself. As the Afghan emerged, she was taken by his lean, taut form. He had to be six feet tall, which was about the top height for an Apache pilot. Most were between five foot seven inches and five foot ten inches tall. The cockpit was cramped, and anyone over six feet couldn't comfortably get into it. She tried to ignore his animallike grace as he climbed out of the cockpit and stood on the dark green and tan metal skirt. The crewman stepped off the ladder and waited nearby.

Emma took in Shaheen's olive skin, military-short black hair and straight, dark brows above narrowed blue eyes. When he smiled and joked with the crewman on the tarmac, her heart suddenly thumped hard in her chest. Shaheen was eye candy, no doubt. And dangerous... His face was narrow, his nose aquiline, cheekbones high and he had a strong chin. When he smiled at a crewman's joke, his teeth were white and even. Emma felt herself melting inwardly. Of all the reactions to have! Shaheen was like a fierce lion moving with a feral grace that took her breath away. There were no lions in Afghanistan, Emma reminded herself.

And yet, she couldn't take her gaze off the charismatic officer. He removed his Kevlar vest and placed

it on the skirt of the Apache. There was a .45 pistol
strapped to his waist. Emma decided that if she didn't
know he was Afghan, she would never have guessed it.
From this distance, he looked like a typical U.S. Army
combat pilot.

The crewmen and Khalid joked back and forth, and
the three of them stood laughing. Warmth pooled in
her chest and Emma unconsciously touched her jacket
where her heart lay. There was such gracefulness to this
tall, lanky warrior. Emma suddenly felt as if she were
standing on quicksand. Her reaction wasn't logical. The
pilot walking languidly, like a lordly lion toward her,
was married. He had to be. He had to have a wife and
children. Afghans married very early. So why was she
feeling shaky and unsure of herself? Emma had never
had such a powerful emotional reaction to a man. Not
ever, and it scared her.

As Emma stepped forward, her mouth went dry. She
forced herself to walk confidently out on the revetment
and meet the foreign pilot. And when his gaze locked
onto hers, she groaned. Shaheen drew closer, and Emma
could appreciate the curious color of his eyes. They reminded her of the greenish-blue depths of the ocean
around a Caribbean island. Not only that, his eyes were
large, well-spaced, with thick lashes that enhanced the
black pupils. She felt as if she could lose herself within
them. Emma jerked her gaze away. What was going on?
Her heart pounded as though she was on an adrenaline
rush. But she wasn't in danger. No, this was excitement
at some unconscious level within her that she had never
experienced. And that made Emma wary.

Shaheen unzipped his olive-green flight suit as he
approached. Black hairs peeked out from beneath his

dark green T-shirt. He reached inside his flight suit. And what he drew out made Emma's jaw drop. Shaheen slowed and stopped about three feet in front of her. In his hand was a huge red rose, its petals flattened from being crushed inside his flight suit, but a rose, nevertheless.

Pressing his hand against his heart, Shaheen bowed slightly and murmured the ancient greeting that all people in the Muslim world shared. *"As-salaam alaikum."* Peace to you from my heart to your heart. "Captain Emma Cantrell?" he asked, smiling as he lifted his head.

Paralyzed, Emma stared up at him. Shaheen held the drooping rose toward her. He'd obviously picked it just before the flight and carried it inside his suit to her. Emma could smell the spicy fragrance of the bedraggled flower. "I—yes," she managed in a croak. Without thinking, she took his gift and responded, *"As-salaam alaikum."* She clutched the rose in her right hand, noting that the thorns had been cut off so it would not prick her fingers.

Scrambling inwardly, Emma tried not to be impressed by this thoughtfulness. When she raised her head, she noticed Khalid's masculine smile and twinkling eyes. "I'm Captain Emma Cantrell," she said in a crisp tone. "Welcome to Camp Bravo." God, she sounded like a teenager on her first date, her voice high and squeaky. Worse, he had the same kind of swaggering, super confidence that Brody had had. They could be twins. Her heart sank. *Not this again.*

"Thank you, Emma. Please," he murmured in a low, husky tone, "call me Khalid once we get out of the military environment."

She stood looking helplessly at the rose in her hand. "Why...I never expected this, Captain Shaheen." Officers simply didn't give other officers flowers. Clearly, he was flirting with her.

Khalid's hands relaxed on his hips, a typical aviator stance. "I went out to my rose garden this morning. I live in Kabul. It is the first rose of the season. I took my knife and cut it off knowing that I wanted you to have something beautiful from me to you."

Emma swallowed hard. Aviators never wore jewelry of any kind. Not even a wedding ring. But this guy had to be married. He was just too charming. The confusion must have shown on her face.

"Rumi, the great Sufi mystic poet, said much about the beauty of a rose." He then quoted her a passage that he'd memorized.

Emma was sure now he was flirting with her. Completely stunned by Khalid's warmth, his utter masculinity and those gleaming blue eyes, Emma choked. "But... you're married!" Well, that wasn't exactly polite, was it? No, but the words flew out of her mouth. Emma took a step away from him. Khalid's face was overcome with surprise, his straight, black brows rising. And then he laughed. His laughter was hearty, unfettered and rolled out of his powerful chest.

"I'm afraid I'm not married," Khalid said and he held up his hands, smiling over her mistake.

Emma didn't know what to do. She knew how she felt toward him—as if he were a conquering Afghan warlord who had just swept her off her feet, stolen her young, innocent heart and claimed her. His smile was so engaging her heart appreciated it by beating erratically. Brody Parker had wooed and wowed her the same way. Oh, God, it was the *same* situation all over again!

Emma gripped the red rose until her fingers hurt. Should she give it back to him? Throw it away? This wasn't military protocol between two officers. Emma furtively looked around her. Who had seen him do this? Had they seen her accept the gift? Things like this just weren't done in the U.S. Army. Could she be more distressed?

"I can't take this, Captain Shaheen." She handed him the rose.

Holding up his hands, Khalid said, "Forgive me, Captain Cantrell. My father is Sufi and I was raised with Rumi. I see all of my life through this thirteenth-century poet and mystic's eyes. I am forever quoting him, for Rumi guides my heart and my life. I hope you do not take offense to my gift. Among the Sufis we believe that love is the only vehicle to touch the face of God and become one with the source. My gift to you was merely an acknowledgment, heart-to-heart, that we are connected. And it is a gift that honors you as a person, to show that you are sacred to me and all of life. Please, do not be pained by the gift."

Stubbornly, Emma gave him a long, steady stare. "It's not acceptable military behavior, Captain. Let's leave it at that, shall we?"

Khalid winced. He pressed his hand to his heart and held her gaze. "I will maintain correct military protocol with you, Captain. Please accept my deepest apology. I am honored that you have agreed to work with me." He tucked the rose back into his flight suit.

Emma wasn't sure about this terribly handsome Afghan standing in front of her, speaking with such candor. Her heart melted over the warmth dancing in the depths of his aquamarine eyes. Given the sincerity in his voice and face, she wondered obliquely if she'd read his intentions wrongly.

"Then we're in agreement," she said in a clipped tone. "I volunteered for this mission to help the Afghan girls get an education." Emma tried to convince herself that he was Brody Parker all over again, only even more charming and smooth than her lover in Peru had been. Emma wasn't falling for it again. Her heart couldn't take the hurt twice. Dallas's words haunted her: *This could be a queen-maker for your career.* And more than anything, Emma wanted to get good remarks from Shaheen after she finished the six-month mission. Now, she felt as though she was literally walking the edge of sword that could cut her both ways. What had she just stepped into?

Chapter 2

Emma tensed. A range of emotions passed across Khalid's rugged face. "Look," she murmured, "I know that in different cultures, mistakes can be made."

"No, no," Khalid said, trying to muster a smile, but failing. "You need to understand the heart of our mission. By knowing what the foundation is, you can appreciate our fierce passion for our people." He held her forest-green gaze. The noise on the tarmac surrounded them. He gestured for Emma to follow him into the Ops building where there would be a room where they could talk.

Emma followed Shaheen. More and more, this felt like doom to her. She was falling fast and she needed to focus on her work. Inside Ops, the captain found an empty room. They went in and closed the door. There was a rectangular table, reports scattered across it along with pens. Emma took a seat and he sat down opposite her after pouring them some coffee.

Taking the lead, Emma folded her hands and met his stare. "My CO told me you were a marked man. I want to know what that means since I'm putting my butt on the line here."

"I have an ancient enemy," Khalid began. "His name is Asad Malik. He was born in Pakistan, along the border in the state of Waziristan. Malik was very poor, and with the Taliban, who make a permanent home in that border state, he found his calling. My father's family are Sufis. They know that education is the door to all fulfillment of a person's dreams and goals. My father has considerable wealth, and he poured it into the border villages of our country a long time ago because the so-called central government of Afghanistan ignored them."

Brows drawing downward, Khalid said, "Malik rose to become a very powerful Taliban leader. He is heartless and ruthless. He began attacking villages to which my father was trying to bring schools and education. There were many pitched battles over the years, and Malik swore to kill every member of my family."

Emma gasped. Although she knew revenge ran deep, the admittance was still shocking. "What?"

Shrugging, Khalid said, "Malik is not a Sufi. He is a terrorist at the other end of the Muslim religion. Our beliefs swing from an eye-for-an-eye attitude to one of spiritual connection with Allah." He pressed his hand to his heart. "I am Sufi. Malik is stuck in a state of twisted hatred and revenge. It would not matter what religion he embraced, he would practice what he is, despite it. He has perverted the Koran for his own goals."

Emma nodded. "Yes, every religion has its fanatics. In my year here in Afghanistan, I've lived among the Muslims and I find them incredibly generous and caring. They aren't the terrorists that the world thinks. They believe in peace."

"Yes, we are peaceful," Khalid agreed. "It will only be through our daily life that we show the Muslim religion is not one of terrorism."

"It's a PR game," Emma said. "And I agree with you, people are educated one person at a time. Religion doesn't kill. It's the individuals within any religion who choose to interpret it according to their own darkness and wounds."

He gave her an intense look. "I have truly made the right decision in asking you to be a part of our mission. I like your free-thinking policy."

Emma tried not to be swayed by his compliment and felt heat enter her cheeks. "I try never to judge a person. I let their actions speak louder than their words." The intensity of his gaze made Emma feel as if she were unraveling as a woman—not as an officer—to this lion of a man. She mentally corrected herself once again: there were no lions in Afghanistan. Instead, Emma regarded him as the rare and elusive snow leopard that lived in the rugged mountains of this country.

"My death dance with Malik," Khalid continued, "took on new dimensions two years ago. Malik stalks the border like the wolf that he is. He continually attacks and kills the villagers who try to better their lives in any way. It is how he stops my father's generosity to lift the poor up and help them succeed. Malik does not care about such things." Taking a deep breath, Khalid continued, his voice strained. "I fell in love with a beautiful teacher. Her name was Najela. I courted her for two years and I asked her to become my wife."

Emma heard Khalid's voice quaver and noticed how he fought unknown emotions, his hands opening and closing around the heavy ceramic mug in front of him. She wanted to reach out and touch him, to soothe away the grief she saw clearly etched in his face. But Emma said nothing. She allowed Khalid to get hold of himself so that he could continue his story.

"Najela and my sister Kinah were the best of friends. And why wouldn't they be? They were both American-educated and trained in education. Najela graduated from Harvard and my sister from Princeton. They were working with my father to help set up village schools for boys and girls. I was away working for the U.S. Army and they were frequently up in this area while I flew Apaches in the southern region of my country."

Emma steeled herself. She leaped ahead and figured out that Najela was dead. At Malik's hands? She hoped not. Her heart cringed inside her chest. "Go on," she urged him, her voice tense.

Nodding, Khalid swallowed hard, took a drink of his coffee, wiped his mouth with the back of his hand and then took a deep breath and released it. "I was on a mission with the U.S. Marines in the south when I got word that Malik had captured Najela in one of the villages." His voice became low and strained. "By the time I was given orders to fly north to the village, Malik had repeatedly raped her and then he…slit her throat. I found her in a mud house that had been abandoned by the family who lived there. All I found…was her…" And he closed his eyes for a moment, reliving that nightmare afternoon.

"I—I'm so sorry," Emma whispered, caught up in his anguish. Without thinking, she reached across the table and touched his hand. And when she realized what she'd done, Emma quickly pulled her hand back. No officer should be seen initiating such an intimate action with another officer. Turning her focus back to Khalid, she thought she saw tears in his blue eyes for just a second. And then, they were gone. Had she imagined them? Emma chastised herself for losing her standards.

"Malik hates anyone and anything who tries to improve upon the villagers' lives," Khalid continued, his voice rough. "As I said, he's sworn vengeance against my family because of my father's generosity to the villagers."

Emma considered his heavily spoken words. "And is Malik out there right now? Will he be our enemy as you and Kinah set up this mission for those same villagers?" A cold chill worked its way up her spine as she saw his expression still and become unreadable.

"Yes, he is our nemesis. You need to know that this mission is dangerous so that you remain on guard. Your CO was correct in telling you I am a marked man. You will be marked too, Captain."

Eyes rounding, Emma sat up. "Aren't you afraid, Captain Shaheen? He's already killed one person you loved. You could be next." Suddenly, Emma wanted nothing to harm this man who had a vision for the girls of his country. She could see his sincerity and the heart that he wore openly on his sleeve. Khalid was priceless in her world because few men could be so in touch with their emotions and share them as he just had with her. Brody had never opened up like this. Not ever. And it threw Emma.

Khalid said, "Rumi would say a real Sufi laughs at death. A Sufi is like an oyster—what strikes it does not harm the pearl within."

Considering the saying from the thirteenth century, Emma grimaced. "Sorry, but I'm not in agreement with Rumi. I don't feel I could be at peace if someone raped and then murdered my fiancée."

"I understand," Khalid said. "You have lived in our country where the threat to your life exists every day." He opened his hand and gestured around the room. "Afghans have been at war with the Russians. Now, we have the Taliban. Do we want to live this way? No. Do we dream of a peaceful life? Yes. I don't expect you, Captain Cantrell, to believe as we do. Najela was Sufi. I know in my heart of hearts that throughout her terrible last hours she felt compassion for Malik. He's a man so filled with hatred and vengeance that I'm sure that her compassion only made him want to harm her even more."

Shaking her head, Emma muttered, "Well, I sure wouldn't be thinking peaceful and loving thoughts if that dude was doing that to me. I'd be looking for any way to protect myself and kill the bastard."

Giving her a slight smile, Khalid nodded. "Sufis are misunderstood even by our other Muslim brethren. In fact, those who choose jihad and become terrorists hate us as much as they do the so-called infidels."

"Which is why Malik hates you?" Emma wondered.

"He hates my family for many reasons and has sworn vengeance against each of us. In part, because we are Sufis and believe in tolerance and generosity toward others. The fact my father is worth billions of dollars makes Malik hate us because he was raised in poverty.

He didn't own a pair of shoes until he was eleven years old when the Taliban leader recruited him."

Suddenly, there was a deafening explosion outside. The sound and reverberation slammed into the room. Instantly, they both dove for the deck, hands over their heads. Emma hissed a curse. Tiles from the ceiling fell around them as a second explosion shook Ops.

"It's the Taliban," she growled, getting to her feet. Automatically, she pulled the .45 pistol from her belt and ran to the door. Swinging it open, Ops looked like a beehive that had been overturned.

Shaheen was at her side, looking down at her. Emma's face was set and her gaze aimed at the windows outside. He saw one of the helicopters burning, the black smoke roiling and bubbling skyward. "Do you get attacks often?"

Grimly, Emma moved toward the center of Ops. Pilots and crews were hurrying out the doors, armed and ready to fight. She knew from being here over a year that such attacks were sporadic. "No," she snapped, moving with everyone else toward the doors. "Come on, we need to help the fire crews."

Khalid didn't know Camp Bravo as she did. He trotted across Ops and found himself outside with her. Emma's eyes were searching the end of the runway and she pointed in that direction. "That's one of the places they hit us. They sit in the brush beyond the runway and lob RPGs, rocket-propelled grenades, this way."

Khalid noted a squad of Special Forces speeding away in a Humvee, armed and ready for battle. He wanted to protect Emma. It was his natural reaction. Telling himself she was a warrior like him, he kept his thoughts and his hands to himself. She was all business now. Another crew rolled up in a fire engine and began spewing foam over the burning CH-47 transport helicopter, already a total loss.

Emma turned. She was glad she had her Kevlar jacket on because gunshots were suddenly being traded at the end of the runway. "Come on, this is under control. No sense standing out here like targets." She gestured toward Ops again.

Shaheen wasn't so sure, for a minute longer, he watched the Special Forces from the Humvee spraying the bushes where the Taliban had been hiding. "Do they get inside the camp?" he asked as he followed her into Ops.

"Not so far, but we're always watching." Settling the .45 back into the holster on her waist, she added, "We're never safe here. Let's get back to discussing the mission, shall we?" Emma stopped and poured herself another cup of black coffee from the urn at the side of the Ops desk. Khalid did the same and they returned to the meeting room.

There were several enlisted men in there. They'd already picked up the ceiling tiles that had dropped from the explosion, so Emma thanked them and, once more, she and Khalid were alone. They pulled their chairs to the table and sat down. Her heart pounded and she felt tense and on guard. As she sipped the coffee, she hoped it would soothe her jangled nerves.

"Will they attack more than once in a day?" Khalid wondered. He found himself drowning in her dark, forest-green eyes, fraught with care and concern. If he read her correctly, it was concern for his welfare. That touched and warmed his wounded heart. There was something ethereal about Emma. Was it how her mussed red hair curled slightly at her temples? Was it her huge green eyes fraught with compassion? Or those lips that reminded Khalid of a rose in full bloom? His inspiration to cut the first red rose of the year from his family's garden hadn't gone as he'd hoped. "Well, let me lay out some information to you on Operation Book Worm," he said, returning to business.

Asad Malik crept away from the end of the runway with his men. Bullets were singing around them, but he knew from long experience that the Special Forces couldn't see them and they were firing blindly into the thick brush. One day, when there was time, such brush would be cleaned away. He had ten men with him. They continued to work their way through the heavy brush, their AK-47s and grenade launchers in hand. Smiling to himself, he congratulated them in a whisper on destroying one of the helicopters. It was a good day!

Dressed in baggy brown trousers, a crisscross of wide leather straps containing bullets across his chest, Malik did not think this attack was done. No. He would wait, skulk through the brush with his men and wait on the other side. Malik knew this forward base was vital to the war effort by the infidel Americans. Until lately, he'd not had enough money to buy more grenades and bullets. Now, he had a new donor from Saudi Arabia who had given him millions to support the Taliban effort.

Grunting and breathing hard, Malik knelt, hidden. He waited for his ragtag group of nine other men to catch up with him. Most were barefoot, their clothes thin and threadbare. They were all skinny, their cheeks sunken, for coming here had been hard on them. Malik

usually worked other areas, but this base was crucial
to the American mission and he'd wanted to strike the
head of the snake finally.

"Everyone all right?" he demanded roughly as they
sat in a semicircle around him. "No wounds?"

"None, my lord," one of the bearded men spoke up.

Malik grinned. "Good. Now, let's sneak around the
other side of the runway. Knowing the infidels, they'll
think this attack is over."

There were soft, knowing chuckles from the men,
all of whom nodded their accord to follow their charismatic and brave leader.

"Come!" Malik whispered harshly, lifting his hand
and moving forward. "I want another helicopter," he
snickered.

Emma could see the burning intensity in Khalid's
blue eyes as they narrowed speculatively upon her.
They'd just finished off their coffees and got down to
the business at hand. She felt giddy and thrilled with his
interest in her. Sure, he respected her as a professional,
but she sensed something deeper. Sternly, she chided
herself for thinking he was drawn to her.

And then her heart contracted. Was Khalid interested in her or was she imagining things? That couldn't
be. Khalid was the head of the mission and held power
over her. His comments would eventually go into her
career jacket. Maybe he was this charming with everyone. She couldn't allow herself to get involved with this
intriguing, romantic Afghan warrior. But why did he
have to be so damn good-looking? She vowed to savor
this rugged male pilot secretly; he'd never know it. She
could hide her feelings. For now.

* * *

Khalid pulled out a map from one long pocket on his flight suit leg and spread it out before them. He stood up and, using a pen, said, "This is the route we're going to follow. We'll move from one village to another." His index finger was on the map, tracing the small villages along the border with Pakistan. It bothered him that he was drawn to Emma, despite her military demeanor. Khalid refused to put another woman in the gunsights of Asad Malik. It would be too easy to become personal with red-haired, brazen Emma Cantrell.

"For the next six months," he said, straightening and moving his shoulders as if to shrug off the tension gathered in them, "you will be with me and Kinah, and you will surely be well-educated into our Sufi world. We believe that all religions have a good message for the spirit. My father, who was born in Kabul, comes from a long line of Sufis. My mother, who is a medical doctor from Ireland, continues to this day to be a Presbyterian missionary. She came to this country after she finished her residency in Dublin, Ireland. Her father is an elder in their tradition. And her entire family has been missionaries here in Afghanistan for nearly a hundred years."

Surprised, Emma's brows rose with that information. "Then…you're half-Afghan and half-Irish?" Maybe that accounted for those dancing blue eyes that always had a bit of devilry lurking in their depths.

"I am," he said with pride. "I am a good example that east meeting west can actually get along."

"Your religions are so different."

"That's what I'm trying to tell you," Khalid said, turning the map over. "The Sufis have no quarrel with any other religion in this world. We accept people as they are and respect their beliefs."

"Too bad that all religions can't hold the same ideas," Emma said. She was thinking of the evil Asad Malik.

"That's why," Khalid explained, "the jihadists who are twisted and out of touch with true Muslim traditions hate Sufis and will kill them on sight. The terrorists among those who profess to be Muslim are threatened by the enlightened ways of the Sufi people."

Emma sat back. "And so you have no trouble being half-Christian and half-Muslim?"

Chuckling, Khalid shook his head. He spread a second map on to the table. It showed close-ups of some of the more major villages along the Afghanistan-Pakistan border. "Absolutely none. Sufis honor and respect every religious tradition on the face of our Earth. We believe all paths lead through the heart to the Creator, no matter what name you call him or her."

Emma watched as he traced a red line around certain areas. "What are those?" she demanded.

"This is Malik's territory, where he and the Taliban are constantly attacking the villagers."

Emma got up and leaned over, their heads inches apart as she studied the map. "This guy is big. I know I've heard his name."

"Yes, he's north of your base camp."

Emma straightened. "Like you said, we'll be alert."

"Agreed," Khalid said. He picked up the papers, neatly folded them once more and tucked them away in the leg of his flight suit. "So, Captain Cantrell, are you ready to fly back to Bagram Air Force Base with me? We have much to do and there's so much to show you about our mission."

Surprised, Emma watched as Khalid stood, lean, strong, his broad shoulders thrown back with unconscious pride. "Bagram? I thought we'd be working here, out of Camp Bravo?"

"Oh, we will," Khalid assured her. "I'm inviting you to have dinner with me tonight at my family's villa in Kabul. You may stay overnight. As you know, there are male and female sections to each home. I have had our housekeeper prepare you a room in the women's part of the house. After we have a wonderful dinner, I will take you to my office and show you Operation Book Worm. I think you will appreciate what I'll show you. Then, you can grasp even more of the mission and its priorities."

Shocked by the offer, Emma sat staring up at him. "But…"

"This is a work invitation, Captain Cantrell. I'm an excellent host. It's easier for me to show you what we will be doing at our villa where it is all stored, than to try and lug it piecemeal back and forth to this camp."

Emma considered the unexpected invitation and her vivid imagination took off. What would it be like to be with this Afghan warrior? And truly, that's what Khalid was. She knew he professed compassion and love for others, but her body was not reacting to him in that way. No, she felt a hunger and drive to know Khalid on a much more personal level. How was she going to keep this fact a secret? Looking deeply into his eyes, Emma realized that this wasn't at all personal to Khalid; it was merely a formality to offer her dinner. After all, Emma knew from experience that all Afghans, rich or poor, would automatically invite her to their home for dinner. It was a custom and way of life in Afghanistan.

"Of course I'll go with you, Captain Shaheen. I look forward to it."

Khalid brightened. "Excellent. If there is anything you need to pack in your flight bag before we take off, why not go get it now. I'll meet you back at Ops."

Good, he was remaining all business. As she walked with Khalid out of Ops and into the warming sunlight over the camp, Emma couldn't explain the happiness threading through her. Khalid bowed slightly where the path forked and led to Ops. The fire had been put out on the destroyed helicopter and there was still a lot of activity on the tarmac.

"I'll see you soon, Captain?"

"Yes," Emma said, "this won't take long." Khalid was all business. All military. That warm smile, those inquiring blue eyes of his were veiled.

"Good, I'll meet you at our Apache." He strode confidently back into Ops to file their flight plan.

Shaking her head, Emma trotted down another dirt avenue between the desert-tan-and-green tents. Khalid and Brody had a lot in common, but she'd never spent too much time with a man who had one foot in the east and one foot in the west. The breeze ruffled her red hair as she continued to jog down the dirt path. Making a left, she found her tent and unzipped it. Worry hovered over her. Above all, she had to keep her silly heart out of this. It was bad enough that Khalid was in the active gun sights of Asad Malik, but the Taliban leader would target her, too. In a heartbeat.

As Emma packed essentials into her canvas flight bag, she couldn't stop thinking about Khalid. He'd loved and lost his bride. That explained why he was still single at thirty, unheard of for a Muslim man. She replayed the grief that was raw and alive in his eyes as he'd shared the tragedy of Najela's death at Malik's hands.

After grabbing her toothbrush, toothpaste, comb and brush, Emma quickly finished her packing. She zipped up her flight bag and took her helmet bag off the make-shift chest of drawers. As she headed outside, she felt the sunlight warming up the coolish temperature. She turned on the heel of her flight boot and walked quickly down between the rows of tents. Despite the unexpected Taliban attack an hour earlier, the air was alive with the puncturing sounds of helicopters landing and tak-ing off once more. The smell of jet fuel was always around. Metallic, oily smoke still hung above the camp from the destroyed chopper. The growl of huge military trucks belching blue smoke, their coughs and grinding of gears, filled the air, too. As she jogged across the camp to the control-tower area, Emma's heart took off.

Why did she feel giddy? Like a schoolgirl who had a crush on the all-star football quarterback? Would she be able to tread on the edge of the sword with Khalid? Separate out her womanly need to know more about him on a personal level from the professional one? Emma wasn't sure. She slowed to a walk and pulled open the door to Ops. As she moved through the busy building and out the other door to the tarmac, Emma sensed her life was about to change. Forever.

Chapter 3

Emma was surprised that Khalid insisted she be the AC—air commander, on the Apache that was to be flown to Bagram. She stowed her bag in a side slot of the combat helicopter. Mounting the helo, Emma was strapped into the back cockpit in no time. She tried to ignore Khalid's charisma as he climbed into the cockpit in front of her. The sergeant helped her and then tended to Khalid's needs. A sudden shiver of warning went up her spine. The whole base was on high alert because of the attack.

Looking around, lips compressed, Emma saw the remains of charred, still-smoking helicopter that the Taliban had destroyed with a grenade launcher. To her left, several Humvees contained Special Forces who were still looking for the terrorists who committed the offense. Something was wrong....

* * *

Malik lay on his belly, the binoculars to his eyes. He studied the Apache combat helicopter, more interested than usual in the pilots. Actually, one pilot. A snarl issued softly from between his full, thick lips. Allah had blessed him! There was his sworn enemy, Khalid Shaheen, in the front seat of the Apache. Mind spinning, Malik watched intently.

So, Shaheen was back in the northern provinces? Malik had his spies and they kept him somewhat updated on his enemy's whereabouts. The last Malik had been told, Khalid was in Helmand Province flying Apaches against his brothers in the Taliban. Malik knew where Shaheen lived in Kabul. He and his upstart, rebellious sister, Kinah, could be found at their family home from time to time. Was that where he was going? A hundred questions ranged through Malik's traplike mind.

"My lord," Ameen whispered near his ear, "it's time to move away. Troops are coming."

Malik growled a response; he didn't want to leave, but he knew he must. Those ground troops would have dogs with them and dogs would find them. Tucking his binoculars away, he got to his feet.

"Where to, my lord?" Ameen asked.

"A change of plans," he told the teenage soldier. "We're going to Kabul...."

Thirty minutes after completing the flight checklist, Emma had taken the Apache off the tarmac. The shaking and shuddering was familiar and soothing to her. She'd felt the Taliban nearby. She'd not seen them, but she instinctively knew they were close. Emma wondered if Khalid was testing her flight skills. After all, he'd been in Apaches for four years and she had only one year of combat beneath her belt.

At eight thousand feet under a sunny April-afternoon sky, Emma relaxed to a degree. Still, she was tense about going to Shaheen's home. This was out of normal military protocol. She had no experience with Afghans except in the villages, and Shaheen was much more powerful than those people who survived in the wild mountains along the border.

"Do you like dogs?" Khalid asked through the intercom.

Emma scowled. Now, what was this all about? Shaheen had the ability to rock her world. "Dogs?" What did dogs have to do with them? It was the last conversation she would think of having with this pilot. If nothing else, Khalid was turning out to be one surprise after another.

"Yes, dogs."

"Why are we talking about them?" Emma demanded, automatically looking around outside the cockpit.

"So you will be well-prepared when I open the door to my family's villa. My father raises some of the finest salukis in the world. Two years ago, he gifted me with Ayesha, a female with a black coat, white chest and cinnamon-colored legs and underbelly. My father gave her to me shortly after Najela was murdered. The dog helped me in ways I can't explain. She gave me back my life and brought me through the darkest tunnel with her love and devotion."

Not wanting to be swayed by his words, Emma swung her gaze across the instrument panel out of ingrained habit. The chances of attack were minimal, but she never completely let down her guard. "I'm sure I can handle your dog," she said, laughing. "Hey, it's kinda nice to have a dog around. We have a few base mongrels that we feed, but they're wild and you can't pet them. I'm always leaving scraps outside my tent for a black dog that comes by every night looking for something to eat. If I try to walk toward him, he takes off at a run and disappears. I've learned to put the food in a pie tin, close up my tent and not try to befriend him."

"Ah, you are a true lover of animals, too. That speaks highly of your heart, Captain Cantrell." Khalid's job in the front seat was to keep watch on the two video screens in front of him. There wasn't much chance of attack at this altitude, but you could never quite relax on the job. He was intensely curious about Emma, but hesitant. She was a by-the-book military officer. Giving her a rose had been a misstep. Khalid had hoped it would open a door to signify a good, working relationship, but Emma had taken it all wrong.

Worriedly, Khalid realized he'd set them on an awkward course with one another. And he desperately needed a woman pilot who could fulfill his vision to inspire the little Afghan girls. How to fix what had already gone wrong? She didn't sound very interested in his dog story, either.

Brows dipping, Khalid asked himself why he was so interested in Emma. She was a tough military combat pilot. Her record showed her abilities and fine skills. He got the feeling she really didn't like him at all and was just tolerating the situation. Maybe it was the attack this morning that had set her off. He shrugged his shoulders to ease them of tension. He simply didn't know how to deal with Captain Cantrell. Most people melted beneath his charm and sincere smile. But all it did to her was make her retreat, becoming stony and unreadable. As his U.S. military pilot friends would say, he'd blown it.

How to repair things between them? He'd spent years in the States being educated. He knew Americans. Khalid sighed. Emma made him feel like a joyous young man. That wouldn't work here. Khalid turned his attention to the screens and did an automatic scan, looking for possible SAM missiles. Taking a deep breath, he hoped what he was about to say wouldn't turn her away from him.

"I did a little research on you, Captain. Your family has a history of service," Khalid said.

Something had told her that as easygoing as Khalid appeared, he was a man who researched the details of any situation.

"Yes, the Trayherns have given military service to their country since they arrived here two hundred years earlier. My mother, Alyssa, was a Trayhern before she married Clay Cantrell, my father. It's a tradition for the Trayhern children, if they want, to go into the military of their choice and serve at least four to six years, depending upon whether they are officers or enlisted. We're very proud of our family's service and sacrifice," Emma said tensely.

"You should be. I'm very impressed, Captain. That's very Sufi-like, to serve others. My Irish mother would say it is what you owe to life. That we all owe others. We can't live life alone or separate ourselves from the poor and suffering."

Emma moved uncomfortably around in her seat. Talking to Khalid was like a minefield. She didn't really want to know anything about him. All she wanted was to do a good job on this mission and then get back to base camp, her military record clean once more. Clearing her throat, she said, "She sounds like a wonderful, giving person much like my mother, Alyssa."

"My mother has red hair and brown eyes," Khalid informed her. "She's an obstetrician and she has set up clinics throughout Afghanistan with the help of her church's ongoing donations. She has spent from age twenty-eight to the present here in Afghanistan. The good she has done is tremendous. I think you must know many Afghan women die during childbirth. Most women have an average of seven children. And one out of eight women dies in childbirth. Very few villages have health care available to them."

"That's so sad," Emma said as she banked the Apache to start a descent into Bagram. They had left the mountains, and now the dry, yellow plains where Bagram air base sat spread out before them. "I can't believe how many women lose their lives. It's horrific. I heard from Major Klein, my C.O., that there are Sufi medical doctors who have devoted their lives to the villages along the border."

"Ah yes," Khalid said, brightening, "Doctors Reza and Sahar Khan. I've met them a number of times. My mother works with them through her mission. They are truly brave. Because they are Sufi and giving service and trying to help the border villages from the farthest south to the farthest north of our country, the Taliban constantly tries to kill them. The only way the Taliban keeps hold over our people is through fear, retaliation and murder." His voice deepened. "Reza and Sahar have a strong calling. As Sufis they render aid and help wherever they can. Reza is a doctor of internal medicine and surgery. His sister, Sahar, is an obstetrician. I cannot tell you how many women's lives she has saved. They drive a Land

Rover that is beaten up and very old. I have offered to buy them a new one, but they said no."

"Why?"

"Because it would stand out like a sore thumb and the Taliban could find them more easily. In January of each year they start in the south of Afghanistan and then they drive along the border from village to village offering their medical services for free. By the time June comes, they have reached the northernmost part of our country, and they turn around and drive back down through the same villages. Each village gets visits twice a year, except of course, the most northern one, but they stay two weeks there to ensure everyone in that village is properly cared for."

"Who funds them?"

"I do," Khalid said. "I also coordinate with several American charities who give them medical supplies. Money's only importance is how it is spent to help others."

Emma said nothing, easing the Apache down to three thousand feet. "That's gutsy, and talk about sacrifice, those two doctors should get medals of valor." Obviously, this officer was generous with his money. Brody's bragging came to mind. Was Khalid bragging to impress her? Something told her he was, and she became even more wary.

Snorting, Khalid said, "The central government refuses to acknowledge their sacrifice to our people. They aren't very happy about Sufis, either. They barely tolerate them."

"Why are Sufis so targeted?" Emma asked. She saw Bagram air base coming up. It was huge and lay on the flat, dirt plain with Kabul about ten miles away. The city glittered in the sunlight. Kabul wasn't that safe, either. The Taliban had infiltrated the city and it was dangerous for any American, military or civilian, to be there without an armed escort.

"What mystic group hasn't been a target?" he asked rhetorically. "Ah, Bagram is below us. We'll be on the ground in a few minutes."

She heard veiled excitement in his voice. Emma paid attention to the air controller giving her landing instructions. Tension accumulated in her shoulders. She really didn't want to go to Shaheen's home. It felt like a trap to her, but Khalid was her boss. If he wrote her up for a glowing commendation after this six-month gig, she'd have a revived military career in front of her. And Emma wanted nothing more than to expunge that black eye she'd given to the Trayhern family, once and for all.

"Come," Khalid said, gesturing toward a large parking lot inside Bagram air base. "My car is over there."

The roar of jets taking off shook the air until it vibrated around them. As Emma walked at Khalid's side, her bag in her left hand, dark aviator glasses in place, she felt nervous. At the Ops desk where they'd filled out the required landing flight forms, everyone seemed to know him. He had joked and laughed with many of the enlisted personnel behind the desk. His sincerity and concern for each of them was obvious. Emma saw how every man and woman glowed beneath his charisma. Brody Parker had done that, too. It seemed people who weren't as rich as he was were always enamored with him. Emma had realized later it had been because they knew he was rich.

As she walked down the line of cars, Emma reminded herself that Khalid was dangerous to her heart. He was far too likable a person. Frowning, she saw him take keys from his pocket and click them toward a Land

Rover. The vehicle was a dark green one that had plenty
of dents and scrapes all over its body. In fact, there was
a lot of dirt and mud on it, too.

"Hop in," Khalid invited, opening the rear so they
could throw all their flight gear into the back.

Emma slid into the passenger side and put on the
seat belt. The dashboard was dusty. She wondered if
Khalid's home looked like his car.

Tension thrummed through Khalid as he drove
through the security gates of Bagram after showing
his identity card. "Have you been in the city of Kabul
before?"

Emma watched him drive with care. "Yes, I have,
but only with an Afghan escort on a day trip. When I
fly in here, I remain on base for safety reasons." He
looked around constantly. In fact, they both had their
side arms on the seat between them. She knew attacks
were frequent in Kabul. The road leading up to the base
was asphalted, but soon they were on another highway
with plenty of potholes to dodge. Heavy traffic came
and went from the busy main air base that served the
country.

"Not many Americans wander off Bagram," Khalid
murmured, nodding. "And with good reason. They are
targets. One day I hope that our country will be free of
the Taliban and you can see the beauty of it."

Emma was as alert as he was, keeping a hand on
her .45 pistol. Too many cars were attacked by the Taliban. That Khalid was a marked man only increased
the chances that they could be attacked.

Khalid motioned with his long hand toward the city.
"My parents' villa is on the outskirts, upon a small hill
ringed with thick, almost impenetrable brush. I also

employ guards at the base of the hill." He grimaced. "Unfortunately, anyone who is rich is an automatic target. But you will be safe at our compound. Ten-foot-high stucco walls completely surround our home. It's all one story so that it is hidden behind the walls. There is a metal gate at the entrance and a guard is always on duty. Each window has an ornamental grate across it to prevent break-ins. The front door is wrought iron, too."

"I don't know how anyone could live this way," Emma muttered. She saw Khalid give his characteristic shrug.

"We have generations of Afghans with PTSD, post-traumatic stress disorder. We all have it," he said, glancing at Emma. "It's just a question of how bad it is and how much of your life it stains."

Shaking her head, she said, "I've always valued being born in the U.S., but after being over here and seeing the poverty, the murders and constant threats that your people live under, I feel very, very fortunate in comparison."

"Yes, I was grateful for my years I spent in your country," Khalid said. He swung off on a dirt road that led up to a small knoll in the distance. The road was rough and rutted because of the spring rains. "The seven years I spent there Americanized me a great deal." He flashed her a sudden grin. "I really miss American French fries."

For a moment, Emma's heart melted. His smile was dazzling and she felt the full effects of it. "You seem very Americanized. Your English is flawless and you use our slang, Captain Shaheen."

Khalid drove around some potholes, the ruts deep, dry and hard. The Land Rover crept forward. "I love

America. I love what she stands for. I want my people to have a democracy just like yours. While I studied at Princeton, I truly understood what democracy was for the first time. I brought my passion back here and Kinah and I have worked ever since to bring our country closer to that vision we hold in our hearts."

"It's a vision worth holding," Emma agreed, hearing the fierce, underlying emotion in Khalid's voice. There was no question he loved this desert country. Emma studied the rounded hill coming up. The shrubs were thick and dark green from the base up to the top of greenish-brown stucco walls. The color of the walls blended into the earthen landscape. If she hadn't been looking for the walls, she probably would have missed them. She wondered what it was like for Khalid and his sister to grow up here under such constant threats. Her admiration for him grew.

The bearded guard at the front entrance opened the gate and saluted Khalid. The sentry stepped aside as Khalid returned the salute and drove the Land Rover into the three-car garage. The automatic door started downward as he eased out of the vehicle.

Emma followed suit. They gathered their gear and he took her to a side door.

"Prepare yourself," he said, a glimmer in his eyes as he opened the door.

Emma didn't have time. The dog, a saluki, Ayesha, rushed out the door, barking joyously around them, her thick, long tail wagging with happiness. It was impossible for Emma to remain stiff and stoic. Khalid had been right: Ayesha would lick her fingers off her hand if allowed to do so.

Wiping her wet fingers on the side of her flight suit,

Emma and Ayesha bounded over the white-tiled hall
with its cool, pale green walls. Khalid's laughter and
playfulness around the saluki automatically made Emma's heart pound a little harder. Truly, Ayesha was a
faithful companion to the Apache pilot who petted her
fondly as she danced and pranced at his side.

The hall flowed in three different directions. Khalid pointed to the left. "Your suite is the second door
on the left. My dear housekeeper, Rasa, has promised
you will be comfortable while you visit us. If there's
anything you need, just press the buzzer on the inside
of the door, and she will come to assist you."

"And you, Captain?" Emma asked.

"I'm going to my suite, get out of my uniform, grab
a shower and I'll meet you in our courtyard in an hour.
There's much to show you before we have dinner at
8:00 p.m. tonight."

Dinner. Her spirit sank. Emma didn't want to spend
too much time with this pilot. He was too mesmerizing. Ayesha bounced around Khalid, her tongue loll-
ing out of her long muzzle, her dark brown eyes alight
with worship for her master. "I'll see you later," she
said, more tersely than she meant it to be. Emma wished
mightily for a bathtub, but they weren't to be found
anywhere. At base camp, there were only showers. Her
flight boots thunked with a slight echo down the highly
polished white-, brown- and orange-tiled hall.

The door to her suite was ajar. Emma pushed it
open and walked in. What she saw made her gasp with
delight. The suite looked like a five-star hotel room!
Across the king-sized bed was a gorgeous lavender-
and-white star quilt. And on the wall above it hung an
art fabric collage of a Rocky Mountain meadow filled

with colorful wildflowers. Setting her bags on the bed, Emma looked around, dazed by the quality of the furniture, the decorations and the sense of peace that filled the room.

Her mahogany dresser was an antique. She ran her hand across the polished surface and figured it had to be from either North America or perhaps Europe. As Emma opened one of the drawers, she noticed the dovetailing on each side, another sign of quality craftsmanship. She tucked away her few clothes, keeping out her silky pink pajamas and her own washcloth. Emma had learned a long time ago to carry one with her since many countries didn't provide them.

The pale lavender walls matched the beautiful quilt on her bed. Fresh flowers in a brass vase adorned the mahogany coffee table that stood between a small purple sofa and a wing chair. Soft music played from a radio. Doilies and a long embroidered runner lay across the top of the dresser. The furnishings gave the room a 1930s flavor. She felt as if she'd walked back in time to an era when everything was made by hand. Even the rugs on either side of the bed seemed to have been handmade from scraps of cloth that had been wound into ropes and then anchored together.

Walking through another open door, Emma sighed. With a Jacuzzi bathtub, the bathroom was as large as her bedroom! She gazed at it longingly. Mentally, she blessed Khalid's westernized parents for their thoughtfulness toward their visitors. There was also a large glass-and-tile shower. The blue tiles on the walls were hand-painted with colorful wildflowers. Emma recognized some of them, others she did not. She walked closer to study them. Some were from the U.S., for sure. Others were jungle flowers and orchids.

A washcloth and a bright yellow fuzzy towel had been folded on a nearby table. Lavender-colored soap sat in a white ceramic dish. She picked up a bar and inhaled the fragrance. It was jasmine, one of her favorite scents. Did Khalid know that? How could he? Emma replaced the soap and turned, suddenly feeling horribly trapped by the assignment. First things first. Emma noticed a range of hair products near the white porcelain sink. She would draw a luxurious bath, soak and then wash her hair in the shower. Still in mild shock over the plush suite, she once again reminded herself that Khalid was a man full of surprises.

What next? Emma wasn't sure. She quickly shed her boots and uniform and turned on the faucet to fill the Jacuzzi tub. As she sat on the edge of the tub and swirled her fingers through the warm water, she felt her heart shrink with fear and dread. What if Khalid made a move on her? Emma could swear he liked her, but so far, he hadn't done anything off limits. The rose told her he was flirting. Did he see her as nothing more than a woman to chase and try to catch in the next six months? Brody had done something similar; he'd chased her for four months before she'd agreed to a date.

Careful. You can't get involved with him. You have your family to think of first. You have to redeem the Trayhern's good name. Never mind Khalid is warm, personable, humorous and kind. Or rich. Groaning, Emma closed her eyes for a moment. This mission was much worse than she'd ever realized.

Chapter 4

"Come," Khalid invited Emma as she walked into the spacious kitchen, "let's go to the garage. I have my storehouse in there." He tried to ignore the fact that she was now in civilian clothes, her red hair still damp from the shower and falling like fiery lava around her proud shoulders. Instead of a baggy olive-green flight suit, Emma now wore a tangerine-colored T-shirt with dark brown trousers. On her, they looked good. Too good.

"I'll follow," Emma said firmly, gesturing for him to take the lead. Emma could smell the wonderful odor of lamb cooking with spices in the oven. With how Khalid's light blue polo shirt showed the breadth of his chest, Emma kept distance between them. He was just too much of a temptation.

Khalid opened the door to the storehouse and stepped aside to allow Emma to enter. He turned on the lights.

Emma halted and stared around the cavernous three-car garage that held only the Land Rover right now. Along the walls in neat rows were thousands of books and boxes of educational items such as crayons, pencils, pens and notebooks.

"This is our vision," Khalid said, closing the door and walking into the room. "Kinah and I bought state-of-the-art printing machines. We gathered a group of Afghan widows and trained them to print out the books for the children." He went to one aisle, pulled out a book and opened it. "We've not only employed six women who had no way to earn any money. Now they are our printers and publisher. The books are written by the best authorities in education, according to Kinah. She worked a year to produce Pashto-written texts and pictures from grades one through twelve. It was a momentous challenge."

Emma nodded but remained distant. She made sure there was plenty of space between them. She heard the pride in Khalid's voice for his innovating and hardworking sister. "This is a major undertaking."

Khalid nodded and slid the book back onto the shelf. "Yes, it is." He gazed down at Emma and had a maddening urge to tangle his fingers in her damp red hair, which curled softly around her face. Did she know how fetching she looked with that coverlet of copper freckles across her nose and cheeks? Emma wore no makeup, but didn't need any. She was beautiful just as she was, Khalid's heart whispered to him. But since he was marked for death, there was no way to fall in love with any woman, not even someone as tempting as Emma Cantrell. He focused on showing Emma the large room of supplies. "Once we begin Operation Book Worm, all the supplies will come from this location. They will be marked, packed by another group of widows and then sent by truck to Bagram for us. From there, we put them aboard our CH-47 and fly them out to the villages."

"And your sister Kinah?" Emma asked. "Where is she in all of this?"

"Right now my sister is working with leaders of the first ten villages along the border where we will set up the schools. She's taking a roster of each child, his or her age, and how many children will be in each school." Khalid said fondly, "My sister is a tempest. She never sits still. Kinah's a fierce warrior for peace and the education of our people. She's a fighter who has vision, strength, intelligence and courage."

"She'd have to have all those things to do what she's doing," Emma agreed grimly, looking around in awe at the room. "Her life is always on the line out there. I'm sure you know that."

Darkness came to Khalid's normally sparkling blue eyes.

"Too aware. I have hired two of the best security guards I can find, but I still worry about her. She refuses to wear a flak jacket, which concerns me. We have ancient enemies out there." His voice lowered. "I know Malik is hunting us, Emma. He's just waiting to spring a trap to capture either or both of us. I worry it will happen when Kinah is alone and unable to defend herself...."

"And yet, you have said Asad Malik has promised your death." Emma looked around. "Where are *your* bodyguards?"

Khalid shrugged. "Now, you sound like my sister, Captain. She is always on me to have them."

"Thanks for the tour, Khalid." Emma sounded less military and slightly breathless. That irritated her a whole lot. Emma felt an unexpected yearning for him that was like a flowing stream that turned into a wild river within her. Khalid was too good to be true. Brody had never been a humanitarian and that's where they were different. In Emma's eyes and heart, Khalid was a true hero, fighting to lift his people out of abject poverty. He had the money, the position and resources to make it happen. There was a generosity so deep within him that it made Emma stand in awe of Khalid. How many men had she met that had all these qualities? Not many. All the more reason to remain at arm's length from this fierce Afghan warrior.

"You're welcome, Captain Cantrell. Now," he said, glancing down at his watch, "I believe Rasa will have our dinner ready for us."

Emma walked toward the door, dreading the meal. Hopefully, she asked, "Are you going to split us up? I'll eat in the women's quarter and you in the men's?" In the Muslim world, men and women ate separately.

Khalid laughed and walked quickly to open the door before she got to it. "No. You are American and I honor the fact that Americans sit as families together. We'll eat in the dining room." He saw a wariness in her eyes and added, "Does this meet with your approval?" No longer could he afford to assume anything about this woman.

Emma kept her sedate demeanor. "This is not military protocol, Captain Shaheen. To tell you the truth, I'm a little uncomfortable with it all." There, the truth was out. Emma noticed the genuine concern in his face and how much her words had hurt him. She knew how important it was for an Afghan to be a host. "But I'll deal with it."

"Yes?" Khalid said hopefully. "For I have no wish to offend you again."

"I'm not offended." Emma hoped she'd smoothed the situation over enough so they could have a quick dinner and she could make a run for her suite.

Asad Malik arrived in Kabul at 9:00 p.m. He and his men had met with a local Taliban sheik at a village outside Camp Bravo. He'd loaned them two pickup trucks so that they could speed their way to Kabul. The stars were bright and beautiful above him as they pulled up at the bottom of the hill where the Shaheen family home sat.

They got out of their pickups and quietly assembled near Malik. He put on a special pair of night goggles stolen from an American soldier during a heated battle. He liked these goggles because, suddenly, night became day. Everything was green and grainy, but he could see. This was the first time he'd ever been this close to the Shaheen estate. As he used binoculars and began a survey of the home, he realized it was going to be very hard to attack.

Ameen, his second in command, came up to him. "My lord, is there a way we can assault the home?"

Malik growled under his breath, "There's heavy brush all around the hill. At the top, there is a ten-foot wall. And on top of the wall is concertina barbed wire." Dropping the binoculars, he handed them to the young man, who wore a worn brown turban on his head. "Stay here. I'm going to look around. With these goggles, I'll be able to see much more." He picked up his rifle and melted into the night, leaving his men standing quietly by the trucks.

Emma walked down the hallway and back into the kitchen. A short, black-haired woman in a long dark blue gown stood at the oven. She wore oven mitts as she pulled out the lamb and placed it on the counter. When Emma saw the housekeeper's face she bit down on her lower lip. The whole left side was terribly twisted and scarred, as if severely burned. What had happened to her? Emma had no time to think about this because Khalid cupped his hand beneath her right elbow and guided her into a huge dining room with its crystal chandelier hanging over a long, rectangular mahogany table.

Once out of earshot, Emma whispered, "Captain Shaheen, what happened to Rasa? Her face is horribly scarred."

Khalid pulled out the chair at the end of the table for her. He dropped his voice. "Rasa lived in a border village. She was fighting to get a school started for girls. Rasa was well-educated and a fighter for women's rights."

Emma sat down and looked up to see darkness in Khalid's eyes. He took a chair on her right and sat down. "Malik, our enemy, heard of Rasa's efforts and he brought his thugs into the village. They found her and poured acid all over her face and told her to stop thinking about educating girls. She was told that women were more stupid than the donkeys that hauled the loads of firewood into the village."

Emma was horrified. "My God, I'm so sorry for Rasa."

He picked up her gold linen napkin and handed it to her. "Rasa lost the sight in her left eye, too. When my father, who was trying to bring education to the villages so long ago, found Rasa, he brought her here, to Kabul. He paid for all of her medical needs. At that time, Rasa was only eighteen years old. She was so grateful that she begged my father to allow her to be the permanent housekeeper for our family. She wanted to repay my father for all his generosity toward her. Rasa remains blind in that eye to this day, and there is nothing that could be done for her. But her face is much improved over what it was at first."

"This isn't right, Khalid. Malik is evil."

Opening his napkin, Khalid nodded. "He's a murderer. One day, I will meet him on the plain of combat."

Startled by his words, Emma realized she was seeing the warrior side of Khalid for the first time. He was a combatant now, his eyes narrowed and dark, his full, expressive mouth thinned with tension. Emma felt the chill of his rage. The light-hearted Khalid had disappeared. Now she understood a little more why this man had been chosen by the U.S. Army for Apache combat helicopter training. This aviator was a consummate hunter, like the legendary and mystical snow leopards who lived in the Kush mountains.

Taking a shaky breath, Emma asked under her breath, "Does Rasa know English?"

"No." Khalid gave her a pleading look. "When Rasa comes to serve us, please do not look into her eyes. She never meets your gaze. Her eyes are always downcast and she speaks so softly that, at times, I have a hard time hearing her."

Heart aching for Rasa, Emma felt how the woman's

spirit had been broken by Malik's attack upon her. "Of course," she promised. "I don't wish to make her uncomfortable, Captain."

Khalid nodded and looked toward the arched entrance that led to the kitchen. "Rasa is painfully aware that no man would ever take her as his bride. She hides beneath a burka so that no one can see her damaged face when she shops in Kabul for us. I have tried over the years to convince her she is not ugly, that she has a beautiful heart and soul. And that any man would overlook her physical face for the unscarred beauty of her heart," he sighed, "but she will not believe me. I have brought potential suitors here for her, but she shuns them." Shrugging, Khalid said, "I've given up at this point."

"Is Rasa happy here?" Emma asked, touched by Khalid's obvious grief over Rasa's suffering. He seemed to hold back unknown emotions.

"Very happy. She has adopted us as her family." Khalid saw Rasa coming from the kitchen with a tray of steaming food. "We'll speak later," he said in a quiet tone.

"Of course," Emma said.

Malik crept silently along the road leading to the estate. Crouching, his AK-47 in his right hand, the butt resting on the earth, he eyed two turbaned guards at a ten-foot wrought-iron black gate. They weren't like most security guards. No, these two bearded men were alert and looking around. Malik knew he was well-hidden by the brush on the dirt road.

After waiting five more minutes, Malik crept into the brush. It was thick but negotiable. He was tall and wiry and able to step softly and not raise alarm. Sitting down, he observed the gate head-on. The guards never left it. He could hear them talking in the distance. They carried AK-47s with two bandoliers of ammo criss-crossing their powerful chests. Judging from how they carried themselves, these were Afghan warriors and not the drivel from Kabul who couldn't fight a fly.

Slowly turning his head, Malik decided to continue to move slowly and quietly around the hill to see if there was another entrance to the estate.

"And so," Khalid said, pointing to the papers spread out on the table after dinner, "this is the full concept of our efforts."

It was nearly 10:00 p.m. as Emma pored over all the information about Operation Book Worm. "This is impressive." She glanced at Khalid, who sat to her right. "How long did it take you two to figure this out?"

"Four years," Khalid murmured. Emma's hair was dry now and curled in crimson around her freckled face. Did she know how beautiful and utterly natural a woman she was? Khalid itched to understand her on a more personal level. He knew she was single because he had looked at her personnel jacket. She had been suggested as the right person to partner with him on this effort. And she was.

It was on the tip of Khalid's tongue to ask if she had a significant other. Just because Emma was single didn't mean she was available. And why was he even thinking in that direction? He could be killed at any moment by Asad Malik. Unconsciously, Khalid touched his chest where his heart resided. Was he finished grieving for his fiancée? Was he returning to life as a man with yearnings and needs? Was his wounded heart truly healed and now calling for him to find another woman who could fulfill his dreams? But that could never happen. Khalid would never put another woman in the sights of Malik.

Emma saw the odd look in Khalid's eyes. What was he thinking? She nervously gathered up the papers and handed them over to him. "It's late," she said firmly. "I know we're getting up early tomorrow. Kinah will be here at 0800? Right?"

"Yes, my sister is flying in tomorrow morning. She'll have the information we require. Then, the widows will be driven over here and, based upon Kinah's assessments, we'll get busy filling orders for each village and boxing them up. Then, you and I will trailer them to the CH-47 assigned to us at Bagram Air Force Base."

Emma rose. "Sounds good, Captain. I'll see you tomorrow morning." All evening she had felt as if Khalid wanted a warm, intimate conversation with her. Oh, nothing overt. Subtle, just as Brody had been. Emma rose from the table and smoothed her slacks.

Khalid quickly stood with her. There was confusion in Emma's green gaze. Why? There was a wariness in her expression as if he had somehow, once more, breached officer-to-officer protocol. Should he apologize? Khalid had treated her with courtesy and kept all conversations about the mission, nothing personal, during dinner. He didn't want to chase Emma off this operation by unmilitary behavior toward her.

Malik hissed beneath his breath. There was no entrance other than the one gate to Shaheen's estate. Making his way back to his men who were patiently crouched and holding their weapons, he took off the goggles. Ameen approached, a hopeful look on his darkened face.

"I will not throw away our lives on trying to get into that castle," he told his men. "I swear blood vengeance on Khalid Shaheen, but this will not be the place to settle that score." Lifting his hand, he gestured sharply to the trucks. "Mount up. We're going back to the base camp. We will watch Shaheen's movements from there and figure out what he's up to now."

By the time Emma got up and dressed in a fresh flight uniform, Kinah and Khalid were already in the dining room having breakfast. Emma had slept hard. She realized how safe she felt in this villa compared to the base camp where mortars would sometimes be lobbed at them by the Taliban. Rubbing her eyes, she smiled a welcome as Kinah rose to greet her.

"Ah, you are the red-haired pilot Khalid spoke of," Kinah said, getting up, her hand extended to meet Emma. "I'm Kinah Shaheen. Khalid's little sister." She grinned mischievously and glanced back at her brother who sat at the table.

Emma grasped Kinah's long, graceful hand. She had nearly waist-length black hair shot through with red strands, green eyes that Emma was sure came from her Irish mother and full lips. Kinah was dressed in a traditional black Muslim gown.

"Hi, Kinah. I'm Captain Emma Cantrell. Nice to meet you."

Kinah stepped back and placed her hands on her hips. "Khalid, shame on you! You did not tell me how lovely this American woman pilot is!" She gave Emma a wink.

Emma decided Kinah was every bit the trickster that Khalid was. It must be that wicked Irish sense of humor in their DNA.

Dressed in his flight suit, Khalid made sounds of protest. "Beloved sister, Captain Cantrell is here as an envoy from the States. Why would I speak of her obvious beauty?" For once, he wished outgoing Kinah would not embarrass Emma. She might bolt and refuse to work on the mission.

As she walked to the table, Emma noticed that a third breakfast setting was there for her. They had not yet eaten and apparently were waiting for her to arrive; such were their manners. "I don't know about you, but I'd love some chai. I need to wake up," she told them, sitting down. Kinah sat at the head of the table this time, her brother on her right and Emma on the left.

"Indeed," Kinah said with a smile, "I believe Rasa is fixing three cups of chai as we speak." She reached over and gripped Emma's lower arm. "We are truly grateful for your presence, Captain Cantrell."

"Call me Emma." There was such warmth in the woman that Emma found herself climbing out of her military decorum.

"Wonderful," Kinah said. "I don't like standing on protocol, either. Please call me Kinah. When we're out in the field together, you must consider yourself a part of our family." She gestured to herself and her brother.

"Well…" Khalid choked, giving his vivacious sister a pained look. "We're in the military, Kinah. I can't just call her by her first name out there."

"Pooh!" Kinah waggled her finger into Khalid's face. "We must appear bonded and friends, brother. After all, it was my idea to bring in an American woman pilot."

Emma saw Rasa come, head down, eyes trained on the floor, bearing a tray with three steaming cups of chai. She could smell the cinnamon and nutmeg fragrance wafting upward in the steam. Kinah's words caught her attention.

"Oh?"

Kinah took her chai and warmly thanked Rasa, who murmured back in Pashto. "I believe," Kinah said, resting her elbows on the table, the chai in her hands, "that little girls out in these villages need to see two strong women from two different cultures." Her eyes sparkled and she said in a whisper, "How else are my little girls to know they can dream as big as their hearts? They see me as an educator. They see you as a woman in the military who can fly a helicopter, who is an officer and who is fully capable. You see," she said, sipping her chai delicately, "little girls in the villages are often told they can't dream of being anything. They see you and me, Emma. They will get it very quickly that they *can* dream! They *can* set a goal through learning to read and write."

Moved by Kinah's passion, Emma said, "I hadn't thought of it in that way, but you're right. Leading by example."

Nodding, Kinah said, "Exactly. I expect you to give a little talk at some point, after we have the schools set up. I would like you to share how you became a pilot. What made you yearn to fly? What dreams did you have as a little girl that fueled your desire to fly a helicopter? You see," Kinah said, smiling softly, "little girls have wings of imagination. You can instill them to imagine whatever it is they desire to become."

Emma smiled a little and sipped her chai. Clearly,

Kinah was a force of nature. Compared to Khalid, she was a ball of energy, hardly able to sit still, her hands always gesturing and her eyes fierce with passion. Khalid paled in comparison to his dynamo sister. The fact that Khalid was the rudder to Kinah's ship of dreams made Emma respect him even more. She could see the doting, loving look on Khalid's face for his beloved sister. She wondered if Khalid took after his Sufi father and Kinah her Irish mother. Clearly, the fire belonged to Kinah.

Emma could understand why Khalid adored his sister. Kinah, although in traditional Afghan dress, was far more a feminist than Emma ever had been. "I wonder if you picked up on your Irish mother's DNA? You're a missionary of a different sort," Emma said. "Is it not a religious calling as much as a humanitarian effort that drives you?"

"Precisely," Kinah said, nodding her head, her dark curls moving across her back. "I may only be small but I am a giant who stands over most others because my heart is connected to my dreams." She gave Khalid a warm, loving look. "And my Sufi brother knows well that when our hearts are aligned with our passions, we can accomplish miracles."

Once Rasa completed delivering their breakfast, Kinah called her over, stood up and gave the housekeeper a warm hug and thanked her. Rasa was bright-red, obviously uneasy and quickly scuttled back to the safety of her kitchen.

Kinah sat down. "You see, women like Rasa deserve more from life than having acid thrown in their face by those bastards."

Emma nearly choked on her eggs. Kinah's language startled her.

Khalid groaned again and gave Emma a look of apology for his sister's bad language.

Kinah merely laughed and ate heartily.

Emma bowed her head and ate her food. She felt caught up in a whirlwind in Kinah's presence. But it was a good one. Now, she grasped Khalid's worry for his fierce, passionate sister. And given that Asad Malik hated this family, Emma understood why. If Malik ever encountered Kinah, it would be a battle of life and death. Kinah was no wilting lily. She would fight to the death rather than allow Malik to rape her, cut her throat or throw acid in her face. No, Malik would have met his equal and Emma bet that Kinah would win the day, if not the war itself.

Chapter 5

Emma tried to still her excitement and fear as she pi-
loted the CH-47 toward their first village. The vibration
rippling through the bird soothed her. The April morning
was crisp and clear. They had left Bagram with boxes
of educational supplies. In the rear, on the nylon seats
along the fuselage, sat Kinah. The load master, Tech. Sgt.
Brad Stapleton, all of twenty-two years old, also sat in
the back. He would be responsible for unloading their
supplies once they arrived at the border village. To her
left was Khalid, her copilot on this mission. They had
just flown past her black ops base camp, and were now
heading toward Asmar and then on to their final destination, Do Bandi.

Asmar was a larger village on a dirt road and further away from the border with Pakistan. Do Bandi was
closer to the border and had been protected by A-teams,
army Special Forces comprised of ten men. These teams

lived in the village, rotating out every thirty days when a new team came in to replace it. Khalid and Kinah felt this village was safer than most and a good one to cut their teeth on. Emma couldn't disagree. There were a lot of logistics and this was their first trial-and-error run.

"Do the village elders know we're flying in this morning?" Emma asked Khalid over the intercom.

"Yes. The A-team stationed there received permission from the chieftain two weeks ago for us to visit him." He flipped her a thumbs-up with his gloved hand. "It's a go." He grinned.

Khalid reminded her of an excited little boy. Emma wasn't sure who was more anticipatory: him or his restless, dynamic sister, Kinah. Neither had barely slept last night, they were so "charged up and ready to rock 'n' roll," as Khalid had put it this morning over breakfast. Emma had slept deeply and had had torrid dreams about Khalid. As a result, she'd awakened this morning in a sour mood. How to keep her boss at bay, do her job and not get involved were *her* logistical problems to solve.

Emma took the CH-47 down to one hundred feet as they approached the first range of snow-covered mountains. They would fly nap-of-the-earth, skimming at that low altitude up, down and around through mountain peaks and passes in order not to be fired upon by the Taliban. Any helicopter that didn't do this type of herky-jerky flying was a sure target for a Taliban rocket. Emma loved flying by the seat of her pants in the hulking, slow transport. The helo was sluggish, but it was steady beneath her hands, which gripped the cyclic and collective. Her intense focus was on skimming the earth and not getting nailed with a rock outcropping or brushing too close to a granite wall with the tips of the helo's rotors.

By the time they reached Do Bandi, which sat down

at the north end of a narrow, green valley, the armpits on Emma's flight suit were wet with sweat. Her heart pounded, adrenaline coursing through her bloodstream. Every time she had to fly nap-of-the-earth, the percentage of a crash rose exponentially. It was life-and-death flying, as she and her cohorts called it. But there was no other choice, was there?

As Emma brought the transport in for a landing outside the village, the twin rotors kicked up thick, choking dust that billowed hundreds of feet into the air. A huddled group of elders hid behind the mud huts to protect themselves from flying dust and debris. The CH-47 hunkered down and Khalid quickly shut down the engines. Emma saw the A-team coming out of the shadows of the line of huts. They were the first to approach. Emma ordered the load master over the intercom to open up the helo.

"I'm bringing down the ramp," Stapleton told her. "A-team is approaching on the starboard side."

"Roger," Emma murmured. She heard the grating roar echo through the helo as the ramp began to descend. The helo vibrated and groaned.

Khalid unstrapped. He wore a Kevlar vest and a .45 pistol holstered across his chest. Grinning, he felt higher than a kite flying off a hill in Kabul. Kite-running was something he'd done as a child. He'd never won, but the exhilaration of flying a kite and then chasing it was always thrilling. That was how he felt now: anticipation and joy.

Pulling off her helmet after unstrapping, Emma quickly ran her fingers through her flattened hair. She'd tied her shoulder-length hair into a knot at the nape of her neck. From her right thigh pocket she pulled out a dark green silk scarf known as a hijab, to wrap around her head. The hijab was a sign of respect to the Muslim Afghan people. Women did not go out into public without their heads being covered. She didn't mind fitting in, although Emma found it ironic in another way. Here she was, a modern-day combat helicopter pilot wearing a .45 strapped across her chest and a delicate, feminine scarf. It was April and cold so the scarf would keep her head warm.

"Ready?" Khalid asked, switching everything off in the cabin. His job as copilot was to power down the helo after it landed. His hands flew across the console, flipping switches and turning off the radios.

Emma turned in her seat. The groaning ramp came to a rest in the dirt with a "clunk."

"Ready," she said. She gave Kinah a thumbs-up, which meant it was all right to unstrap. The woman smiled and nodded, quickly removing the harness and getting to her feet. There were about fifty boxes in the hold of the transport. Only about half were actual school supplies. The rest were donations from America of clothing and shoes for the children. There were also medical items for the A-team sergeant who was responsible for the health of the villagers. Penicillin and other antibiotics were treasures out on the frontier and Emma knew their worth was as gold to the Afghan leaders. Antibiotics were desperately needed by all border villages, but few ever received them. Death by infection was a common way to die, unfortunately.

Kinah walked down the ramp. She was dressed in a black wool robe with a bright red hijab over her thick, dark hair. She shook the hand of the captain of the A-team and then walked quickly toward the wall of old men, the elders of the village.

Emma could see her breath and knew that at this altitude, the temperature was still at freezing. She would be glad to see May arrive and warmth grudgingly coming back to these mountain villages. She had pulled on her thick, warm green nylon jacket and left it unzipped in order to reach for her .45 in case she needed it. Although Khalid felt this was a highly secure village, no one took it on faith. The Taliban had made repeated attacks on it, only to be repulsed by the A-team stationed here. The BJS Apache combat helicopters spewed out their bullets and rockets at the enemy when called in by the A-team to chase them away.

Khalid came to her side as she stood just below the lip of the ramp. "Come, let me introduce you."

"Kinah already has the elders smiling," Emma observed, giving him a slight grin. "Your sister should run the United Nations."

Khalid laughed heartily. "My sister is a one-woman army, no question. She's like a laser-fired rocket—she knows her destination and nothing will stop her from reaching it." Khalid walked toward the huddled group near the huts. "I love my sister dearly. I worry about her, though. She disdains having guards to protect her."

Emma nodded. Today, Kinah had ordered her two Afghan guards to remain in Kabul. She did not want them near her on this first, important step of their education mission. And worse, Kinah would remain behind in the village after all the supplies were removed by the load master and the A-team members. She saw the worry banked in Khalid's eyes. Border villages were not safe and they never would be until the Afghanistan government turned its eyes and heart to them. These villages took the brunt of the Taliban attacks.

Emma stood at Khalid's side as he greeted the village elders in Pashto. She was glad she could understand what was being exchanged. There was much hand-shaking and touching of cheeks between Kinah, Khalid and the elders. Khalid ensured that Emma was introduced and she went through the same greetings with the elders. She could see that hope burned bright in their aged eyes. Not only was this village receiving protection from the A-team and the army from the air, but medicine was now available. The next step was education for their children. Emma knew that Afghans fiercely loved their children and wanted only the best for them.

Khalid turned to Emma. "Would you like to work with the wives of the leaders to distribute the clothes and shoes?"

"Of course," Emma said. Behind the elders was a group of their wives dressed in burkas, only eye slits to see through. The burkas were only worn outside; in their homes, they came off. Emma went and introduced herself. She led the four women to the supplies being stacked outside the CH-47. There were fifteen boxes of clothes and shoes. She watched as the women reverently touched the cardboard boxes. Their voices were low and filled with excitement.

Khalid was busy for the next hour. It was important to get the helo unloaded and back into the air. They couldn't remain on the ground for fear of a Taliban attack. He'd lost sight of Emma, who had gone into the village with the women. The elders had chosen an empty mud hut for the school, which was where Kinah had gone with the boxes and many curious, excited children.

Finishing up, Khalid walked down the rutted main street with huts on either side. A donkey pulled a creaking cart, the owner walking beside the gray beast. He was heading down the slope below the village in search of firewood. Dogs barked and ran excitedly up and down the street.

Khalid remained anxious since the Taliban were always nearby; it was just a question of when they would sneak in to try and attack these good people. Leaping over several ruts, Khalid walked to the house of the chieftain, sure that Emma would be there. The children were all lined up at the door, giggling and expectant. Some of the children had shoes, others didn't. Mothers with their wriggling, restive children stood patiently, hidden beneath their burkas, waiting for their turns to get their children fitted for shoes.

Khalid squeezed through the door, and Emma realized how handsome he looked. His short black hair was mussed, giving him a boyish look. She forced herself to remain neutral toward him by repeating Brody's name in her head.

"Ready?" Khalid called to her over the noise of the children. The wives of the leaders had opened many of the shoe boxes. A child sat in a chair as the mother tried on pair after pair until they found the size to fit her child's feet.

"Yes," Emma called over the din. She turned and warmly thanked one of the wives and told her she had to go. The woman smiled and pressed her burka-covered cheek against Emma's. One thing Emma had learned was that if one could befriend Afghan people, they were loyal to the death. A fierce love welled up in her chest. These villagers had courage to survive despite the terror of the Taliban always skulking nearby, hidden and deadly.

"How about a quick lunch at your base camp?" Khalid suggested on the way back to the unloaded helo.

She shrugged. There were so many fine lines to walk with him. Emma knew if she turned him down, he might get upset. For a C.O., an invitation was often an order. "Sure," she said.

"It's not a death sentence," Khalid teased her as they walked shoulder-to-shoulder down the main street. There was such struggle in Emma's face, and he tried to put her at ease.

"Captain, you have a dry sense of humor," Emma said.

He sighed and pressed his hand over his heart. "I've been so charged," he admitted, wishing for some relaxation between them.

Though she felt bad, Emma forced herself not to feel sorry for him. Khalid was her boss, pure and simple. She wanted high marks from him after this six-month gig. He obviously saw her reluctance.

Khalid performed the mandatory walk around the helo, part of his copilot duties. He would look for anything loose, oil leaking or flight surfaces that weren't secure. Emma went directly to the cockpit. Sitting down in the right-hand seat, she got ready to perform the takeoff checklist once Khalid finished his inspection tour outside the CH-47.

For the next five minutes, they were too busy to talk. Khalid called the black ops base and let them know they were taking off. Sometimes, an Apache helo would escort them, but today, there was high demand up north near Zor Barawul. The Taliban had launched another offensive against the village and it was currently being repulsed by a lot of air power. Their next stop tomorrow was that very village. Danger was always near.

"So," Khalid said as he sat opposite Emma in the chow hall back at base camp, "what would you tell the little girls about yourself?" He was obviously casting around for a way to ease the tension between them.

Emma had lifted her fork halfway to her mouth and stopped. She had spaghetti with meatballs. Khalid had the same, adding four pieces of buttered garlic bread, as well. She frowned momentarily, ate her food and considered his request. His question seemed innocent enough.

"I'd tell them that my family is a military one," she said between bites. "Nearly all the Trayhern children serve at least one tour in the service of their choice."

"So," Khalid said, relishing the warm garlic bread, "little girls would think that this career choice is expected?"

Emma shrugged. "I guess it is. My youngest sister, Casey, wasn't interested in being in the military. She joined the Forest Service and is a ranger currently stationed at Grand Tetons National Park in Wyoming."

"Is she considered an outcast?" Khalid wondered. While he hungered for a more personal connection, Khalid resisted his impulses.

Emma shook her head. "No, of course not. My Uncle Morgan Trayhern is fine with whatever we kids want to do with our lives. He loves Casey as much as any of the rest of us. His adopted daughter, Kamaria, never went into the military. She's a professional photographer and was a stringer for a number of top-flight news organizations around the world before she settled down at a Wyoming ranch."

"The girls would probably like to know how many children are in your family."

Emma smiled and explained. "Let's see. I'm the oldest. Then came the first set of twins, Athena and Juno. Two years after that, Casey and Selene. There are five daughters in our family. My mother loves the Greek myths so she named each one of us after a goddess. In my case, my middle name is Metis. She was a goddess and mother to Athena. Casey hated her name, Castalia, and so she shortened it to what it is now." Emma grinned. "My poor dad had five girls running under his feet, but my mom thought it was great," she laughed. "We're a very close, tight-knit family."

Khalid had watched her relax slightly and dared to ask a personal question. "Are you the only daughter with red hair?"

"No. My mother, Alyssa, said she has red hair and twins in her DNA. Two of my twin sisters, Casey and Selene, have red hair, too. Athena and Juno have my dad's black hair. Why?"

Khalid shared a slight smile with her. "I like the combination of your red hair and freckles. It makes you look like a young girl despite your being a mature woman, Captain."

Grimacing, Emma growled, "Don't remind me!" She sopped up some of the marinara sauce with her garlic bread. "All my life I've had to fight that little-girl look. I'll probably have to have gray hairs before anyone gets that I'm not a teenager."

Chuckling, Khalid felt his heart expand. He saw the righteous indignation gleaming in Emma's green eyes. Her mouth was beautifully shaped. He entertained the dream of someday kissing her, just to discover how soft and luscious she was. What was it about Emma that made him realize he was a man with needs once more?

As he twisted his spaghetti around his fork, Khalid asked, "They will probably ask if you have a man who loves you." He knew he was taking a chance with such a question. Emma's eyes flared with surprise. Khalid added a coaxing smile with his request, and her fine, thin red brows eased. He was glad he could influence her mood. Did he dare interpret that look to mean she was interested in him? Khalid felt torn. Half of him wanted a personal relationship with Emma. The other half did not want to put her life at risk.

Pushing her plate away, Emma picked up her mug of coffee. "No, not presently," she slowly admitted. And then the words leaped out of her mouth before she could stop them. "What about you?"

"I'm like you," Khalid offered.

"Because of Najela?" Emma guessed. She saw pain come to his eyes for a moment.

"Yes. I am just now realizing that I am ready to face life on the personal front again." Khalid did not say, *Because of you, I am inspired not only to live again, but to allow my heart to dream of you....*

Emma didn't know what to say. Clearly, Khalid liked her. She saw it in his hooded gaze, the desire banked in their blue depths. Paying strict attention to her coffee, she hoped the moment would pass.

"Now that we've started this mission," Khalid said,

"you are welcome to stay as my guest at our home in Kabul. You don't need to remain here at the base camp."

"No," Emma said with finality, "I want to stay here." *That way, you won't be so available.* She was afraid of herself. Afraid of what she might do because Khalid clearly desired her. The man was more than capable of sweet-talking her into something that couldn't— shouldn't—happen. Seeing the regret in his expression, Emma steeled herself against Khalid. The man oozed charm and sensuality.

"Well," Khalid said, setting his emptied plate to one side, "if you want, my home is always available to you. I know you loved the bath."

Groaning, Emma held up her hand. "Don't remind me! I'm a bathtub baby. I hate showers."

"Then," Khalid said, his voice low and smoky, "perhaps once a week you will consider coming to take advantage of the bath in my home?"

Emma managed a polite smile. "I don't think so, Captain Shaheen. It wouldn't look proper to the military. Thank you, though, for the offer." Emma couldn't afford to make him angry at her. Yet, she was walking the edge of the sword with this very available male pilot who was interested in her.

"Pity," he remarked. "Well, then I will fly the CH-47 back to Bagram alone. I will miss you, Captain Cantrell."

"Oh," Emma said lightly, standing and picking up her helmet bag, "I think you'll have plenty to keep you busy, Captain Shaheen."

Back at her tent, Emma threw her helmet bag on her cot. She turned to sit down in the camp chair at her desk.

Upset with herself, she decided that she was too easily swayed by Khalid, for whatever reason.

Tomorrow morning, he'd fly in at dawn with another load of boxes for the village of Zor Barawul. They would continue this pace daily or every other day, depending upon the distance involved.

"Hey, Emma!"

Emma turned toward the open flaps of her tent. Nike Alexander poked her head in. "Nike, come on in! How are you?"

The BJS woman pilot slipped in, threw her helmet bag next to Emma's on the cot and sat down in the extra chair. "Okay. Just got off a hot firefight around Zor Barawul. We kicked ass. How are you? I haven't had time to catch up with you lately. What's happening?"

"Just delivered our first boxes of books to Do Bandi. I had lunch at the chow hall and was coming back here to drop off my helmet and then go to the BJS HQ to fill out my report." Emma watched as Nike pushed the black curls off her sweaty brow. She saw the armpits of her flight suit were wet with perspiration. Flying an Apache in a firefight made the adrenaline rocket upward. She saw pink spots on Nike's olive-skinned cheeks. Her friend was still caught up in the adrenaline charge from the firefight.

"Was that your boss I just passed out there?" Nike hooked a thumb toward the tent opening. "That eye candy that's long and lean? Black hair? Blue eyes?"

Groaning, Emma nodded. "Yes, that's Captain Khalid Shaheen."

Nike gave her a wicked look. "Hey, if I hadn't met the man of my dreams recently, I'd definitely give that dude a second look. He's absolutely handsome."

Sighing, Emma gave her friend a dirty look. "Don't make this any worse than it is, Nike. Think about me. I have to work with the guy for the next six months and remain immune to him."

Laughing, Nike slapped her knee. "Oh, Emma! You're single. You're not involved with anyone. Why wouldn't you think about getting hooked up with him?"

Emma explained all the details to Nike about Brody Parker. As she did, she watched her friend become more serious. At the end of her explanation, she watched the excitement die in Nike's eyes. "So you see, I need a good recommendation from Captain Shaheen for my personnel jacket. I have to dig myself out of the black eye I gave us," she said, desperate. Opening her hands, Emma added, "And I don't dare let him know I like him, Nike. I fight it constantly. But I'm afraid he's just another player in disguise."

"I see," Nike muttered, sitting up, hands on her knees. "I'm hoping in my own way to overcome our mistake, too. But at least I don't have to worry about falling in love with my boss. That's an extra added strain on you."

"I'm not falling in love with him," Emma said more sharply than she'd intended. "I like the guy, yes. But love? No."

"Hmm," Nike murmured, a grin pulling at her lips, "sure don't look like it from my end. Every time you talked about him, your voice went soft and your eyes got that faraway, dreamy look."

Emma stood up, scowling at her best friend. "Nike, you're wrong."

Nike stood, laughed and picked up her helmet bag. "Okay, then prove it."

Chapter 6

"When does Shaheen arrive at Zor Barawul?" Asad Malik demanded. He sat crouched in front of a small fire, warming his hands. The cave where he and his men hid sat across from the Afghan village, which was perched on top of a hill.

Merzad, a trusted warrior, stood attentively by the Taliban leader. "My lord, our spy in the village told our man that next week Captain Shaheen, his sister Kinah and an American woman pilot are to fly educational books and desks into this village."

Scowling, Malik took a tin cup filled with steaming chai from the cook, Omald. He looked across the fire as the boy fed the fifteen men under his command. Omald was only thirteen, an orphan Malik had taken under his wing. He had been ten when Malik had found him in a burned-out border village. He had brainwashed the child and turned him into his personal servant. Omald's job was to make him chai, feed him, take care of his horse and serve his soldiers whatever scant food they could steal.

"Do you think that they will arrive with an Apache escort?" Merzad asked, taking a proffered cup of chai from Omald.

Shrugging, Malik enjoyed the warmth of the fire. The cave was dry and cold. Outside, April rain fell. There was a gray pall over the entire area and Zor Barawul was hidden in the mists and cold mountain air. "I hope not. We never know," he muttered, stroking his black-and-gray beard. At fifty, the harshness of his life as a leader in the Taliban was catching up with Malik. His joints ached in the winter snows and it worsened during the spring rains. Now, he looked forward to the summer heat when his arthritis stopped bothering him as much.

Merzad crouched down next to him, his narrow face set in a deep scowl. The black beard on his face was fuzzy and unkempt. All the men smelled. They went days, even weeks, without a place to clean themselves up or comb their beards and hair. He looked over at his beloved leader, a giant of a man with broad shoulders, a deep chest and powerful, sun-darkened hands covered with scars. Merzad felt a brotherly love for his fellow Pakistani. They'd grown up in the same village, survived terrible odds and gone on to carry the jihad into Afghanistan. Like Malik, Merzad felt strongly that the Taliban needed to be back in control of the country before the U.N. came in with troops to "free" the people from them.

Continuing to stroke the beard that fell nearly to his chest, Malik murmured to his best friend, "I hope to fulfill my promise to Shaheen and his sister. I killed Shaheen's fiancée two years ago. I've waited patiently, praying daily to Allah to give me another chance to kill him and his infidel sister. We were blessed when we hit the base camp to spot Shaheen there. Our spies have kept good track of him since then."

"They are both infidels," Merzad muttered. "They might be born to a Muslim father, but he's a Sufi." The word *Sufi* came out like a growling curse from the lean forty-five-year-old soldier.

Snorting, Malik sipped the delicious cinnamon-sprinkled chai. "Sufis are our enemies," he acknowledged. "I have no use for mystics of any kind." He smiled, remembering his rapes of Najela. She had fought him, and, to this day, he bore four fingernail marks on his right cheek where she'd clawed at him. No matter, he'd had his way with her. His loins warmed to the memory of taking the feisty black-haired beauty. She'd fought every time and Malik had enjoyed the encounters. Finally, he'd grown bored with her bravery and had slit her throat as she slept. They'd thrown her body into a village where he knew his archenemy, Khalid Shaheen, would find her. Again, his lips twitched with those fond memories. He anticipated capturing Kinah. She was fiery and gave no quarter. Malik, in his own way, admired the Sufi woman, but his hatred was even more intense toward her than it had been toward Najela.

"According to our source," Merzad said, pleased, "you will have them all coming to Zor Barawul."

"Yes," he muttered, "but the leader of that village is pro-American. His village, over the last year, has been protected by A-teams, given medical and dental care from the Americans." Shaking his head, he said, "We must be careful here, Merzad. We can't just openly walk into their village and threaten them as we used to. We tried that just this week and got nowhere. I've lost half of my men to the Apaches. We must rethink and try a different strategy."

Agreeing, Merzad sipped his chai, deep in thought. "It used to be easy to come across the border and threaten the leaders of these villages. Now, this past year, they have received all kinds of aid from the U.N., the U.S. Army and charity organizations from around the world. They no longer fear us." His mouth dipped downward as did his thin black brows.

"They will fear us again," Malik muttered, finishing off his chai and handing the cup back to his servant. He slowly rose on painful knees and rearranged the two bandoliers of ammunition across his chest. Looking around the large, dry cave, he saw that his men had bedded down and were sleeping, their rifles next to them. They'd just suffered a terrible defeat at the hands of the American Apache helicopters. The best thing to do, Malik knew, was to let them heal and lick their wounds, give them hot food and chai to rebuild their confidence. He silently cursed the combat helicopters. They were the bane of his existence. His mind spun with possible plans.

Zor Barawul was considered an American stronghold now. Malik could recall when he had owned that village. The old, crippled leaders cowered before him as he rode through like a conquering hero, his men following him. *No longer.* Allah would show him a way to infiltrate the village. His whole focus was on capturing or killing Khalid and Kinah Shaheen. Then his revenge would be complete.

After ordering another cup of chai, he watched the young lad quickly pour it from the teakettle across the grate of the fire. Malik took it and scowled. The Shaheens were infidels. They weren't even full-blooded Afghans. The blood of the Irish ran through their veins. Malik hadn't liked it when the Shaheens began to come regularly to the villages along the border. First, it was the elder Shaheen who had thrown his money at the villagers. Malik cursed the Sufi. All of them were stupid dreamers who thought love could solve the world's problems. How wrong they were! All of the money the elder Shaheen had given the villages had created schools. Malik had been livid with rage when he'd found out that girls were being taught, and he'd come in and destroyed every one of those schools.

Of all things! Malik was enraged to find out that five years later, the stupid girls were going to be educated once more by the Shaheen son and daughter. What an utter waste of time! A donkey was far more valuable than an accursed woman! Women had little value except as brood mares to bear a man's children and further the male family line. *Stupid women! Women must know their place. I will show them, once and for all. Once I capture Kinah Shaheen I will use her and kill her. Once she's dead, I will dump her body in Zor Barawul and let the women there see what will happen to them if they so much as pick up a book.*

Emma moaned. She turned over in her cot, the layers of blankets keeping her warm. Khalid was with her in her dream. He was touching her cheek lingeringly. She could feel the roughness of his fingers as they curved and followed her cheekbone. The look in his blue eyes, hooded with intent, reminded Emma of a summer thunderstorm. Skin tingling wildly in the wake of his slow caress, Emma sighed and leaned forward. She was naked and so was he. They knelt in front of one another on a sunny, grassy slope. She didn't know where they were, only that it was warm, beautiful and the fragrance of roses surrounded them.

"You are my beloved rose with freckles," Khalid murmured, watching her cheeks turn pink as he whispered the words. "The sun may rise and set, but the rays of love emanate from your heart to mine."

As her breasts brushed his dark, hairy chest, they tightened and a deep throb began in her lower body. Oh, how Emma wanted his hand to trail downward, hold and caress her taut breasts. A softened sigh slipped from between her lips. Khalid smiled into her eyes.

"You are the rose who grows in my heart, beloved."

Her mind was starting to come unhinged as his fingers trailed across her eyebrow, down her temple and back to her cheek. "Rumi...was that Rumi?" she managed in a whisper.

His smile increased. "Rumi talks of the rose. Do his words not touch your heart, also?"

Nodding, Emma moved her hands up across his shoulders. She felt the warmth of the sun upon them. Khalid was so strong and steady, as if he knew who he was and where he was going in his life. Emma wished she felt that way. Confidence radiated from him like the sun itself. As she absorbed a sense of protection and love from him, Emma's lids shuttered closed. His fingers outlined her lips and she wanted to kiss him.

"Not yet, beloved. Allow my hands to remember every inch of your beautiful being. My heart needs to map you, remember you and breathe you into itself...."

Heat throbbed through her womanly core. Fingers

digging into the hard flesh of his shoulders, Emma whimpered his name, begging him to kiss her. She was not disappointed. As Khalid's strong mouth brushed her lips, she trembled. She felt him smiling against her. She smiled in return. With her eyes closed, Emma simply wanted to feel the texture of his mouth, the heat of his ragged breath whispering across her cheek, the male fragrance that was only him.

She opened her lips and pressed into his smiling mouth. They slid and melted together as if in a slow-motion dance of fusion. Emma realized in some far corner of her barely functioning mind that Khalid was courting her slowly, enjoying her with a thoroughness she'd never experienced before. There was no hurry. No rush. Just…timelessness and being rocked and cradled with his mouth sliding upon hers. There was such strength and yet incredible tenderness as he asked her to open her mouth more so that he could take her fully into himself.

Had she ever been kissed like this? No. Every sip of his lips upon hers sent wild tingles down to her breasts and fueled the need to take him completely within her. Khalid's slow exploration of her lips now moved to her cheeks. His mouth scorched a path of neediness with each caress upon her skin. He traced the outline of her brows with his lips. Soft, rose-petal touches grazed her closed eyelids. Strands of hair caught beneath his seeking mouth as he lingered on each of her delicate ears. Emma surrendered to the slow, delicious seduction by Khalid.

"You are honey, my sweet, sweet woman," he whispered into her right ear. Moving his fingers upward from her jaw, Khalid framed her face and pulled back just enough to drown in her dark green eyes that were sultry with need—of him. "The sweetness of your heart bathes my wounded heart. Honey heals. The sugar of life nurtures new bees into being born and birthing. You are no different...." He trailed a series of kisses from her brow down to her parted lips. There, he halted and barely grazed them with his own. "And like the bees, the honey of your heart allows me to be reborn anew...."

"Emma! Wake up!"

Emma jerked into a sitting position, completely disoriented.

"Over here!" Nike called, her head sticking through the opening in the tent. "Wake up!"

"Oh," Emma gasped. "What time is it?" Khalid's words and fiery, evocative touches were real. Her body throbbed and ached. Embarrassed that Nike had had to awaken her, she looked at her watch.

"Oh, God," Emma groaned, "I'm late!"

"No kidding," Nike said. "What's the matter? You having a sexy dream about Khalid?"

Emma leaped out of bed and fumbled for her flight boots beneath the cot. Shocked at Nike's intuitiveness, Emma muttered, "Oh, forget it, Nike! I was up late last night writing reports, that's all."

Nike grinned. "Oh, sure. Well, hey, Khalid's on the tarmac waiting for you."

"Okay, okay." Pulling out her boots, Emma twisted around. "Can you tell him I'll be there in ten minutes?"

Laughing, Nike said, "Yeah, no problem. Was it a good dream?"

Emma glared at her. Nike chortled and disappeared. How could her girlfriend know about that wonderful dream? Stymied, Emma tore her mind from that to getting dressed, getting to the toilet and grabbing her flight bag. She was late! She'd never slept through the alarm on the bedstand! Ever. Grabbing the clock, Emma realized with a sinking feeling that the alarm was on, but she hadn't heard it.

With a moan of trepidation, Emma hurried to make up for lost time.

Emma was breathless as she arrived at Ops. As usual, it was a beehive of nonstop activity, planes and helos landing and taking off in an invisible dance known only to air-control-tower personnel. She saw Khalid leaning against the fender of the Apache, reading a book. He was relaxed, his head bent down, his helmet bag sitting next to him on the skirt of the helo. The April day was cloudy and chilly. It had rained all night. Puddles lay everywhere on the asphalt landing strip. Ragged, scudding clouds hid the mountains that surrounded the base camp.

Sucking in a breath, Emma walked quickly toward Khalid, her flight boots splashing through several puddles. She saw him lift his head. Instantly, her heart rate doubled. Why did he have to be so handsome? Just looking at the man, who was all warrior and yet so incredibly sensitive, made her feel even more breathless than the run from the tent to Ops had. Emma girded herself for his censure.

"Good morning," Khalid greeted, giving her a warm and appreciative look. "Nike said you overslept."

"I did." Emma pushed several strands of hair off her face. "I'm sorry. I set my alarm but I slept right through it. That's never happened before."

Khalid saw how upset Emma was, her cheeks stained

with heat. It only made her freckles more obvious and gave her a decidedly girlish look, at variance with the competent combat pilot she was. "Relax," he urged quietly. "We are in no rush. The weather is bad and we are going to have to wait for the clouds to rise more before we can fly nap-of-the-earth." CH-47s did not have all-terrain radar to see where they were going, and flying a hundred feet off the ground required a good set of eyes and no fog or low-hanging clouds obscuring the terrain.

"Oh," Emma said, relieved, "that's good news."

"Here," he said, handing her the book, "this is a gift for you. I realize it's not military protocol, but I would like to share my world with you a little bit. Take it. We'll go to the chow hall and get some chai and wait until the clouds lift." He picked up his helmet bag.

Emma looked down at the book. She nearly dropped it. It was a paperback called *Rumi: In the Arms of the Beloved*. Stunned, she looked up at Khalid.

"How did you know?" she croaked, confused as she held the book. How could he know about her torrid dream of this morning? Was it all over the internet? Nike had known too. Now, Khalid, of all things! Emma stood there feeling stupid for a moment. She stared at the cover. It showed several men in tall, red, Turkish caps wearing white clothing and whirling around in long skirts. Because of her one-year saturation into Pashto, Emma realized these were Sufi whirling dervishes. They would whirl around and around to music and it allowed them to go into a mystical trance to connect with the Beloved, a direct connection with God.

"Know what?" Khalid asked, confused, as he walked at her side. Emma's brow wrinkled. There was shock in her green eyes. She kept turning the book over and

over, as if it were too hot to handle. Khalid wondered
if he'd overstepped her personal bounds again. Was
giving her a book such a crime in the military's mind-
set? After all, they were both captains, of equal rank.
He saw no reason to think a book was too personal a
gift. But, judging from the rush of redness to Emma's
cheeks, the way she tucked her lower lip between her
teeth, maybe it was.

Gripping the book, Emma muttered, "Oh, nothing.
I'm still waking up." She hoped the excuse would sail
with Khalid. It did. The worry dissolved from his handsome features. And then, abruptly, she said, "Thank
you. This was a very nice gift." They were love poems!
Inwardly, Emma felt as if Khalid could see straight
through her, to her heart, and was fully aware of the
throbbing ache that still lingered in her lower body.
His eyes at times made her think he truly had paranor-
mal abilities. Had his intuition whispered to bring her
a book of love poems because, somehow, he knew how
she felt? Emma always felt out of step in Khalid's presence. He thrilled her, mesmerized her, made her want
him in every way possible. And he was off-limits to her
for a damned good reason. Emma wasn't ready to toss
her wounded heart into any relationship yet.

"Ah, yes. Well, a good, bracing cup of delicious chai
will cure your sleepiness," Khalid chuckled. They made
their way through muddy ruts, leaping over puddles and
walking around the larger ones.

Emma glanced at her watch. It was barely 0800. The
chow hall would be packed, the noise high and it was
the last place she wanted to be. Right now, she felt terribly vulnerable. Was it the dream? Or something more?
Emma swore she still felt every touch of Khalid, her

skin still retaining memory of it. "Sounds good," she managed, her voice sounding strangled even to her.

To her relief, Khalid found an empty table in a far corner. She sat down with the book on the table and watched him thread through the men and women to get to where the Afghan widow sold the chai. Khalid had such grace. He walked with pride and almost always had a smile lurking at the corners of his sensual mouth. Fumbling with the book, Emma finally opened it. She began to read some of the poems. Instantly, heat nettled her cheeks and she slapped the book shut and pushed it away, as if would incriminate her. The memory of that very real dream was still too close, too evocative. Reading Rumi's poems was like fanning the fires of her desire once more.

Emma shook her head. Somehow, and God only knew how, she had to erase Khalid from her body and her yearning heart. But how? Emma couldn't blame Khalid for how her body was behaving. Did he know that casual smile of his just made her ache to grab him and haul him into her bed? Emma was sure he'd be shocked by her very brazen instincts. Khalid was a gentleman, a throwback to another century where a man smoothly courted a woman with flowers, gifts, looks and compliments without ever touching her.

Sighing, she rubbed her face with her hands. What made her situation worse was that Emma wanted to be in Khalid's world. It was more than just sex. The mystery of the man himself compelled her. Not that he hid any aspect of himself, but her curiosity went much deeper. If Emma was honest with herself, she wanted to hear every thought Khalid had. What were his growing-up years like? How was he able to adjust to American life? What adventures had he had in the U.S. Army while learning how to fly the Apache? And how could a Sufi be a warrior? There was so much Emma wanted to know. And it was all personal. She spotted Khalid coming back, moving as quietly as fog around groups of people coming and going from the chow hall. In his hands, Khalid held two cups of chai.

Emma felt as if she were sitting on a volcano about to erupt. As Khalid handed her the chai and sat down opposite her, Emma did all she could to ignore her attraction.

"The chai will help you wake up," he observed wryly, lifting his cup in toast.

His teasing eased her anxiety. "Salud," she muttered, clinking the rim of his cup.

Khalid sat with his elbows on the table. "Have you looked at Rumi's book yet?"

"No," Emma lied. She didn't want to get on the topic of love with him. That would be like holding a grenade with the pin released from it. "These are whirling dervishes on the cover, aren't they?" Emma hoped this safe conversation would steer him away from the main topic of the book.

"Ah yes, the young men who spend years learning how to turn in a circle, remain grounded and yet, open their hearts to Allah." Khalid smiled. "They are the role models for the rest of us. I have seen some twirl for an hour or more without stopping."

Emma drank her chai, relieved the conversation was on religion and not her. "That's an amazing feat in and of itself. I couldn't twirl in a circle for probably more than thirty seconds before losing my balance and falling down."

Chuckling, Khalid said, "At one time, I begged my father to send me to a Sufi learning center. From childhood on I had seen the whirling dervishes at the festivals. They were magical! I remember standing in front of my father, his hands on my shoulders, and my eyes were huge as they whirled past us like tornados."

Emma sipped more of her chai. "I can just see you as a little kid: all eyes. That would be an incredible thing to experience." Emma recalled the magic carpet and genies of the *Arabian Nights*, and felt those myths were still alive—between them, for whatever reason. The magic seemed to leap to life every time they talked to one another. And now, she'd dropped their conversation to the personal level. Groaning inwardly, she felt trapped.

Khalid drowned in Emma's warm forest-green gaze. "Yes, I fell in love with the mystical segment of our Sufi way of life. My father gently turned me away from becoming a dervish."

"Do you regret that?"

"No. In reality, my father saw I was not ready for such schooling. I was a very adventurous boy given to taking risks and boldly exploring where few ever went." His smile increased. "He knew my love of flying. I thought as a child I could fly in the invisible ethers that the whirling dervishes flew on. My father was far more practical. He harnessed my love of flying with military service with the U.S. Army. I hadn't thought of that path, but it felt like the right one for me." He pointed his index finger upward. "When I'm flying, I feel like the dervishes, held in the invisible mystical hands of the universe. There's nothing quite like it."

"I agree," Emma said. "The sky takes away all my fears, worries and anxieties about the future."

"Hmm, perhaps we're both eagles of the Kush, eh?" he teased.

Emma laughed, and the words flew out of her mouth, "Oh no, you're a snow leopard! No doubt about that." And then, she gulped, set her mug down and realized her gaffe. Amusement glimmered in Khalid's expression.

"Indeed. You see me as a beautiful and rare snow leopard?"

Emma froze. No matter what she'd say, she would incriminate herself. *Damn!* Her heart sank into her boots. What had she just done? Was she so exhausted that she was unable to erect her defenses, keep the conversation strictly focused on their mission?

Khalid leaned forward, his voice dropping to an intimate whisper. "I often wondered how you really saw me, Captain Emma Cantrell. Snow leopards are perhaps the most beautiful and rarest of cats in the world. There are only a handful who live in the Kush. I was fortunate enough to see one, once. His coat was of soft gray-white with spots of brown that matched the mountain slope. He blended in so well that at first I did not spot him. But my friend, who was a biologist, did. I watched that cat move from one side of the rocky, unstable slope to the other. He had such feline grace, such quiet power and authority, all I could do was stare with admiration at him." Khalid sat up and gave her a dazzling smile. "So, you see me as a snow leopard. What a wonderful compliment. Thank you!" There was no question; his heart was opening to Emma.

Chapter 7

When they landed at Zor Barawul, the April showers had eased up. It was almost noon when Emma powered down the CH-47 and shut off the engines. The village was a hub of activity. Two days earlier, it had been under attack by the Taliban. Now two A-teams were present. One was stationed on an outpost that overlooked the valley where Zor Barawul sat. The other team lived in the village itself.

It seemed nothing could dampen Khalid's spirits. He unhooked the jack from his helmet, pulled it off his head and seemed utterly unaffected by the violence that surrounded them. Emma marveled at that, but she figured, as her hands flew over the controls, that his Sufi perspective gave him that sense of protection.

The rains of April made the village a sea of mud. Warm in her thick nylon jacket and glad to be wearing it, Emma heard the ramp grinding down. On this particular flight, they had brought a dentist and a dental hygienist from Bagram. Emma wasn't happy about keeping the CH-47 on the ground all day, considering the recent attacks. Too often, if a bird stayed on the ground, the Taliban would sneak up and lob mortars at it. However, they'd be staying to help out and, near sunset, they'd fly the army dental team back to Bagram.

Turning in her seat, Emma stood up and saw her load master, Sgt. Steve Bailey, unhooking his harness. The twenty-two-year-old blond was tall and gangly. When Khalid walked back to help him organize the boxes to be off-loaded, she thought they looked like brothers body-wise. As always, Emma remained alert and on guard. She swept her gaze around the area where the helo was sitting. It was parked on the tip of the hill. There was a fifty-foot-diameter landing area. The rocky slopes dropped off steeply to a valley a thousand feet below them.

Khalid eased between the cargo boxes. They were battened down with sturdy netting and nylon straps that kept the boxes from flying all over while they were in the air. He saw Abbas, a tall older village leader with a deeply lined, narrow face, waiting for him near the ramp. He wore a dark gold wool turban, a gray robe and wool cloak over his proud shoulders. His black and gray beard was neatly trimmed, his eyebrows straight and thick across his dark brown eyes.

Emma smiled to herself as Abbas shook Khalid's hand, pumping it up and down. The leader then leaned forward and kissed the pilot on each cheek. This was a common Afghan custom and a sign of friendship. She heard Khalid murmur, *"As-salaam alaikum."*

Abbas returned the warm greeting with *"Wa alaikum as-salaam wa rahmatu Allah,"* in return. That meant "And to you be peace together with God's mercy."

Emma liked the sincere greeting. Khalid had already prepped her for the important people who ran this village. At Abbas's side was his wife, Jameela. She was dressed in a black burka, only her cinnamon-brown eyes looking out through the cross-hatched material. Jameela had been college-educated in Pakistan and spoke fluent English. At her side was Ateefa, their daughter.

Emma felt her heart contract with pain at the sight of the five-year-old girl with a prosthesis on her right leg. Her black hair was clean, brushed and hung around her small shoulders. There were shoes on her feet. Emma knew most children in these border villages went barefoot all year long, even in the harsh, icy winters and cold, rainy springtime. Today, as she pulled the green scarf from the thigh pocket on her flight suit, Emma smiled to herself. A gaggle of wide-eyed, curious children of all ages peeked around the adults huddled near the last mud hut at the end of the village. They too had shoes. Not only that, they were dressed warmly in clothes that had been donated by Americans. Emma knew a lot had been done for this village and the people were grateful.

Placing the scarf around her head, Emma walked down the ramp. The A-team helped bring the boxes out of the cargo hold of the helo. Several wooden pallets had been set up by Bailey where the boxes would be placed. That way, the boxes remained dry and protected from the mud. There was an air of excitement, as if a festival were in progress. The U.S. Army dental team, consisting of two men, forged ahead of Emma.

They would give their greetings to Abbas and then get on with their work. A dental hut had long ago been set up and they came in monthly to help the villagers.

Emma waited to present herself to Abbas. When she was next, she murmured the same greeting, her hand pressed to her heart and giving Abbas a slight bow, a sign of respect. He'd never met her before and official salutations were a must.

Abbas thrust his hand out to her. *"Salaam,"* Emma said, as he shook her hand, warmth dancing in his dark eyes. He then leaned down and brushed a kiss on each of her cheeks. His beard tickled her. She returned the greeting and then stepped back. Her ability to speak Pashto to him made his eyes light up with surprise.

"Ah, you speak our language, Captain. That is an unexpected gift."

Emma smiled. "I'm working with Captain Shaheen and his sister Kinah for the next six months. He asked for someone who could speak Pashto. It makes it easier on everyone."

Abbas looked over at his wife. "Indeed, it does. Please, this is my beloved wife, Jameela. She will take you to our home where you will share a cup of hot chai with her. As I understand it, the desks for the children's school have arrived today. Perhaps you two can decide where they need to be set up? I will have my men take them out of the boxes and assemble them."

Emma nodded. "As you like, my lord. I'm here to serve." She saw the old man's expression soften and seemed grateful for their presence. Khalid had told her that Abbas was highly educated and had a degree in biology. He'd received university training in Pakistan and returned to the village of his birth. He had been responsible for breeding better animals, improving sheep's fleece and his progressive leadership had influenced a number of other border villages. The man was courageous in Emma's eyes. He had fought against the Taliban, but had caved to their demands when his people's lives were threatened. Now, with over a year's worth of U.S. Army protection and help, this village had flourished.

Jameela stepped forward and shook Emma's hand. "Welcome, Captain Cantrell. I'm so thrilled you are here with us. I am Jameela."

Smiling, Emma shook her hand. They traded kisses on the cheeks. Jameela brought her daughter forward. "And this is Ateefa, our youngest. Her leg was destroyed by a mine when she was three years old. Last year, thanks to Captain Gavin Jackson, a prosthesis was made for Ateefa. And look at her today! She has thrown her crutches away and can run and race with all her friends."

Emma crouched down and took Ateefa's small hand. The little girl was beautiful, with large black eyes and a sweet smile. "How do you do, Ateefa? I'm glad you have a leg to run around on now. How are you getting along with it?"

"Fine, soldier lady," Ateefa said shyly, putting her fingers in her mouth.

Emma chuckled. "You have a beautiful daughter."

Abbas touched his wife's shoulder. "Beautiful children from my beautiful wife. Go, Jameela. Take our guest and allow her to warm up in our house."

"Of course, my dearest husband," Jameela said. She held out her hand to Emma. "Come. This is an exciting day for all of us. The children have been longing to see their new desks. After some chai, I'll take you over to the house we have chosen to become our school for our children."

The excitement was palpable as Emma walked at Jameela's side. Ateefa and several other young children raced ahead. The main street had deep ruts created by the donkeys who pulled the carts. It seemed everyone was out to greet them. Emma felt her heart lift. This was what life was really about: helping those who had less than she did. She followed Jameela to a beautiful two-story stone building with a red wooden door. It was the only home that had two stories. All the rest were made of adobe mud bricks, or, for those who could afford it, built from stone.

Looking over her shoulder, Emma noticed Khalid with a heavy box balanced on one shoulder, leading the A-team down the street with their own boxes of desks. A number of children across the street stood at the opened door of what would become their school. They were like excited little puppies wriggling around, giggling, excitement shining in their faces. Emma smiled. It was a great day for Zor Barawul. Still, she felt tense. She sensed that the Taliban was nearby monitoring them and this sent a chill up Emma's spine as she entered the warm home.

Asad Malik watched the activity at Zor Barawul through a set of Russian binoculars. The beat-up set had served him well over the years. He'd killed a Russian officer with his pistol and divested him of anything of value, including his binoculars. It reminded Malik of their victory over the Russians who had tried to tame the wild Afghan people. They hadn't succeeded, and if he had anything to do with it, the Americans and the U.N. would leave with their tails tucked between their legs, too.

"What do we do?" Merzad asked as he stood near the opening of the cave looking across the valley to Zor Barawul.

"Nothing," Malik murmured. "Not yet…"

Frowning, Merzad offered, "You know, we have two new boys, orphans, with us. Why not send them into the village as our spies? Let them pretend to be hungry and lost. Someone will surely help them. With all the food, money and medical gifts old Abbas has gotten in the last year, they will take in our 'lost' boys. They could become our eyes and ears, Lord Malik."

The plan wasn't a bad one. Malik dropped the binoculars back on his chest. Turning, he nodded. "That's a good plan. Our only problem is we haven't had either boy long enough to brainwash them properly. What if they run away and side with Abbas? What then?"

Merzad shrugged. "When you rescued them three months ago, they were starving. They've been treated with nothing but discipline, been given food, a blanket and I believe they can be our spies without concern."

Rubbing his beard, Malik glanced over his shoulder. Both boys were sitting near the fire, recently fed and cleaning some of the weapons for his soldiers. Their jobs were to clean weapons, help the cook, water the horses and do the bidding of his soldiers. Soon, they would be taught how to fire the weapons. For now, cleaning a rifle was crucial because it taught them about the weapons and it gave them prestige within the group. Being trusted to handle such weapons earned them respect from his soldiers. The boys desired to be a part of his family.

"Benham is thirteen. He's got the slowness of a donkey pulling a cart, though."

"Agreed," Merzad said in a low voice so no one could overhear them. "He's slow but very loyal to us."

Malik's gaze moved to the ten-year-old boy crouched nearby with a partly dismantled AK-47 on a thin, tattered blanket before him. "Fahran is the smart one." The scrawny child wore a dark blue woolen robe, his feet bare and sticking out from beneath the dirtied material. He had black hair, startling green eyes and he reminded Malik of a wily fox.

"You have doubts about Fahran?" Merzad probed. "When you say nothing but you look for a long time, I know there are problems you are contemplating."

Malik gave his compatriot an appreciative glance. Merzad was forty-five years old and his best friend. Having been born in the same village gave them a bonding like no other. Merzad had saved his life a number of times and vice versa. Malik trusted few, but Merzad had earned his trust. "I'm unsure about him, that's all. He's very young."

"But alert and smart," Merzad offered. "He's learned how to take apart an AK-47 and put it back together as no one we've ever seen. Even now, he instructs Benham on the next step. That older boy has been at it as long as he, but Benham stumbles and is forgetful."

"Mmm," Malik said, hand on his beard, studying the two youths near the fire. "The real question is: do I trust Fahran on such a spy mission?"

Saying nothing, Merzad stood quietly. He knew better than to argue Malik in or out of anything.

"Benham comes from a farm-laborer background," Malik said, talking to himself. "He has no education whatsoever. Our men are teaching him to read by learning the Koran. Fahran has been schooled and comes from a well-educated family in his village. He reads, writes and speaks several dialects already."

"Do you think he knows English?"

"How could he?" Malik said, looking over at his friend. "He comes from an Afghan border village in the north. According to him, his parents took their schooling in Pakistan. No, I doubt very seriously if he knows English."

"If you are considering him for this mission, I can ask him," Merzad suggested. "If he does, that would be a strong reason to have him go. He could eavesdrop on the Americans. They'd never suspect someone like him would know English, much less understand it."

Nodding, Malik said, "Have one of our men ask him. Then, let me know."

"Of course," Merzad said, leaving his side.

Malik turned and placed the binoculars to his eyes once more. How badly he wanted to sneak over under the cover of night and lob a rocket or mortar round into that helo. Chances were that it would lift off before dark. They rarely left any helicopter on the ground overnight.

His mind turned back to the ten-year-old Afghan orphan, Fahran. Malik didn't fully trust anyone that smart. His loyal soldiers could read the Koran but few knew how to write. He wanted to keep them dumb. It suited his purpose. Merzad, of course, knew how to read, could write and spoke a number of different dialects, but Malik trusted him.

The boy with the bright green eyes, his black hair

straight and shaggy around his head, was quick and agile. His small, greasy fingers flew over the weapon with knowing ease. Malik had entered a village one night where his men had killed a number of Sufi families. One of his soldiers found Fahran hidden beneath a bed, shivering like a dog. They'd dragged him out, kidnapped him and brought him along with them because they needed young boys for their unit. Benham had been found in shock, wandering around outside the village, crying for his parents, who had been killed.

At first, Malik recalled, Fahran had tried to run away several times, and each time, he was caught. Finally, the soldiers kept a rope tied around his thin ankle. If Fahran tried to escape, the rope would tug in the soldier's sleeping hand and awaken him. Fahran had tried it once and was whipped soundly, his back bleeding from ten lashes. After that, Fahran seemed to accept his fate. But had he really surrendered? Malik didn't know and wished mightily that he had the answer to that question.

With a sigh, he returned to watching the activity across the valley. Merzad would find out if the boy knew English. For Malik, that would seal the deal one way or another.

"Look! Look!" Ateefa cried, sitting down at the first assembled desk. She beamed with excitement at her parents who stood in the large, cold room smiling down at her with pride. All around her men were tearing open boxes and everyone was assembling the wooden desks. Children were barely able to stand still as they waited to be assigned a desk by Jameela.

Emma stood near the wife of the leader, smiling. There was an air of celebration, the room filled with men, the laughter of children and as many families who could squeeze in to watch the miraculous event. She thought about American children who took a school desk for granted. Much of the world did not possess the riches of America, and watching Khalid and the A-team work to assemble the desks made Emma's heart warm with pride.

Jameela joined the wives of the other children and asked them to open several boxes that held crayons, notebook paper, pens, pencils, rulers and erasers. The small group of younger women eagerly descended upon the huge box, glad to be part of the activity. Immediately, all their children gathered around the boxes, touching the cardboard and anxious to see what was inside.

Emma couldn't help the men with the desks, although she wanted to. That was considered a man's job, not a woman's. Several more A-team members set up the newly assembled desks. Others hauled away the cardboard and placed it in neat rows in front of a huge green chalkboard that had been hung in place earlier in the morning.

She saw the joy in Khalid's ruddy features as he crouched and gathered the pieces to assemble another desk. Emma didn't want to feel so good about watching him. His long fingers moved with an assuredness and precision that made her crave his touch. She couldn't erase the haunting dream of him courting her, kissing her. Every time his gaze met hers, she quickly averted her eyes so that he couldn't, somehow, read what was in her thoughts and heart. What to do? This wasn't getting any easier, Emma realized with a sinking feeling.

Of course, it didn't help that she was drawn to the

man who read love poems by Rumi, either. In her foreign language class she had read his poems, and she understood why Khalid was a devout reader of his work. The ancient mystic touched her heart and soul as well. Who wouldn't be touched by this man's greater awareness of the human condition, his acceptance of the fact that no one was perfect, and yet that we all deserve another chance? Emma liked Rumi a lot, but she wasn't about to confide that to Khalid since it would make their relationship that much more personal. Right now, she had enough to juggle emotionally about the Afghan pilot.

Emma watched as several children mimicked the A-team members by helping them haul the cardboard out of the classroom. It wouldn't be wasted. The cardboard would be taken to a barn for future use by the villagers. The mountains in this area had a lot of brush and very few trees. Wood was hard to come by. The cardboard would be a welcome fire starter in the mornings around here, Emma realized.

Khalid set up another desk. As they were put into working order, Jameela announced the name of the next child to be assigned that seat. Emma watched the pride and excitement in the eyes of the children, and the hope mirrored in the faces of the proud parents. Her heart opened to Khalid, who dusted off his hands and walked toward them. Kinah had the supply box. She handed out all the items to the parents, who in turn, gave them to their children. Truly, Khalid and his sister were changing the world one child, one village at a time.

The warmth in his sparkling blue eyes stole Emma's breath for a moment. It was a fierce, burning look Khalid gave only to her and it made her feel so special.

Blessed by her lover's gaze, as Rumi would say. Khalid moved over the cardboard debris to reach Abbas's side. How shaky she felt after that hooded look that had lasted only a fraction of a second between them. Emma tried to ignore it.

If only she could find something to dislike about Khalid and focus on that. He was terribly human, but as for a real flaw? She couldn't detect one—yet. It could be the one thing to protect herself from wanting a personal relationship with him. The more she worked with Khalid, the more Brody Parker dissolved into her past.

Chapter 8

"Come," Khalid entreated Emma as she stood near the edge of the village. The sun had just set and the grayish dusk was upon them. "Let's give the sergeant relief from staying with our CH-47. He needs to eat before we leave."

Emma hadn't seen Khalid the rest of the day. The men had been busy over at the schoolroom, and she'd been with the women and school supplies at another nearby home. Her heart beat a little harder to underscore the dark and light playing across his face. Those dark blue eyes were narrowed and filled with desire—for her. Gulping, Emma nodded. They fell into step while avoiding the donkey-cart ruts down the center of the muddy street.

"So, how was your day?" Khalid inquired. Up ahead their transport helicopter sat like a dark hulk. As soon as the load master who guarded the helo returned from eating in the village, they would lift off and fly back to the base camp. No one kept a helo on the ground overnight out here.

"Busy," Emma admitted, smiling a little. "The women got all the school supplies divided among the children. They'll have everything they need for tomorrow's first class."

"Good. We got the desks all assembled, finished off some last-minute things in the room itself and now it stands ready for use." Khalid rubbed his hands and gave her a satisfied smile. "We've done good work today, Emma." And then he grimaced. Khalid hadn't meant to call her by her first name. That was personal, not professional. Giving her a quick glance, he saw her eyes widen considerably over the gaffe.

"I apologize for that slip," he murmured.

Emma couldn't be angry at him. The way her name whispered from his lips sent a tantalizing sensation across her skin. "I guess when we're alone, we could use first names," she said.

Holding up his hands, Khalid said, "I want what makes you comfortable. I know you prefer professional military conduct between us." Khalid didn't want that, but he had no choice. And it formed a buffer zone between them so that his aching need to kiss her, to court her, was stopped cold.

As she reacted to Khalid's earnest look, an old block in her heart melted. How long could she go on pretending she wasn't drawn to this heroic man? No matter what Emma tried to do, she could no longer erect Brody Parker's face and memory as a wall between her and this handsome pilot. "It's okay," Emma reassured him.

Relief and terror surged through Khalid. This was new footing, and it was like going down slopes with rocks that slid from beneath him. Instantly, he felt thrown into turmoil because the expression in Emma's eyes rocked his foundation. He saw desire in her eyes. For him.

As they approached the helo, the load master came out to meet them. Emma ordered him to the chieftain's house for dinner. His face lit up and he eagerly trotted back into the village. They climbed into the fuselage via the lowered ramp. Emma automatically swept her gaze around the bird to ensure all the cargo had been removed. The fuselage sounded hollowly as they walked toward the cockpit.

Emma took the right seat and sat down. Khalid hesitated a moment, pulled something out of his large right leg pocket and then sat down. Curious, Emma saw he had a small book in his hands. Looking out the window, she searched the area for movement as a matter of habit. The A-team had a member out on guard walking the perimeter around the helo. She knew the Taliban was active at this time of day. Like nocturnal animals, they stirred at dusk and hunted throughout the night.

For the first time, Emma spoke his first name. "Khalid, did you see those two boys? Those two poor little orphans who came in earlier today asking for help?"

Nodding, he placed the book on his thigh, his hand across it. "Yes, Benham and Fahran. Abbas took them in. With so many family members being killed by each side, children are left to fend for themselves."

"It's horrible," Emma muttered. "It just tears my heart out of my chest. Those two children had no shoes and they were wearing such thin clothes. I don't know how they survived the nights in these mountains."

"That was curious to me, too," Khalid murmured. "It's freezing at night. What they wore wouldn't keep them from dying of hypothermia."

"They probably slept in tight little balls against one another," Emma said. "They're so cute. Benham is shy. He wouldn't look anyone in the eyes."

"That's not uncommon. These children have PTSD and they're traumatized to the point that they don't know who to trust anymore. They're orphans of war."

"Fahran told Abbas that they came here because they heard that Americans were giving food and clothing away."

"Word carries fast," Khalid said. He watched the soft gray dusk accentuate Emma's freckles. Once inside the helo, she'd removed the hijab and ruffled her fingers through her hair, catching the strands and taming them into a ponytail. Soft, curled tendrils along her temples emphasized the anguish in her green eyes. "Well," he said, "let me read to you from Rumi." He held up the book. "My father gifted me with this set of poems when I was five years old. You can see how dog-eared and worn the book is." He gave it a fond look as he lifted it toward her to inspect.

Emma could see that the title on the small red leather book was nearly worn off. She couldn't make it out. "Oh, so you're going to read to me?" Thrilled by the offer, Emma wondered why, but didn't want to spoil the magic of the moment. She was exhausted trying to ignore his masculinity, his worldliness and kindness toward others. Maybe, just this once, it would be all right, she told herself. All right to let down her walls and just be with him in this stolen moment.

"Of course," Khalid said. He opened the book and gently laid it across his thigh. The light of dusk filtered through the Plexiglas to highlight the words written in Pashto. "He is our greatest Persian poet and mystic. His words touch the soul of a person, regardless of their faith and beliefs. He was so connected to the Creator that he transcended his own Sufi boundaries to see that all of us are loved."

Sitting back in the seat, Emma watched Khalid's darkened form in the copilot's seat. She absorbed the grace of Khalid's long fingers. He reminded her more of an artist than a combat helo pilot. "I haven't had anyone do this for me except when I was a little girl. My parents would come in and read to me. I loved that time. I remember being in bed with my stuffed bear, Mr. Brownie. Mom would play the part of the woman in the story and Dad would be the man." Emma smiled in remembrance. "That was so much fun...."

"Reading is a way to open a person's heart," Khalid agreed. "It shows care, respect and love."

Emma felt her heart thud on that comment. Khalid's warm look stirred her body. He touched her on a level no man had ever reached. Emma was afraid to tell Khalid that, for fear that she would lose control. And that just couldn't happen.

"Well," Khalid murmured, "I have chosen some of my favorite quotes from Rumi that I'd like to read to you."

Just the way Khalid softly spoke the lines in his husky voice made her feel as if warm honey were being poured over her. Touched beyond words, Emma struggled to find her voice. "That was a beautiful poem." She considered Rumi's words for more than a minute. Khalid sat quietly, hands resting over the book balanced on his thigh. He seemed at peace, undisturbed by the war-torn world that surrounded them. "It sounds as though Rumi knew through experience about love."

Nodding, Khalid said, "Yes, Rumi knew the great highs and lows of loving another just as we do. He had a great love and then it was torn from him." Khalid touched the edge of the book with reverence. "Rumi led a hard, demanding life. That is why I believe so many people around the world, regardless of their personal belief system, can relate to his poems."

Sighing, Emma looked through the Plexiglas at the graying world, "I've never known that secret sky he spoke about in his poem...." Then she caught herself, blushed and gave Khalid an apologetic look.

"There are many types of love," Khalid agreed. "Rumi, because he was a mystic and desired to know the Creator, walked through trials by fire in order to fulfill his desire. To do that, one has to experience these things as other people do. But—" Khalid smiled a little "—he knew love and many of his poems are a reflection of that. It isn't always love between a man or woman, it can be the love you have for your parents, your friends or your relatives."

"He sounds like he was a very astute observer of life," Emma said. "I really wish now that I had studied Rumi more back at language school. I like how he sees our messed-up world."

"Let me read you another poem," Khalid said, and carefully turned the page on the very old, well-used book.

Emma felt as if that poem was about her, about the walls she was trying to build within herself to stop herself from liking Khalid. Shifting uncomfortably, she refused to meet Khalid's inquiring gaze after he finished the reading. His expression softened.

"I know that something exists between us," Khalid began gently, getting Emma to look into his eyes. "I feel you pulling back, Emma. I think I understand why, or perhaps I don't at all."

Ouch. Emma sat up, hands clasped tensely in her lap. "Are you always this direct?"

"I speak from my heart," Khalid said. "I know no other way. Do you?"

The man was so open and vulnerable right now that Emma couldn't just fire off some sniping comment and escape from the helo. The sincerity in his darkened eyes called to her. "I…well…" She hesitated. And then, she knew she had to be equally honest with him. "Look, Khalid, you're my boss. I don't think a personal relationship is appropriate. Do you?"

"I wasn't expecting to be attracted to you, Emma." He never broke eye contact with her. "For so long, I felt nothing at all after Najela's death. In fact—" and he straightened and looked out at the darkening world beyond them "—I did not realize my heart was healing from that tragedy until I met you."

Emma sat immobile, confused. "Oh…" was all she could manage.

Khalid wrestled mightily with his past. After Najela's death, he'd sworn never to fall for another woman and put her into danger. Now his resolve was disappearing. All he wanted was a closer connection with Emma. The more he tried to stop himself, the more he felt driven to do the unthinkable.

Khalid could see the bewilderment on Emma's face. Without thinking, he stood and leaned over her. His hand slid across her jaw to cup her cheek. Bending his head, he gently placed his mouth across Emma's parted lips. Her breath was warm and sweet, her mouth soft and tasting of cinnamon chai. He felt Emma stiffen and then, surrender to his kiss. There was such hesitancy and, yet, a sense of yearning as her mouth slid provocatively against his. The moment felt torn out of time and place. All Khalid could do was taste Emma, absorb the perfume of her skin, her hair and the silk of her mouth into his wildly pounding heart.

Emma suddenly jerked out of the woven heat of the moment. She looked up into Khalid's hooded, dark eyes that burned with need—of her. "We can't!" she cried.

Khalid stepped back, hearing such fear in her voice. His mouth throbbed with the kiss, the taste of her on his lips. The book was still gripped in his hand. "I'm at fault," he murmured apologetically. "After Najela's murder, I swore I would never get involved with another woman. I never wanted her harmed as Najela had been." He gave Emma a helpless look. "I'm so sorry, Emma, I don't know what happened."

Emma felt panic. She could still feel the masculine stamp of Khalid's mouth on her own. Oh, how she wanted him! All of him! The unexpected kiss broke open the lies she'd been telling herself. His mouth resting lightly on her own, his male scent consuming her, all conspired against Emma. The raw pain in his hoarse tone was evident. Najela's death had changed him forever. Opening her hands in desperation she said, "We've both got good reasons not to do this. I'm relying on you to give me a positive rating after this mission."

Khalid shook his head, his emotions still gripping him in a powerful hold. "But I will give you an excellent report for your personnel jacket. Why are you so worried about that? You are a good pilot, you care and you're an excellent officer. How could I not give you a glowing report?" Khalid knew from many earlier heartbreaks that some women could not tolerate his Muslim-Christian background. Maybe that's what this was all about. He borrowed from both great religions, but primarily was guided by his Sufi heart and soul. His heart never led him wrong, but Khalid had encountered a few women in his life who were not as tolerant as he was, and those relationships had broken up as a result. Was Emma wrestling with this issue, too? It didn't matter. He had to be responsible. Never would he place Emma in Najela's place. He just couldn't!

Khalid sat down. Emma looked as if she wanted to run away. Searching her face, he asked, "Is it because of my religions that I embrace, Emma? Does that offend you?"

Brows rising, Emma gasped, "Why—no! Of course not!"

"What then?"

Emma sighed. She had to tell Khalid why it was important to get a good grade on this mission. As quietly as she could, because she didn't want her voice drifting out beyond the helo to other ears, she confided in Khalid how she'd allowed Nike Alexander to give up her seat in the Apache to save a Special Forces sergeant's life last year. As she finished the story about the punishment she'd gotten, the demotion and the black eye it had given her famous military family, Khalid's expression changed from confusion to surprise and then, finally, understanding.

"Ah," he said, "I see why you are so distraught. It creates great pain for you to hurt your family's untarnished reputation. I get that." Khalid sat for several moments digesting Emma's conundrum. He could still taste her on his lips. He never wanted that sweet cinnamon taste to go away. The barrier between them was greater than he'd anticipated. And now he understood Emma's fear of intimacy with him.

"Can I convince you that I will give you a good mark for this mission?" he asked in a hopeful voice.

Emma grimaced. "So many things could go wrong, Khalid. It's not a matter of trust. It's about life. What if we got together and then broke up three months from now? You'd be hurt. Angry. And you could get even with me by giving me a very bad mark on the report." Emma shook her head. "No, I can't risk that. I'm sorry."

Tapping his fingers softly on the book, Khalid said, "I wish I could regret kissing you. But I cannot." His stomach roiled, his heart pounded as if he were being pushed in several directions—between the horrific past, wanting to love Emma and knowing he never could.

Emma shrugged, dodging his inquiring gaze. She stared down at her clenched hands in her lap. She could feel Khalid struggling with these issues. Emma felt she owed him the truth. Looking up, she held his gaze. "No, I can't regret it, either, Khalid. But there are other things involved."

"Such as?"

"Such as I'm on a second tour over here. In nine months, it's finished and I'm being rotated stateside. I have three more years on my officer's contract with the U.S. Army. I have no idea where I'll be sent."

"I understand. Many hurdles."

"Yes," she whispered, feeling emotionally exhausted. "And they are all out of my control."

"But," Khalid persisted with a gentle smile, "life always throws hurdles at us. I swore on Najela's grave not to fall in love with another woman and have her harmed by Asad Malik."

Now more than ever, it was time to tell Khalid everything. He needed to know about her own heartbreak. She couldn't hold back. Emma finally broke down and told him about Brody Parker. When she was finished with the deeper explanation, she said unsteadily, "Just as you have your own reservations about getting involved again, I feel the best thing to do is to walk away. We can't jeopardize this mission...or our wounded hearts."

The words were like ice. Khalid realized he was just coming out of two years of grieving over the loss of Najela. He was acting irrationally and expecting too much from Emma. It was her right to set the agenda. "I understand," he said. "I will honor your needs, Emma. I will remember our kiss forever." Moving his shoulders, as if to remove an unseen load, Khalid added, "I do not want to be a dark shadow that stains your life and stops that wonderful smile from giving others sunlight."

Feeling miserable, Emma muttered, "I appreciate it, Khalid. I'm just sorry it couldn't be what we wanted."

Khalid rose because he saw the sergeant returning from the village. "I am, too. Here comes our load master. We need to fly back to base camp now."

"Hey," Nike Alexander called, sticking her head inside Emma's tent, "how are you?"

Emma was just easing her flight boots off her feet

when her best friend slipped through the tent flaps. "Hey, Nike. Good to see you."

"Girlfriend," Nike murmured, putting her hands on her hips and studying her, "you look like hell warmed over. Bad flight back from Zor Barawul?"

Sighing, Emma gestured to the chair next to her cot. "Have a seat," she said. After she kicked her boots beneath the cot, she got up and tied the tent flaps together. She'd just arrived back to Bravo an hour earlier. It was cold, nearly freezing outdoors. As soon as Emma had got in her tent, she'd turned on the space heater to warm it up.

Nike put her helmet bag next to the chair and sat down.

Emma poured herself some water. "Want some?"

"Yes, thanks. We forget we're in a desert, and none of us drinks enough to stay properly hydrated," Nike said.

Emma poured a second glass and handed it to the Greek pilot. "You look like you saw some action. There was a lot of chatter on the channel as I was flying back."

"Yeah," Nike said, drinking the water in gulps. "The crap hit the fan over near the border about three miles west of Do Bandi." Nike gave her an evil grin. "We creamed about fifty Taliban who thought they could sneak across the valley in the dark."

"Wow," Emma murmured, "that's good."

"Fifty that won't be harassing those poor Afghan villagers in that area," Nike said. She placed the emptied glass on a table next to where she sat.

"Yes, and Do Bandi is one of the villages we're working in to bring education to the children," Emma said, worried. She sat down on the cot next to her friend.

"So, what's with you? Catching the flu? Rough flight back? Get shot at?"

Mouth quirking, Emma growled, "I wish it was one of those things."

"Uh-oh," Nike said, grinning. "Man trouble."

"It's Khalid."

"Yeah, remarkable dude, isn't he? A stud. If I didn't love my guy like I do, I'd sure consider chasing him myself," she chuckled.

Emma searched her friend's face. "From the moment I saw him, I felt my heart twang like a harp. I fought it, Nike. I put up good reasons not to even think about being with this guy."

"But?"

"We were in the cockpit at dusk tonight. He came and sat down in the copilot's seat and started reading Rumi's love poems to me."

"How sweet!" Nike got excited. "Emma, that's wonderful! How many American guys would think of doing that?"

"Oh, you would react that way, Nike. Dammit! I need a little pity here, okay?"

Nike chuckled darkly. "What's standing in your way, Emma? You're not attached. And if you like him, what's the problem?"

Emma told her. She saw Nike lose some of her ebullience over the event.

"Oh yeah, I forgot about that. He is your boss, after all. And Brody Parker led you on and then crushed your heart. He was a sonofabitch."

"I really hurt Khalid's feelings tonight. He asked me if I trusted him to do the right thing. And I said I couldn't trust him."

Nike shook her head. "I feel for both of you. Right now, you're caught between a rock and hard place. Your first duty is to your family and expunging the bad name we managed to give it."

"Yeah," Emma sighed, "I know it. To be fair to him, he's fighting his attraction to me because he lost Najela to Asad Malik. He doesn't want to put another woman in that bastard's gun sights."

"Mmm," Nike said. "He's caught between a rock and hard place, too."

"Yes," Emma said, feeling glum.

"Well," Nike said, patting her friend's sagging shoulder, "you do the best you can, Emma. The way I look at it, if it's meant to work out, it will. No matter the reasons, if it's meant to be, it will happen. You have this mission to toe the line on and get glowing commendations."

Giving Nike a warm look, Emma gripped her hand, squeezed and released it. "I just want to try and get my career back on track and get my family's good name polished up again."

"Right on," Nike agreed.

Emma pressed her hand to her heart, her voice low with unshed tears. "The problem is I like the guy. More than a little. This sucks."

"Doesn't sound like a problem to me." Nike gave her an encouraging wink, which didn't help matters.

Chapter 9

"Brother," Kinah called to Khalid from the door of the school, "come visit with me."

Khalid halted in the center of the muddy street in Do Bandi. The late-April rains were starting once more. He wore his dark green nylon jacket and a black baseball cap to shield himself. As he glanced over his shoulder, he saw that Emma remained at the CH-47, helping a group of medical people get their supplies. He hadn't seen Kinah in two weeks and he waved to her.

When Emma looked his way, Khalid motioned with his hand, signaling where he would be if she needed him. Today, he was the pilot and she was the copilot. It was her duty to deal with the details while he could be somewhat free from those responsibilities. Emma raised her hand in return and nodded.

Happiness thrummed through Khalid as he turned.

A cluster of children surrounded him at the door where his younger sister stood. He pulled out handfuls of candy from the thigh pockets of his flight suit. Little hands opened. They didn't grab or fight. Instead, Khalid could see Kinah's firm but loving training.

"Well, well," Khalid said to them, "I believe you all need this." He handed out all the candy to the children. They were polite, smiling and they thanked him. Then, they scattered to the four winds, sweet treasures in hand.

Kinah laughed and stood aside so her brother could enter the now-empty classroom. "You are like Santa Claus to them, brother. And you spoil them. Every time you fly in here, they know it's you. I can hardly keep their attention when they hear your helicopter coming toward the village."

Khalid grinned, shut the door and embraced his tall sister. She was dressed in a cinnamon-colored wool robe and a bright red hijab covered her black curls. "I can see your handiwork, sister," he whispered, giving her an evil grin as he stepped back. "They are acting with manners. Well done." Khalid scanned the area. "This looks great," he said. There were three large green chalkboards hung on three walls. Twenty-five desks were arranged in tidy rows. Kinah was one for insisting that children learn to be organized. Each desk had a notebook, a pen and a pencil on top of it.

Kinah slipped her arm around her brother's arm and walked him to her desk at the front of the room. "Do you have an apple for the teacher, too?"

"No," Khalid admitted, still smiling. "No apple."

Pouting, Kinah released his arm and sat down in her chair. She gestured for him to sit down in the sturdy wooden chair next to her desk. "I know, you save all your gifts for Emma."

Khalid sat down and took off his baseball cap. He shrugged and said, "Well, perhaps I did remember to bring you something." He dug into the pocket of his jacket. Kinah had a great love of Kit Kats, the chocolate wafer bars. She'd been able to get them only rarely after leaving America when her education was complete. He saw Kinah's winged brows rise, and she looked with curiosity at him.

"I met Steve Hudson, an army major at Bagram. He's assigned to fly with the Apache squadrons in the south. He just happens to be a good friend of mine. So I asked a favor of him...." Khalid drew out four Kit Kats and handed them to his sister.

Kinah gasped. "Khalid! You did it!" She grabbed them. "Oh, you are such a jewel, beloved brother!" Rapidly, Kinah tore off the wrapping and took her first bite of the Kit Kat.

Khalid laughed. "You look like an addict getting her fix, Kinah."

Giggling between bites, Kinah said, "Oh, I am! But better to be addicted to chocolate than opium."

On that note, Khalid lost his smile and became more serious. "Indeed," he murmured. It did his heart good to see his vibrant, feisty sister once more. Since Operation Book Worm had begun on April second, nearly four weeks ago, he'd rarely seen his sister. Kinah's job was to bring in teachers, create an atmosphere of learning and organize everything having to do with the children's education. Her tasks were at an end today at Do Bandi. Khalid and Emma would be flying her to Zor Barawul, where she would manage the educational program for two weeks, before they headed home today.

Kinah sighed, finishing off the first Kit Kat. "That

was pure heaven. Thank you, brother." She reached over and pinched his cheek.

Khalid caught his sister's long, fluid hand and placed a kiss on the back of it. "You were looking tired. I knew Kit Kats would refuel you." He released her hand. Kinah colored fiercely and pretended to give him a stern look.

"Brother, I fly on the wings of my heart's passion. You know that. And when you love what you do, all the energy in the world is available to you."

"You have always been guided by your heart."

She returned his look. "Is there any other way?"

"No," he agreed. Gesturing around the room he asked, "So, how are you? Have things been quiet here?"

Kinah sighed. "The last week has been peaceful. The Taliban, I think, realize that with an A-team stationed here, they cannot ransack and harm the villagers. It has been a very happy, relaxed place for once."

"Mmm," Khalid said. "The Taliban goes where there is no threat to them."

"That's getting hard for them to do with the border villages," Kinah said. "You should see the difference in the people here, Khalid. They are protected for the first time in many decades. They laugh. They smile. It truly warms my heart." She pressed her hand to her breast, tears in her eyes.

"The children look clean and their hair is cut and combed," Khalid agreed. "They are joyous. I can see it deep in their eyes."

Reaching out, she gripped Khalid's arm. "What we are doing, brother, is helping. I hope you know the extent of it."

"I do. But I always worry for you. Being out here alone…"

Kinah snorted. "I'm fine, Khalid! Do not look so anxious. Save your worry for that red-haired woman who stirs the fires of your heart." Kinah saw her brother suddenly lose all his vitality, his eyes dark. "What?" she demanded, leaning forward. "Khalid, what's wrong?"

"Oh," he murmured. "There is tension between Emma and me." Giving her an uncomfortable look, Khalid added, "We're drawn to one another, but neither can do anything about it for different reasons."

"What? The most handsome, richest man in all of Afghanistan? I know hundreds of young Afghan women who dream of you being their husband!"

Twisting in the seat, Khalid grimaced. "It's not that simple, Kinah. You know the military."

"Ohhh, my poor older brother! What could she possibly not like about you?"

Khalid held his sister's indignant look. "Emma likes me—"

"Well, there you go!" Kinah said, triumphant. "I was right! No woman worth her salt will not be swayed by your looks and kind heart."

"Kinah, let me finish...."

Pouting again, Kinah sat back in her chair. "Go on."

"Emma has a six-month mission assignment. Technically, I'm her boss as the military sees it. At the end of those six months, I must write a recommendation based upon her performance over that time."

"Emma is a hard worker!" Kinah said. "She's kind, responsible and cares. I'm sure you'll give her the praise she deserves in that report."

"Yes, I will." Khalid gave his sister a look, pleading with her to stop interrupting him. He told Kinah the rest of the story. When he finished, he added, "And so, she cannot get involved. If she did and we broke up, she's afraid I would give her a bad grade and recommendation. That would hurt her military career. And frankly, I hadn't thought of that angle at all. But she's right."

Snorting again, Kinah leaped out of the chair and began to pace the room. "This is silly stuff, Khalid. I see how Emma looks at you. I certainly see the look on your face. Clearly, you are both falling in love with one another!" She threw up her hands and looked at the ceiling. "Surely, Allah, you can get these two stubborn donkeys together? Rip off their individual blinders so they can see?"

Khalid chuckled over his sister's dramatic antics. "Kinah, come, sit down...."

"How can I, brother? Surely," she protested, turning and standing in front of him, hands on her hips, "this is really about trust."

"Yes, it is," Khalid said, looking up at her demanding features.

"Emma doesn't trust you."

"That's right. She says I'm like the man who broke her heart. He too was rich and powerful. Only, he was married with two children, and he lied to her."

"Of all things!" Kinah stamped her foot and then said, "I will talk to her. I will tell her how sweet, how kind and how sensitive you are. That you would never break someone else's trust."

"No," Khalid said, "you can't talk to her, Kinah. It wouldn't be right. I'm hesitant to get into a relationship, too." He frowned and his voice lowered with anguish. "I can't because I want no woman murdered and tortured as Najela was. As long as Asad Malik lives, I will put no other woman beneath his sword. You know that. I've purposely avoided getting back into a relationship for two years now because of that price."

Rolling her eyes, Kinah muttered, "Men! You're all alike. I swear by Allah, you are!" She cupped his jaw and looked into his anguished blue eyes. "This must stop, Khalid. You can't put your life on hold because Malik is a threat. We may never see him die, and what will you do then? Live life as a monk? Deny yourself the happiness you deserve?" Removing her hand she straightened. "Khalid, do not be afraid to live once again. Don't be scared of reaching out to Emma if she stirs your heart. Asad Malik wins if you deny yourself any sort of personal life." She marched to the door and pulled it open.

Alarmed, Khalid leaped to his feet. "Kinah! Where are you going?"

"To see your beloved," she sang out, sailing out the door and disappearing.

Khalid groaned, knowing he couldn't make a spectacle of himself by rocketing out of the room and running down the street after Kinah. What had he done? It would only make things worse if he intercepted Kinah in front of Emma. And his sister wasn't one to be stopped from her trajectory. Khalid knew she cared for him and she liked Emma. It was Kinah's way of caring: getting involved as a possible future sister-in-law. Frustrated, he stood looking at the light filtering into the classroom. Emma wouldn't be happy about this. And his sister had a goal in mind, Kinah was mission-oriented. Groaning again, Khalid decided the best thing he could do was visit the chieftain of the village, give his regards and find out if he needed anything from the U.N. forces.

"Emma!" Kinah called, waving at her. Emma stood near the ramp after giving the medical team directions into the village.

"Hey, Kinah!" Emma's smile blossomed genuinely for the firebrand woman. "How are you?"

"I'm fine, my sister." Kinah gave her an American hug and then the Afghan greeting of kissing her cheeks. Gripping Emma's upper arms, she said, "Are you feeling well?"

Emma laughed. "Yes. Why? Do I have dark circles under my eyes?"

Kinah took her hand and pulled her away from the A-team members who were walking the perimeter of the helicopter. "Come with me," she whispered dramatically. "We must talk."

Emma warmed to the small Afghan woman. The bright red hijab reminded her of a red light flashing on a police cruiser. Smiling to herself, Emma allowed Kinah to pull her aside. The rainy skies threatened. A shaft of sunlight shot through like a beam down into the green valley far below. The wind was chilly and Emma was glad to have on her thick nylon jacket.

"Now," Kinah said, releasing her hand and remaining near Emma, "it appears to me that your heart has dark circles beneath its eyes!"

Studying Kinah's narrowing gaze, Emma said, "What?" Sometimes Kinah spoke in symbols and she couldn't follow the intelligent woman at all. Plus, Kinah, who loved all things American, mixed and matched Afghan sayings with American slang and sometimes, it all got jumbled for Emma.

"Do you like my brother?"

Before Emma could speak, Kinah held up her index finger the way a teacher would to a child.

"Before you say anything, my sister, I want to know how you feel. Not what you think." Smiling brightly,

Kinah pressed her hand to her heart. "And no, Khalid did not send me out here to harass you. I've decided to find out the truth for myself."

Unable to stop her smile, Emma quickly grasped what was happening. Sometimes, Kinah's excitement and sureness sent her like a juggernaut into a situation or, in this case, into a person—her. "Did Khalid tell you why I can't like him?"

"Oh, pooh!" And Kinah waved her hand impatiently and wrinkled her fine, thin nose. "Whys do not count, sister. Only your heart counts!"

Emma rested her hands on her hips and appreciated Kinah's misguided efforts. "I'm sure he told you why I can't cross that line."

Widening her large eyes, Kinah whispered fiercely, "Yes, he told me. Emma, why do you deny your heart its yearning? My brother likes you. Allah knows, he moons like a dog that has lost its mate. He told me why you think you cannot like him, but I say this is foolishness. How often do you think love happens between two people? Not often. And you deserve happiness, Emma. I know my brother will make you ecstatically happy."

Emma held up her hands. "Whoa, Kinah. Slow down, okay?"

Laughing, Kinah shook her head. "Slow down? Does the heart ever slow down? Of course not. Emma, I know you care very much for my brother. When you think I do not see the look you give him, or that he gives you, I remember it." Kinah tapped her temple. "You are suited to one another. Perfectly. I see no reason not to allow Khalid to court you as is our custom."

Emma saw the burning hope in Kinah's eyes. She was incredibly beautiful, with a square face, a stubborn

chin, gorgeous high cheekbones and a broad brow. Emma
had wondered many times why Kinah had never married. Surely, she'd had suitors. Emma made a mental note
to ask Khalid sometime about that. "I love you dearly,
Kinah, but there can't be any courting. I'm sorry, but
my life belongs to the U.S. Army. I'm not as free to follow my heart as you think." She touched Kinah's proud
shoulder. "I think the world of Khalid. You're right: he's
an incredible man and truly deserves happiness after
losing Najela. But I'm not in a position to do anything
about it, Kinah."

Touching Emma's reddened cheek, Kinah whispered,
"You are wrong, but I understand better what Khalid had
told me about the two of you. I see that there are other
priorities that must be sorted out first."

Emma smiled gently. She loved Kinah's fierce inde-
pendence, her willfulness, her heart brimming over with
a desire to lift others and give them a better way of life.
"That's a nice way of putting it," she told her.

"And what if these priorities sort out?" Kinah asked,
slyness in her tone.

Emma chuckled. "Oh, you're such a crafty fox, Kinah!
Just be patient. I don't know what the next minute will
bring. Or the next hour. In our world of the military, all
I can count on is change."

"But you like my brother?"

"I do," Emma hesitantly said.

"Does he not melt your heart?"

Sighing, Emma nodded. "He can melt butter with
those looks he gives me sometimes."

Clapping her hand, Kinah said, "Wonderful! I have
prayed to Allah daily that my dearest brother would
be healed of his wound and loss. I prayed that a new

woman might enter his life, awaken his numbed and shocked heart." She gripped Emma's arm, giving it a small shake. "My brother is one of the finest men you will ever meet. He appears kind and gentle, but he carries the heart of an Afghan snow leopard. He is a warrior, but he knows when and how to display that side to himself. He can be your best friend, Emma, if you allow him that. Perhaps that is all you can share with one another right now, but allow him that at least."

"You're such a used-car salesman, Kinah."

Kinah laughed. "Thank you, dear sister. That is a compliment! Afghans are great traders, as you know."

When the Silk Road existed, Emma knew, Afghanistan was little more than four hundred different tribes. And they traded lapis lazuli, the bright blue stone, for much money and goods. Trading was, indeed, in their DNA. "Yes, *you* certainly are." She looked at her watch. "Kinah, I have some things I have to attend to."

"Of course," Kinah said. "I'll meet you here once I find my handsome brother."

Emma watched the elegant Kinah turn and walk with pride in her steps. Unable to be angry over her overture, Emma hurried up the ramp to find the lists that she had to check. She wondered if Khalid knew that his sister had come to plead his case with her. Somehow, Emma felt Khalid would be embarrassed by it, but who could stop Kinah?

Chapter 10

Back at base camp, Emma walked with Khalid over to Ops. There they had to fill out the mandatory after-action flight reports. The April skies had cleared and now a cool breeze blew across the area. Helicopters of all types were coming in before night fell. Only the Apaches with their 24/7 ops ability ruled the night air.

Khalid opened the door for her and they made their way to a small room off to the left of the busy Ops desk. After shutting the door, Emma set her helmet bag on an empty table, grabbed the report forms and sat down. Khalid did the same.

"So," Khalid said as he looked up from his form, "my sister grilled you. I'm sorry, Emma, I didn't want her to say anything."

Touched by his sincere apology and the worried look in his blue eyes, Emma stopped herself from reaching across the table to touch his hand. How easy it was to let herself simply be lulled into Khalid's world of the heart. "Don't worry about it." Emma pushed some strands of hair off her brow. "Kinah is a force of nature that no one can stop. She was very nice about selling you to me."

Khalid sat back and looked up at the ceiling for a moment. "I knew she'd do that...."

"Hey," Emma murmured, sympathetic. "She loves you, Khalid. She's a great sister. I have sisters, too, and I'd want them to circle the wagons to support me."

"Do they?" he asked, resuming work on his report.

"Yes. We're tighter than fleas on a dog."

Laughing at the slang expression, Khalid shook his head. "Well, I ask your forgiveness for my beloved but impetuous younger sister."

"I weathered it," Emma said dryly.

After filing their reports, Khalid prepared to check out an Apache helo. He would fly it back to Bagram Air Force Base. Emma rose and collected her gear and walked to the door. Outside the thin wooden door she could hear the noise of Operations: the laughter, the people talking, along with the sound of airplane and helo engines.

"I'll see you tomorrow at 0800?" Khalid asked as he opened the door. How badly he wanted to romance Emma, but he knew it was folly. If anything, Khalid realized his growing desire for Emma would truly have to be tabled forever. The pain in his heart was constant over that realization.

"Yes," she called over her shoulder. Emma lifted her hand in farewell. "Have a safe flight home, Khalid."

He watched Emma disappear in the crowded Ops and his heart contracted with sadness. Turning, he walked up to the Ops desk to fill out a flight plan before he left for Bagram.

* * *

Emma was jolted out of her early-morning sleep by a sergeant who came to her tent.

"Captain Cantrell?" the woman sergeant called.

Disoriented for a moment, Emma said, "What? What's wrong?"

"Ma'am, Zor Barawul is under attack. We need every available pilot!"

Adrenaline shot through her and she leaped off the cot. "Has Captain Shaheen—"

"Yes, ma'am. He's on his way to pick you up right now. You have about ten minutes before he arrives here at the base."

Emma turned on a small lamp that gave her enough light to get dressed and hotfoot it over to Ops. "What's the report on the village? Do we have Apaches in there?" Grabbing her flight boots, she jammed them on her feet.

"Yes, ma'am. Two Apaches were sent there about thirty minutes ago when the attack by the Taliban began."

Emma quickly caught her red hair into a rubber band at the nape of her neck. She stood up, grabbed her helmet bag and rushed out the tent flap. The sergeant trotted alongside Emma. Overhead, the night sky twinkled with bright, white stars. A thin slice of moon hung in the sky. The air was cold but not freezing.

"What else?" Emma demanded, jogging down the road between lines of tents.

"Ma'am, they think it's Asad Malik attacking. It's his signature and the A-team is calling for reinforcements."

"Dammit," Emma muttered. Her brow wrinkled. One of the things they had done after they left the village of Do Bandi was to take Kinah north to Zor Barawul. She was to spend the next two weeks helping to get the teachers set up to teach. Was Kinah okay? Emma's heart contracted with fear for the woman.

The sergeant said, "Ma'am, I need to get back to BJS HQ."

"Fine, I'll be in radio contact with HQ on this, too." Emma lengthened her stride, fully awake now. By the time she arrived at Ops and signed in, she saw Khalid's Apache landing outside the doors. Once outside, Emma stood impatiently on the tarmac and waited until the blades had stopped turning. The flight crew quickly placed chocks beneath the three wheels.

As she quickly climbed up on the helo, she saw Khalid's dark and tense face. The other cockpit behind his had the canopy open. She hesitated for a moment. "Khalid, have you heard anything on the attack?"

"No, climb in."

Nodding, Emma swung into the seat and quickly got settled. A crew woman helped her strap in and then closed and locked the canopy before hopping down off the helo and pulling the ladder away. Time was of the essence. As soon as Emma got the helmet on her head and plugged into the communications system, she asked, "What's the last you heard, Khalid?"

"Let's do the preflight check. I'll tell you more after we get airborne," he ordered tersely.

The tension in his voice heightened Emma's worry for Kinah. Oh, God, what if she was hurt? Emma's hands flew with a knowing ease as she went down the checklist for preflight with Khalid. Her heart pounded like a drum and speed was important.

The Apache shook and shuddered around them as

Khalid, the air commander, got the helo up to speed. Emma received permission from the control tower to take off. She noticed that the Apache was loaded with weapons. They were flying into combat, no doubt.

As the helo took off beneath Khalid's hands, Emma switched to the green light across her instrument panel and two screens in front of her. The green color was less harsh on her vision. Blackness surrounded them, the base camp quickly disappearing. They would fly at nine thousand feet toward Zor Barawul. Emma felt safe within the shuddering vibration of the Apache. She could sense Khalid's worry. What must it be like for him? He'd already lost the woman he loved. Now, he could lose his sister. Emma knew how close they were, how much they loved one another. "How are you doing?" she asked.

"The best I can," he growled.

Emma heard the terror in his low, husky tone. She could hear his fast and shallow breathing. "Does Kinah know what to do in a situation like this?"

"My sister is a survivor, if nothing else."

"And she's gone through attacks like this before?"

"Yes."

His voice was raw and strained. How would she feel if one of her sisters was in a firefight with the Taliban? If the Taliban broke through, they'd kill Kinah on the spot. Lips tightening, Emma said in a soothing voice, "I know she'll be okay, Khalid. I feel it in my heart."

"Let us hope you're right," he rasped.

There was little else she could do. Emma felt a special kind of helplessness. She knew all the people at this village. Good, kind and generous Afghans who wanted nothing more than a life better than the hard-scrabble

one they had to eke out in these desert mountains. And
what of the A-team stationed there? Had they taken casualties? Emma couldn't stand not knowing so she dialed in the A-team frequency. Instantly, her ears were
filled with the sound of gunfire, explosions and the
yelling of orders between the captain and his men. No
doubt, a fierce, ongoing battle. Gulping, Emma began
to pray because at this point, that's all she could do.

Khalid circled the village of Zor Barawul, high up on
a hill far above a narrow unseen valley below. His heart
centered on Kinah, but he couldn't afford to go there.
Right now, he was coordinating with the two Apaches
already on station and working to kill the Taliban who
had gotten very close to the village itself. In his gut,
Khalid knew it was Asad Malik. Just the other day on
a Taliban website, he'd read that Malik promised to kill
him and Kinah. Was this the beginning of his campaign
against them? Khalid had read Malik's spewed hatred
against the education of girls. He'd railed against Kinah
because she was a woman leading a fierce battle for
peace and education.

Khalid had not told Emma about this website or Malik's promise. Grimly, he swung the Apache around as
the air commander, Major Klein, ordered them to hover
and fire rockets into a hillside about two hundred feet
below the village. Unable to do anything but focus on
the attack, Khalid worked constantly with Emma, who
would handle the ordnance and fire the weapons.

Emma watched the explosions walk across the rock,
dirt and thick scrub brush on the steep slopes. She heard
Major Klein ordering another set of Apaches out of this
firefight, saying that they were low on ammunition.

They would have to fly back to the base camp, take on another load of ordnance and then fly back here. Emma was amazed at the ferocity of the battle. The winking red and yellow lights of A-team members firing down the hill looked like Christmas sparkling in the night.

Emma worried for all the villagers, like Ateefa, the little girl with the prosthetic leg. How was her mother, Jameela? Was she holding her children and trying to keep all of them safe? In the mud homes, bullets could easily fly through the walls and kill someone trying to hide. Abbas had one of the few stone houses, but it had windows and bullets took no prisoners.

Her headphones jumped with more frantic calls from the A-team. A group of Taliban had breached the slope! She felt Khalid moving the Apache in that direction. With a sinking feeling, Emma saw the other two Apaches who had been on station flying off because they were out of ammunition. Now, it was up to them. Could they repel this attack? Hundreds of infrared bodies showed up on the slope via the one screen. The Taliban were like relentless ants crawling up the hill and cresting it.

"Medevac's on the way," Emma reported, hearing another channel. "A-team has four men wounded."

"Roger," Khalid growled. "Switch to Gatling gun. Hose that area where the enemy is getting over the top of that hill."

"You got it," Emma said. She felt the Apache bank, heard the engines thunder as her fingers flew over the console to engage the huge gun beneath the belly of their helo. At least twenty Taliban were now running full tilt toward where the A-team had made their stand. If they got past the A-team, they were into the village itself. And Emma knew they'd go house-to-house, firing inside and killing everyone without mercy. The villagers had some weapons but could never repulse an attack like this. They were helpless against these thugs.

Khalid took a big risk by flying in low. They were well within range of the enemy firing a grenade up at them or, worse, a rocket. It was a chance they had to take. The helo shuddered violently as Emma triggered the Gatling gun. Khalid felt the floor of the helo vibrate heavily as the gun continued to fire. His feet grew numb from the shudder. He watched his other cameras because he knew Emma was engaged with the gun.

Suddenly, a bright light popped off the slope about two hundred feet below. "Rocket launch!" he yelled. Instantly, he shoved the throttles to the firewall, hit the rudders and made an effort to evade the fired rocket.

Emma cursed and quickly turned her attention to it. She hit the flares in the nose. They could possibly detour the rocket. Red flares lit up the sky. Her fingers flew to the trigger to fire their own rockets. She punched the button. Instantly, the Apache bucked from the rocket's fire. Bright yellow light momentarily blinded her. Her harness cut deeply into her shoulders as Khalid worked frantically to get the Apache out of the way of the oncoming Taliban rocket. Her eyes widened and her heart banged violently in her throat. Would the rocket hit them?

A million thoughts jammed into Emma's head as she watched, almost fascinated, as the ground-fired weapon hurtled up toward them. A rocket had heat-seeking abilities and she was sure it had locked on the Apache's overhead engines. Mouth dry, Emma suddenly felt her entire world slow down to single frames from a movie.

She heard Khalid's heavy breathing. Felt the Apache screaming in protest as he continued violent, evasive maneuvers to try and outwit the oncoming rocket.

Then, at the last second, the Apache rocket locked onto the enemy fire and struck it with full force. The entire night lit up like a Fourth of July celebration. Emma gasped and threw up her gloved hand to protect her eyes from the red, yellow and orange fireball that was no more than three hundred feet to their starboard. The resulting explosion sent a massive shock wave through the night air. It struck the Apache broadside. The helo shuddered and shook. Khalid wrestled with the controls in order to ride out the shock wave.

"Direct hit!" Emma yelled, her adrenaline pumping through her, making her anxious and yet angry. She had no time to sit and gloat over the fact they were still in the air.

"Back to work," Khalid snarled. "Gatling gun. We're going back in. The Taliban is still on top of the hill. We've got to stop them!"

For the next ten minutes, Emma's world revolved around halting the Taliban attack. Her headphones crackled with other communications. There were three medevac helos on the way. Khalid asked BJS 60 to send more reinforcements, saying that they were running low on ordnance. Emma was careful with the Gatling gun. Prolonged firing would only waste the precious ammunition. Instead, with Khalid's expert touch at the controls, she was able to use the infrared camera that showed body heat and fire it in short bursts. It saved their ammo and targeted the running groups who were trying to penetrate the village itself.

Sweat poured down Emma. Her gloves were wet,

and she felt the trickle from beneath her armpits. Her gaze was glued to the television console, slipping back and forth between it and the infrared screen. Emma saw the Taliban being driven to a standstill. In the back of her mind, she worried that another rocket would be fired at them. They hovered less than four hundred feet above the fray and directly over the A-team like a big, bad guard dog. Bullets pinged off the Apache's resilient skin. The Taliban were now firing up at them, hoping to hit the rotor assembly above the cockpits and bring them down.

Time became suspended. All Emma saw was gunfire back and forth. The shuddering of the Apache vibrated through every cell in her tense body. Khalid's breathing was ragged and so was hers. This was a life-and-death effort. If they couldn't stop the Taliban from coming over the slope, the A-team would be overrun. Already, the A-team leader had called for reinforcements. They needed more ammunition. A CH-47 had been launched from the base camp with a resupply of ordnance for them, but none of it would get here in time. Emma knew it was only their being on station above the team that might tip the balance in their favor. If they hadn't hovered and stood like a gate guardian, the Taliban would have surged like a tsunami into the village, murdering men, women and children.

"Fire a Hellfire missile into that area where they've breached it," Khalid ordered her.

Emma rasped, "Roger that..." She quickly dialed in the Hellfire II. It was a brilliant idea. Why hadn't she thought of it?

"After firing it, I'm going to fly us around to attack

that slope with what we have left in ordnance. If we can't stop them, everyone's toast."

"Roger," Emma said sharply, her mind focused on the missile. She flipped the switch. The Apache jerked as the missile slid off the rail. Light flared beneath the stubby wing. And then, she watched it hunt down the mass of men coming over that slope like a dark, malevolent ooze toward the village.

The entire night sky lit up again. Blinded, Emma couldn't know how many that rocket had killed, but it had to be substantial. Rock, dirt and dust flew skyward. She felt Khalid wrenching the Apache in a sharp bank to the left. The shoulder harness bit hard into her and Emma tried to brace herself. Khalid was a skilled pilot and he knew how to push the limits of the Apache to get the maximum performance.

The helicopter thumped down, down, down the slope where there was no longer any enemy left alive. Emma tensed and held on. She worked to get the gun back online. In seconds, Khalid whipped the combat helicopter around to the slope where the Taliban had breached the hill. On the screens in front of her, Emma observed a lot of unmoving bodies. Down below them, however, was another mass trying to climb upward.

"Fire at will," Khalid muttered.

"Roger," Emma said, her voice taut. She triggered the gun again and again. The knot of Taliban scattered like a flock of birds that had had a rock thrown in their midst. "They're on the run!" she yelled triumphantly.

"Keep at it," Khalid ordered in a tight voice.

Between her skill at hitting targets and Khalid's ability to make the Apache dance like a ballerina in the sky, Emma was able to beat back the rest of the attack.

In minutes, the charge was over. They swung around and around the hill looking at their infrared screens for any moving bodies trying to form another attack. Sweat ran into her eyes. Emma blinked several times. She pushed the perspiration away with her trembling, gloved fingers. She felt the Apache surge upward into the darkness.

"I think we got them," she told Khalid. Her voice was shaky; the adrenaline made it that way.

"Roger that," Khalid agreed, his voice thick with unspoken emotion.

"We're down to dregs on ordnance," she warned him.

"In five minutes, two more Apaches will arrive on scene."

Five minutes could be a hell of an eternity, but Emma remained silent. They kept flying around the thickly brushed slope below the village. Who was dead in Zor Barawul? Who was injured? She could hear the chatter between the A-team leader and the medevacs that would arrive on scene in ten minutes. Before they could land to take on the injured men, the place had to be secured and safe. That was their job: fly around and continue to be a threat to the Taliban, should they think of trying a second assault.

"Helluva night," Emma whispered into the microphone on the inter-cabin frequency.

"Yes. You're a good shot."

She heard a little relief in Khalid's voice. He was on an adrenaline high like her. Emma smiled a little. "You're one hell of a pilot, too."

"Thank you. Now we're a mutual admiration society."

Chuckling, Emma felt some of her own relief tun-

neling through her. "I'm worried about Kinah. I wish
we could know how she is."

"I know..."

"Maybe we can get one of the A-team to go check in
the village as soon as medevac arrives and takes their
wounded back to the hospital at Bagram?"

"That's what I was thinking," Khalid said. He swung
the Apache out in wider arcs as they approached the
base of the hill where the village sat. "I wish we could
land. But I know we can't."

Emma grimaced. "Take it from one who once did
and suffered as a result, you don't want to do that."

Khalid smiled, but grimly. He kept his hands on the
collective and cyclic, continuing to widen their hunt for
whatever was left of Malik's group. He hoped Malik
was dead. "No, I don't want to go there. When things
get organized and calmed down, we can ask the captain
to send a team member in to locate Kinah."

Emma saw the other two Apaches arriving on station. It felt good to see the combat helicopters loaded
down with ordnance. "Whew, the cavalry has just arrived. Good to see them."

"Hey, Red Dog One," Nike Alexander called to them,
"I hear you've been stomping the hell outta the Taliban.
Good work. Doesn't look like there's anything for us to
do. Bummer! Over."

Chuckling, Emma keyed her mike. "Roger, Red Dog
Three, we didn't leave much for you to clean up. Over."

"And here I wanted to dance on those bastards'
heads," Nike chortled. "Over."

Khalid laughed and so did Emma. "We're going to
hang around for a while longer, Red Dog Three. Over."

"Roger that. More Apaches are good. It will give

those bastards second and third thoughts about regrouping to hit this village again. Any idea of casualties yet? Over."

"No, Red Dog Three. No sense of how many are dead or wounded. Over."

Emma sat back and tried to relax as Khalid urged the Apache to five thousand feet. She watched as the other two combat helos scoured the area, hunting like hungry wolves for any survivors. Grateful to this incredible machine, Emma knew they had saved Zor Barawul. At least this time. She wondered how Khalid was handling the fact his sister might be dead or injured. How badly she wanted to land, but they didn't dare break that regulation.

Emma switched to inter-cabin and asked Khalid, "You doing all right?"

"As best as I can. I'm worried for Kinah...."

"What if we get permission to fly back to camp and then we pick up a CH-47 and fly back out here? It will be dawn by that time and we'll be able to do it. That way, we can land and you can find Kinah. It might take an hour, but at least you'd be on the ground." A CH-47 had no nighttime gear on board and was only flown in VFR conditions where the pilot could do a line-of-sight visually.

"Good idea, thank you."

"I'll call BJS and get permission to head back to base," Emma said.

Chapter 11

"Kinah!" Khalid called as he ran into the village shortly after Emma had landed the CH-47. Dawn crawled up the horizon, allowing them to fly back to the battered village. The A-team leader, Captain Jason Cunningham, had radioed in just as they landed the Apache at their base camp. They'd found Khalid's sister. Kinah had been wounded in the fierce fighting but had waived her right to be brought back on the medevac. There were men on Cunningham's team that needed medical treatment before her own wounds, she'd told them.

As he rushed into the schoolhouse, Khalid saw that hundreds of bullets had punctured the mud walls.

Kinah sat holding the two orphan boys in the schoolroom. "Khalid!" she cried, relief in her tone.

"Sister!" he rasped, his voice cracking with emotion. Kinah's hair was in disarray. Small oil lanterns burned and shed light into the gray space. Beneath each arm huddled one of the young orphans, Benham and Fahran. Both were pale, their eyes huge with fear. She sat on the floor, her back to one wall near the desk. She was not wearing a hijab. Tracks of tears streaked down her dirtied, tense face, making Khalid even more anxious.

"They said you were wounded," he whispered, kneeling down and tentatively touching her shoulder. He tried to keep the fear out of his voice as he searched for blood.

"Just a scrape," Kinah protested, sniffing. She held up her hand and showed him a graze of a bullet across her wrist area that had been hidden by her robe. As Khalid gently cupped her shoulders, she struggled to battle back her tears. Her lower lip trembled. "Khalid, it was awful! So many people were killed! I hate the Taliban! They did this to us!" More tears fell and made tracks through the fine dust across her face.

"I know, I know," Khalid soothed. He crouched before them. Gently touching each boy's head, he asked them in Pashto if they were all right. Each jerkily nodded they were okay. Khalid could see they were in shock by the glassy look in their eyes.

"I was in here," Kinah whispered, "with them. They wanted to help me clean up the room. Such good boys." She wiped her eyes and sniffed. "It was just shortly after dusk." Looking around at the holes and the cool air flowing through the schoolroom, Kinah sobbed once and then gulped back the rest of her tears.

"I dragged the boys beneath my desk and huddled with them in my arms. We were all crying, Khalid. We were so afraid. I've been in firefights before, but this one was the worst I've ever weathered. I was fearful of the Taliban overrunning the A-team. Poor Captain Cunningham! He and his men fought fiercely. All I wanted to do was keep the boys safe and survive this awful hell on earth!"

Touching her curly, dusty hair, Khalid gave her a sad smile. He pulled a green linen handkerchief from his pocket and gently dabbed her dusty cheeks. "It was bad," he agreed. "But you survived, Allah be praised. And so did these boys." He gave them a smile in hopes of letting them know they were now safe. "Are they wounded?"

"N-no," Kinah sniffed. She took the handkerchief and wiped her eyes. "A medic already came by and checked them over. He wanted me to leave for this silly scratch on my wrist and I told him no. The boys are fine. Just scared."

Who wasn't? Khalid nodded and helped each boy to stand. They shook like leaves in the wind. He then gripped his sister's hands and pulled her to her feet. Khalid briefly held her, placed a kiss on Kinah's damp cheek and looked deeply into her frightened eyes. His sister had been in two other villages where firefights had broken out a year ago. This one, however, had scared her even more and shadows lurked in her brown eyes. "I want you to come home for a while, Kinah. Let the U.S. Army get this place more secured. Then come back here."

"No," she muttered, giving him a defiant look. Breaking free of his embrace, Kinah brought the two boys to her side and held them. Each clung to her robe.

Sighing, Khalid nodded. "I thought you'd say that."

"We can't leave. That would be a sign of defeat, Khalid. You know that." Kinah scanned the room riddled with bullet holes. "No, I refuse to run! I would say this is the work of Malik." Her brows dipped and anger tinged her husky tone. "That desert rat is behind this, Khalid. My gut tells me so. Last year up north at the other village where I worked so hard to get the people to build a schoolroom, he came in and shot hundreds of holes through it."

"Yes," Khalid said quietly, "I believe he's behind this attack." And he said no more. Both of them were aware of Malik's promise to kill them. It had almost happened last night. Khalid wanted desperately to remove Kinah from the village. As he looked into the stubborn set of her chin, he knew it was useless to insist.

"Where's Emma?" Kinah asked, wanting to move on.

"At the helo. We brought in a medical team and other emergency supplies." He glanced toward the door that had been splintered by gunfire. "I need to get back to help her. Will you be all right here?"

"I'm fine, brother. Go. I'm taking these boys to my home. They need to get washed up, find clean clothes and be fed some food. That's where I'll be."

Khalid leaned over and pressed a kiss to her damp cheek. "We will come to see you later," he promised, his voice thick with emotion. Turning on his heel, Khalid left the nearly destroyed classroom. A number of the desks were in shattered ruins, too. His heart ached for his sister. This time around, Kinah had been brutally impacted by the attack. The other two times last year were nothing in comparison to this one. Khalid could see that she grappled with the trauma of it all. Who didn't in this demoralized village?

Emma glanced up to see Khalid striding down the muddy street toward where she stood with the list of supplies in hand. How was Kinah? Anxious, she passed the list to her load master. A number of men from the village assisted what was left of the A-team to offload the emergency supplies. Five soldiers were on their way to Bagram for treatment of their wounds. The medical team, consisting of a doctor, a nurse and a medic, was already in the village helping those who had been hurt, but not badly enough to be medevaced to Bagram for treatment.

Meeting Khalid, she asked, "Kinah? How is she?"

Khalid told her. The morning was dawning clear after the storm clouds of yesterday. Emma's fine, thin brows moved downward as he finished.

"She's been traumatized," Emma growled, unhappy.

"Yes, this time it really got to her," Khalid agreed, his voice distraught.

"She won't leave?"

"No. Wild horses wouldn't drag her out of here now."

Seeing Khalid's worried, forlorn eyes, Emma wanted to reach out and embrace him. "I'm sorry, Khalid. War is ugly business. Everyone is hurt by it," she said, hurting for him.

"You should have seen those two orphan boys. They were shaking like little trees in the aftermath."

"The worst is how the children are affected," Emma agreed. "But they're with Kinah. She'll be a rock for them and she'll get them through this."

Khalid looked around. Bodies of the Taliban had been put to one side of the flat landing area. A number of Afghan national soldiers had come with them on their flight, and now they were going through each man's clothing to find identification. It wasn't a job he would want.

"Malik's behind this," he rasped to Emma as they walked back to the helo. Most of the crates were out of the bird and the last of the A-team men hefted supplies on their shoulders and took them into the busy village.

"It sounds like his signature calling card: destroying the schoolroom. The bastard," Emma whispered, angry.

Walking up the ramp, the load master, a twenty-year-old blond technical sergeant, handed her another list. Emma stopped and signed it. She was AC, air commander, and therefore responsible to see the shipment was out of the helo and delivered to the proper village authorities. Khalid walked past her and sat in the left-hand seat. He moved his knees aside so she could slide between the seats and sit down in the right-hand seat. Even though she was the AC, Khalid was the head of this mission.

"What now?" Emma asked. Khalid's profile was silhouetted against the sunlight suddenly flooding into the cockpit.

"I need to talk with Abbas. By the way, their family is okay. Shaken up, but no injuries. Many of their windows are shattered, but they can be replaced."

"Good," Emma sighed. "I'm relieved." Living in a stone house rather than a mud one had its advantages in a firefight.

Khalid glanced around. No one was near their helicopter. Driven by the anguish of his sister facing death so bravely, he couldn't help himself. Last night as he and Emma had fought the Taliban, he'd known that they, too, could die. And they nearly had when that rocket was fired at them.

Khalid's eyes narrowed upon her, burning with desire. Taken off guard by his sudden predatory look, she didn't see it coming. One moment he was in the chair and the next, he was standing. He cupped her face with his long hands and leaned down, sweeping a powerful kiss against her mouth. Emma stiffened momentarily. The heat of his mouth rocked her lips open. She felt his warm breath, smelled his spicy scent and tasted chai.

Her world dissolved beneath the swift, hungry kiss, his mouth sliding hotly against hers. Oh! Emma didn't know what to do. For so long, she had yearned for Khalid's mouth on hers once more. She wanted to feel his sensuous, exploring lips against hers, inciting her, teasing her and letting her know just how much he loved her.

Mind spinning as she hungrily returned his passionate kiss, his fingers moving through her hair and holding her prisoner against his searching mouth, Emma heard the word *love* reverberating through the halls of her wildly beating heart. Right now, Khalid's mouth was playing her as if she were a beloved instrument in his hands. His lips drifted from her mouth to her cheek, to her closed eyes and finally, back to her parted, wet lips. There was such tenderness in Khalid's slow exploration of her as a woman. And Emma wanted this. She wanted him.

Khalid's soul absorbed Emma. Never had he wanted a woman more than her. That shook his internal world. His grief was gone. In its place an assuredness that this magnificent and courageous red-haired American woman was priceless to him. Her mouth was soft and pliant, giving and taking. He'd been afraid she'd reject him, but, to his relief, once his mouth slid across hers in invitation, she'd responded just as eagerly and passionately as he. Perhaps it was the combat last night, their near-death experience? Khalid wasn't sure. What he did know without reservation was that he was falling in love with Emma.

As he sipped at her wet lips, Khalid smiled and whispered against them, "You are the sunlight to my darkness, beloved."

Just the way he whispered *beloved* made Emma moan with pleasure. As she drew away, his face inches from her, the tender light burning in his blue eyes, she didn't know what to do or say. "Oh, Khalid," she managed in a strangled tone.

"I know," he said apologetically, releasing her. "We're in a very confusing situation." He stared down at her full mouth glistening in the wake of his worshipful kisses. Fighting himself, Khalid sat down. He reached out and gripped her hand. "We could have died in combat last night."

Emma closed her eyes, as she heard the urgency in his voice. She worried about someone seeing them kiss or holding hands. It was forbidden by military law. Opening her eyes, she cast a quick glance around. They were alone, and relief sped through her. She drowned in his pleading gaze. "In our business," she said in an unsteady tone, "we can die at any time, Khalid. You know that." He had been right, though. Last night's combat had been raw and violent. She was still edgy from it. So was he. Plus, Khalid had thought his sister might have died in the attack. Emma realized the pressures upon him and knew that he needed a safe harbor. She was that harbor.

Nodding, Khalid forced himself to release Emma's hand. It was a hand he wanted to kiss, one finger at a time. His dreams were erotic, with his loving Emma an inch at a time. "Yes, you're right. I'm still on an adrenaline high from it."

Emma tucked her hands in her lap. "We're both jumpy. We have a right to be." She lowered her voice and searched his stormy gaze. "You could have lost Kinah last night. I understand, Khalid. We all need someone at times like this."

The silence settled in the cockpit. Khalid's heart pounded with love for Emma. He knew he could not speak of it. Not yet, at least. And he had to get past the six-month mission before he broached it with her. "People need people," he agreed, his voice suddenly weary. "I'm just glad you're here. Thank you." He reached out and grazed her hand. "I didn't exactly give you warning, did I?"

Emma drowned in the heat of his voice and eyes. Khalid's ability to seduce her was more than impressive. She'd never met a man who could touch her heart and soul at the same time. But Khalid did. "No, you didn't," she admitted, her voice barely above a whisper. What should she do? As much as she tried to push away her desire for Khalid, their attraction kept growing. Emma felt out of control, but reasoned that it had to do with the combat.

"It was good."

His eyes crinkled at the corners. Sometimes, Khalid reminded her of an Irish elf, a trickster who was completely unexpected in his actions. Like this kiss. How long had she waited for it? Emma wanted to tell Khalid of her dreams of making love with him, but she didn't dare. "Yes, it was very good," she said. "But I'm confused, Khalid. I'm not sure what to do."

"Then," Khalid said, hope in his voice, "perhaps we

can learn to be good friends who support one another in times like this?"

"I don't know where professionalism and personal needs begin and end with you. I'm at odds with myself." She touched the area of her heart. "I wish we'd met somewhere else. The military is a rough place to find romance, much less keep it and grow it."

Joy raced through Khalid as he heard Emma's softly spoken admittance. She couldn't look at him, her gaze down on her tightly clasped hands. He wanted to unleash his excitement and hope, but he reined it all in. He had to respect Emma's need to get past this mission. "You have trusted me with yourself, Emma. I will hold you in my heart and hands as if you were a dear friend."

Tilting her head, Emma studied Khalid's serious features. "I've been in other situations where my boss and I did become friends. It never influenced us when we were flying or what we had to do in our respective jobs."

"And you are okay with that between us? To allow our friendship to flourish like a red rose bud?" Khalid asked hopefully.

She melted beneath his burning blue eyes that spoke so fervently of untold and unexplored possibilities. Perhaps, someday, Emma cautioned herself. "I can't think of having a better friend than you, Khalid."

Chapter 12

"You're looking pretty down," Nike observed of Emma as they sat in the chow hall at dinnertime. The place was noisy, crowded and plenty of A-teams were mingling with the combat and transport pilots.

Emma pushed the mashed potatoes around on her aluminum tray. "Yeah, some stuff happened in the last twenty-four hours, and I'm conflicted about it."

Nike had her appetite. She dove into the steaming mashed potatoes and gravy. "Khalid?" she guessed.

Looking up, Emma frowned. "Yeah. How'd you know?"

Nike wiped her mouth with a paper napkin. "Oh, come on! He's in love with you. Don't you see it?"

"Mmm...."

Nike cut into her sirloin hamburger. "The guy clearly loves you. Now, I wouldn't ordinarily judge things like that, but it's written all over his face every time I see him with you. Has he let you in on his secret?" She grinned wolfishly.

Unhappy, Emma set her cutlery aside and sighed. "Yes and no. He kissed me this morning." Emma saw Nike's black, thin brows rise with surprise and then she saw fear in her friend's eyes—for her. Holding up her hand, Emma quickly added, "No one saw us."

"That's good. Because you think getting busted over us landing on that hilltop was something? If Dallas hears about you kissing another officer in a combat zone, your ass is grass, my friend. You'll never be more than a captain, even if you're allowed to stay in for your twenty years."

"I know, I know."

"So, you want his attention? He seems like such a heroic figure, Emma. He's doing so much for his people here in his country. He and his sister are out on the front lines every day making a difference." Nike popped some food into her mouth, chewed for a few moments and swallowed. "What's not to like?"

"I didn't want his attention, Nike, but he's a man with a mission."

"You like him?"

"Yes." Emma's brows curved downward and she stared at the food on her tray, her stomach in knots. "There's nothing to dislike about Khalid. That's the problem."

Nike studied her critically. An entire A-team took up the picnic tables to their left. She lowered her tone and leaned forward so only Emma could hear her. "What is the problem? That he's Afghan and you're an American citizen? That your family, if they heard about you fall-

ing in love with a foreigner, would go bonkers? Or...?
You supply the third reason."

Emma glanced toward the A-team. A sergeant came
and sat to her right, his tray filled high with food. She
knew these men ate MREs out on their thirty-day missions and that hot food was a rarity in their lives. "My
family is very open-minded about whom I might fall in
love with. My mom and dad aren't prejudiced."

"Yeah," Nike said, "but he's a Muslim, Emma. Did
you consider that angle? I mean, the Trayherns are a
military dynasty. I'm sure you probably don't have that
religion in your family."

Emma shrugged. "Not yet. My family accepts all religions, Nike. They have a live-and-let-live attitude. I
like my parents' take on it: a religion is something you
live daily. It's not about going to church once every
seven days and then not living your beliefs the other
six days. In Khalid's case, I respect and admire him for
his dedication and beliefs. He clearly lives them every
day whether it's dangerous to do so or not. That's com-
mitment."

Nike considered her words. "I just wonder if your
parents would be so open-minded if you married the
guy, though."

Shocked, Emma sat up. "Married?!" She'd said it a
little louder than she'd thought. The entire A-team to
their right collectively lifted their heads and stared at
Emma. They soon turned, bent their heads and continued to shovel in the food as if they'd never get any more.

Heat flushed from Emma's neck upward and stung
her cheeks. She rolled her eyes, having no one to blame
but herself for speaking too loudly. Nike grinned,

clearly enjoying her reaction. Emma leaned forward and whispered, "I haven't thought of marriage, Nike."

"Well, I didn't either when I met Gavin, but that's what happened," Nike chuckled, resuming eating her meal.

"Did your family have issues with him being an American army captain because you're from Greece? Did your parents get upset with the fact you are going to marry someone who isn't Greek?"

Nike wiped her mouth, took a sip of her coffee and said, "No, they didn't. My dad was in the military for twenty years and is now a commercial pilot for a major Greek airline. He flies around the world. My mother is cosmopolitan, too. The only thing that gives them stress is that when I marry Gavin at the end of our tours, we'll continue to be in the army. And so, we're not going to be home in Greece. They'd like that, of course, but understand we have to go where the army assigns us."

"Yes, but eventually, you will retire," Emma said. "Would you live in Greece or the U.S.?"

"We don't know that yet. My parents want us to live in Athens near them. But Gavin's farm parents want him to come and settle down near them in Nebraska. We're not promising either set of parents anything at this point."

"And Gavin isn't Muslim," Emma muttered.

"True, but you know what? I have a lot of friends who worship different gods. As long as they don't push their religion on me and I don't push my beliefs on them, we're fine. Everyone has to be more open-minded."

"It's only the fanatics of any religion who cause trouble," Emma agreed.

"So, if Khalid's religion isn't really an issue with your parents or you, why are you so hesitant?"

Emma picked up her fork and ate a few kernels of corn from her tray. "I just need time, Nike. I didn't expect to like this man. I didn't realize how heroic he really was deep down. Khalid has worked for the good of the common people here in his country ever since he returned from the U.S. And it's not like he doesn't have money. His father is a billionaire times ten. He uses the money to lift people out of the terrible poverty we see here."

"Yeah, he'll need billions to do that," Nike muttered. "With all the bribes that are expected, I'm sure he goes through plenty of dough."

Emma groaned. "Yes, bribery has been a way of life for Afghan people for thousands of years. It's awful. I don't see what or who is going to break this cycle, Nike. The chieftain of the region is always looking for money from Khalid."

"Oh, you mean Jawid Khan. He's a crafty devil," Nike agreed with a slight smile. "But he's like all chieftains. They have over four hundred and fifty different tribes that make up the country of Afghanistan. They've had this system enforced for thousands of years."

Emma continued to nibble at the corn. "Khan is only forty-five years old and, really, he's the one who is part of the Northern Alliance that has been fighting the Taliban for the last decade after the Russians gave up and left."

"I heard he's a pretty colorful guy. I've never met him."

"I haven't, either," Emma said, "but Khalid knows

him well. He can't do business in Khan's villages without his blessing."

"And of course," Nike said, smiling, "the blessing is in the form of money greasing the chieftain's palm."

"Right on," Emma said.

"But I hear from Mike, Dallas's husband who works up the strategy with the general, that Khan is a pretty decent fellow. He's continued to use his five hundred horsemen to seek and root out Taliban all along the border."

Emma nodded. "Khan is a good guy of a sort. I just wish this bribery would go away."

"But how else is Khan going to feed his men, take care of his horses and get ammo to fight the Taliban?"

"I know, I know," Emma muttered. "It's a system. I don't have to like it."

"It's so old that I don't care what the commanders say about winning the hearts and minds of Afghans. I don't think it's ever going away," Nike admitted.

"I understand from Mike that Khan is coming to Zor Barawul. After this last attack on Khan's main village, he's shifting his forces to protecting them in a proactive manner."

"He's going up against his old nemesis, Malik," Nike said.

"Yep, those two hate one another. I'm hoping that with five hundred horse soldiers in the valley, Malik will think twice about doing what he just did to that village."

"Malik's not dumb. He's a cagey fox," Nike agreed. "He'll probably shift his force north or south of Zor Barawul."

"Yeah," Emma said unhappily, "to Do Bandi, another of Khan's villages he's sworn to protect."

"At least we know the players," Nike said, lifting the cup to her lips and sipping. After she set the white mug down on the table, she added, "And Khan is a pretty good guy. Maybe Zor Barawul will get the peace it needs in order to really establish that school for the girls and boys."

Emma lifted her fingers and crossed them. "I hope so."

"You going out there tomorrow?"

"Yes, with Khalid. Kinah's in the village and we're bringing in a dental team for the children."

"You'll probably meet the colorful Khan, then. He's supposed to be arriving there by tomorrow morning, from what I understand."

Emma at his side, Khalid stood by the ramp of the CH-47 as Chieftain Jawid Khan, astride his prancing white Arabian stallion, rode up. In his hands, he had a box of dates from Saudi Arabia, one of Khan's favorite delicacies. The forty-five-year-old chieftain was tall and erect in the saddle. He wore a dark green robe embossed with gold threads. The geometric designs across his powerful chest and sleeves emphasized his authority. On his head was a turban that matched his intelligent forest-colored eyes. Khan's beard was trimmed and neat but showed silver among the black hair. Khalid smiled to himself. Khan was from a thousand-year-old family line that had ruled this part of Afghanistan. The man was married and had ten children. The last twenty years of his life, he'd lived on horseback and fought, first, the Russians with the Mujahadeen, and for the last ten years, the Taliban, whom he hated with equal ferocity.

The stallion snorted and danced to a stop. It was decked out in a dark green leather bridle and martingale, with gold tassels sparkling in the morning sun. The entire village of Zor Barawul had come out to welcome their leader and his five hundred horsemen now surrounding the entire mud and stone village.

Khan's narrow face broke into a smile. He'd lost one of his front teeth many years ago to a bullet that had grazed his mouth as he'd charged up a valley to destroy a Taliban machine-gun position. The bullet had chipped the tooth, but that hadn't stopped him from continuing the charge up the hill. When the fight was over and won, Jawid Khan celebrated with his men. He'd had his second-in-command, Naraiman, pull what was left of the tooth without any anesthesia. Out here there were no painkillers. Khan's men had roared and cheered as Naraiman used a pair of rusty old pliers to get the job done. Khan knew men would only follow a leader who didn't show weakness to pain or suffering.

Dismounting with a flourish after two of his soldiers ran up to hold the stallion's reins, Khan grinned widely. He opened his arms toward the lean pilot in the dark green flight suit. "Khalid, my brother!"

Khalid bowed his head to the mighty warlord and handed him the box of dates. "My Lord Khan. Welcome."

Khan looked at the dates and grinned. He handed them to another awaiting soldier. "Brother, you look well." He moved forward, kissed each of Khalid's cheeks and then shook his hand. Then, he turned and studied Emma whose red hair flashed like fire in the morning sunlight. She wore a hijab to match the color of her hair. "So, who is this beautiful red flower?"

Emma held out her hand to the warlord. She murmured the usual words of welcome and expected him to shake her hand. Instead, after giving her the formal greeting, Khan swept forward and kissed each of her cheeks, denoting that he considered her a trusted friend, not just an ally.

Breathless, Emma felt the soft brush of his beard against her cheeks. The man was very good-looking, despite the gap in the front of his upper teeth. His skin was darkly tanned, the squint lines at the corner of his green eyes deep and fanned out. Khalid had warned her that Khan was a flirt with all women, whenever he could get around Muslim law. In his position of power and authority, he regularly broke Muslim customs.

"So, Captain Cantrell, you are more beautiful than the stories that are carried to me." Khan stepped back and grinned up at the tall Afghan pilot. "Khalid, you are a blessed man."

"I think so," Khalid said with a slight bow of his head. "Come, we have gifts for you, my lord." He led Khan to the rear of the helo. "We have five hundred pounds of grain for your horses. We've brought in a pallet of five-gallon plastic jugs of water." Khalid knew that in this desert, food and water were scarce for man and animal. It was a worthy gift for the warlord, who appeared properly impressed.

"Very good, Khalid!"

"And," Khalid said, walking up inside the helo and bringing out a gunny sack that he held gingerly, "a special gift for you."

"Eh?" Khan's thick black brows rose as he took the

gunny sack. Bottles clinked inside. "Is this what I think it is, brother?"

"It is," Khalid said, smiling. Khan had gone to school in France. He had a degree in Business Administration. While there, Khan had acquired a taste for good burgundy. Oh, Khalid knew that Muslim law forbade the drinking of alcoholic beverages, but that had never stopped Khan. "There are six bottles of burgundy in there, my lord. I think you will enjoy tasting them. A little reminder of France."

Khan grinned. He had sent his family to live in France. He left them every spring and returned to them as winter set into his country. No one fought on horseback during the season of ice and snow. In France, his family was out of harm's way. In the winter, Khan ran several multimillion-dollar businesses in France that kept his family accustomed to their rich life. "Thank you, brother. You make my heart smile." Khan handed over the gunny sack to another soldier. He gave him orders to take it to the stone house which was always maintained for his visits to Zor Barawul.

Turning, Khan rubbed his hands together. "So, let us sit, have hot chai, breakfast and discuss things." He turned and gestured toward Emma. "Come, sister. You will join us as we talk strategy against my brother, Malik."

Emma was shocked by the invitation. Khalid had warned her that the westernized Khan paid no attention to the Muslim law that said men and women should not eat together. She saw Khalid barely tip his head forward. "I'd be delighted," she told the warlord in Pashto.

"Excellent! Come!" He slid an arm through one of each of theirs and led them through the village. The villagers lined the rutted, dusty street. They cheered their proud warlord, for without him, they would have been destroyed by the Taliban long ago. If not for Khan's threatening presence, his five hundred loyal men on horseback, this village would have been utterly destroyed long ago. They had reason to cheer for their brave and caring warlord.

"And so, Malik attacked with at least two hundred men last night?" Khan asked, popping a date into his mouth. His men hovered nearby. The room had been prepared with expensive Persian carpets and many pillows and the scents of chai, curry and honey filled the air.

Khalid sat in the position of honor to the right of the warlord. Emma sat on the left. "Yes, my lord. And they almost overran us. Our three Apache helicopters made the difference."

"I wish I'd been here!" Khan said. He smiled over at Emma. "I understand you fly this Apache?"

"I do, my lord."

"Isn't that amazing, Khalid? A woman flying a combat helicopter."

Khalid understood Khan's amazement. In his country women were kept back from such achievement, something he wanted to change one village at a time by educating the women. Once they were educated, they could take places of more power, and their voices would be respected by the elders. "As you know, women in the Americas and Europe are not held under a man's thumb."

Grinning, Khan took a cup of chai from an old, bald

man who was his chef. "Yes. One day, brother, I hope to see our women in those powerful machines."

Emma gulped and hid her surprise. Was Khan that forward-thinking? She stole a look over at Khalid, who seemed pleased. She knew these two men had at least a fifteen-year relationship with one another.

"I believe we will see our women rise to whatever they dream of becoming," Khalid murmured tactfully. "I hope in another decade, our country can be at peace, not at war."

Frowning, Khan sipped his chai. "So, tell me of Malik. Give me the details."

Khalid told him everything. When he was done, he added, "If you are going to stay in this area, it will be helpful. My sister, Kinah, refuses to leave this village until all is in order. We have teachers coming in to teach and they must feel safe here. Otherwise, they will leave."

"Of course, of course." Khan handed the emptied china cup to his cook. "But you know I have many villages to protect. I cannot remain here forever."

Khalid nodded. "How long can you stay?"

Pulling thoughtfully at his beard, Khan said, "Perhaps a month, brother. But I will need your help. I intend to root out Malik from the caves on the other side of this valley. I will not sit idle. And to do that, I need ammunition, food for my men, water and grain for my horses. We will hunt by day and return back here to Zor Barawul at dark."

"Whatever you need," Khalid promised, "you will have." Ammunition for their AK-47s and older rifles was vital. "And we have an A-team who will ride with you. They can call in bombs from B-52s and other air-craft should you flush out Malik and his men."

Khan rubbed his hands together in glee. "Excellent! We had another A-team ride with us for a month up north and they did a good job of calling in the bombs on the Taliban."

"Captain Cantrell and I will fly back to the base camp," Khalid said. "We'll let General Chapman know what your needs are. It may take three or four days to get in all your supplies...."

"That is fine. My men could use a few days of rest," Khan said before smiling over at Emma. "We will rest. I will pay my respects to Abbas and the other elders. I will find out Malik's tactics from them. And then, when you return with our supplies, we can make our plans."

Getting up, Khalid said, "We'll leave now, my lord. Thank you for your generosity and food."

Emma quickly rose, bowed and murmured parting words to the smiling warlord. Outside the rock house, Emma walked at Khalid's side. The everyday rhythm of the village was once again in place. The children were playing, dogs were barking, women in burkas were hurrying down the street. Several carts drawn by small gray donkeys moved along the main thorough-fare. "Wow, Khan is something else!" Emma exclaimed.

"Yes, he's quite a colorful character," Khalid said, smiling. Down at the end of the street sat their emptied CH-47. The load master waited near the ramp. "Khan liked you."

Emma snorted. "I respect him for what he's done to try and keep his people in his villages safe."

"I meant," Khalid amended, grinning, "he was very

drawn to you. I think he was enamored with your red hair."

Groaning, Emma muttered, "Great."

Khalid chuckled. "Don't worry. He knows that I favor you."

Feeling heat tunneling into her cheeks, Emma gave him a dark look. "We're friends, remember? Not an item."

Holding up his long, expressive hands, Khalid laughed as they stepped out of the village and onto the landing zone where their CH-47 sat. "Yes, yes, of course." Emma's worried look dissolved. Khalid was falling in love with this red-haired woman, with her dancing green eyes. For her sake, though, he had to slow down. She was obviously tense about the possibility of their relationship going beyond a friendship. He'd given much thought to Najela's murder and now was awakening from his loss. Kinah's words had shaken him. She had been right: he couldn't continue to live in a vacuum and ignore his need for a deep, satisfying relationship. Still, Khalid was nagged by Malik's presence and worried for Emma.

As Khalid entered the helicopter, Emma on his heels, he cautioned himself to remain patient. He had. Yet, he wanted to kiss her again. This time, he would trail a series of kisses from her silky, flame-colored hair all the way down every inch of her body to her toes. Khalid did his best to tuck all his longing away and sat down in the left seat as the copilot. Today, Emma was the AC of this mission. As he slipped into his harness and Emma sat down in the right-hand seat, Khalid wondered privately if she was falling in love with him. Was there hope for them despite this war?

Chapter 13

The early-June weather was welcome to Emma. She pulled off her helmet as Khalid squeezed between the seats and walked toward the opening ramp of the CH-47. The sunlight was bright and she was glad to have her aviator glasses on. Getting up, she set her helmet in the copilot's seat and smiled to herself.

Ever since Jawid Khan had made his presence known in the southern part of his territory, the warlord seemed to have chased Malik and his men out of the area. Despite Khan's presence, Emma didn't trust Malik. He had twenty years of hard-earned camouflage techniques and could dig in, hide and still be nearby without anyone knowing about it. On the other hand, Khan knew how to dig rats out of a tunnel and he and his men had systematically scoured every cave along the other side of the valley, ridding themselves of pockets of Taliban. Khan took no prisoners and Emma saw the fierce horsemen in a completely new light. They were ancient warriors come to life. There was no mercy between enemies. Ever.

Today, MREs—Meals Ready to Eat—oats for the horses and more burgundy for Khan had been flown into Zor Barawul. Pulling the rubber band off her ponytail, Emma allowed her shoulder-length hair to flow free for a moment. She then combed her fingers through the strands and whipped her hair up into another ponytail. She grabbed her green silk scarf and wrapped it around her head. Once it was secured, she set off to visit with Kinah and see how things were going with the school.

There was an air of celebration in the village. A number of children who had been let out of school early were with Kinah, waiting anxiously at the edge of the landing area. The dust had cleared. Khalid worked with the A-team Special Forces soldiers and the load master to remove the supplies from the bird. About fifty of Khan's horsemen sat just out of range of where their helo had landed, their faces alight with expectation. They didn't necessarily like the MREs, but it was food. Many times, the horsemen had only meager supplies to last days at a time when out hunting the Taliban. Some days, they had nothing to eat.

Kinah waved and grinned. She refused to wear the burka that the other women of the village donned when outside their house but she wore the hijab. Her bright red scarf emphasized her black hair and flashing eyes.

"Emma!"

Emma grinned. "Hey, Kinah! How's it going?" The knot of children remained around her friend. She spotted the two orphans, Fahran and Benham, among the group. Ever since the horrific attacks by Malik a month earlier, the two had seemed inseparable. Kinah had saved their lives and they doted upon her.

Emma handed out candy to the children. Little hands shyly reached out, along with murmurs of thank you. She loved that these children were always polite and didn't grab a handful of candy and then run off. They knew how to share.

"I'm fine, sister." Kinah embraced Emma and they shared cheek kisses with one another. "Look at you! How long has it been? Two weeks? And Khalid looks very happy, too." She gave Emma a sly look. "So, love flourishes, eh?"

Emma stepped back and smiled. "We are just *friends,*" she emphasized.

"Mmm, friends. Indeed." Kinah smiled and looked across the sun-splashed narrow valley at the caves that were a part of the rocky landscape. "Friendship is always a good beginning basis for a relationship."

"It can only be friendship," Emma said. She fell in step with Kinah, the children providing a phalanx around them as they walked into the village.

"As you say, my sister," Kinah murmured, a sly smile still lingering across her mouth.

Emma wasn't taking the bait. She knew Kinah wanted her to fall in love with Khalid and marry him. Emma waved as a number of women in burkas came outside their mud homes to greet them. The village had a palpably, happy atmosphere. It was amazing how the people rebounded once the Taliban threat had been removed. Apaches had flown in almost daily during the first two weeks when Khan had begun to root out Malik and his men from the valley caves. The Americans had worked in concert with the warlord to eradicate the threat.

Kinah stopped at the school, opened the door and stepped inside. Emma followed and so did the curious children. Closing the door, Emma saw that all the bullet holes had been patched over with new mud. The temperature was pleasant, in the seventies, and the windows in the schoolroom provided good light.

Emma scanned the room and looked approvingly at Kinah. "This is a wonderful space. It's as good as new. How are the kids doing?"

"They are learning to read and write not only in Pashto, but in English. I have told them that English is the accepted universal language for our globe. They must learn it in order to grow."

Emma nodded, glancing toward the books, the chalk, the crayons and at the children's art that adorned the walls. "Good. That's a wise move. Little kids are sponges and it's the right time to teach them foreign languages."

Kinah counted heads and then gave the children an unexpected recess, much to their delight. They would get fifteen minutes to go out and play. The classroom fell into silence as the last child left and closed the door. Kinah sat down at her desk and gestured to Emma to take a seat on the wooden chair next to it.

"My brother looks very happy, my sister. Have you two been growing closer as friends?"

Emma cleared her throat and sat down. "Yes and no. The military doesn't foster much else between officers other than follow the Code of Conduct. Fraternization is not allowed."

"Yes, that is what Khalid said."

The door opened. It was Benham, the thirteen-year-old orphan.

"Mem sahib, come quickly!" he called urgently. "There is a baby goat stuck in a thick bush down on the side of the hill. We need your help in order to free it."

Kinah frowned. "But, Benham, where is the boy who tends those goats? It is his job to free it."

"No, no, mem sahib. This baby is far down the hill. Fahran and I can hear it bleating. It is in trouble! Can you help us? Please?" He gave her a pleading look.

With a sigh, Kinah got up. "Very well. I'm such a sucker for babies who get tangled up in all that brush."

"I'll go with you," Emma said, rising. She pointed to her flight uniform. "I can probably thread those thickets a lot more easily than you can in your robe."

Grateful for the company, Kinah nodded. They followed Benham out the door. He led them down behind the classroom. Emma saw nothing but a lot of thick green bushes. Some were two or three feet high and others, six to ten feet high. She saw holes in the ground where brush had been blown away by Apache rockets earlier. The wind was breezy as they stood on the lip of the hill. It was a steep, rocky descent. Benham scrambled like a mountain goat in his new leather shoes down the reddish slope.

"Come, come!" he hollered enthusiastically, waving them to follow him.

Emma heard a faint bleat. It was way down the hill. She wore a .45 strapped over her Kevlar vest across her chest, and she swept the area critically for enemy. Yes, Malik and his men had just been cleared, but Emma sensed the enemy was never very far away. Malik was a coyote. Looking over at Kinah, she saw the woman scowling.

"Over here!" Benham called pleadingly, as he slipped and slid farther down the rocky slope. "You don't want the baby goat to die, do you? I'll need help!" He slipped in between two thick bushes and disappeared. The goat bleated again.

"Let me do this," Emma said, holding out her hand as she took a step down onto the narrow, sliding earth and rock. "You stay up here, Kinah. You'll just get in trouble with that robe you're wearing."

"Are you sure, sister? This isn't the first time I've helped untangle a baby goat or sheep from that awful brush."

Grinning, Emma slid farther down the slope, arms out for balance. "My turn."

"Be careful..."

"Don't worry," Emma muttered, sliding and correcting constantly, "I will be."

Kinah noticed the other orphan, Fahran, suddenly appear out of the brush. He was farther down from where Benham had disappeared. His face was white and he seemed frightened. Kinah waved to him and called, "Emma is coming to help you. Just stay with the baby. She'll be there in a moment."

Fahran looked back toward the brush. He clung to a branch in order not to fall farther down on the steep talus slope. He opened his mouth and then shut it. Then, he looked at Emma who slid down the slope toward him. Dust rose in her wake. Rocks tumbled all around where she placed her flight boots. More than once, Emma fell on her butt, got up, dusted herself off and kept moving toward where Benham had disappeared earlier.

"It's all right," Kinah called reassuringly to Fahran. The ten-year-old orphan had a soft spot for all babies, animal or human, she had discovered. Maybe because he had lost his own family, he was sensitive to the plight of others. Fahran clung to her gaze as if she were going to cast him off someday, but Kinah always reassured him that she would be there for him. "Emma is coming! Just stay where you are, Fahran!"

Emma disappeared into the brush. The shrubs were long-armed, poking at her, and the leaves swatted her face. Breathing hard, she watched where she put her feet. She could barely see anything, the brush was so thick. The goat bleated frantically now, but she couldn't see him, only hear him.

"Benham?" she called.

"I'm here, I'm here," the boy's voice drifted toward her.

"Keep talking so I can find you!" Emma called, holding up her arm to protect her face from thick foliage.

"You're coming the right way," Benham shouted. "Hurry, hurry! The baby goat is bleeding! You must rescue him!"

Groaning, Emma threw caution to the wind and crashed forward through the brush. She heard the baby goat. It was shrill and bleating, as if completely frightened out of its wits. "Damn goats," she muttered.

Just as Emma turned around to avoid a huge group of limbs and allow her body to create an opening, a man's hand grabbed at her shoulder.

Emma was jerked hard into the brush. Grunting and terrified, she looked up to see an Afghan soldier grinning at her. His fist was cocked, and it smashed down into her face. The moment his fist connected with her cheek, Emma felt an explosion of pain. And then, darkness.

* * *

"Khalid! Khalid!" Kinah screamed as she ran down the street toward the helicopter.

Khalid jerked around. His sister was white-faced, her eyes wide with fear, her hands above her head to get his attention.

As he handed the load master the supply list, Khalid stepped off the ramp. What was wrong?

Kinah raced to him, out of breath. "Khalid, something terrible has just happened!" She rapidly told him the story.

Frowning, Khalid knew that slope was precarious and steep. "Are you sure?"

"Yes, yes," Kinah sobbed worriedly, "I kept calling for Emma. She never replied!"

"What about the boys?" he demanded, feeling sudden fear.

"They're gone, Khalid!" Kinah pressed her hands to her mouth, tears streaming from her eyes. "Oh, brother, I think Emma has either been killed or taken prisoner by the Taliban! Otherwise, she would have returned my calls and the boys would have reappeared."

A cold terror bolted through Khalid. There was no way to get a horse down that slope. He ordered Khan's soldiers to get off their animals and follow him. As he raced down the center of the village, his throat ached with fear—fear for Emma. Khalid jerked his pistol out of the holster.

Kinah watched from the top of the hill as Khalid and fifty of Khan's men searched every inch of that slope over the next half hour. She had directed them to where she last saw Emma, and they had literally torn the shrubbery apart looking for her.

After a frantic search across the slope, Khalid scrambled back up the hill. He was breathing hard, his face a mask of fear. "I'm going to call this in to our base," he told Kinah. "Emma is gone."

"Oh, no..." Kinah moaned. She grabbed Khalid's arm. "I'm so sorry, so sorry. I should have known it was a trick. This is Malik's work. He's used the two orphans to lure Emma into their trap. Oh, Khalid, why didn't I see it? Why didn't I recognize this was a trap? What will they do to Emma?" Her eyes were wide with terror.

Khalid gulped hard and pulled loose from his sister's grip. "I've got to go. I'll get back to you as soon as I can. Use the radio I left with you if Khan's men find anything or if you hear anything from a Taliban envoy."

Kinah gulped and rasped, "Yes, yes, I will, my brother. This is terrible! Emma's in danger!"

She was in more than that and Khalid knew it as he raced down the dusty road toward the helicopter. His mind spun with what had to be done first, second and third. His heart was pounding in agony. *Oh, Allah! Emma is a prisoner of the Taliban!* He knew it in his gut and heart. Najela's dead body swam in front of his eyes. Running up the ramp, Khalid snapped orders to the load master to get the supplies out of the helo pronto. Fifteen men from the village raced forward to follow him.

With a steady voice, Khalid talked to BJS 60 ops, telling them everything. A CH-47 did not have infrared or television cameras. He couldn't just lift off and fly around to try and find Emma and her abductors. He'd have to wait until an Apache was free of other duties to fly over here to begin a search pattern or he'd be shot out of the sky.

As he sat there in the cockpit of the helo, Khalid felt

as if his whole world had turned black. Fear gripped him. Instinctively, Khalid felt this was Malik's work. The man was a sly enemy. And despite Jawid's best efforts to purge the valley of the Taliban, Malik had somehow managed to avoid detection.

He knew Khan and his soldiers were down in the valley. He picked up the radio and called the warlord. There was no signal. That wasn't unusual; among the sheer cliffs a radio signal could easily get lost. Khalid wiped his dry mouth with the back of his hand. His heart ached with fear for Emma. Malik would kill her. Worse, he would probably behead her. That was what the Taliban did to infidels. And especially if a woman soldier or pilot was captured, they were broadcasted as examples.

Khalid felt his heart explode with new grief and awareness. For so long, he had tried to tell himself he was not falling in love with Emma. That they were from very different worlds and countries. Yet, he *had* fallen in love with her! He closed his eyes, his hand pressed to his chest. There was such agony that he could barely breathe. He wanted Emma in his life. For the rest of his life. How could she be gone, ripped suddenly and unexpectedly from his life, from his heart?

Opening his eyes, Khalid felt a new emotion. It wasn't love. It was hatred. Despite only being half Afghan, the blood of the warrior was genetically as much a part of him as his Irish mother's side was. His eyes narrowed as he looked out over the green floor of the V-shaped rocky valley. Emma did not deserve this. None of it! She loved the Afghan people and these villagers loved her in return. She had made so many friends. True, loyal friends for life among them. She had done nothing wrong, and yet, Malik had captured her.

Getting up, Khalid cautioned himself to wait. He couldn't just take off and go find Emma. The infrared on an Apache could spot body heat miles away. It was their only chance to find her. Without hesitation, Khalid skidded down the ramp. The men had made short work of getting the rest of the boxes out of the hold of the cargo helo. His boots created a metallic echo as he left the ramp and stood in front of the men who had finished searching the slope.

One man, who had part of his arm missing, came forward and handed Khalid a green scarf. "This belonged to mem sahib," he told him. "We found it among the brambles near the base of the slope. There are footprints of five men. And we found where they hid their horses." He pointed toward the other side of the valley. "We can track them, Captain Shaheen. We have good daylight, half a day. Can we go after them?"

Khalid felt torn. The Afghan warrior in him wanted to leap upon a horse and lead these crafty men who knew how to track in even the worst of circumstances. Yet, as an officer in the U.S. Army, he had to wait for that Apache gunship to arrive. None was available for at least three hours. By then, Malik would escape. Holding up his hand, he told the man, "Hold on. I'll be right back. Mount up and get me a horse."

Khalid made a radio call to BJS 60 and told them what was going on. To his relief, Major Klein gave him permission to ride with Khan's men to start tracking Malik in hopes of finding Emma. She ordered him to take a satellite radio with him so they were in contact at all times. Klein understood there were no Apaches presently available and their only chance to find Emma was to do it the old-fashioned way: with men on horseback tracking their enemy.

Khalid pulled open his helmet bag. Inside was a curved dagger in a leather sheath. He removed it and set it on the seat. Glancing over, he imagined Emma sitting on the other seat. His heart contracted with such anguish that tears drove into his eyes. Khalid blinked them back, forced down all his emotions. He jammed all the extra cartridges for his .45 pistol into the leg pockets of his uniform. He found it comforting to strap on the dagger to the right side of his waist. This dagger had been in his father's family for eight hundred years. It had belonged to a caliph and had been a present to one of Khalid's relatives who was a powerful warlord in the region. Touching it, his fingers brushed the jewel-encrusted leather sheath. Khalid silently swore he would use it to cut Malik's throat.

Chapter 14

Fahran bit down hard on his lower lip. He crouched within a grayish cave that had poor light. For an hour, they'd ridden hard with their prisoner—the woman he and Benham had lured down the slope of Zor Barawul. Frightened, he watched as Lord Malik shoved the woman, Captain Emma Cantrell, off her feet. He hid his face, his back up against the cold, jutting rocks. Fahran felt no pain for himself, but anguish for the semi-conscious woman.

He saw Benham standing near the knot of Taliban soldiers who encircled the woman. Her hands were tied in front of her and she was helpless against the jeering, cursing men. How could he have done this to Emma? How? Tears leaked into Fahran's eyes and he looked away as Malik lifted the toe of his boot and savagely kicked the woman in the ribs.

He heard Emma cry out. Suddenly, she went limp

within the circle; dirt was smeared across her face and through her hair. Gulping and sobbing, Fahran stood up on tiptoe to see if she was dead. He bobbed his head from one side to another to see if she moved. Oh, why had he been talked into this by Lord Malik? Emma had always been nice to him and Benham. She'd brought both of them special gifts that no one else received. She'd even brought him the pair of fine leather shoes and the socks he now wore with pride.

Guiltily, Fahran gazed down at his shoes. They had been expensive, that he knew. To denote their worth, there was fine leather craftsmanship and colorful stripes on either side. Fahran had never had a pair of shoes in his life until Emma brought them for him. And how had he repaid her? Wiping his eyes, he crept closer. Was Emma dead? Had Lord Malik killed her with his boot? Gulping, Fahran wedged in between two soldiers.

Emma Cantrell lay unconscious within the circle of men, her face dirty and pale. Fahran thought surely she must be dead. His gaze shot to Malik who swaggered into the circle. The warlord's eyes were black with hatred. He kicked Emma again, this time in the shoulder. She moved like a rag doll, no sound issuing from her slack lips. Benham was grinning like the idiot he was. He liked hurting Emma.

What could he do? Fahran blinked back the tears, for he knew if any of these rugged, hard soldiers saw him cry, they would give him the boot, too.

"Leave her," Malik boomed. He looked around. "Come, let us eat in the other cave. They will never find us here." He grinned triumphantly.

The soldiers shouted a roar of approval. This cave was a very secret place and to get to it, one had to follow a series of tunnels. Their horses were tied up in a smaller, nearby cave. They would eat a hot meal, the smoke being carried down into another cave that no one could climb into.

Malik spied Fahran. "You!" he growled, pointing his finger at him. "Take care of this bitch when she wakes up."

One of the soldiers next to Fahran gave him a pistol from his belt.

Fahran gulped and nodded. "Y-yes, my lord," he whispered.

Suddenly, everyone was gone. Fahran could smell the wonderful scent of curry on the cool breeze moving silently through the series of caves. He stared down at Emma, who was motionless. Frightened that she was dead, Fahran dropped the pistol onto the dirt floor and knelt at her side after everyone had left.

Gently, he put his dirty hand on her shoulder. "Mem sahib Emma? Are you all right? Please wake up? Please," he choked in a whisper as he leaned near her ear, "don't be dead...."

The cave was cold. They always were. Fahran took his jacket, which Emma had brought him, and he carefully laid it across her shoulders and back to try and protect her from the draft. Hesitantly, he touched her cheek. She was so pale. Her freckles stood out in dark brown spots across her ashen flesh. Terrible memories of his family dying a year ago slammed into him. He had leaned over his mother who was bleeding from the mouth, ears and nose after the bomb had exploded. She too had had her olive skin turn ashen just like Emma's. *Oh, Allah! Emma cannot be dead!* Why, oh why had he listened to Benham when he was given the order by

Malik to lure either Emma or Kinah down the slope?
Benham had swaggered, proud that he, of all people,
had been chosen to initiate the trickery.

Malik had told Benham to take Fahran, too. Benham, of course, was in charge, Malik had assured the
thirteen-year-old, patting him on the shoulder. Fahran
hadn't wanted anything to do with the plan. Yet, he
knew Benham would kill him if he didn't go along
with it. On the way across the valley, Fahran had tried
to find a way to detour Benham from the plan, to no
avail. Benham had captured a baby goat and tied it in
a thicket. He would jab it every once in a while with
a sharp stick to get it to bleat. They'd hunkered down
with the baby and watched Emma coming their way.

Two of Malik's best soldiers had then sneaked up
and waited for Emma. When she'd gotten tangled in
the thick brush, they'd attacked her. In seconds, she had
been knocked unconscious. It had been easy to drag
her to the horses tied below. One soldier mounted and
the other hung her across his horse's withers. Benham
leaped upon his horse and Fahran rode behind him,
clinging for dear life as they thundered down a narrow
trail that would lead them across the valley to their hidden cave complex.

Emma groaned. Pain made her open her eyes. At
first, everything was blurry. Pain was radiating from
her left shoulder. Her left hand felt numb and she
couldn't feel her fingers. Her head throbbed. And so
did her cheek and jaw. Blinking, she realized Fahran
was kneeling next to her, his little face anxious.

"Mem sahib! You live!" He touched her jacketed
shoulder.

It took long moments for Emma to realize what had

happened—and where she was. Fahran jabbered on in Pashto, telling her everything. Her ears were still ringing, probably from the blow she'd taken earlier to the head. Fahran started to cry.

"I—I'm so sorry, mem sahib Emma. You did not deserve this. I—I couldn't do anything. I tried to get Benham to stop the plan. Oh! I thought you were dead after Lord Malik kicked you in the back."

Emma lay with her cheek against the fine, cool dust of the cave floor for nearly five minutes, trying to absorb what had happened. Fahran's tears rolled down his taut face making tracks through the dust on his cheeks. She tried to reach out with her left hand, but pain made her grunt. Her arm fell helplessly to the floor.

"Fahran," she croaked, "help me stand up. Can you do that?" Emma saw the pistol lying in the dirt about fifty feet away. She knew from Fahran that he was supposed to guard her. A mere ten-year-old. Hatred for Malik gave Emma the strength she needed. As she sat up, holding her left arm tight against her body, she closed her eyes until the dizziness passed.

Fahran anxiously circled her. "What are you going to do, mem sahib?" He told her what Malik had done to her. That he'd kicked her twice.

Emma opened her eyes. She knew her left shoulder blade had been dislocated by Malik's kick. "Help me stand. I need to reset my shoulder blade."

Fahran gripped her right hand. Between them, Emma got to her feet. She staggered. Fahran threw his small arms upward and around her hips to steady her. It was enough. Emma heard voices wafting through the cave complex. She guessed the Taliban soldiers were not very close. The voices were muted. *Good.*

"Help me get to the wall," she ordered, her voice low with pain. Every time she took a faltering step, the agony made her groan. Gritting her teeth, she relied on Fahran's strength to get her to the wall of the cave.

Leaning against it, breathing hard, she felt Fahran's hands continue to steady her. "I'm—okay," Emma told the boy. "Stand back."

Fahran backed away. He gave Emma a quizzical look. What was she going to do?

Emma sucked in a breath. *Oh, God, this is going to hurt....* She hurled her back against the cave wall as hard as she could. There was a *snap* and her shoulder blade seated back into its correct position. Emma blacked out from the overwhelming pain and fell, unconscious, to the floor.

Fahran cried out and raced forward. Emma was dead! What had she done to herself? She lay on her stomach, her arms flung away from her body. Dropping to his knees, he sobbed out her name and shook her shoulder, trying to awaken her.

Emma groaned. She felt Fahran's small hands gripping her flight suit near her right shoulder. The moment she groaned, he leaped way, frightened. The pain in her shoulder ebbed now as she pushed herself up into a sitting position. Fahran's eyes were huge. Tears glimmered in his dark eyes. "I'm okay," she rasped.

With a moan, Fahran walked toward her, unsure. "A-are you dead? Or are you alive?"

Emma forced a smile that was more like a grimace. "I'm alive, Fahran. I dislocated my left shoulder." She vaguely gestured toward the cave wall. "I threw myself into the wall to reset it. Do you understand?"

"N-no."

Emma felt stronger, more clear-headed. Her left shoulder ached, but nothing like before. She tested her left arm and lifted it a little. There was pain, but it was now manageable. Worriedly, Emma couldn't feel three of her fingers on her left hand. Had there been nerve damage when Malik kicked her unconscious? Had his boot severed those nerves? Fear struck her as she slowly opened and closed her left hand. If she couldn't get back sensation in those fingers, she would never be allowed to fly again.

"You must come with me," Fahran urged, coming over to where she sat. He whispered the words fiercely and kept looking toward the exit where the Taliban soldiers had left.

"Where? Where am I, Fahran? Can you help me get out of here?" She saw him screw up his small, thin face. He looked down a dark tunnel that lay opposite. Some grayish light came through it.

"You are on the other side of the valley opposite Zor Barawul," he told her. Anxiety raised his voice and he sounded reedy. "You must follow me, mem sahib Emma. I know another way out of here! But it is dangerous. And only small people can slide through the opening."

Emma nodded. "Am I small enough?" Her heart beat with hope. She heard the drifting voices of the soldiers. Would they come back and check on her? Emma knew Malik would kill her.

"Yes, yes, you are." Fahran held his small hands about an inch apart in front of her face. "It is late afternoon. We can wriggle like escaping rabbits away from Lord Malik." Anxiously, the boy looked at the opening. "They are eating and drinking now. There's a great celebration because you were captured."

Grimacing, Emma got to her feet. She gripped Fahran's slender shoulder. "Show me the way to get out of here. Can you take me out of these caves and get me clear of Malik and his men?"

"Yes, yes, I can." Fahran walked over to the pistol and then brought it back to Emma. "You keep this. I cannot kill anything."

Her heart broke over the boy's sudden, sagging face, tears in his eyes. Emma took the pistol and made sure there was a bullet in the chamber and the safety was off. "I understand," she told him gently. Patting his dusty hair, she added, "Let's go to Zor Barawul, Fahran. Take me home."

The sun slanted steeply on the western horizon when Malik heard the cry of a guard. It was the soldier standing at the mouth of the second cave. Malik had been crouched in front of the fire, eating a juicy, warm rabbit leg. The scent of curry and hot tea filled the small, warm cavern. Malik stood up, the leg of the roasted rabbit in his left hand.

"Lord Malik!" the soldier panted, running into the cave. "Riders! Lord Khan and his men! They're coming our way!"

"Mount up!" Malik roared. He took several more tearing bites from the rabbit and then threw it away. Turning, he said to Benham, "Get the American bitch. Bring her here to me."

"Yes, Lord Malik!" Benham pirouetted and raced for the smaller cave via a tunnel.

Everyone else quickly stored their meager utensils

in rags and hurried down another tunnel to where all
the horses were tethered. Malik scowled. It would be
impossible for Khan to find this place. This cave complex had never been discovered. Touching the dagger
at his waist and then his pistol next to it, Malik picked
up his AK-47 and ran down the tunnel toward the sad-
dled horses.

Benham gasped as he skidded to a halt in the other
cave. Breathing hard, he looked around. Where was the
American pilot? And Fahran? Suddenly scared, Benham wondered if she had overpowered Fahran and run.
But where? Anxiously, Benham searched the entire
cave. Nothing. There were no voices, no noises. No—
anything. Suddenly afraid, Benham spun around and
raced as fast as he could. Lord Malik needed to know
his prisoner had escaped.

Malik had just grabbed the reins of his white stallion
when Benham burst into the cave. His black-and-gray
brows drew down. "Where's the American?" he roared
at the approaching teenager.

"Gone!" Benham cried, sinking to his knees. All
around him, riders and horses swirled. The tension was
electric, dust raised by the horses suddenly whinnying
and prancing around.

"What are you talking about?" Malik thundered as
he mounted. He rode over to the cowering youth.

Benham choked out what he'd seen. "I-is there another way out of there, my lord?"

Scowling, Malik snarled, "Yes. It's a small, narrow
passage." He glowered at the big, lumbering Benham.
"You're too large to go in there to see if you can find
them." He jerked his head around and barked orders

above the din. A very small, wiry soldier came running forward.

"Siamak, go into the tunnel where the American was being kept prisoner. She's escaped into it. Find her. Kill her. Then, join us near Do Bandi. I'll see your horse is left here for you."

Nodding, Siamak bowed and took out his curved dagger from his belt. "As you wish, my lord." He turned and ran out of the cave.

Turning, Malik raised his hand and roared, "Follow me!" He jerked his stallion's reins and then trotted down another twisting, winding tunnel. Someone had lit a torch, the yellow and red flames flickering ahead of Malik.

Malik grinned savagely. He knew that this half-mile long tunnel, barely ten feet high, would lead them to a brush-covered opening that Khan knew nothing about. Within half an hour, they would be gone. Malik seriously doubted if Khan would even find this cave. It was all but impossible.

Gasping for breath, her shoulder burning, Emma crawled and wriggled through the blackness. Only Fahran's small shoes near her face kept her hopes up.

"A little more!" Fahran gasped.

Hope sprung up in her. It felt as though she'd wormed her way through the narrow, twisting tunnel forever. Every time she reached with her left hand to pull herself forward, the burning sensation deepened in her shoulder blade. She tried to use her right arm, but it was difficult. Her head throbbed and Emma wished mightily for some aspirin.

As they inched around a curve, Emma gasped. Light!

She saw sunlight coming in through massive bushes that grew in front of the entrance. She saw Fahran's head bobbing up and down as he quickly scooted forward on his belly. Within three minutes, they were out of the tunnel and standing outside the thickets.

Holding her left arm against herself, Emma looked around. It was near sunset. The sky was a deepening blue as the rays of the sun shot across the tops of the peaks above them. Fahran dusted himself off the best he could. Emma glanced down at her flight suit: she was dirty from top to bottom. She turned toward the small, narrow inlet. "Fahran, is there a trail down to the valley?"

"Yes," he said, suddenly smiling, relief in his face, "this way!"

Khalid rode with Jawid Khan, who had shown up with more men as they rode down through the valley. Khan's white stallion was a pure Arabian, small and powerful. Khalid's black gelding scrambled to keep up as they took a narrow, steep and rocky path up the side of a hill. Above them were caves. His terror over Emma being taken had tripled in the last two hours as they rode at high speed.

At the top of the hill, Khalid pulled his stallion to a skidding stop. His eyes were narrowed and he jabbed his finger to the left. Khalid squinted. He could see dust clouds rising far above them.

"What?" Khalid demanded, coming abreast of the panting white stallion.

Khan grinned. "Dust clouds indicate a large group of Taliban, brother. That is Malik! Let's go!" He spurred his stallion up the steep hill, pulling out his rifle from the sheath as he did so.

Khalid didn't question the man. Khan knew signs of Taliban better than anyone. His gelding was shiny with sweat, foam on his neck as he plunged up the hill on the heels of the white Arabian.

Khan gave a war cry of triumph as he breasted the hill. Khalid quickly saw why. There, no more than a mile away, in a slight meadow area, were twenty fleeing Taliban. And leading them on a white stallion was Malik himself.

"Do you see Emma?" he shouted to Khan, who was busy cocking his rifle.

Looking through his binoculars, Khan shook his head. "She's not among them. Once we get them, we'll find her location!" Khan whirled around, gesturing violently to his two hundred horsemen. For once, the odds were on his side. Normally, the Taliban outhorsed them and had more ammunition than they did. But not this time.

"Lord Khan!" Khalid shouted and pointed to the sky as two Apache helicopters hove into view. He pulled out his radio to direct the pilots to fire on the Taliban. "Malik is mine!"

Grinning wolfishly, Khan nodded. "As you will, brother. Let the Apache helicopters finish him off!"

Khalid knew he shouldn't feel happy about killing twenty people, but he did. Since Emma wasn't with them, he had the luxury of using the Apaches. As he called in the air strike, he wondered where she was. Had Malik hidden her in a cave? More than likely. Was she even alive?

Chapter 15

Emma was startled by two Apache helos flying overhead. They were firing off major expenditures of rockets. She heard the thuds, the explosions high up on the ridge above where they stood on the valley floor. Fahran clung to her, his head buried against her. Emma held him with her right arm, her left arm nearly useless. For about ten minutes, the combat helicopters circled like buzzards over an unseen prey. She couldn't see who or what they were targeting, but guessed it was Malik and his horsemen. Grimly, Emma watched. She hoped the son of a bitch died.

"Come on," she urged Fahran. Looking up, she noted that the sun had set, but the well-used trail was easy to see. "We've got another mile before we reach the village," she told the boy.

Where was Khalid? Emma knew he'd be looking

for her. They scrambled up the steep and rocky shrub-strewn slope. Breathing hard, slipping and sometimes falling, Emma thought she might be more mountain goat than human. Fahran, who was much lighter and smaller, climbed ahead. Sometimes, he would turn and hold out his small hand toward her. Emma's left shoulder ached badly and her left arm felt better if she didn't use it. She had to get to a doctor as soon as possible once she got back to the village.

As they huffed up the last, steep slope, Fahran cried out and pointed to the left. "Riders!"

Emma gasped and hunkered down on the gravel slope, the sharp stones biting into her knees. About a mile away on another trail that led directly to the village, she saw a band of over two hundred riders at a hard gallop. In the lead was Jawid Khan. Her eyes narrowed. Yes! Khalid rode next to him! Her heart tumbled and for the first time, Emma allowed the suppressed emotions to surge up through her. Khalid! He'd gone out on horseback hunting for her. And he was safe. Gulping, Emma fought away the tears.

"Come on, we'll meet them at the village," she told the smiling Fahran, her voice hoarse with tears.

The last thing Khalid expected to see when he galloped into the village of Zor Barawul was Emma standing in the center of the village with bedraggled-looking Fahran in hand. He skidded his gelding to a halt and leaped out of the saddle, his booted feet hitting the ground at a run.

"Emma!" he called, his voice cracking with emotion. How pale she looked. Emma held her left arm against her body, her right hand protectively drawn across Fahran's thin shoulders.

"Khalid!" Emma didn't care who in the village saw them. She rushed forward after releasing Fahran. Emma extended her right hand toward him. Khalid's eyes filled with anguish and joy. As he approached, he gripped her hand and then closed the distance.

"You're alive," he whispered, leaning down and kissing her mouth tenderly.

Emma's world anchored only to Khalid's warm, cherishing mouth against hers. She moaned softly and leaned against his strong male body. He took all her weight and carefully held her, as if she were a priceless glass vase that might shatter at any moment. The warm moistness of his breath reminded Emma of life, instead of death. She could have died. She knew that. Emma loved Khalid with a fierceness that swept through her as he took her mouth commandingly a second time.

Breaking contact with her, Khalid looked critically into Emma's softened and teary green eyes. They were marred with pain. And relief. And love—for him. Was that really possible? Stunned, Khalid hadn't expected to see that. Did Emma love him? Her eyes were shining with joy—for him alone. Her lips trembled and then she fought back the tears.

"Malik dislocated my left shoulder in the cave," she whispered. She looked down at Fahran. "He helped me escape, Khalid. He's the real hero here. Fahran risked his life to show me another way out of that cave complex."

Khalid tousled Fahran's dusty hair. "Thank you, my brother."

Fahran looked shyly up at the pilot and managed an embarrassed shrug.

"There's a medevac flying in right now," he told Emma, his fingers wrapping around her right arm. Sweat and smudges of dirt covered her face. Even her red hair was dust-coated. "Can you walk? Or do you want me to carry you?"

Giving him a half laugh, because it hurt to move with the inflamed and injured shoulder, Emma said, "God, no. Just keep a steady hand on me, Khalid." Worried because three of her fingers were still numb, Emma wanted to see a doctor as soon as possible. The people of the village came out and offered help. Khalid thanked them and told them that Emma would be flown back to the base for medical treatment.

Near the edge of town, Kinah rushed over. She had concern on her face and her eyes were dark with worry. Emma assured her she would be okay after they carefully hugged one another.

"Malik's dead," Khalid told his sister with grim satisfaction. "The two Apaches came in and destroyed his entire army. There's not much left of any of them." He had wanted to race down that slope and meet Malik on the field of battle. Instead, Khalid had called in the combat mission over his portable radio. The two Apache helicopters had loosed an arsenal of ammunition that had killed every Taliban rider. Including Malik.

Emma closed her eyes for a moment. Then, she looked down at Fahran, who refused to leave her side. "Benham was with Malik?" she asked the child.

"Yes, he was, mem sahib."

Nodding, Emma told Khalid what had happened. She saw the medevac flying over the mountain crest and heading directly for the landing zone just outside the village. Khalid gently placed his arm around Emma for just a moment, his embrace butterfly-light.

"We'll get you to Bagram. I know all the doctors there. We'll get you to an orthopedic and neurology specialist, Emma. He'll make you well." He bored a look into her fatigued eyes. All he wanted to do was kiss her senseless and hold her tightly against him and protect her from a world gone mad. But he could do none of those things right now. Khalid swallowed his frustration. He had to be patient. Emma was worried about her numbed fingers. All he could do was be at her side.

Kinah came forward and grasped Fahran's hand as the medevac landed, the blades whirling and kicking up dust clouds. "I'll take care of him," she called to them. "Be well, Emma. Brother, let me know how she is?"

Khalid nodded. Kinah had a military radio that was always on her person. Plus, the A-team that was stationed at the village could always be contacted to let her know the latest news. "I will, my sister."

Once the medevac had shut down, Khalid led Emma to the open door. Welcoming hands ushered her into the helo. As Khalid climbed in and made sure Emma was being taken care of, a bit of relief sank into him. Khalid had terrible memories of finding Najela dead. He didn't think he could go through the same thing again.

"I can't believe it," Emma told Khalid as she walked into his home near Kabul. "Thirty days leave." Her left arm was in a sling and she had been given pain medication for her dislocated shoulder.

Khalid opened the door. "I can. Come, we'll get you into your suite and you can take a long, hot bath." The sky was dark, with sparkling stars, the wind hot off the desert. Inside, air conditioning welcomed them. He shut the door. Rasa, his housekeeper, had been called earlier, and she stood attentively at the end of the hall near the living room.

In Pashto, Khalid asked Rasa to escort Emma to her suite. He leaned over and pressed a kiss to her hair. "If you want to go directly to bed, do so. I will be up for a while." He motioned toward the kitchen. He'd eaten little in the last twenty-four hours.

Emma nodded as she noticed the darkness beneath Khalid's eyes. "Okay," she whispered. "I'm not hungry, just dirty and tired. The bath sounds perfect. Good night." After hours in the medical facility at Bagram, being poked, prodded and X-rayed, Emma felt so fatigued that her feet moved like chunks of concrete across the tiled floor. She'd had serious bruising on her cheek and ribs, but nothing was broken, thank goodness. Bath and bed sounded wonderful. She smiled at the housekeeper, and the woman nodded and smiled shyly in return.

"Only good dreams," Khalid said, giving Emma a raw look of love.

"Good dreams," she murmured. Emma looked over her shoulder to see Khalid striding silently into the kitchen. What she wanted was to be with him. To bathe, get her hair washed and slip into Khalid's bed and be held in the loving protection of his arms. It was another dream....

Swallowing, Emma understood that it couldn't be. At least, not right now. The doctor at Bagram said she'd suffered nerve damage to the three fingers of her left hand. Worse, he had no idea if she would get feeling back in them or not. And, the final blow to Emma was that she could not fly until—or if—she got full use of her fingers back. Emma felt as though the world had crashed in on her. She reminded herself she'd get out of the dirty flight suit, clean up and, she hoped, sleep deeply. Tomorrow morning, she would be in a better frame of mind.

Emma sat up screaming. The shout that erupted from within her startled her awake. Breathing raggedly, she shakily touched her perspiring face. Even with her eyes open, the light from the moon coming in the window, she could still see the hatred for her in Malik's eyes. That had been seconds before he'd kicked her in the ribs and knocked her unconscious.

"God," she muttered, throwing off the sheet and planting her bare feet on the cool tile floor. The slight movement of air conspired to help her focus on the present, not the past. Emma moved her left arm tentatively. She was on pain medication and now it moved easily and without any problem. Getting up, she found the lavender silk robe at the bottom of her queen-sized bed. As she pulled it on, Emma wanted to escape the room—and Malik's leering face. Maybe a hot cup of tea would help.

Heart pounding, Emma made her way through the darkened halls to the living room. This was her favorite place in Khalid's home. There were leather couches strewn with colorful pillows and a beautiful Persian rug lay between the two massive couches. She halted and gasped. "Khalid!"

"Emma." Khalid swallowed his shock at seeing her and quickly stood up. He'd been leaning against some

pillows propped up against one of the massive sofas.
Dressed in a dark blue cotton robe, he stared at her in
confusion as she anchored at the door.

He saw the dark circles beneath Emma's eyes even
as the moonlight sprawled through the massive picture
window. Her flesh gleamed. It was then that it hit him:
she'd had a nightmare. More than likely a reaction to
her trauma. "Please," Khalid whispered, "come in. I can
leave if you like?" He had no desire to make her feel
trapped. The wildness in her dark green eyes haunted
him. Khalid saw the fear etched in them. Praying it was
not fear of him, he lifted his hand and opened it to her.

"I—uh...no, stay." Helplessly, Emma said in a shaky
voice, "I had a nightmare about Malik just before he
kicked me. I woke up screaming. Did I wake you up,
too?"

Khalid watched her with such gentleness in his eyes.
"No. I've been up for a while." He motioned to the book
near the pillows. "I was reading and hoping to get tired
enough to go to sleep."

Emma saw how very old the book was. The leather
was frayed and worn. Somehow, just talking with Khalid was helping calm her down. "I wish I could read a
book and feel safe...feel...okay," Emma gulped. Clinging to Khalid's dark gaze, all she wanted to do was run
to him. As if reading her mind, he walked toward her,
his arms opening, silently asking her to come to him.
Emma didn't shy away from her raw feelings for Khalid.

Moving into his arms and feeling his strength and
tenderness, her face pressed to his neck and jaw, Emma
released a long, trembling sigh.

"You're safe with me, beloved," Khalid rasped near
her ear. Tendrils of her unbound hair tickled his chin

and lips. Inhaling her feminine scent, he felt Emma sag completely against him, her arms sliding around his waist. He closed his eyes and savored her trust of him. Without thinking, he pressed small kisses upon her mussed, clean hair. "It's going to be all right," he breathed against her ear. "We have one another, Emma. The world might unhinge, but we love one another. And with love, we can get through anything. Together."

Tears beaded along Emma's lashes. "I feel so weak, Khalid. So scared. My whole life is upended. What if I don't get feeling back into my fingers? My God, I can't fly. The army won't allow it. Where will I go? What will I do? All I've known is the army and flying."

Khalid absorbed her sob. Emma's fingers dug into his robe and chest. "Let it out, Emma. I'm here...I'll hold you against the storms."

Emma had never felt so safe or so loved as in that moment. There was something so exotic and ancient about Khalid. He was a warrior at heart. A man who could wear his heart on his sleeve without apology. And he knew when to be tender and sensitive. She had never found all these qualities in one man before. She had in Khalid. As hot tears spilled out of her eyes and streaked down her cheeks, Emma trusted Khalid with her life. She cried out her fear of having no future as a pilot, of having her world suddenly turned upside down and not knowing where she was going to land. Only the safety, the stability of Khalid's strong arms holding her tightly against him was real.

Eventually, Emma's sobs ceased. She hiccuped a few times. Khalid gently moved her toward the sofa and they sat down together. She eased back into his arms and he simply held her. With her head resting against his shoulder, her silky hair against his jaw, Khalid closed his eyes. He could feel Emma's heart pounding against his chest. Felt the touch of her hand against his damp robe. He tenderly slid his fingers through her mussed hair. This was the first time Khalid had explored her and it made his heart swell fiercely with love for Emma. He felt her nestle her cheek more deeply against the crook of his shoulder. The fast beat of her heart was slowing now.

"Crying is a good thing," he told her. "I remember when I was a little boy and my pet canary died, I cried for days afterward. He was my friend and at seven years old I didn't understand that things could die. My parents encouraged my tears and they held me. I was lucky to have their understanding. I learned about death and that I could be held with love in the aftermath."

Just hearing Khalid tell his story soothed Emma's fractious state. She sat up and wiped her cheeks free of the spent tears. "I feel like I'm dying, Khalid." Emma held up her left hand and looked at it. "I have this horrible gut feeling that I'm not going to get rid of the numbness in my fingers. That the army will ask me to give up my commission." Emma searched his eyes. "What will I do then?" The question was hard to ask, but she felt as if Khalid saw into her soul and never judged her.

Reaching up, he pushed a few errant tendrils of hair away from her face. "Beautiful Emma, you are young. You have your whole life ahead of you. Sometimes, we have one door shut in our face. But as soon as that happens, another will open. That is the way it is."

Emma nodded, barely able to keep from staring down at her hand. "My family is a military one, Khalid. Most of us serve our country. Casey didn't, but that's okay, too. She's my younger sister." Dragging in a deep breath, Emma expended it and frowned. "The army won't wait long to see if I can fly again. If I can't, they'll release me. What good to them is a pilot who can't fly?"

Touching her left hand, Khalid stroked each of her long, artistic fingers. "Listen to me, Emma. I have had many dreams for you—and me." He snagged her glance and smiled unsurely. "I have dreamed of asking you to marry me. To be my partner. I have dreamed of us flying books and school materials all along the border of my country—together." He held her left hand. "The military might not let you fly, but there is nothing to say you can't fly a commercial helicopter. You know, I own a fleet of them. I have three. I have used them for years to help Kinah fulfill our destiny with our Afghan brothers and sisters. You know me as flying for the military, but my life is much broader and deeper than that."

Amazed, Emma stared at him. Her heart pounded. Khalid wanted to marry her! She vaguely heard the rest of his words, her gaze locked with his. There was such tenderness in his eyes for her. Real love. Not some passing infatuation, but love. Emma knew the difference. She twined her fingers between Khalid's. "From the moment I met you, Khalid, I fought my attraction to you. At first, I thought you were just like Brody Parker. But over time, I knew that wasn't so. Every time we kissed, I wanted so much more from you. I wanted to know everything about you. How you grew up. What held your interest. What experiences you went through to make you the man who is sitting here with me now."

Lifting his hand, Khalid cupped her cheek. "And I fought loving you, Emma. After Malik murdered Najela, I felt as if my whole life was over. I couldn't conceive of ever loving another woman." He grazed her cheek. "Until I met you. Then, everything changed for me, Emma." Touching the area of his heart, Khalid whispered unsteadily, "I felt as if my life were given back. A second chance. And once I realized I loved you with a fierceness to match the breadth of my life, I wondered if you loved me. You know in the military we can't show our affection with one another. It's not allowed."

Emma nodded. "I know...and I wanted so badly to tell you, Khalid, but I was scared. We're from different countries. Different worlds. I was worried how our parents would get along. I was worried about a lot of things, so it stopped me from telling you how I really felt." Emma closed her eyes as his fingers trailed down her cheek to trace the length of her slender neck. Khalid had to know the truth. "Where would we live? What kind of life would be expected of me by you? I had so many questions and no answers."

Khalid dropped his hand and held on to her searching gaze fraught with worry. "My mother is Irish. My father is Afghan. I was raised in a home where nothing but love and respect ruled. My father, whom I know you will love, is a man of great heart. He respects everyone. Their beliefs. Their individualism. My mother is tolerant of all peoples. She sees only their hearts and their dreams."

"Your parents are like mine in that way," Emma said.

Khalid managed an unsteady smile. "When one is raised in such an environment, Emma, how can one have problems with any other? I believe you have the right to ask those questions, but you must base the answer on your experiences with me. I can't believe that your family is prejudiced against anyone from a foreign country. You show a tolerance and respect similar to mine, so I know your family is heart-centered too. It's not the color of a person's skin or their particular beliefs that really matters."

"It's the only way I want to see the world, too. My parents taught us the real measure of a person was their humanity to others," Emma whispered.

Khalid tapped his heart with his hand. "Yes. The only question I ever have of anyone is whether they are coming from their heart. You come from your heart, beloved, just as I do. Is it not possible that two people who come from the heart can love and marry? That their families would also be celebrating such a union? When you marry for love and come into that sacred union with only love, then the best of all worlds has been born."

Emma saw how her doubts had no merit whatsoever. Khalid's voice was low with feeling. The more she knew the man, the more deeply she fell in love with him. Khalid was complex, with so many layers, and yet, he had a global perspective she didn't see as often in others. And that drew her powerfully to him. "You're right," Emma admitted quietly, brushing her fingers across his hand.

"Love moves mountains," Khalid told her. "No one can be untouched by love. I have dedicated my life, Emma, to doing things from my heart for others. Yes, I am rich monetarily, but I prefer the richness that comes from the heart. It's not something money can buy. That is why it's so important to help my people here in Afghanistan. Kinah is the same. She sees our money as simply a way to a means. One that will lift our people, one child at a time, to be educated. Because getting an education will lift our nation out of the past and bring it into the present."

Emma saw the fervency in Khalid's narrow eyes. And she heard it in his voice. "You're a family of dreamers who put your vision into reality."

Smiling faintly, Khalid took her hand and pressed a soft kiss to the back of it. "I like that. Yes, that's true, beloved. Right now," he whispered, sitting up and framing her face, "all I want is you at my side, Emma. I want you as my partner for life. I cherish your ideas, how you see the world and how you see me. I want to fulfill your dreams, too. What is a life lived alone? It is empty and hungry. I want my life entwined with yours, Emma. Will you marry me?"

How could she say no? Khalid's words fell gently across her heart in such a way that Emma could not see her life without his larger-than-life presence in it. "Yes, I will marry you, Khalid. I'm not sure where our lives will lead, but it's going to be an adventure."

Leaning forward, he brushed her lips, parting them. "Beloved, no matter what we do, we will allow our hearts to lead the way...."

Chapter 16

Khalid picked Emma up and cradled her in his arms. She kissed his cheek and inhaled his dizzying male scent as she wrapped her arms around his broad shoulders. There was joy in his eyes, a fierce love for her that stole her breath. This man, who bridged two major religions, was living proof that east could meet west from the heart. Khalid was unique and Emma sighed as she rested her brow against his cheek. Her mother, Alyssa, had always said that whomever she married had to be more than just a man. She had been right: Khalid was archetypal in the best of ways. Having been born and lived in such a loving home where the Christian and the Muslim religions were joined, he'd absorbed the best from both. And now, she was going to live with this man who held the hope of the world in his heart.

Emma smiled faintly as Khalid nudged the door to

his master bathroom open with his toe. "Ah...water. I like where this is going, Khalid..."

He gently placed her on the thick blue Persian rug in front of a huge glass-enclosed double shower. "Care to join me?"

Grinning, Emma watched as he stepped into the blue-and-white tiled shower and turned on the water. The multiple shower heads released warm water that fell like soft raindrops. "Just try and stop me."

Khalid smiled in response, then felt the temperature of the water. "Just right. Are you ready, beloved?"

Without hesitation, Emma slid the lavender robe off. She wore only a silky tank top and shorts that fell midway on her thighs. "I am. You?" She gave him a challenging smile.

Khalid had no shyness about removing his blue robe. He was completely naked beneath. If Emma was disappointed in him, her large, beautiful green eyes did not reflect that. As her gaze moved from his throat, down across his darkly haired chest to his flat stomach to his narrow hips, he saw her cheeks turn pink and those copper freckles darkened. Reaching out, he settled his hands lightly on her shoulders.

"Do I pass your inspection?"

His teasing made her laugh. A sudden, happy giddiness surged through Emma as she looked up into his glinting, narrowed gaze. "Oh, yes, you do." She saw how pleased Khalid was, and maybe, a bit relieved. After all, he was a flesh-and-blood man and Emma knew he was probably worried she might not be pleased with his body. She felt him move the thin silk from her shoulders. Her skin flushed and then prickled pleasantly as he coaxed the material off her torso and exposed her breasts. In a moment, Khalid had removed the soft material and set it on a nearby shelf. His gaze moved hungrily across her body. She felt his desire even though he hadn't made a move to touch her. Her breasts tightened and the nipples hardened beneath his intense look.

Pushing the silky pajama pants off, Emma let them pool around her feet. She smiled and moved into the warm streams of water that issued from opposite walls within the huge shower. Gripping his hand, she said, "Come on in. The water's fine."

In moments, Khalid had closed the shower door, and the steam began to gather, moving in fine, thin ripples around them. Emma moved boldly into Khalid's arms. She wanted him and wasn't going to be coy about it. To her delight, his very male mouth curved over her brazen move. As soon as she slid her wet body up against his, his arms circled her. Leaning up, she claimed his smiling mouth. Emma unleashed all the hunger from the last months against Khalid. His mouth was strong, giving and taking against her own. As his tongue moved across her lower lip, she felt his hand slide teasingly down her spine. His fingers splayed and outlined each of her vertebrae, the water intensifying his burning touch. Khalid drew her powerfully against him and Emma gasped. She felt him smile and returned it. The water was like another set of her lover's hands as it curved and curled around her face, wetting her hair, the strands thickening and lying in fine sheets across her shoulders.

Khalid's mouth tore from hers and he trailed hot, hungry kisses from her jaw down the graceful line of her neck to her shoulders. With her left shoulder, he was tender and careful. Her skin sizzled with pleasure and danced with each slight brush of his exploring mouth.

As Khalid eased her back, his hand splayed out against her spine to hold her steady, their hips melted into one another. His kisses sought and found each of her taut breasts. Emma sighed and gripped his tense arms that held her captive.

He tenderly mouthed each of her nipples, making her moan. The water sluicing across her face, down her shoulders and trickling in and around her breasts only increased her pleasure. Each kiss along the curve of each breast heightened Emma's need of him. Khalid's masculine power was nearly overwhelming. She felt him trembling and Emma intuitively understood he was holding back his fierce love for her. Because of her injured shoulder, she knew he was being gentle so that he wouldn't create more injury for her.

As Khalid brought her back against him, the water spilled over them, the heat and steam curling around them like the fingers of a thousand other tantalizing hands. He slid his hands down, down, down until he cupped her hips. And then Khalid lifted her against him. Her arms slid around his shoulders as he gently settled her against him. Inch by inch, he slowly lowered her down upon himself.

A raw, guttural sound of pleasure rose in Emma's throat. She threw her head back, her body melted hotly against Khalid's as she brought him within her throbbing core. The moment was powerful, the water running around them, fusing them even more wonderfully to one another. Emma leaned her head downward, found his mouth and kissed him hard. She didn't want him treating her like some fragile glass that might break. After all, it was only her shoulder. Emma felt him smiling beneath her mouth. In moments, Khalid was moving her, holding her and kissing her hungrily in return.

The steam swirled around them. The silken water fused and inspired them. Emma gripped Khalid's broad, powerful shoulders, suddenly tensing as the heat of her body burst open and flowed in a tidal rhythm. A groan of complete pleasure tore from her wet lips. She felt Khalid tense, a growl from deep within him rolling upward. The sound was like thunder, shared and absorbed between them.

Closing her eyes, taut as a bow against Khalid, Emma surrendered all her love into this man who held her in his arms. For long, golden moments, only he existed—a part of her, a part of her pounding heart rhythm in tune with his. She thought she'd known love before, but she really hadn't. The love that Khalid had shared with her, the respect, the joy was rare. And beautiful. And fulfilling.

As water coursed down her head, the strands of her red hair clinging to her wet face, she leaned over, framed Khalid's face and kissed him. Nothing had ever been as wonderful as this moment for Emma. She understood now what Khalid had said earlier about living from the heart. It was effortless and joyful. As their mouths cherished one another, took and gave, Emma knew this man was greater than most. Her spirit had seen his. She truly saw Khalid's heart and his love for her. And searching his soft blue eyes, Emma knew he looked into her soul with nothing but love. Together, they could do a lot in their own unique ways to help the world. What else was there but love? In her dizzied mind, her thoughts disjointed, Emma was ready to accept whatever life would hand her. After all, she had a man who loved her with a fierceness that took her breath away. All else would fall into some kind of order after that.

"I'm really sorry," Nike told Emma as they stood outside the HQ of the BJS 60 squadron. "I know Rachel would be here to support you today, but she's off on a mission."

"Don't be," Emma told her best friend. She smiled a little. On her left hand was an emerald ring that Khalid had given her a month ago. Rachel, her cousin, had wanted to be with her when she found out the army's decision, but a sudden firefight along the border had broken out and all available women pilots were called to the Apache gunships to go help turn the tide.

Nike grimaced. The July sun was hot overhead, the nonstop sounds of helicopters landing and taking off nearby permeating the vibrating air. "You got feeling back in one finger, but not the other two. I don't know why the army refuses to let you fly. This is so stupid."

"Let it go," Emma counseled gently. "The army says a pilot has to have feeling in all ten fingers. Not eight. I'll be okay."

"I won't be," Nike griped. Upset, she jammed her hands on her hips. "The army should give you more than four weeks to heal up! Who's to say you won't get feeling back in those fingers two or three months down the road?"

"What are they going to do with a pilot who can't fly?" Emma asked. "Major Klein was very sorry she had to give me their decision. She said if it had been up to her, I'd still be with BJS 60."

"I know. Everyone in HQ knew when the decision

by the army higher-ups had come down. Major Klein was in a really ugly mood for a couple of hours after that. That's how we all knew they'd decided against you staying. You seem to be at peace about this," Nike said. "Khalid's influence?"

"In part, yes." Emma put on her aviator sunglasses and settled the black BJS baseball cap on her head. "My family is fine with what has happened. Khalid and I have a plan. I'll now be a part of his family nonprofit charitable organization. I'll be allowed to fly commercial helicopters that he and his family own. And really, it's a good thing because I can fly into the safe villages with resupplies and the army won't have to do it." She grinned and began to walk with Nike toward the tent area. Emma would pick up the last of her clothes and other personal items from the tent she'd lived in for over a year, and then be escorted off base. For a new life. A new adventure. And with a man she loved and who loved her with a fierceness that made Emma feel as if she were floating on a cloud of nonstop joy.

"When it's all said and done," Nike told her, brightening a little, "you'll be allowed back on base because Khalid is assigned here."

"Yes, I will." Emma gave her an evil grin. "Down, but not out, Nike. I'm going to move my stuff into his home in Kabul. A week from now Khalid gets thirty days of leave from the army and we're going to fly home to San Francisco to be married. My entire family, uncles included, are coming. Even Rachel, my cousin, is being given leave to attend, thanks to Major Klein. She knows how much it means to my family to be there for our wedding."

"That's great. I wish I could be there, too."

"So do I. I was surprised Major Klein let Rachel go. This is our heavy season for Apache demands and we're now a pilot short because I had to resign my commission."

"I think Major Klein is a good C.O. I know she didn't want you to resign, but she can't buck army regs as much as she might have wanted to. You and Rachel will be back a month from now," Nike said, gloating. "And we'll just pick up where we left off, girlfriend." She threw her arm around Emma's shoulders and gave her a quick squeeze.

"We will," Emma promised her, voice thickening with tears. Nike was an incredible friend, someone she never wanted to lose touch with. Today, her life would change forever. It was a bittersweet moment for Emma. She'd been the casualty of this war in one way. In another way, this war had brought her the man she would love forever. And she would have her cousin Rachel here with her. If she had learned anything, Emma had learned a long time ago that the only thing she could count on was change.

Emma opened up her tent. Nike followed and in quick order they had her personal belongings in the duffel bag. Her shoulder had healed up completely in the past month and it was easy enough to carry it over her right shoulder. Nike walked with her in the hot sunlight. The smell of aviation fuel, dust and the noise of trucks coming and going was a constant.

Emma was glad to be going home. Her family was in high gear to give them a July wedding at Golden Gate State Park near San Francisco's Golden Gate Bridge. And San Francisco was one of Khalid's favorite cities in the world. Yes, Emma thought, it would be a whirlwind month filled with overflowing happiness for her entire family. But especially for her and for Khalid who loved her tenderly every night before they slept in one another's arms. She was excited to have the Cantrells and the Trayherns embrace Khalid and his family who would also be there for the wedding. They were a global family in so many ways already. Now, east was marrying west. She liked being a forerunner. And she loved Khalid, a man who had one foot in western civilization and the other firmly rooted in his beloved Afghanistan. She would love this fierce global warrior forever.

* * * * *

We hope you enjoyed reading this
special collection from Harlequin® books.

If you liked reading these stories,
then you will love
Harlequin® Romantic Suspense books!

You want sparks to fly!
Harlequin Romantic Suspense stories
deliver strong and adventurous women, brave
and powerful men and the life-and-death
situations that bring them together.

Enjoy four *new* stories from
Harlequin Romantic Suspense
every month!

Available wherever books and
ebooks are sold.

ROMANTIC suspense
Heart-racing romance, high-stakes suspense!

SPECIAL EXCERPT FROM

H HARLEQUIN®
TM

ROMANTIC suspense

To bring down a serial killer, two detectives must pose
as husband and wife. They infiltrate a community, never
expecting love to intrude on their deadly mission!

Read on for a sneak peek of

UNDERCOVER HUNTER

by *New York Times* bestselling author
Rachel Lee, coming January 2015!

Calvin Sweet knew he was taking some big chances, but
taking risks always invigorated him. Coming back to his
home in Conard County was the first of the new risks. Five
years ago he'd left for the big city because the law was closing in on him.

Returning to the site where he had hung his trophies was
a huge risk, too, although he could claim he was out for a
hike in the spring mountains. There was nothing left, anyway. The law had taken it all, and the sight filled him with
both sorrow and bitterness. Anger, too. They had no right
to take away his hard work, his triumphs, his mementos.

But they had. After five years all that was left were some
remnants of cargo netting rotting in the tree limbs and the
remains of a few sawed-off nooses.

He could close his eyes and remember, and remembering
filled him with joy and a sense of his own huge power, the
power of life and death. The power to take it all away. The
power to enlighten those whose existence was so shallow.

They took it for granted. Calvin never did.

From earliest childhood he had been fascinated by spiders and their webs. He had spent hours watching as insect after insect fell victim to those silken strands, struggling mightily until they were stung and then wrapped up helplessly to await their fate. Each corpse on the web had been a trophy marking the spider's victory. No one ever escaped.

No one had escaped him, either.

He was chosen, just like a spider, to be exactly what he was. Chosen. He liked that word. It fit both him and his victims. They were all chosen to perform the dance of death together, to plumb the reaches of human endurance. To sacrifice the ordinary for the extraordinary. So he quashed his growing need to act and focused his attention on another part of his life. He had a job now, one he needed to report to every evening. He was whistling now as he walked back down to his small ranch.

A spiderweb was beginning to take shape in his mind, one for his barn loft that no one would see, ever. It was enough that he could admire it and savor the gifts there. The impulse to hunt eased, and soon he was in control again. He liked control. He liked controlling himself and others, even as he fulfilled his purpose.

Like the spider, he was not hasty to act. It would have to be the right person at the right time, and the time was not yet right. First he had to build his web.

Don't miss UNDERCOVER HUNTER by *New York Times* bestselling author Rachel Lee, available January 2015 wherever Harlequin® Romantic Suspense books and ebooks are sold.

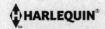

ROMANTIC suspense

Heart-racing romance, high-stakes suspense!

BAYOU HERO
by *USA TODAY* bestselling author
Marilyn Pappano

Available January 2015

One family's scandal is responsible for a rising body count in New Orleans's Garden District...

Even for an experienced NCIS agent like Alia Kingsley, the murder scene is particularly gruesome. A man killed in a fit of rage. Being the long-estranged son of the deceased, Landry Jackson quickly becomes a person of interest. But does Landry loathe his father as much as the feds suspect?

It's clear to Alia that Landry Jackson has secrets, but his hatred for his father isn't one of them. Alia feels sure Landry isn't the killer, but once more family members start dying, she's forced to question herself. What if the fierce attraction she has developed toward Landry has compromised Alia's instincts?

Don't miss other exciting titles from
USA TODAY bestselling author Marilyn Pappano:

UNDERCOVER IN COPPER LAKE
COPPER LAKE ENCOUNTER
COPPER LAKE CONFIDENTIAL

Available wherever Harlequin® Romantic Suspense books and ebooks are sold.

www.Harlequin.com

HRS27902

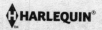

HARLEQUIN®

ROMANTIC suspense

Heart-racing romance, high-stakes suspense!

HIGH-STAKES PLAYBOY
by *New York Times* bestselling author
Cindy Dees

Available January 2015

Who will get this Prescott bachelor first—
the girl or the killer?

To help his brothers, marine pilot Archer Prescott goes
undercover to find out who's sabotaging their movie set.
But the die-hard bachelor isn't ready for what he finds
in the High Sierras: his doe-eyed girl-next-door
camerawoman is the prime suspect.

Marley Stringer isn't as innocent as she seems.
As Marley turns irresistible and the aerial "accidents"
turn deadly, Archer begins to wonder who's more
dangerous—the perfect woman who threatens his
heart...or the desperate killer who threatens his life.

Don't miss the first exciting installment from Cindy Dees's
The Prescott Bachelors series:

HIGH-STAKES BACHELOR

Available wherever Harlequin® Romantic Suspense
books and ebooks are sold.

HRS27903

JUST CAN'T GET ENOUGH?

Join our social communities
and talk to us online.

You will have access to the latest
news on upcoming titles and special
promotions, but most importantly,
you can talk to other fans about your
favorite Harlequin reads.

Harlequin.com/Community

Facebook.com/HarlequinBooks

Twitter.com/HarlequinBooks

Pinterest.com/HarlequinBooks

HSOCIAL